I0760645

Amazon Reader Reviews
For Earlier Works In This Series

"Reading Tom Corbett's work will have you impressed and awed by his superb literary skills . . . the book is so engaging and captivating that one can only wish to read more from this author. *Ordinary Obsessions* will have you engrossed . . . as the plot is perfectly executed, and the story line flows well."

Aaron

"The author honestly does a wonderful job of making the reader relate to each character and fall absolutely head over heels for each one and their journey through the book! With politics, power, religion, family drama, romance, and cultural struggle, this book exceeds expectations. I look forward to more by this author and cannot wait for the next gem he writes."

Veronica White

"Fast moving political drama that will keep you turning the pages. I do not read a lot of political drama novels, but I could not put this one down. Ordinary Obsessions by Tom Corbett is engaging . . . it pulls you in with the emotions of the characters."

Karen A.

"The author's writing style flows naturally and . . . the story develops with perfect pace. There is not one thing I would change about it."

M.C.

"This book is inspirational as it relates to knowing ourselves better, understanding the world we want, and more so the things that most of us would love to do in life. Corbett's polished writing style alone will get you hooked but his sense of humor and passion for writing will keep you reading."

Trizah Kelvin

"The author's writing style is so unique that I love to read his works. I get lost among the pages so easily."

Carleen Makivich

"I . . . have always been impressed with his talents . . . and found myself drawn into each character's struggles and triumphs."

Stacy E. Vance

"An awesome read! Five out of five stars!"

J. Lantin

"An utterly compelling narrative of two disparate families separated by culture and experiences who come together by circumstances and serendipity."

Amazon Customer

"It is easy to understand why this book comes so highly acclaimed. And the author's background as a professor of social sciences really comes into play . . . he has masterly shared the plight of two families who could not look more different."

Erin P

"Tom Corbett's *Palpable Passions* is the perfect combination of fact and fiction as it educates its readers about current events in our world today."

Lillie S

"The rhythm of the words attracted my attention and pulled me to the end. When I was done reading, I felt I had learned something new. Once you start reading, it is very hard to put down."

Jengel 106

"*Palpable Passions* is truly a great read that will leave you feeling empowered and determined to make a difference in the world in your own way. *Highly recommend* everyone pick this up."

Kimmy 4077

Amazon reader reviews of an earlier version of *A Clueless Rebel*: 4.9 out of 5 stars!!!

"Another winner from Tom Corbett. I've read several of Tom Corbett's books and I've enjoyed them all. He's a very talented author and storyteller."

"Tom Corbett is a gifted storyteller. He pours raw honesty and cleverness into his writing that both amuses and inspires you."

"An insightful and hilarious coming of age memoir set mostly in the decades after World War II."

This book has a close connection to the author's earlier work, Confessions of a Wayward Academic, where he gives insights into policymaking and welfare reform."

"Corbett does an excellent job weaving his tale in a way that both inspires and amuses, heartens and saddens."

"I found myself on an emotional roller coaster throughout the story."

"Reflective, insightful, and intimate. Experience nostalgia even if you are 46 years younger than Corbett, like me!"

"Corbett is a great storyteller who knows how to connect memories and ideas to find meaning and to make his ordinary life entertaining, relatable, and amusing."

"Never a dull moment and I found it hard to put down."

"Reading Confessions of a Clueless Rebel makes me feel I'm at a coffee shop with the author, swapping stories about life."

Amazon reviews of an earlier version of *Our Grand Adventure!* 4.4 out of 5 stars!!!

"The writing is moving, engaging, and I found it to be immersive with every page. Corbett is wonderful with his narrative skills, the details he conveys throughout the text with just the needed information and not too much nor too little."

"Author Tom Corbett … depicts the past with wit, charm, and insight, weaving humor with gravitas in his unique manner."

"This book is amazing! Tom Corbett writes his recollections in such a humorous and sarcastic way that it was impossible to put down."

"Great Book!! This book is full of history lessons … Corbett references the past with wonderful prose and helps the reader to understand how things were."

"The book tells the story of the author's firsthand experience of joining the peace Corps at its inception. Never thought learning about this period could be so funny, entertaining, and insightful. Truly a good read."

"(The book) … does not read like an autobiography/ memoir/ reflective/ history piece, though it has all these elements. This can be credited to Corbett's irreverent style which makes it a page turner."

"The volunteers who left home out of a to do good came home with experiences that you can't buy at a store or glean from a textbook. Tom Corbett's ability to see the humor in humorless circumstances touches off universal questions about the meaning and mystery of life."

Reviews of the author's other works:

"Palpable Passions delivers a compelling story arc infused with historical fact that should appeal to readers…"

Blue Ink Reviews

The book…feels like a screenplay; its dialogue is abundant and punchy, its landscapes well defined, and its characters have significant bonds. Palpable Passions uses bright, earnest characters to show that a microcosm can be as complicated as the big picture."

Foreword Book Review

"Corbett has created a captivating novel. The book title perfectly describes the fragile thread that spirals around each individual…to create an enthralling story that anyone will love to read."

U.S. Review of Books

"This is . . . a fully rendered tale. Those interested in the complexity of relationships …will find some rewards here."

Blue Ink Reviews

"…Tenuous Tendrils, by Tom Corbett, is a compelling journey from exile to redemption. Like its characters, the book is quite clever and features an abundance of humor. Many heavy scenes are punctuated by conversations about the futility of war and the humanitarian failings of government also feature omniscient narrative wit that keeps the text from being bogged down by sentiment and allows the characters' personalities to shine."

Clarion Review

Amazon Readers' Reviews
of author's other fictional works.

"I loved how the author told each family's story back and forth chapter by chapter. The characters are so well-formed, and the accurate descriptions of life in Afghanistan really drew me in. Finished book in one day. I didn't want to put it down."

"This is truly a great read that will leave you feeling empowered and determined to make a difference in your own way HIGHLY RECOMMEND that everyone pick this up."

"It's easy to understand why this book comes so highly recommended. Palpable Passions is a powerful book. I highly recommend it to anyone who loves literary fiction."

"A penetrating look into the human soul and the fragility of relationships."

"This book was incredibly personal on so many levels. Overall, I found this to be an extremely touching and educational read."

"I personally loved this book. It was refreshing and thoughtful."

"The overall story is incredibly genuine, realistic to the time limits it covers and thoughtful. Each time I put down the book I found it moderately difficult since I wanted to know what would happen next."

"Excellent characterization and historical facts make this a compelling story as hope overcomes despair."

Selected Praise for the Author's Non-Fiction Works

"A wonderful first-person account of the ground-level of welfare reform in recent times. It was a momentous time for reform of the nation's welfare system and Corbett was in the thick of it. He relates what happened with a wry, self-deprecating of humor, but there are serious lessons to be learned..."

—Robert Moffitt, Ph.D., Professor of Economics, Johns Hopkins U.

"The subjects author tom Corbett tackled were both relevant and deep. [He]...is a brilliant writer [and] Confessions of an Accidental Scholar is an original book. [He]... blended the academic, professional, and personal perspectives when writing about the subject matter."

—Pacific Book Review

"Tom Corbett exposes the reader to the raw reality of confronting our most difficult social issues in this engaging, compelling, yet witty book. He brings the doing of policy alive, going beyond the dry numbers to reveal the human side of the equation."

—Dennis Dresang, Ph.D.,
Professor of Public Policy,
U. of Wisconsin

"...throughout the memoir, Corbett's prose remains engaging, consistently mixing insight with the familiar jokes that one would from

a close friend. A thoughtful memoir about life and politics told in a (n} ... endearing style."

—Kirkus Review

"Corbett's stories from the front lines of policymaking, like All Quiet on the Western Front or The Things They Carried, provide great insight into the way the world actually works, not what the generals or policy planners think is happening."

—Matt Stagner, Ph.D. Policy Fellow
Mathematica Policy Research, Inc.

"...the emergence of Corbett's humanistic world view...gives Ouch, Now I Remember intellectual gravitas. Corbett imparts an enormous amount of wisdom and humanity."

—Clarion Review

"...I found "Ouch. Now I Remember" to be a witty yet edifying read, riddled with some funny moments... with many of them making me laugh out loud. I enjoy his writing style, it was comforting yet candid, like listening to a respected relative recount their own life with unabashed honesty."

— Pacific Book Review

"*The Boat Captain's Conundrum* is a winning performance."

— Forward Clarion Book Reviewv

"Corbett takes a topic often shrouded in numbers and dense writing and turns it into an intellectual, yet conversational memoir."

—U.S. Review of Books

"Corbett's reflections, woven together with great insight and humor, transform public policy from a class that is boring and mundane to a career that can be engaging and germane."

—Karen Bogenschneider Ph.D., U. of Wisconsin

"I enjoy his writing style, it was comfortable yet candid, like listening to a respected relative recount their own life with unabashed honesty."

—Pacific Book Review

"If you truly want to understand how public policy works, read this book. Corbett's descriptions about how laws and programs are developed gives readers a real take away—genuine insight into the discipline of public policy."

—Mary Fairchild, Senior Fellow National Conference of State Legislatures

Selected Works by the Author

Oblique Journeys (Revised edition, Papertown Press, 2022)[1]

Our Grand Adventure (Revised edition, Papertown press, 2022)[2]

A Clueless Rebel (Revised edition, Papertown Press, 2022)[3]

A Wayward Academic: Reflections from the policy trenches (Revised edition, Papertown Press, 2021)[4]

Evidence-Based Policymaking: Envisioning a New Era of Theory, Research and Practice (2nd Ed.) with Karen Bogenschneider (Routledge Press, 2021)

Felicitous Fates (Papertown Press, 2021)

Confessions of an Accidental Scholar (Revised edition, Papertown Press, 2021)[5]

Ordinary Obsessions (Papertown Press, 2019)

Palpable Passions (Papertown Press, 2017)

---

1 Originally published as ***Tenuous Tendrils*** by Ex Libris and later as ***Casual Choices*** by Hancock Press.

2 Originally published as ***It Seemed Like a Good Idea at the Time*** by Hancock Press.

3 Originally published as ***Ouch, Now I Remember*** in 2015 by Xlibris Press and rereleased under the current title by Hancock Press in 2018.

4 Originally published as ***Browsing through My Candy Store*** in 2014 by Xlibris Press and rereleased under the current title by Hancock Press in 2018.

5 Originally published as ***The Boat Captain's Conundrum*** in 2016 by Xlibris Press and rereleased under the current title by Hancock press in 2018.

Return to the Other Side of the World with Mary Jo Clark, Michael Simmonds, Katherine Sohn, and Hayward Turrentine (Strategic Press, 2013)

The Other Side of the World with Mary Jo Cark, Michael Simonds, and Hayward Turrentine (Strategic Press, 2011)

Evidence Based Policymaking: Insights from Policy-Minded Researchers and Research- Minded Policymakers. With Karen Bogenschneider (Routledge Press, 2010)

Policy into Action. With Mary Clare Lennon (Urban Institute Press, 2003)

REFRACTIVE REFLECTIONS

by:TOM CORBETT

Refractive Reflections

To order additional copies of this book, contact:
www.amazon.com
www.barnesandnoble.com
www.papertowndigitalsolutions.com

Published in the United States of America

ISBN:

Paperback: 9781956895322
Hardback: 9781956895360

"If one man can destroy the world, why can't one girl fix it?"

—Malala Yousafzai

"If you have any young friends who aspire to become writers, the second greatest favor you can do for them is to present them with copies of The Elements of Style. The first greatest, of course, is to shoot them now, while they're happy."

—Dorothy Parker

"Life is the best novelist."

—Honore de Balzac

"I screamed at god for the starving child until I saw the starving child was God screaming at me."

—Anon

"The test of a first-rate intelligence is the ability to hold two opposing thoughts at the same time, and still retain the ability to function. One should, for example, be able to see that things are hopeless yet be determined to make them otherwise."

—F. Scott Fitzgerald

DEDICATION

For Mary…

CONTENTS

Forward I

Part I – 2021 1

Chapter 1 – Kabul (Summer 2021) 3

Chapter 2 – Vancouver (Months Earlier In The Year Of 2021) 20

Chapter 3 – Connie 43

Chapter 4 – They Are Coming 62

Chapter 5 – Celtic Musings 78

Chapter 6 – Azita's Reflections 96

Chapter 7 – A Temporary Peace 128

Chapter 8 – The Crawford Home 148

Chapter 9 – Heathrow Airport [Summer 2021] 172

Chapter 10 – The Kabul Airport [August 2021] 194

Chapter 11 – Balliol College [Fall – 2021] 211

Chapter 12 – The Masoud Center [End Of 2021] 247

Part II – 2022 265

Chapter 13 – The Hairy Hare (Winter 2022) 267

Chapter 14 – A Discrete Visit 296

Chapter 15 – Connections 314

Chapter 16 – Farzana 337

Chapter 17 – Conversations 360

Chapter 18 – Ominous Signs 399

Chapter 19 – Connelly's Vision 420

Chapter 20 – Intimations Of The End 445

Chapter 21 – Shadows 463

Chapter 22 – Hegira – Preparations 478

Chapter 23 – Hegira – Flight 496

Chapter 24 – Refractive Reflections 519

Epilogue 549

The Players 561

About The Author 567

FORWARD

"Why do people always expect authors to answer questions? I am an author because I want to ask questions. If I had answers, I'd be a politician."

Eugene Ionesco

Refractive Reflections can be read as a self-contained work. It also can be considered the fifth volume in the saga that covers the story of three families ... the Masoud, the Crawford, and the Connelly clans. Five books in all, *Oblique Journeys, Palpable Passions, Ordinary Obsessions, Felicitous Fates, and now Refractive Reflections* constitute an interrelated set of works that explore the complex evolution of these three distinct families and the relational, political, and philosophical subthemes they embrace or reflect. While these works touch upon the stories of individuals and families, they also bring us deeper into a set of larger issues and challenges common to the human condition. In short, the entire series is multi-layered ... serious in substance, yet oft told with wit and well-paced drama.

The ***Connelly*** children (Joshua and Rachel) were raised in a gritty, blue-collar family in a Boston area ethnic ghetto who came of age during the turbulent 1960s. The ***Crawford*** siblings (Christopher, Katherine, Katerina, and the late Charles Junior) were born a short generation later. While enjoying a childhood of wealth and privilege in Chicago, they were torn apart by family dynamics that would dramatically impact their lives. The children of the ***Masoud*** clan were raised in Kabul during the worst days of the first Taliban era as we entered the 21st century.

Pamir and Madeena had three offspring (Majeed, Deena, and Azita). The two girls (Deena and Azita) pursued their dreams despite all odds. Three distinct cultures, separate generations, yet brought together by universal aspirations and challenges.

My first fictional work, now rereleased under the title ***Oblique Journeys***, introduced readers to Jeremiah Joshua (Josh) Connelly, his paramour Corinthea (Connie) Chen, his sister Rachel, and her daughter Cate, along with several other relevant characters that revolve about these main characters. The crux of their story focused on personal decisions made during the height of the Vietnam war crisis in the 1960s and how those decisions played out over the succeeding decades. The narrative primarily focuses on a single week during Joshua Connelly's retirement from the University of British Columbia around 2010.

I then moved on to the story of the Masoud and Crawford families in ***Palpable Passions*** and ***Ordinary Obsessions***. In these works, a more complex, multi-level, story line emerges involving these two quite different families separated by geography and culture. The Masouds, specifically the daughters Azita and Deena, struggled in Afghanistan during the Taliban reign of the late 1990s while the Crawfords grew up earlier in Chicago though the younger son (Chris) had already emigrated to England as their story unfolds. The complex stories of these two families encompass and reflect the tragedy of religious extremism in one country and the descent into a potential authoritarian rule in the other. This tale of the Masoud and Crawford families spans three volumes, over two decades, and three countries in the telling.

In a 3rd volume focusing on the Masoud and Crawford tribes, ***Felicitous Fates,*** I bring the two-story lines and the three families together. That is, I incorporate the main characters from the Connelly family story with that of the Masoud and Crawford clans. The narrative takes place in the recent past (ending with the 2020 U.S. Presidential election) and several subthemes are brought to an apparent close. At the close of Felicitous Fates, I thought this saga was at an end and that I would move on to other topics.

I discovered, however, that no great story ever ends. They simply evolve. Alexander McCall Smith, a gifted Scottish storyteller, started what he presumed to be a short series of stories to be published serially in an Edinburgh newspaper. As it happens, he came to love his characters and their situations. Now, the series runs into well over a dozen books. This is a malady suffered by many writers, they fall for the products of their imaginations.

It soon was clear to me that at least one more work touching upon these three families was necessary. Their story was not at an end. The Taliban surged back to power in 2021 and the major players in one American political party fomented an insurrection on the American Capitol building and then refused to acknowledge the legitimacy of the 2020 election results. Themes that appeared resolved at the end of Felicitous Fates soon began to unravel and the optimistic note on which Felicitous Fates had ended was thwarted by subsequent reality. Life has a way of interrupting both our dreams and the denouement of our creative endeavors. My saga, it struck me with considerable urgency, was not at an end.

I must note that each book can be read, understood, and appreciated as separate or individual works. I hope so at least. There is plenty of backfilling to keep the reader from getting lost. Besides, I fill in most of the essentials below. If you first stumble across this literary gem, you can start here. If the themes and characters appeal to you, one can always go back and explore the deeper backstory. It is a journey of the imagination worth taking which one can start at any point.

Introducing some of the key players ...

The patriarch of the Masoud family, Pamir, was a physician who grew up in humble circumstances. His talents, when recognized by his community, enabled him to be medically trained in England before returning to Afghanistan to aid his homeland and raise his children. Pamir's wife, Madeena, was a mathematician who taught at university level in the pre-Taliban era. We tend to forget that this beleaguered country once had a substantial secular population. In the 1970s, before the monarchy fell and the Communists gained power in a revolution that sparked a religious backlash, urban women experienced considerable freedom. They went to university, found careers, wore Western fashion, and dated on their own. Such freedoms are long lost now.

The Masouds, as noted, had three children: a son, Majeed, and two daughters, Deena and Azita. The youngest, Azita, was passionate about following in her father's footsteps despite the obstacles imposed by a totalitarian religious regime. In the first volume, we picked up the Masoud's story during the height of Taliban rule, but prior to Osama Bin Laden's 9/11 attack on the United States. The Masouds were determined to escape Kabul and the oppressive rule under which they felt captive. The family's goal was to flee to the area still held by the Northern Alliance or *Shura Nazar*, a group of tribal clans who bravely fought the Soviet invaders in the 1980s, and who fiercely opposed Taliban rule when it first came to power. His family story is rooted in the Panjshir Valley, which resisted Taliban extremism in the 1990s. This remote and rugged northern area in Afghanistan is where Pamir was born and raised. It is home to him, a place where he hopes to find comfort and safety in troubled times, and where his children might pursue their dreams.

The Crawford clan is headed by Charles Crawford, Sr., who was born in Poland as Karol Chrezsinski just as Europe spiraled into World War II. Charles was spirited to the United States after his father, a leader in the anti-communist and exiled Polish government, was killed by Stalin at the end of the war when he returned to establish a new Polish government. He naively believed Stalin's promises of free elections. The fatherless boy grew up determined to accrue personal power and great wealth, part of which he obtained through a calculated marriage to Mary Kelly, a rich Catholic socialite from Philadelphia. Charles and Mary have four children: Charles Junior (Chuck), the oldest (and married to Beverly), followed by twins, Christopher (Chris) and Kristen (Kay), and their youngest daughter, Katerina (Kat). The Crawford family members know extraordinary comfort and privilege in Chicago but are gripped by serious internal divisions that eventually mushroom into outright rebellion.

Other prominent characters in earlier volumes include Richard (Ricky) and his sister Juliana (Jules) Jackson are unlikely childhood friends of Chris. Ricky and Jules are black and from very modest means, growing up in a tough Chicago neighborhood just west of the Loop. Chris and Ricky bonded at a high school summer basketball camp and remained the best of friends throughout adulthood, until they meet their ends in the violence attending the Crawford drama. Early on, the Jackson home provided a milieu of love Chris never experienced with his own family. Chris and Jules enjoyed a long on and off romantic relationship over the years.

Other primary characters featured in this work include Karen Fisher who is Chris's assistant in his international service organization. From a working-class British family, Karen is a tough, yet perceptive, professional partner, who also happens to be a lesbian. Amar Singh is an Indian-born doctor whose struggle to become a physician was made more difficult by her conservative family who wished little more than a good marriage for her. Chris's twin sister, Kay, is a talented trauma surgeon who earned her medical expertise by attaching herself to the emergency room of a Chicago public hospital, partly out of dedication and partly to spite her father by working for the public good, something she knew her father would never understand. Kay married James (Jamie) Whitehead, a British Military doctor whom she met in Afghanistan. Readers will meet other fascinating characters along the way.

Refractive Reflections focuses a lot on the Connelly clan, mostly Jeremiah Joshua Connelly or Josh. He was born and raised in the Boston area, became involved in anti-war activities in college where he befriended several other would-be revolutionaries such as Morris Greenstein, Carla Shapiro, Bob Wilson, and Peter Favulli. Josh flees to Canada when he becomes overly conflicted by the violence of the movement. He does not reconcile with his sister Rachel, or his college revolutionary friends, until he retires from the University of British Columbia. Rachel's daughter, Cate, remained his sole family tie during his exile. In this work, the main surviving characters unite in England as Josh's health declines, and he faces his mortality.

The story line so far …

Palpable Passions traces challenges and struggles in both the Masoud and Crawford families. With the help of her biological parents, Azita violated the strict rules governing the proper behavior of Muslim girls. She stubbornly insisted on being educated at home by her mother and on helping her father with his medical work, sins that will no longer be tolerated by the Taliban as she approaches puberty. Azita will then be expected to become a servile and obedient woman as Taliban orthodoxy dictates. After Azita is almost killed by the religious (or morals) police while she is under Majeed's protection, Majeed is determined to fight these oppressors. The Masouds decide to escape Kabul and the Taliban when Majeeb is about to be forced into military service for a system he abhors. Under false pretenses, the Masoud family makes a dangerous escape to the Northern Alliance.

Following the tragic suicide of Chuck Crawford, who had been the forced heir apparent to the Crawford dynasty, much reflection takes place among the remaining Crawford offspring who come to reject their father's antisemitism and obsession with right-wing causes. Christopher, a Rhodes scholar with a doctorate from Oxford, uses his wealth and connections to develop an international service organization. He is devoted to helping the world's most vulnerable people and is most gratified that his father dismisses these ambitions as soft and ridiculous. Chris makes his home in London and Oxford, England.

Kay has also rejected her father's ideals by her choice of medical specialties. After a tenure as an ER doctor in a Chicago public hospital, she decides to escape the family drama by joining Chris's international organization where she manipulates her initial assignment in Pakistan to relocate to Afghanistan, an extremely dangerous site at that time. There, she becomes friends with Dr. Amar Singh and the two risk all to help those desperately holding out against the Taliban. Chris is outraged when he discovers that his sister defied him and joined Amar Singh in the conflict torn and dangerous country. Frantic for her well-being, he travels to Afghanistan to remove Kay from harm's way.

The Masoud and Crawford families connect in this desperate and conflicted part of the world. Representing radically different backgrounds, they find much in common. However, fate, as it so often does, intrudes in the most disturbing ways. Majeeb Masoud dies fighting for the Northern Alliance. Pamir and Madeena Masoud are murdered by the Taliban in the tumultuous days following 9/11. Kay stays in Afghanistan with Jamie Whitehead, and Chris loses his heart to Amar Singh, something that shocks all who knew him. Moved by the intelligence and drive of young Azita, Chris and Amar bring her to England where she can receive the education about which she has always dreamed but did not think possible. After some time, Deena (now living with Karen as loving partners, joins Azita, Chris and Amar in their international work. Palpable Passions ends with Azita Masoud finishing her pre-medicine studies at Oxford University and giving a university-wide talk about the obstacles she overcame to pursue her passion of becoming a physician against all odds.

Ordinary Obsessions moves the timeline forward to the run-up to the 2016 presidential election. By this time, the roles and situations of the main characters have changed. Azita Masoud is well into her medical studies at Oxford and is thinking hard about her future as her medical degree approaches. Her relationship with Benjamin Kaplan floundered given his Jewish family's reservations about her religious and cultural background. Moreover, she feels increasing reluctance to being swept into a medical research and academic career that might keep her from her homeland and thus following closely in her deceased father's footsteps. Deena had advanced her education but remains working on education opportunities related to Afghan girls. Strains begin to develop in her relationship with Karen.

Charles Crawford Senior has been removed as head of the Crawford financial empire in a family-initiated coup. At first bitter, he soon turns his energies and resources toward advancing his long-espoused hard-right political agenda, including supporting, though with some reluctance, the candidacy of Donald Trump. As this hard- right agenda appears to gain further traction, Katerina (Kat) Crawford, now titular head of the Crawford empire, lures her brother back to the States, where Azita will do her medical internship in Madison Wisconsin at the University's Children's Hospital. By this time, he is ensconced in the academy at Oxford University, writing books and still consulting with the ISO. Reluctantly returning to the States, Chris heads up a team whose mission is to tease out the reach of suspicious political activities designed to manipulate the election. His wife, Amar, reluctantly agrees to what is supposed to be a temporary exile back to America.

Karen Fisher has assumed day-to-day responsibility for running ISO, the service organization Chris founded. Ricky

Jackson, who had left the financial world in Chicago to help her, returns to help Kat run the Crawford empire after the two of them marry. Karen, meanwhile, is gradually building up the management staff of ISO with an international team of talented people including Carlotta Ciganda from Spain and Atle Bergstrom from Norway.

Throughout *Ordinary Obsessions,* the characters struggle with issues related to their professional roles, personal relationships, and their futures. Chris and Amar are concerned that Azita will return permanently to Afghanistan, particularly after she meets a boyhood friend, Ahmad (Abdul's son), as her relationship with Ben ended very badly, with his suicide. Kay finds that domestic life and wife and mother leave her unsatisfied and she takes up with Karen after she and Deena had grown apart. Not surprisingly, Deena gets more involved in educational issues for girls, while her bond with her sister, never totally smooth, finally begins to strengthen. Azita and Deena form connections with Bahiri and Ferhana Gupta, two doctors who have picked up the practice once run by Pamir and with Archie and Agnes Singletary, who are managing the Panjshir Valley site. The pull for Ferhana to remain connected with their homeland is strong.

Yet, danger is real and ever present. Kat fears she narrowly escaped attempts on her life. Deena is shot by an assassin and nearly killed during a visit by her and Azita to Pamir's historic family village. And Beverly, who remained close to her father-in-law, Charles Senior, used her feigned relationship with her father-in-law as an opportunity to spy on him for Kat and Chris. Beverly was found dead after Christmas 2016, having fallen from her penthouse balcony. No one can tell if it was an accident, suicide, or homicide. Tensions come to a boil at her memorial service when the Patriarch, who finally realizes that his son will never join him, baits Chris into attacking him in this public venue. Charles Senior has Julianna Jackson, Chris's former lover and long-time friend who is now a network star reporter, banned from the memorial. She has been reporting unfavorably on the Patriarch's activities and those of his uber-wealthy allies. Then, in front of Amar, the father taunts his son that Jules has remained Chris's lover. Chris attack's his father, leading Ricky to break his best friend's nose as a security guard for Charles Senior drew a weapon to strike Chris down, thus averting a greater tragedy.

Trump's surprise election changes everything. Kat and Chris realize that the right-wing insurgency in America might be on the verge of an ultimate triumph. America's fragile democracy is on the edge. They feel compelled to initiate a longer-term oppositional initiative to the decades-long effort to redefine American politics in a conservative direction including, as demographics threaten Republican political hegemony, subverting American democracy. Chris and his family return to England, but he will remain involved with his younger sister to thwart a growing international agenda to impose oligarchic control over the major countries around the world. The Putin-Trump conspiracy has ever widening implications.

At the same time, Chris works out a deal with his colleagues at Oxford, particularly Sir Charles Howard and Professor Shahed Al-Hussein, to establish an international initiative to advance the cause of Muslim women. He anticipates that this will induce Azita and Deena to remain connected to England and ISO, which will partner with this initiative. He and Amar know that this will not keep these two young women, whom they dearly love, out of harm's way completely. It will help to do so, or so they hope. The volume ends with Azita completing her internship and becoming engaged to Ahmad.

In *Felicitous Fates*, the Crawford clan prepares to return to England though realizing that this will not be a return to domestic serenity. Politics both in the US and in the UK continue to deteriorate while Trump and Brexit weave their evil potions around the souls of these two nations. In a unique narrative twist, several of the main characters from *Oblique Journeys* are woven into this story line. Retired Professor Jeremiah Joshua (Josh) Connelly, his sister, Rachel, along with her daughter, Cate, and Cate's partner, Meena Muhaisin find their way into the domestic and international intrigues explored in this third volume. It is a seamless interjection that brings a third major family theme into this political and personal drama.

This third volume takes us to the present day and peers into the future. Joshua Connelly joins forces with Chris Crawford to battle the surge of popularity for right wing demagogues in America and the slide toward fascism. The two work ever more closely with Kat Connelly and the Jackson twins to take back the political narrative in the U.S. that had been hijacked over the previous few decades through an increasingly effective set of conservative news outlets. Behind the scenes Charles Crawford Senior, smarting from losing control of his financial empire to his children plots to further a right-wing coup to establish an authoritarian form of government.

At the same time, Azita and Deena Masoud continue to risk their lives to help women in the middle east, the greatest dangers they face is in their homeland, Afghanistan, where the Taliban is making a comeback and America is making sounds that it will withdraw from the longest war in its history. Eventually, with the help of Professor Shahed Al-Hussein (Ali), they form a new initiative through ISO, Chris Connelly's international service organization, to identify young Muslim women to educate and nurture for future leadership positions. Rachel Connelly, Usha Nayer, along with Rachel's daughter and her partner join this effort.

During all this, two dark shadows arise. First, the Covid pandemic sweeps the world, shifting some attention to working with Toynbee Hall to serve vulnerable Muslim populations in London. Meanwhile, Charles Senior breaks his final ties with his wife and offspring and goes full out for a right-wing revolution. In Afghanistan, old animosities boil which threaten Azita and Deena's work there and their lives.

As 2020 unfolds, a series of catastrophes occur. The son of a Taliban extremist tries to kill the Masoud girls with a bomb at a Kabul medical facility run by ISO. They escape but Azita's husband, Ahmad Zubair, and Rachel Connelly are killed. Later, Azita is tracked down in her family village and once again escaped death at the last moment. In the U.S., Charles Senior goes after those within his family he feels betrayed him. Several attempts to kill his own children fail but, in the end, Ricky Jackson, Chris's best friend and brother-in-law, is killed by a car bomb. Amar, Chris's wife, who had been weakened in the Kabul blast, contracts Covid while treating patients back among the immigrant population of East London. As she is dying, she asks Juliana, Chris's old lover, to marry her husband. That is not to happen since Jules soon is assassinated on orders from Charles on a Chicago Street while Peter Favulli, Josh's old friend, is wounded as he tries to protect her. Mary Crawford, the matriarch of the clan, fears that her son will now try to go after her estranged husband, or the reverse will occur. She knows that things have reached a breaking point. She takes a preventive move, tracking her husband down at a breakfast place he frequently haunts, and shoots him through the head.

Felicitous Fates ends with a series of tantalizing events. Chris and Ali, longtime colleagues with no apparent previous romantic attachment marry. Kay Crawford, who had divorced Jamie Whitehead some years before and experimented with a lesbian relationship, reunites with her husband. Chris finds that his father had never got around to changing his will and that he inherited the bulk of his dad's fortune. And Donald Trump loses the election, thwarting a rightwing takeover. The battle for the soul of America remains in doubt as Trump refuses to accept defeat.

The Masoud, Crawford, and Connelly families face new questions in the aftermath of all these events. What will happen to the Crawford family now that the patriarch is dead? Do his dreams for an authoritarian takeover of America disappear with his assassination and the outcome of the 2020 Presidential election? That outcome quickly faded given the post Presidential election events, especially the insurrection on the U.S. Capitol of January 6? And how will the central characters of our saga respond to the loss of several loved ones such as Chris's wife Amar and his lifelong friends Ricky and Jules Jackson; Josh's sister Rachel and Azita's husband Ahmed.

Most importantly, how will the dreams of Azita and Deena Masoud survive with the resurgence of the Taliban after the American withdrawal after two decades? Existential questions and relational challenges must be faced and addressed. The question is, as it always is, how will the human spirit respond to our ultimate challenges? Are final ends predestined or do we shape the arc of our lives? What about us is chosen, and what dimensions of our lives are based on choice as opposed to fate?

The saga continues …

The dawn of 2021 spoke of a sense of hope that was liberally mixed with uncertainty. American democracy appeared to survive the assault from the right, though concerns remained. Donald Trump was soundly defeated in both the popular vote and the electoral college though at least five states were close enough to cause anxiety and drive those on the losing side into deep denial. While a solid majority had rejected his white nationalism, Trump would not, or could not, admit defeat and began beating the drums for the BIG LIE. After a direct assault on the Capitol by his followers fell short on January 6, his acolytes continued to cajole and even threaten officials in contested states. Highly publicized private recounts were held in Arizona, Wisconsin, and other states to no avail. There was no widespread fraud. The Trump believers soon began preparing for future elections, clinging to the belief that their failure at the polls meant rampant fraud, though never documented but widely believed to exist. This could only be rectified by direct action outside to the Constitution. For many, democracy now clung to life but clearly was on life support.

In England, the Connelly clan regrouped after several personal losses, especially the death of Amar, Chris's wife, Ahmad, Azita's husband, and Ricky and Jules Jackson, Chris's best friends and confidants. Ricky's death was particularly difficult for Katerina (Kat) Crawford who had taken over the Crawford financial empire. She had come to depend on him as a partner in life and as a valuable associate in running this complex organization. The death of the patriarch, Charles Senior, at the hands of his own wife, had simplified many things for her. Still, she considers relocating her headquarters to London, both to be closer to family and the world's financial markets. It wasn't only business considerations prompting this move, though. She found herself alone and missing her two remaining siblings, as did Mary, the aging matriarch of the family who was beginning to fail.

Azita and Deena Masoud once again found themselves at a crossroads. The earlier institutional focus on providing a coherent set of integrated services to highly distressed communities had matured. The early so-called lighthouse sites had proven successful for the most part and that part of Chris's vision seemed stable. On the one hand, their newer initiative of integrating Muslim girls into as full members of mainstream society remained highly vulnerable, especially in Afghanistan as subsequent events came to pass. The Masoud sisters, based on their own experiences, had formulated with Chris Crawford's new wife, Professor Shahed Al-Hussein developing, an exciting concept. They would identify promising young Muslim girls, many from rural schools they had sponsored. With tutoring and hands-on help, they would sponsor further education abroad to help develop a cadre of female leaders for the next generation.

As 2020 segued into 2021, few could have predicted that Trumpism would continue to dominate the Republican Party. But such things happened. With few exceptions, mainstream Republican politicians defended the Big Lie that the 2020 election was stolen even as the evidence that this allegation was patently false grew. Alarmingly, the right worked to take control of the electoral mechanics in many swing states, vowing to overturn the results they would not accept. American democracy was on the brink. Even sober political pundits and observers commented that the American experiment might well be on its last legs. The real enemy of America did not identify with the hammer and sickle, nor Islamic Terrorism. No, the threat came from within and was carried by white, evangelical nationalists who sought authoritarian rule when democracy failed to create the nativist society they craved.

Even fewer expected that the Taliban would retake power in Afghanistan. But they did, as the U.S. tired of the endless conflict with no definitive resolution. Once the troops were gone, the secular government evaporated like moisture in the summer heat. And with that collapse went so many dreams of ordinary Afghani women who enjoyed a small and brief taste of freedom and opportunity. And so, the saga continues for the Crawford, the Masoud, and Connelly clans. Their story is not at an end.

This work, in the end, is more than the continuation of a long-established narrative. It is a reflective journey through the soul as one ponders mortality and the meaning, if any, of one's life on this earth.

Tom Corbett
Madison, Wisconsin
March 2023

PART I
2021

CHAPTER 1

Kabul

(Summer 2021)

"As far as we can discern, the sole purpose of human existence is to kindle a light of meaning in the darkness of mere being."

Karl Jung

It was that deceptive part of the day. The dark and quiet of a Kabul night could not fully conceal the challenges to come. Still, the blackness afforded a disingenuous form of calm even though not all suggestions of what might be coming could be obscured. Sounds of an uneasy city murmured about the sleeping forms at the medical complex run by Doctors Bahiri and Ferhana Gupta. Human forms were everywhere, on cots and in sleeping bags arrayed in every nook and cranny where space might be found. As the ancient cliché went, it was a case of necessity being the mother of invention.

There also were the commonplace sounds of distant babies crying, domestic and public arguments in remote locations, dogs barking and vendors up early while preparing for the day's labors. This night, however, there were additional and potentially more sinister interruptions. Sounds of cars and trucks in greater numbers could be heard coursing through the streets. Gunfire, often part of the background noise on a sweltering summer night in larger Afghanistan cities, were now heard with more persistence, and closer than might be anticipated. To those awake at this hour, the staccato shots on this night punctuated and accentuated the normal cacophony to a more pronounced and unsettled degree.

Doctor Azita Masoud had hardly slept. She wanted to. She had tried. God knows what lay ahead that day and some of the possibilities rushed through her head in an unwelcome manner. She tried pushing them away since having her wits about her might be critical this day of all days. But that made rest even more elusive. It cannot be willed, especially when one's mind typically is restless and so many alternatives, most of them horrific in nature, seemed not only plausible, but likely to occur.

In addition, the summer heat was insufferable even at this hour of the night. While the clinic had air conditioning, electricity was a sometime thing in these troubled days. The portable generator was reserved for the patient wards and the areas where medical procedures were to be performed, especially at this hottest time of year. Azita momentarily wished she had stayed another night at that Western style hotel in the city center but that could not be done. Beyond worrying that she had become spoiled, soft even, they had to prepare everyone to leave today. It was all happening so suddenly. Any luxury of considering alternatives had expired. They simply had run out of time and options. It was either escape or … she cared not to think on the other possibilities.

Azita decided she should get up but found she was unable to will herself into action. Rather, she lay as still as she could so that she might not disturb others and so that she could preserve whatever coolness the night hours offer.

This had been the Masoud family home and medical facility when she was a child. The heat had never bothered her then. Was it warmer now, a function of climate change, or had she softened given the years away from her homeland? Let's see … how long had she been in England, some two decades now, not including the time in America as a medical resident. *Oh yes,* she worried, *she had been an exile long enough to forget what it had been like as a child, both the weather and other things.* Was she still an Afghani or was she now a Westerner who merely had been born in this strange land? Knowing she could not answer that conundrum, she focussed on the more pleasing memories suggested by this place. Her mind began to wander.

It was here that her original family was together for most of her childhood. True, those early years were scarred by memories of the oppressive Taliban in the late 1990s but there were so many comfortable memories as well. Most occurred within these very rooms, though the overall facility was larger now. She, along with her older sister Deena, and her even older brother Majeed would squabble and struggle for the attention and favor of their parents whom Azita never ceased to miss, not for a single day. Her mother Madeena had taught at the university level until that option was snatched away by the religious extremists. Her father was a physician revered by his patients and adored by his youngest child.

Azita had been inspired by Pamir Masoud. He had received his medical training in England and could have stayed had he wished. He had been a prodigy, coming from a respected family of much local note, but of modest financial means. They had lived for generations in the Panjshir Valley located in northeast Afghanistan where they exerted authority but, given the poverty of the area, had fewer resources than affluent urban families. Upon achieving his medical credentials, Pamir might have stayed abroad, that was an option. He could have acquired great wealth by Afghani standards. That prospect, however, never tempted him. His people, his community, had invested in him and he felt a tug to return to his roots. He would return home, marry Madeena whom he met at university before heading to England, though it was she who pursued this shy young man. That was possible in those days among the educated, a freedom that disappeared along with elite women wearing Western style clothing. Educated females had rather independent lives at the end of the monarchy a half century ago, now a long-forgotten memory. Pamir would start his medical practice in Kabul and, when established as a professional, would return to his own valley … to serve his people. That only happened after the Taliban took control.

Azita mused that Pamir and Madeena could easily have remained part of the Afghan elite but chose to work among the regular folk overlooked by most. Fortunately, Pamir's reputation brought to his practice many affluent clients which gave him the resources to help those less well off. Madeena, after being deprived of her academic position, would educate local girls surreptitiously, especially her two daughters. She would later find out that Madeena had encouraged the education of several neighbor girls including one named Ferhana, who eventually fled to India to get her own medical degree long before Azita had developed clear memories of her. In medical school, Ferhana met her husband Bahiri. So inspired was she by the Masouds that she convinced her husband to return to Kabul with her after the Taliban had been ousted in 2001. Ferhana eventually returned to her childhood neighborhood where she and her husband set up a practice in Pamir's old facility.

Azita smiled as she thought of the day when she and her sister returned to the family home, simply as a sentimental exercise. The two siblings were shocked and surprised to find their former neighbor plying her father's trade on that very spot. A tradition had continued. It was a no brainer for the Masoud girls to bring this practice into the orbit of the international service organizations, ISO for short, that her adoptive father, Christopher Crawford, had set up. Now, the Gupta's would have sufficient resources for their work.

A frisson of fear and despair now seized Azita as she sat in the darkness. What would happen now? Would this medical tradition end? The dreaded Taliban once again were sweeping across the country. The last American's were leaving as 20 years of effort and a trillion dollars in investment was being washed away with little protest and only mild regrets on their part. In her native land, on the other hand, uncertainty and fear rippled across the land. She pushed that thought out of her head.

Rather, she thought of her original family and the days they were together here. Even at an early age, she would follow her papa around as he did his medical work. Despite all his efforts to dissuade her, he realized early that you cannot drive out what god has put in a person. Nor can you ignore it. Azita relentlessly pestered her physician father to teach her his trade. Eventually, she wore him down.

Her ambitions to become a doctor seemed hopeless in those early days of the 21st century, given Taliban control of most of the country except in the north, where Pamir had grown up. Nevertheless, to humor her, he relented and began to tutor her while the mother taught all the children English, math, and other subjects. To his amazement, she stuck with it. Neither the sight of pain nor blood diminished her obsession. And to Azita's delight, Pamir began to treat her as the prodigy that, in fact, she was.

Azita always lamented that he never got to see what she would become, nor would her mother, or the eldest brother. Majeed would die fighting the Taliban after the family fled Kabul to escape their despotic rule. And then, on a night that she could not recall absent many tears, Pamir and Madeena were slain in the traditional family home amongst the mountains that gave them such comfort. They were assassinated by the Taliban who were seeking revenge while Azita and Deena barely escaped. Pamir had lied to the authorities in Kabul to get his family to where the 'Shura-e Nazar' continued to resist Taliban oppression. If it were any consolation, they did pass on back in the ancestral lands of Doctor Pamir Masoud, working among the people he loved so much.

Now, in the seeming nothingness of night, in the place of her childhood before the family made a tense *hegira* to escape Taliban rule and to join those fighting them in the north, tears flowed down Azita's cheeks. The blackness and despair were back. The Taliban who had wreaked such pain upon her and so many others were sweeping back into power. Nothing could stop them. But, as she and her sister had escaped, they could at least help other young girls desperate for an education and a future to find their way to some morsel of hope. If not, she would die trying. That was a small price to pay.

"Sister," Azita heard in the darkness, "are you awake."

She recognized Deena's voice. "Of course. Who can sleep this night?"

A form appeared from deep inside the inky blackness. "Apparently, most can. I hear deep breathing and snoring all around me. Let's make our way to the small office Bahiri uses. We can talk there."

With difficulty, they felt their way around slumbering bodies to the small room that was used as an office. When they opened the door, they were surprised to see four pairs of eyes staring at them in the dimly lit room. "Oh, you are all awake."

Bahiri and Ferhana Gupta, who had expanded this medical facility originally started by Pamir Masoud, were along one side of the single desk that dominated the room. Along another side were Doctors Carolyn Watanabe and her physician husband Kenji (Ken). Carolyn was the daughter of Doctor Archibald Singletary and his nurse wife Agnes who ran a similar medical and educational facility in the Panjshir Valley, both operating under the aegis of the International Service Organization (ISO) that Christopher Crawford had initiated almost three decades ago upon completing his studies at Oxford. That facility in the North was the very spot where the Masoud girls had met Chris and his wife-to-be Amar Singh so many years ago, the two people who would bring them to England and to a life of opportunity. "Oh, so glad you two sleepy heads are up," Ferhana said with a smile.

"You should have gotten us," Azita uttered a bit sharply, then transitioned quickly into a smile. She was a bit embarrassed for indulging herself with idle thoughts of the past when the others were working on the escape plan.

Ferhana chuckled with a soft sound. "We all know that Deena needs her beauty sleep and that Azita is cranky when awakened." Everyone now smiled since the elder Masoud sister clearly was a beauty and Azita an easy victim of harmless sarcasm. "But come closer. We are looking at routes to the airport."

Now six people hovered around the desk. All the usual patient reports and medical journals had been swept aside, replaced now with a detailed map of Kabul. Ferhana spoke. "We are not sure of how many girls have made their way here, since some may show up at the airport. This is such a difficult decision for them and their families, to uproot and leave with only the faintest hope for something they can hardly imagine. Can we really expect them to appreciate what awaits them beyond their life's experience? I remember being that young myself, about the age of many of these girls, and trying to decide whether to leave my family for India and there were cousins there to take care of me though I did not know them well. I could see what would happen under the Taliban, but it was still difficult, better the devil you know and all that. I almost did not go until Azita and Deena's father, Pamir, took me aside. I still remember his words. '*Young lady, the Taliban are about to take control. They will crush your spirit and keep you a prisoner. Whatever you fear, these are things of your imagination. But the Hell offered by the religious zealots is utterly real. Go, find your dream. I beg you. You have such promise.*' He said those words to me in this very office. You were here at that time, Azita. You always seemed to be with him, following him around."

"I was such a pest to him. I wish he were here so I could apologize." Ferhana lamented.

"Banish such nonsense from your mind." Deena interjected. "You were a jewel in his eyes."

"I always suspected papa had eye issues." Azita offered with an impish smile.

Ferhana chuckled softly as she finished her thought. "Azita, I suspect you were too young that day to remember the conversation."

"I am afraid you are correct though I retain a memory of you. I was jealous back then since you were a favorite of papa and I wanted him all to myself."

"Oh yes," Deena giggled, "Sigmund Freud would have interesting things to say about you."

"Oh shush, dear sister." Azita then became reflective. "I was too young to understand the Taliban threat in the beginning or why papa insisted you leave. Only later ..." Azita stopped.

Deena's expression turned grave. "You mean when those extremists almost beat you to death for reading in the public square."

"I had been convinced before then."

"Our dear brother Majeed carried you home all covered with blood. I almost died that day even though I didn't like you at the time."

"You were just jealous." Azita poked at her sibling.

"Jealous! Me! No way," Deena retorted. "You were shameless around papa, always seeking his favor. It was disgusting. Mama and I talked about it."

"Enough of the sibling rivalry," Ferhana interjected. "You should have seen these two when they were children. Their poor mother's hair turned grey trying to keep these two from killing one another. Besides, now we have work to do."

Carolyn spoke in her yet distinct Australian accent. "We brought as many girls from the north as we could, those we thought were the most eager to be educated and had the maturity to do well abroad. Their parents would like to follow one day but that likely is a hollow dream."

"Yes," her husband Bahiri took over. "It likely is. Many will be left behind, both girls wanting out and so many parents. We have gathered several buses. Two are here. The others are here and here," he said as he pointed at two medical facilities located in other parts of the city. "I will take one bus, Ferhana another, Azita and Deena will each take control on the buses here. There are four natural leaders we have selected from among the students ... Tahera Delawarzag, Makruh Sultana, Manzha Sultani, and Shekiba Nazari. They are older, very mature, and many of the girls know and trust them. One of these girls will be assigned to each bus."

"I know we have been over much of this before, but I am still not clear why I should not take a bus?" Ken Watanabe asked.

Ferhana spoke firmly but warmly to him. "We appreciate you and Carolyn getting some of your students here from the medical center in the north. However, as I said earlier, you do not know the city and you clearly are not local. Each bus will have to negotiate roadblocks and check points which will demand some negotiation. Local knowledge may be critical."

"But Bahiri is not an Afghan." Ken tried weakly.

"True, but he has been here long enough to fake it, or at least I hope so." Ferhana smiled at her husband. "Carolyn and Ken, I will ask one more time. Won't you get on a plane and get out now. We don't know what will happen a week from now, or tomorrow?"

"No way, my parents are still at our facility in the Panjshir Valley. They are old and stubborn. It exasperates me but I love them. I must stay with them. I suggested to my husband ... ."

"I love them as well." Ken said in a way that, knowing where the discussion was headed, hoped to end that topic.

"Okay, then," Ferhana continued. "You and Carolyn will stay here to look after any patients who come by and need immediate care along with any girls who make their way here at the last minute."

Bahiri pointed to the map. "I have traced out four routes from the starting points to the airport. If we make it there, not a guarantee given the chaos, there should be two planes waiting. We will fill the first up with the early arrivals and get it off the ground. Some buses may have to make two trips, there are students from the Asian University for Women yet expected but we don't know how many. They may be at the airport and have their own transport. All this is so rushed, chaotic. The first plane will take off when it is filled. A second plane will wait if it can until we see how many others make their way to the airport. But we are running out of time. Many girls will be left behind."

Deena spoke with conviction. "They will have to smuggled out later, if we can find a way."

"Yes," Azita said with equal conviction, "it would kill me to leave anyone behind."

Deena reached across to squeeze her sister's hand. "I understand."

Carolyn Watanabe spoke at this point. "What happens after they leave. I was not in on the early planning."

Deena picked up the discussion. "The plan is for them to go to Spain first. There, they will be met by Carlotta Ciganda, and Malala Yousafzai, among others. Besides heading the service side of the Crawford organization, Carlota is a Spanish citizen and has many contacts in Madrid. And Malala, as we know, has enough clout to open doors. Karen Fisher, our CEO, will be there to see things get done. She is so forceful. Another critical person is Kamal Ahmad. He is an Afghan national who, after his education in England and at Harvard, is now based in Boston. He will be handling the girls who will go to the U.S. As I understand it, Malala has been making arrangements on the continent for some of the girls, finding homes and tutors and, when possible, schools where they might succeed. While all that sorting out may seem complicated, they have been discussing that on their end for some time now. They are all good people, it will work. Oh, and I should mention that Professor Shahed Al-Hussein is coordinating things back in England, making housing arrangements, finding tutors, and the usual. She is less known to some of you but has been working on Muslim women's issues for years. And she is Christopher Crawford's new wife."

"We found it remarkable he remarried so quickly after the tragedy with Amar." Ferhana said with a touch of surprise or was her tone less generous?

"You can say that again," Azita murmured.

Deena spoke up, hoping to negate any further digression on that topic. "All this planning on the other end, only makes sense if we get the girls to the airport and on those planes." Azita said in a voice that she hoped did not reveal the tension she felt. "It will be chaos with the regime collapsing like it is. We all thought there would be more time. The Americans alone expect some 80,000 to 100,000 refugees, mostly people who helped them and now face retribution. Such people will be desperate. Others just want out for all kinds of reasons so there will be mass confusion at the check points. Who should go, who should not? Some of those decisions will be life and death."

Everyone looked at the maps in silence. They had been over these details before. It was mostly anxiety now driving this attention to detail as if thinking things through might sway the gods of chaos. Each person around the table knew one truth. All this was a bit like war. Plans only last for the first few minutes before a fog on uncertainty and random chance assumes control. Then Providence takes over.

"I think," Ferhana said softly, "we each should pray to our personal God. That would be the Buddha figure for me."

"I have many Hindu gods from which to pick," Bahiri uttered with a sheepish grin.

"Allah for me." Deena said in a whisper, causing Azita to glance in her direction.

"Christ for me." Carolyn said. "Though, I must admit, I haven't spoken to Him in a while."

"I will speak to my ancestors." Ken nodded.

After a silence, Azita wondered aloud. "Well, we seem to have the heavens covered. We'll need their intervention for sure. I wonder if Allah would recognize my voice after all this time."

After some time, there was nothing more to discuss. Azita and Deena then drifted outside to catch whatever refreshment the morning air might offer. The faintest suggestion of a lighter sky was perceptible to the east if one looked closely. This would be the first signal for the city, the nation, to arise and begin another day of struggle. The two women breathed in deeply. There was little relief even at this early hour. This parched land seldom offered escape for an oppressive torpor, except in the mountains to the north and east in the winter months.

In most of the country, the first suggestion of dawn signalled initiation of human activity. On cue, they could hear an increasing chorus of sounds and the murmur of restless human activity in the surrounding streets. Further away, the more distinct hum and cough of engines starting and cars coursing through city streets that would soon be clogged with human and vehicular traffic.

Deena turned to her younger sister. “I'm not sure we are Afghani anymore.”

“Don't be silly, we shall never be anything else.”

Deena did not look convinced. “Yes, you are right I suspect. But I must say I do not look forward to another scorching day. And we will have to dress as the local women. Even if the Taliban are not yet officially in charge, they shall be everywhere. Perhaps this time it will be my turn to be beaten within an inch of my life for some imaginary infraction.”

Azita looked at her sister with a smile. “Then I shall take immense pleasure in beating the remaining life out of you.”

“Great pleasure?”

Azita chuckled. “Great pleasure indeed. You have always been more trouble than you were worth.”

Deena took her sibling's hand. "Do you ever pray to Allah anymore? We used to talk about beliefs and faith. It has been some time."

Azita sighed. "I think, in the room, when we briefly touched upon the gods we look toward, or once looked toward, I tried a brief invocation."

"It seemed futile, did it not?"

"Yes," Azita sighed, "it was so much simpler when we were children. Our Gods seemed real then. Mine were since I worshipped papa as one. I can feel him here. After all, he did his medical work in this building."

"And you would follow him around like a puppy dog until he gave in and began teaching you, at great danger to us all. The Taliban could have punished the entire family for what you were learning."

"Were you any different once you found your own voice. After that, mother began spending endless hours teaching you. You were rather slow."

"Not slow, but I did have some catching up to do. I started later than you," Deena added defiantly. "I think mother realized at some point that I preferred girls to boys, which she apparently realized even before I did. When she suspected I would never marry, or try not to at least, she desperately hoped to create an independent woman out of me."

"Hah, mama never had to spend hours on my lessons. I was the good student." Azita said with distinct pride.

"You were just the teacher's pet. Besides, you had time to study. You were a lazy cow who never did any chores about the house."

There had been a time when Azita may have disputed that assertion. She might have pointed out what a quick study she was, how learning came so naturally to her, and that she helped papa in his work. But now she looked upon her sister with affection. "You, my sweet Deena, always had one thing I never did …"

"What nonsense are you talking about?"

Azita brushed a tear away from her eye. "A huge heart."

"Posh," Deena brushed aside the complement.

"I am totally serious. Do you remember the time that Chris talked about people with brittle intelligence? Not important that you recall. I remember. He said they are people who can easily solve complex mathematical puzzles but stumble over the simplest human challenges. You have a quality I lack, the ability to see inside people. I mean, this whole project with the education of Muslim girls is all yours, no one else but yours. It was your kindness and vision that has brought so many together for this. I am proud of you."

It was just now light enough for their two faces to be seen. Deena could apprehend that her sister was serious. "Be that as it may, now we must get these girls out. And then we must see about how much of our programs here we can salvage with the new regime. I'm not giving up you know. If we must smuggle half the girls out of this country to save them, we will, or die trying."

"See, right there." Azita touched her sister's face. "I would be calculating the probabilities of assorted options and dismissing many, if not most, as infeasible. You always go right to the heart of things."

Deena looked to the heavens. "Perhaps a good thing or perhaps something that will get us all killed. Sister, if you find any god in your heart, now would be the time to talk with him."

"I'll try, for you." Azita murmured.

"Good! Now let's go and get this started. I can hear that most are up and about inside."

CHAPTER 2

Vancouver

(Months earlier in the year of 2021)

> *"Do not grow old, no matter how long you live. Never cease to stand like curious children before the great mystery into which we were born."*
>
> *Albert Einstein*

Jeremiah Joshua Connelly, known universally as Josh, stared out the window at the nearby harbour below before shifting his gaze to the mountains that lay to the north of the city. Vancouver never failed to touch him with its beauty. Over four decades earlier, he initially embraced this panoramic scene in awe. That long-ago moment happened just a few blocks away, from an upper-story suite at the Blue Horizon Hotel. He had been gratuitously upgraded to a fancy suite since it was the off-season and there were few customers. Perhaps, as he preferred to think, the young female clerk was taken with his Irish charms and boyish good looks. On checking into the hotel, he had tried to appear shocked by the nominal asking price, especially when the demand for rooms clearly was down. After all, he was a poor student, and the trip would be a splurge for him. It struck him that the clerk, an attractive if a bit plump female his own age, had smiled at him. Was she flirting or merely acknowledging his transparent attempt to negotiate a better deal? He preferred the former explanation.

In any case, this rather transparent tactic worked. He had an upper-floor suite with floor to ceiling windows looking out upon scenes of breath-taking beauty, at least when he was not dizzy with vertigo. He made a quick mental note to employ such a stratagem in the future. That, it turned out, was a lesson quickly forgotten as he made his way up the economic and professional ladder. He soon could afford better rooms since most trips were on someone else's dime. Moreover, he quickly realized that money and material possessions meant little to him. He often found himself amazed that his well to do peers spent so much energy looking for monetary deals, how to get something cheaper. If he needed something, he went out and bought it. There was no haggling and no endless searching for a better price. He knew where his disdain for money and material things came from … his mother. She was so unhappy that life had not afforded her the finer things. It reduced her to a shell of bitterness, something that Josh would not permit in himself.

These moments of discovery began at the very beginning of his academic career, during his first visit to the city. He had arrived for a job interview at the University of British Columbia, a trip conducted more to please his academic advisor at the University of Toronto than from any desire for a career in the academy. In that long ago moment, he still had no idea what he wanted in life. He yet labored under the premise that he was not cut out for the rigors of a faculty position at a topflight research university. In his mind, he still was a working-class kid who had charmed his way through a terminal and rigorous academic program while remaining utterly amazed that his doctoral committee had not discovered that he was a fraud. He was shocked that the faculty had seen any promise in him at all if he were being honest. He found it impossible to shake his working-class roots … this self-image that he was little more than an Irish-Catholic tough guy from the streets.

As he looked at the visage before him on his first visit that day so long ago, he was smitten by what he saw before him. No matter his doubts in the moment respecting career and one's purpose in life, he would not leave this paradise. No way, not unless there were no choice. That seemed like a lifetime ago, he told himself. Then he realized that it was exactly that … a lifetime ago. His first vision of Vancouver's environs happened just as he emerged from a period of confusion and doubt from his early struggles as an émigré to Canada. As had many others of his generation, he had fled the Vietnam draft and from his impetuous acts of outrage that put him outside the law. When he first fled over the border, leaving family and fellow revolutionaries behind, he thought it was temporary. America surely would return to normal, and then he could return to repair the family and collegial ties he had severed. That was not to be. America did move on easily from the war, but not the enmities it generated. Nor could he move on with ease from his personal guilt and shame.

This vision before him on that long ago day seemed to justify all that he had been through over the decade after his hegira into a new land and life … his exile from all he knew and his struggle to regain his footing in a new country. His convictions, his personal acts of conscience against a war he considered an ill-conceived folly, had cost him his family, the one woman he loved dearly in his youth, and his circle of friends and fellow conspirators. Rather than face the moral conundrums that were driving him half mad, he ran away from everything and everyone. Silently, in the middle of the night, he escaped to Toronto. Not long after, he descended into his personal nadir, and after hanging on the precipice of suicide, slowly climbed out of a pit of despair in which he found himself. Eventually, he earned his Doctorate before stumbling into a position at a world-class University in this beautiful city, a situation that left his fellow doctoral students green with envy. He ascribed his fortune to the 'luck of the Irish,' rather than skill or effort. He remained crippled by the imposter syndrome.

In the arc of his life, that moment where he first viewed the environs of Vancouver was seared into his soul. It had proved an inflection point where his world would shift in both trajectory and meaning. As he, for the first time, stared at the panoramic view before him all those years ago, he saw the possibility of a fresh and less ominous future. It suggested hope and a promising career that was within the grasp of his metaphorical reach. He could imagine an end to the demons that had been chasing him remorselessly, to be replaced by a sense of acceptance and a career as a perhaps disingenuous academic and a happy, if peripatetic, policy wonk. He would join the ranks of the successful and the accepted. He would be normal. That became his plan at least.

Yet, inside, he knew that was not true exactly, likely more illusion than reality. His oppressive sense of guilt would remain, often finding its way into nightmares that woke him bathed in sweat and self-recrimination in the middle of the night. After all, he was Irish and had been raised Catholic. Self-forgiveness was the one personal aspiration almost impossible to secure no matter how diligently sought.

Now, high up on the 10th floor of this medical facility located just east of Stanley Park, there was a sense of melancholy, of loss, of an ending from which there was no exit. His just punishment had come due, as all the sons of Eire knew it must at some point. There was no ultimate escape from sin, and sin he had accumulated in abundance. No amount of absolution could wash away that stain of betrayal attached to him. No degree of penance could obviate his original transgressions. Those around him had, as he found out late in his life. That was a blessing he could not understand, not really, and therefore their forgiveness remained more of a curse. His own soul, by his own reckoning, remained tainted.

On cue, his oncologist confirmed what he already knew … it was payback time. His penance was announced with appropriate solemnity and professional gravitas typically attached to medical professionals. Jeremiah Joshua Connelly was dying. Only the final details needed to be prescribed, the inevitable minutiae that accompanied each of our endings. There were, as Josh imagined, the rituals of death to be honored.

He had sensed the diagnosis would be bad even before arriving, a pessimism cemented when this specialist suggested he bring his spouse for this consult. That was new, or at least the tone in his voice was different. Now alerted, he next asked just how dreadful things were. *'Don't be overly alarmed,'* the specialist had said, *'but we will be discussing treatment options, so it would be useful to have Professor Chen there. A second set of ears is useful for such discussions'*

Naturally it would. The doctor wanted an ally as he pushed invasive techniques for keeping his patient alive for a bit longer. That is what doctors did despite the wishes of the patient and the futility of the exercise. *'What folly,'* Josh had thought in that moment, *'keeping the condemned man alive for a few more weeks or months or even a few years.'* He knew, however, that a stay of execution did not eliminate the inevitable. It merely postponed what must be at great economic cost to society and considerable suffering to those immediately involved.

He had lied to Connie, his wife. He hated doing that. It was one of the few fabrications he could recall since they wed over a decade earlier or was it even longer than that. After a lifetime of avoiding emotional commitments, he finally had succumbed to this most basic of human needs to commit emotionally to another being. He first had reached out to repair things with his younger sibling, Rachel, during his retirement week from the University. In truth, it was she who did the reaching. Then, he finally acknowledged feelings for this woman known as

Professor Connie Chen, an academic peer with whom he had previously lived for a while but then pushed away in a panic as the relationship deepened. Or did she initially dump him as an emotionless robot? Now, the details were fuzzy in his remembering of them.

No matter, to his astonishment he responded positively to both attachments … the one with his only sibling and with the one female who managed to penetrate the defences carefully erected to support his commitment phobia. Affection, even love, turned out not to be an illusory *bete noir* of his personal existence. He had fought against such emotions which, to his shock, turned out to be acceptable in the end. This epiphany began when the sister who had meant so much to him in his youth forced the issue upon him. He was so grateful to her for this but, of course, the cruel divinity who hands out justice snatched her away from him all too soon with sudden and cruel ferocity. He still had not forgiven God for that.

He now wondered if perhaps God balances the scales somehow. He lost his only sibling, Rachel, suddenly and tragically but soon came to realize that he really loved this comely Asian woman … an academic colleague with whom he had danced about in an emotional tangle for years but had kept at arm's length. These feelings of attachment surprised him. He had thought himself incapable of such commonplace emotions … filial and erotic love. In the end, though, he was like other men, not so special and surely not unique. And finally, during that same retirement event, he reconnected with old peers and associates from his youthful revolutionary days, those whom he had hid from for decades out of shame. Those reconnections were cathartic and liberating. He thought they would never forgive him, but they did, or it seemed as if they did. He still could not quite accept that nor understand their capacity for such a love.

Having Connie in his life made his impending end more difficult. His sister Rachel, now only a sweet memory, had been blown apart by a bomb while working in Kabul. That had broken his heart. Finally, having rebuilt their connection after so many decades, it was ripped from him in a moment. Her sudden demise now seemed more a blessing in some warped way. He would not have to tell her he was abandoning her again, even if there would be less personal guilt associated with this leave-taking. There was no choice in death, perhaps in the timing, but not in its finality. Then there were the friends and fellow revolutionaries from his youth. He had reconnected with them a decade or so ago. They were in another country, back in America. They would be solicitous, but the looks of concern and pity would, at best, only be experienced through cyber-space, not up close and personal unless, of course, they chose to be with him. Would they? No, he doubted that. That would be asking too much.

Connie was a different matter. He knew she would not let him go in peace. On his own, he could determine his own fate. But she was his partner, and she loved him. He never quite could understand that. Yes, he was extremely popular among acquaintances, colleagues, and former students. He had always been affable, insightful, and so witty. But love … for him? Could she not see how undeserving he was? What was wrong with her? She saw him daily. Did she not see him for what he was … a deeply flawed man? And what about Rachel. She had also forgiven him far too easily. Not only had he run away from her when he fled north but he kept her at arms-length for decades out of shame and guilt. But she had pushed through his shell and reached his heart. That was all her doing, despite his resistance. She loved him, at least until that terrorist explosion took her away in an instant. He never felt deserving of such love.

Every time Rachel came back to his memory, a frisson of pain coursed through him. He had let her down when she needed him. He had run off and, even worse, did not reach out to reconnect. He remained mostly silent except for perfunctory offerings of the meaningless detritus that constitute the ordinary aspects of life. He did not know how to say sorry, so he said little. And she still forgave him. They all forgave him. That was a fresh kind of hell, was it not?

Connie would want to keep him alive for as long as she could, a sentiment that Josh admired and resented in equal measure. And Rachel, if she were still with him, would share that same purpose even, as a physician herself, she might understand the hopelessness of the situation. People were funny about death, he thought. They were so reluctant to let go, so resistant to reality and the inevitability of events. We all die. That is our one inescapable truth. And still, we fight it so desperately. It is inevitable, the one dimension of life's cycle that is undeniable. Still, we resist it so fiercely. 'Was that merely a fear of what was next?'

Nevertheless, there was something affirming about this passion to keep the other alive, to sustain life in any loved one. In his case, it testified to her love for him, an attachment that he did not doubt but would never completely understand. This form of reluctance by others to not let go was such a selfish emotion in his mind. It was like they were saying I want to keep you with me no matter your suffering. That is how it struck his cynical side. Josh thought of an old aphorism. 'We celebrate at the birth of a child and cry at their passing toward the end of their life because we are not the one involved.' Would we not be more honest to weep at the suffering to be endured in life and cheer when one is released from this mortal toil? That struck him as a more genuine appraisal of what life and death offered. That, however, was his dark Irish cloud talking.

No matter, he had lied to his wife about the visit to his specialist. '*This is just a routine follow-up visit,*' he told her. She looked sceptical. How did women see so easily through the men they loved? What magic powers did they possess, able to peer so easily into a man's heart and soul? No matter, he managed to keep his demeaner calm, his tells hidden. He sensed that she rejected his lie but neither did she push the issue. She would find out soon enough, or might she call his specialist on her own. That struck him as more than likely.

"You didn't bring your spouse?" The specialist asked with disapproval.

"She is a busy woman," Josh tried. "She still has her research and continues to write academic papers." Then he added a bit of wit, his go-to position. "Hell, I have to make an appointment to see her most days."

Unlike his internist, with whom his light humor worked, this oncology specialist was decidedly serious. Perhaps he had delivered too much bad news over the years. Most likely he had heard every manner of evasion and denial imaginable. Joshua Connelly was clever but not that clever. Without further comment, the physician launched into a clinical discussion of Josh's condition with appropriate, yet practiced, sympathy. Upon finishing, he added. "With your permission, I will be in touch with your wife to let her know."

Josh suddenly felt like the schoolboy caught using a trot for his Latin lesson. "I will let her know. I want to tell her in my own words. I know how to talk to her, break it gently."

At this the specialist sighed. "I understand where you are coming from. I really do. At the same time, I also know that patients are not always in the best position to be totally … accurate in these discussions."

"I …" Josh tried.

"Go home. Break the news to your loved ones. We won't discuss treatment options today. But I want her here when we do? Is that understood? And have her call me."

Clearly, the specialist doubted Josh's good intentions.

Josh stood in the waiting room as others had replaced him in the inner sanctum where news, hopeful or doleful, was being doled out. What would he say to Connie? What message did he have for himself? In the moment, he did not know. He presumed he was prepared but realized one never is. Reality is a demanding mistress that takes few prisoners.

His mind drifted toward thoughts that typically occupied him when unduly stressed. In such moments he often contemplated those bigger questions like *Where had we come from? What was our place in the universe? And where we were going?* These impossible questions were what … perhaps his coping mechanisms. Whatever they were, he felt his mind drifting inexorably in that direction.

He usually had felt sophomoric when focusing on such unanswerable conundrums, much like he did during those boozy, late-night conversations back in college, at least after he had sobered up. He smiled at the recollection where some faux intellectual among his college peers would suggest that our whole cosmos might be the experience of another being in some larger, parallel cosmological location. Perhaps all that we have measured both across time and over vast galactic distances was nothing more than an atomic explosion in a parallel universe. Our Big Bang was the ignition point, the impact at ground zero. The moments of the mushroom cloud in that other universe were experienced by us as billions of years in our world. Time is relative after all. Didn't Einstein tell us that?

This had a certain plausibility to it. Our own galaxy, the Milky way, has some 200 to 400 billion stars, The so-called Sombrero Galaxy contains another 200 to 300 billion stars. Our neighbor, the Adromeda Galaxy might have more than a trillion circling stars if he recalled correctly. While still 2.5 million light years away, we are destined to collide with our nearby galactic giant some 5 billion years in the future. More mind blowing was the reality that there are billions of these galaxies throughout the Universe, some colliding with one another but most racing away into the unknown. He was told by an astro-physicist, the brother of the late wife of his good friend who was teaching in Canada at the time, that there are 400 billion times a quintillion stars throughout the universe. Aji Singh, which was his name, had told him that a quintillion was a billion times a billion of something and that there were about 400 billion times a quintillion stars out there. That was a ten with some 24 zeros after it, a large number indeed.

Aji then said that we hadn't yet captured them all yet. Quite clearly, we hadn't. After all, our known and measured universe expands by the decade, perhaps it is now by the day, with each new picture taken in deep space by the James Webb telescope. He just ran across an article showing how the earlier Hubble telescope in deep space focused on what appeared to be a small empty spot out there. After four months of capturing whatever light could be detected from this apparent dark and empty area, they found thousands of additional galaxies, some populated by up to a trillion stars. Yes, the broiling masses of gas and heat of an atomic mushroom cloud just might look like our universe in a perverse way.

Back in school, he had smiled back at such idle musings. But now this image captured him anew, a swirling mass of stars and nebulae where most galaxies and celestial objects are flying from one another in some infinite time and space … or was it some soup of dark matter. Is it not unlike the image of a nuclear blast with the hot gases and radiation expanding in a widening path of death and destruction? What if we were some other universes version of our Hiroshima … our galaxy being one tiny part of a growing mushroom cloud which destroyed that Japanese city in 1945. Could it be that our whole experience of where we are is merely an insignificant speck in someone else's mushroom cloud?

If true, Josh thought to himself, then our perception of time is also illusory. Those mountains he was looking at across the bay were millions or even billions of years old. The earth itself was 4.5 billion years old since gravity had collected circling gases and debris into a sphere while the time elapsing from the Big Bang ran some 13.5 billion years. He couldn't quite retrieve the moment when primitive life emerged, one cell organisms but it was a long time ago. He did recall that dinosaurs disappeared suddenly some 65 million years ago, likely when an asteroid struck the earth creating a dramatic climactic disaster. That was lucky for our ancestors who, at the time, were tree hugging shrews who could survive the disaster. Eventually, over an extended period, they morphed into the genus homo some 2.5 million years in the past.

In some ways, it all struck Josh as painfully glacial but remarkably immediate in geological terms. It was another 4 to 5,000 thousand years before groups of our ancestors had any luck hunting larger game and another 300 thousand years before fire was commonly used by members of the Homo-Erectus and Neanderthals, those who came before us. Then, fortuitous climactic conditions in East Africa led to the emergence of homo sapiens about 200,000 years ago after which the pace of change picked up. About 70,000 years ago, what we now think of as humans began migrating out of Africa to other parts of the globe before clashing with related species like the Neanderthals and eventually prevailing.

There were competing theories on how our ancestors prevailed. Josh always preferred the disease explanation. They brought diseases for which the original inhabitants of the new lands they 'discovered' had no resistance. I mean, Josh murmured to himself, that's what worked for the first Europeans who arrived in the Americas. The germs they brought killed 80 to 90 percent of indigenous peoples while butchery subdued or eliminated the rest. We humans were a two-edged sword, bringing both uniqueness as well as death and destruction wherever we roamed.

Josh shook his head and looked at his watch. He should head back, talk to Connie, but he wasn't ready quite yet. Now here was the benefit of a febrile imagination, he realized. He could evoke all manner of arcane thoughts to keep him occupied and away from the pressing matters of real life. It was a refuge into which he had retreated to all his life. Now he needed it more than ever. His gave full permission to his imagination to wander as it would, and as it did with the effortlessness of gods when he got into one of his moods.

About 10,000 years in the past, migratory tribes who had survive by hunting and stealing from others began settling in Mesopotamia, the fertile crescent of modern Iraq. They gave settled agriculture a try which, in turn, permitted larger groups to collect in each location leading to the rudimentary elements of civilization. Nevertheless, civilizations emerged and the development of recognizable cities a few thousand in size soon followed some 7,000 years ago. Josh wondered anew as to how such inflection points happened. Was it some prescient individual who struck on a new idea or way of doing things? Or maybe the time was right, or some other climactic or demographic pressure required adaptation to survive.

He realized how much we like the story of some early genius striking upon the wheel, or fire, or agriculture, or fashioning man-made weapons. But maybe it was merely time to move ahead, no genius required. He recalled how Thomas Edison was awarded credit for inventing the electric light bulb, a breakthrough which transformed society. To Josh, that was a simple-minded attribution, as with so many other discoveries during that era. Josh searched his memory to recall that as early as 1808, English electrochemist Sir Humphrey Davy created an incandescent lamp by passing a current through a thin strip of platinum. There were subsequent improvements on this basic concept on nine other occasions until Edison's engineers got around to coming up with a similar innovation that stuck. Why then and not earlier? Probably it all came down to the fact that society was finally prepared to invest in the infrastructure to make it practical. Even then, Edison fought hard for his direct current option against Nikola Tesla's for more efficient alternating current option. And Alexander Graham Bell got credit for the telephone though insiders credit an inventor named Meucci who developed the concept some 60 to 70 years earlier. Josh often wished he could transport himself back to answer such imponderables such as how did progress really happen. Ideas were not accepted until the time was ripe. After all, the Vikings were in North America several centuries before Columbus, but their discovery didn't take.

Humans, particularly the early city dwellers, became interesting as they started creating myths, narratives, and primitive religions to explain their world. Well, it was more than an effort to understand things but also to control them. And it gave the priests and shamans an elite place in society, much as some academics like himself enjoyed in the current era. The first written narrative for a culture, the story of Gilgamesh, was written in about 5,000 years ago while the more advanced cultures of Greece, Egypt, China, and Central and South America popped into existence some 2 to 3 thousand years ago. We know so much more about them because the written language was more universal. Yet, others may have been as advanced. In fits and starts, civilization started forward, hitting another inflection point some half a millennium ago with the development of inductive reasoning and the invention of Gutenberg's printing press. Then, it was off to the races toward the modern world and just a matter of time before the technological world emerged.

And yet, Josh thought, we are still caught between the brilliance of our scientific sophistication and the barbarity of our ancestral imperatives to dominate and destroy. ***'Which will win out, our better angels or our inner devils?'*** *He would have to ponder this conundrum more.*

A voice broke his reverie. "Professor Connelly, are you waiting for someone, do you need a cab. I can call one."

"Oh, sorry," he mumbled in embarrassment. "Just daydreaming. My car is downstairs." Embarrassment motivated him to move.

When he slid into his vehicle some ten minutes later, he did not start the engine right away. He wasn't ready. Rather, he sat there while his mind yet churned.

How could his conflicted thoughts and theories be sorted out … a universe billions of years old while, at the same time, being part of another's nuclear blast which was a mere moment in their time. It took Josh a moment to seize on Einstein's insight. Space and time were not constants. A static understanding of things was Newton's universe. Reality was relative, with space and time somehow related to the observer's perspective. He could not fully fathom such matters, but he decided to accept what his mind rebelled against. Our billions of years could be a moment or two in some other reality. Really, doesn't string theory posit these parallel universes with realities smallest concentrations of energy existing in more than one place at a time. Mathematics somehow suggest impossible scenarios. Yes, this fantastical sense that we are some other world's Armageddon might not be totally ridiculous.

As it did when Josh got into such moods, his mind began to hurt as it raced through possibilities divorced from constraints. He loved these internal monologues, they represented some of the more exciting intellectual ventures he experienced. At the same time, they caused him pain, mostly in the recognition of his own limits ... how little he still knew after a lifetime in the academy. And now he had such little time left. Anger suddenly flushed through him. Perhaps he should go for aggressive regimen of treatment. He needed more of life's most precious commodity ... time. He needed so much more if he were to understand his world and put his thoughts to paper, to share with others. He had no children, except for his niece Cate. But she was not his biologically. He only had his accumulated wisdom to leave. He laughed grimly. That would be his only legacy.

Time, he thought. There wasn't enough, ever. He recalled another conversation with his Aji. At the speed of light, it would take us one second to reach the moon, 8 minutes to get to the sun, some 20,000 years to escape our own galaxy, and 46.5 billion years to reach the boundary of the known cosmos. And maybe there was more out there we hadn't measured yet.

Yikes, he exclaimed to no one, this does hurt my brain. Just get back to the task at hand. No, he was not ready to let this go. Not yet. He was not quite ready to face what had to be faced. So, he let his mind wander to the biggest question of all ... *is there any purpose to all this?*

This conundrum hurt his brain more than any of the others. On the one hand, he was told that the entropy was the ultimate end of things. The universe will continue to expand and cool until it reached a steady state of nothingness. All would be cold and lifeless. Now that struck him as particularly pointless. Perhaps he could take a lesson from the Hindus. The image of Chris Crawford popped into his head. Now, there was a man who was my equal in terms of intellectual masturbation, he said out loud to no one. Then he chuckled at the fact that he was talking to himself. But he and Chris would share such musings, and he had loved his discussion with Amar, his friend's late wife, and her brother Aji Singh, the cosmologist whom he met at the University of Toronto and who now was at Cambridge University on sabbatical.

It was Amar who told him about Brahma, and the ancient belief that this major Hindu God would breathe in and out every 80 to 85 billion years. Did he recall that correctly? Just how did the Hindu's have such a sense of immense time when some Christians still see a world some 6000 years old, created on October 23rd to be exact, in which dinosaurs and man competed for God's favor. No matter, if you take this story in some allegorical sense, our universe is at some part way point through Brahma's breathing cycle. As this God exhales, the universe expands, and stars and galaxies and all manner of cosmological wonders rush into seemingly infinite space or what may be dark matter. Then, as Brahma inhales, it all begins to contract again. First at a slow pace, then with increasing celerity, until it all collapses into a finite point of unimaginable density, heat and potential integrated, something like the singularity of an immense black hole. It is now once again ready for a Big Bang. As with reincarnation, the cycle of creation and destruction is endless which mutes concerns over what preceded our Big Bang. It was another Big Bang.

Josh shook his head to clear it of the thoughts rushing through. He started the car and started east before swinging south and then west toward home and the University of British Columbia. He tried to focus but his mind kept wandering. The route was second nature to him, hardly demanding much attention. Cold entropy or endless repetitions of expansion and contraction. Not much of a choice. The major religions offered little more … obey some invisible master who issued amazingly confusing edicts in ambiguous language or else. What kind of omniscient God would demand servitude from still evolving life forms on a speck located in an insignificant solar system circling a minor league star in an immense universe. The earth is just a speck, an atom, within this cosmos so big the human imagination cannot comprehend it. It was inconceivable to Josh that any deity would even notice this speck or the current dominant life form on it, never mind whether Johnny managed to cop a feel from Susie on a Friday night. And yet, that was what he was taught in the Catholic church of his youth.

But there was always one thing that intrigued him and caused him pause. Humans were evolving toward the singularity, or so he was told. This was another of those inflection points in the arc of the human experiment where consciousness would be melded and enhanced by technology in some synergistic form. He read that there was a 50-50 chance of creating a machine-based entity to replace or, more accurately, house many dimensions of human intelligence by 2050 followed by a form of super-intelligence by 2075. Who knows what might be possible when kids born today reach the end of their human days? Perhaps that was where hope for escaping some inevitable and pointless end. Humans can create an artificial intelligence that somehow, in ways that Josh could not imagine, could counter what seemed inevitable … the extinction of one's consciousness.

Right now, there were some 72 studies of which he was aware working to create advanced forms of computer-based intelligence. Long ago, they had developed machines that could beat the best humans at chess and certainly outperform man and women at complex calculations. Now they were well along on the path of developing systems that could learn, correct their mistakes, and so much more. Arthur C. Clarke's mechanical character HAL in film classic 2001: A Space Odyssey portrayed that future moment when a form of artificial intelligence would outmatch its human competition and assume command. This was a universal theme that initially frightened audiences in those 1950s sci-fi movies about a scientific community out of control while inadvertently creating monsters that could not be mastered. Hadn't the recently invented atomic bomb threatened to annihilate all of us?

On the other hand, what could such a superior intellect accomplish if used for good, with all data at its command and no death and decay to worry about? Sure, there were hurdles to overcome. Humans were still more skilled at making fine differentiations that demanded refined perceptions, distinguishing a wolf from a coyote. But those skills could be learned after thousands of comparisons are made and then handed off to other machines as given skills. It takes years for a human child to develop such skills. Could not a machine, with its incomprehensible computational speed, do the same in seconds. The possibilities seemed endless as human limitations were surmounted, and the potential of human thought given over to its full potential. In that moment, Josh ached to know the outcome. Could the species not kill itself off before it moved toward becoming an avatar for God?

The question, and this was always the question in Josh's mind, was how an inanimate object might develop moral judgments. Could they understand compassion, caring, empathy? Were these uniquely human attributes that inanimate machines could never comprehend. Or could our future machine-based life forms embrace such norms far better than the species they might come to dominate and replace. After all, humans had not done such a great job with their presumed intellectual attributes, and certainly not with their presumed moral and ethical sensibilities. While science was reaching out to the edges of the cosmos with new-fangled technological wonders, the American public had elected a demented pervert, Donald Trump, to the highest office in the land. That was the ultimate conundrum, he decided. Which would prevail … paradise realized, or opportunity squandered.

Suddenly, he was home. How had he gotten there? This always frightened him. He often lost awareness as his mind raced through thoughts and theories while his body negotiated real life. It was one thing to lose himself as he walked down a street or along the shore near his home. Doing the same while driving a car was a different thing all together. Yet, he did so all the time. How had he not killed himself in the past? Then it struck him. Perhaps that would not be such a bad thing now … to end things quickly.

He paused to think on this notion … suicide. That had many positives to be considered. In this moment, though, such was not to be.

"What did the doctor say?" Connie asked.

Josh looked at her in confusion. He had taken a long time to return home and gave not a thought to how he would tell his wife. No, he had run to that place which always provided comfort, his febrile imagination. He had to say something. With no alternative at hand, he told her the truth. When she remained calm, he added, "You don't look surprised, sad, or angry."

"That's because I already knew."

"I should have guessed," he said weakly. "You called him, or he called you."

She betrayed a hint of sadness. "I didn't have to call him, especially when you didn't return right away. I assumed you lied to me before going and then you were reluctant to return home. I'm not Sherlock Holmes but this wasn't hard to figure out."

"Sorry..." he mumbled and stopped. Communicating with a spouse was like interacting with one's mother. You might command respect in the wider world, but you become a child again in when facing the woman who brought you into life or with whom you chose to share that life.

Connie sighed. "Josh, I know you, the peculiar Irish places where you run and hide, that mind of yours that races ahead of others. But at the end of the day, I love you. I mean, really, who else would marry such damaged goods. I could have had a sensible physicist after all."

"Harold?"

"Of course, Harold. I'm shocked you recalled his name." Connie managed a tiny smile.

Now Josh smiled back. "How could I forget it now. I almost lost you the last time I forgot."

At this, Connie chuckled. "Yeah, you really pissed me off then, making fun of my fiancé, such as he was. But I knew, even as I was screaming at you, that it was hopeless. You were inside my head, and my heart. We ... I... just had to go through my emotional hoops first. That old saying is true ... the heart wants what the heart wants."

Josh went to her, taking her in his arms. "I love you."

"I know. After all this time I know. If I didn't, I'd be separating your family jewels from the rest of your body right now, you shit." She pulled away revealing tears flowing down her cheeks. "No more hiding. You got that mister."

"Yes ma'am. Old habit I suppose."

"So, what are you going to do?"

Josh looked at her as if her question made no sense whatsoever. He hadn't considered at all the most pressing issue in his life. "I'm not sure."

She looked at him for what seemed an eternity. "But you're not going to fight this, to stay alive even for my sake?" Then her face flinched. "I'm sorry. That was unfair."

He sighed. "No, Connie, that was eminently fair." He lowered his head for a moment before raising it again with a more resolute expression on his face. "After he told me I thought about some of the things that have always puzzled me, and there are many. It grieved me that I won't have time to figure them out. That has always been one of the things that has driven me in life, figuring out horrendous puzzles."

"We are similar in that way," Connie interjected.

"But you address answerable questions that involve chemical functions. By that I suppose I mean questions that have answers. I keep getting stuck on those damn conundrums that are beyond our reasoning. I remember Rachel when she was a young girl following me around. She was always asking these questions like *'can God create a rock so heavy He can't lift it?'* She was a pest as a younger sister, but I loved her so. That she could even come up with such questions at that age was a marvel to me."

"How did you answer that one?" Connie asked softly.

"When she was young, I made crap up. But later, I got smart. I would answer with another question, mostly with *'what do you think?'*

"You always were a clever lad."

"Not so clever but I became increasingly fascinated with her answers. She was a prodigy. And then, and then I betrayed her, betrayed them all."

"For Christ's sake, don't go there again." Connie said sharply then visibly softened. "Rachel loved you, as did your friends from college."

His chest heaved. "For me, there were never enough apologies. There never could be enough. And then she went and died on me. Perhaps that adjusts the guilt scales."

Connie embraced her husband again. "And I ask again, what are you going to do?"

"Not quite sure, not just yet." He said softly.

Connie smiled. "Of course you have. You simply haven't acknowledged it yet."

CHAPTER 3

Connie

"I have a religion; it's called love. I have a church; it's called earth. I have a scripture; it's called a heart. I have a prayer; it's called compassion."

Sofo Archon

After Josh left the house, Connie Chen immediately sought out her contact list. Her husband, as much as she loved him, was a male and thus beset with usual limitations universally found in that gender. He would not face unpleasant tasks and, being an accomplished procrastinator, would find endless ways to put off what had to be done. He was, for example, better at delivering a witty remark to sharing hard news about himself. She would let people, some people at least, know his bad news, and now rather than later! Her urgency was more than merely dealing with an unpleasant task, which was her style in any case. For a moment, she pondered whether this trait was part of her Chinese heritage. She could not recall anyone claiming that to be an ethnic attribute, but the hypothesis sounded reasonable to her. She would have to explore that possibility when she had more time,

No, there was another reason. She feared her husband might go to some remote and ominous place inside his head when facing the end. He might drift toward an emotional pit preferred by those of the Irish persuasion. *Now,* she said silently to herself, *that is an ethnic fact recognized by all.* If that dark fate were to occur, she wanted allies on her side. This was not a battle she preferred to wage on her own.

She was glad that he was old fashioned. Yes, he had a contact list on his phone. However, he yet maintained a written list of essential people in his life, along with a host of personal information such as financial account numbers, passwords, frequently used vendors, medical and legal and accounting contacts, and all manner of other essential data needed to keep a person going in the modern age. She shook her head. It was likely that this list was on his computer which, if it found its way into the wrong hands, would enable a miscreant to walk off with his life and his fortune. Good thing she was honest.

She looked through the names. There were many professional colleagues and associates, either in academia or government. She noticed immediately that this enumeration was dated. Even she knew that some were deceased or had long abandoned any active place in his life. Others were current, but Connie paused. He was friendly with these people, but they were not friends. She had to think harder on this matter.

Why was she even doing this, or doing it so quickly? There were those who would be saddened by the news. A few would reach out to help, perhaps more than a few. And yet, as Connie reflected on the names, she sensed a truth about her husband's world. For someone so nominally popular and charming, he was a man unto himself.

At first, that epiphany saddened her, though not for long. Her immediate reaction was replaced by a more sanguine response. She treasured deeper relations and good friends. Josh. On the other hand, seemed beyond those ordinary emotions in some odd way that never ceased to perplex her. He seemed content in his own world, comfortable in his own emotions and thoughts. That struck her as cold and lonely, but was it? He never seemed to mind being self-contained. She had been with him long enough to realize that, as good as he was in a crowd, and he was a schmoozer par excellence, it drained him of energy to be with others except for a chosen few.

She had seen him come back from public talks or academic conferences exhilarated and yet spent. While he usually was a hit, a fact that buoyed him given his natural tendency to feel unworthy, he also would express how much the effort had taken out of him. They had talked about this on several occasions. She found that being around others tended to lift her up, energize her. He was depleted by others. When she pushed him, he had trouble explaining why, so she watched him closely.

She supposed that is what wives did, or all women did, as a matter of course. They watched the man to which they had attached themselves closely. She doubted men did the same with those females who were significant in their lives. Perhaps that is what explained the difference between men conversing and women conversing. Males focused on outside topics … sports, business, hobbies. When Connie conversed with her female acquaintances, their chatter touched on academic topics for sure since, after all, her friends were drawn mostly from the academy. But they also talked a lot about relationships and feelings and the deeper emotional pools within. Men seldom went there. Were men that shallow? Was Josh an outlier? She thought over the males she had gotten to know well but could never arrive at a definitive conclusion.

She smiled as she reflected on one telling aspect of their relationship. She would ask him how things went at the university or at some meeting or conference with public officials and he would say 'fine.' That designation sufficed for all no matter whether the event was a spectacular success or an unmitigated disaster. Everything was 'fine.' Perhaps Josh was little better in that regard than her first husband, a successful businessman. He would be incommunicative most days though she concluded that was because he could not believe a female, certainly not an academic, could possibly understand his world. It was a massive put down that wore on their relationship. They parted without much acrimony, and hardly any emotion. They simply arrived at a realization that they did not mesh well.

On the other hand, Connie would disgorge her day's events to Josh in detail, including the reactions of all who fell within her orbit that day. What happened to that Asian inscrutability? In truth, she could not recall doing so with her first husband, a sign that their partnership was doomed from the start. As she talked, Josh would smile and nod, as if listening. Only on occasion, would she become suspicious and try to test how attentive he really had been. Often, he surprised her by providing just enough feedback to convince her he had not tuned out completely. He was crafty, she concluded. More importantly, when she went to him for serious feedback and input, he would be there for her. He knew when the moment was serious, and she loved him for that.

Most of these people on his list could wait. Several undoubtedly were important to him, but few were critical. She knew the ones that were. This was not difficult. There were the few remaining from his revolutionary days as a college student in the Boston area. He had reconnected with them after a life of estrangement to find the bonds just as strong. She understood that. Early friendships are special. She had lost most of her early connections since they had been stuck in Communist China and she lost contact over the years. That continued to bother her. Yes, she would have to contact them even now if that were possible.

Of course, she must let his niece Cate Connelly know. She was now like a daughter to him. He had never wanted children even as all around him enthused about what a great father he would be. When he did talk about this matter, he would give stock responses; he was awed by the responsibility, the world was a harsh place and going downhill, and he was so busy with life to raise kids of his own. As she talked with him over the years, another factor seeped out. He had been deeply unhappy as a child. He could not get outside his personal world of hurt and imagine an alternative experience for any issue he might sire. It was as if his personal experience of the world was universal or all that mattered.

Funny, Connie thought, many couples in unimaginable circumstances have children absent much thought as to how they all will fare over time and certainly with little regard for their own likely experience with this life-long obligation. Here was a man with so much going for him believing, and she thought he was serious in this, that he could not provide a modicum of happiness to a child he might sire. Early scripts can be devastating, she mused, and so difficult to erase, or write over, or suppress.

From Connie's conversations with Cate, it was clear she had always seen Josh as her real father. Her biological father had been to the manor born who somehow had chosen a scholarship student at Johns Hopkins medical School as his trophy wife. Rachel, Josh's sister, had worked her way out of a Boston Irish ghetto to the top of the medical world. She confided to Connie that her selection as the spousal choice of Evan Ballentine III always remained a mystery to her. While she remained perplexed by his attentions, he seemed like a catch to her in that moment. Perhaps her judgment was clouded by the fact that all the other female students gushed over what a catch he was. She had won the prize and lost all.

She had doubts at the last moment, thinking seriously about calling it off. But these things have a momentum of heir own. It was not long before her fears were confirmed. When Rachel was anything but a compliant spouse, the relationship unravelled. Cate was the only good to come of this ill-starred marriage. Unfortunately, the Ballentine family could not forgive Rachel's unwillingness to play her assigned role as subservient spouse, nor Cate's unwillingness to play the dutiful daughter worthy of the clan's name. The final straw was Cate bringing home a Jordanian as her lesbian partner whom, while belonging to the elite in that country, could not be explained easily to the east coast elite in which the Ballentine tribe functioned. Cate cut off her association with her father's family, changed her name to Connelly, and embraced Josh as the male figure in her life. It was, after all, a role he had played for some time.

Connie scoured her mind and the contact list for connections from all those decades Josh spent at the University of British Columbia, working as a respected academic and an influential policy wonk. Here, she came up dry. There were dozens of names, some who had been relatively close to him, but she knew most were peripheral acquaintances or professional colleagues. They were not people in whom her husband would confide, but only consult on intellectual matters. Only Usha Nayer stood out, his good friend and a companion whom he married as a matter of convenience to give cover for her lesbian lifestyle. Usha's conservative Indian parents would have never understood such a life choice or so she thought. In the end, after several years in this faux arrangement, she came out of the closet and moved on to a female partner. That relationship didn't last either. Usha and Josh remained close friends even after she left for the University of Toronto and her short, tempestuous connection with a female partner.

There was one relatively recent bond Josh had had created which could not be ignored. Now this was intriguing, very much so. Early in his retirement, he brought home to dinner another academic named Chris Crawford. Connie had heard the name on a few occasions even before he arrived in their lives. She knew he was at Oxford University, had come from a prominent and very wealthy family, and that he ran some important international service organization in addition to being a scholar. On the day she met this man, all she knew was that Professor Crawford had spoken at the University after visiting Bill Gates south of the border in Redmond Washington. Josh never even mentioned that he intended to bring this man to his home, he just did. She was not prepared that Chris and Josh would bond in a way that would upend their lives.

With Chris Crawford eventually came others in what she thought of as the Oxford orbit. There was Kay, Chris's physician sister, Kat, the younger sibling who runs the family financial empire, Azita and Deena Masoud, his adopted children, Professor Shahed Al-Hussein, his new wife after his first spouse died tragically from Covid. She had met them all, and others, when she suddenly found herself in England working with Chris's international initiative, shortly after her own retirement. It had been an unexpected immersion into a new world. Just as they all became fully entangled within this new and exciting world, Josh decided he would return to Canada at the end of 2020. That had surprised her and especially Chris whom she could tell was confused and hurt. She also had been perplexed. Only now did an answer come to her … he might have sensed something was wrong with his body even then.

Of all these people, Chris was the most important. He had touched Josh the most deeply, reached him in places she could not. It was a primal male bond no woman could compete with nor threaten. As Connie reflected on it, Chris was like a son to her husband. Cate may be the daughter in his life but there is something special about a father-son relationship. But how could she possibly know about that? Her only issue was a daughter who was an economist at Cal-Berkely. They were reasonably close though she knew the frantic lifestyle of an academic at a research university. There was little spare time for family niceties.

Connie had her list. What would she say when she called? Hi, how are you doing? By the way, Josh is dying. Have a nice day.

Okay, that was a non-starter. It struck her that giving people a stark message might prove counterproductive. The last thing Josh would want would be people tramping to Vancouver to hover over and about him as he died. In any case, she had no idea when that would be. Now, reflecting on her conversation with the oncologist, she recalled the man being irritatingly vague. Then again, medicine was not an exact science. Most prognoses this far out were given in ranges which were impacted by far too many variables to count. *Besides, the damn Irish are a stubborn lot,* she thought. *That alone might be worth an extra six months at least.*

Regardless, if she somehow made this a maudlin event, she would precede him in death, as he would somehow manage to poison her Starbuck's latte. No, this had to be done in a way that he did not put a curse on her as he left this earth.

Then it hit her. *He will go back to England.* That is what he will do. Of course he will. Quickly, she spun a logical story out in her mind. He knew something was wrong at the end of 2020. In response to his concerns, and without confiding in anyone, he insisted on heading back to his familiar haunts until he found out for sure. That is why he secretly started making doctor's appointments even before their return, since getting medical appointments take forever.

Connie recalled asking him why not in England. Doctors surrounded him there. They could have expedited matters. But he waived off her concerns and she let it drop. He had to find out on his own terms, and absent the prying eyes and questions of others. Another frustrating Irish disposition, she thought ruefully. *But he knows now. Yes, she was certain of all this now. He will go to Oxford where his ersatz family and children will be.* Connie smiled. Knowing how much Josh's father hated the Brits, his son heading there to die would have the poor man turning in his grave.

Connie started by composing an email to herself. She wanted to get the tone right, letting people know that Josh did have a medical issue, nothing immediate but nothing to sneeze at either. No need to get in touch now, you know how he is. She went on to stress that she would update folks on matters as they developed. In the meantime, they are likely to travel a bit. Yes, she must prepare others for the departure she now knew was imminent. Most likely they will return to England to see their good friends there, it is so easy to hop over to the continent from the U.K. Still so many places to see.

When she was certain she was being sufficiently obtuse and disingenuous, she typed in some addresses and poised over the send key. Then she hesitated. He will not be happy. He seldom got very angry, but this might do it. *Screw it,* she said to herself. This is why she was in his life. This is why all women were in their men's lives, to do the things men put off. In the end, they were babies who needed attention and direction. She hit the send key.

Some contacts needed more attention, an individualized touch. She picked up her phone, looked up a number and punched the digits in. Again, she paused with uncertainty, reconsidering her next action. Then she hit the green icon on her phone.

Her heart pounded faster as she waited for a connection, which came as she was about to give up. "Is this Morris Greenstein?"

"Yes," and after the briefest of pauses, "is this Connie?"

"Why yes, you recognized my voice." Connie was surprised.

"Why not, you are family now." Mo said graciously though he sounded hesitant. "Wait, is this about Josh?"

Connie waited too long; she should have anticipated that a call unexpectedly from her would raise concern. Josh normally called his college friends. Now she kicked herself for not preparing a response to such an expected concern. "Yes."

"Something bad?"

"Well," her voice caught, which upset her. Connie now struggled how to continue.

"Hold on," came from the other end.

Connie waited for what seemed like forever. She was grateful, though. It gave her time to think about what she wanted to say. It was moments like this she wished she were more like her husband. She saw him in front of many audiences, even attending a few class lectures at the university, mostly out of curiosity. He almost never prepared talks like she did. He would make notes, points he wanted to cover, but that's as far as he went.

She asked him once, *how can you go into these talks with so little preparation?* She recalled him looking at her as if she had asked a dumb question. *'I'm prepared'* he had responded. *'But if I wrote things out, or even had detailed notes, then I would be compelled to cover everything. I did that at the beginning of my career and found that cramped my style. I'm better when I improvise.'*

"I'm back," came a voice that shook her back to reality. "And I have Carla. I'm putting you on speaker phone. What's up."

Connie summarized what she knew about Josh's condition, though she realized she had softened the news quite a bit. Still, she made it through while keeping her voice reasonably steady. It would get easier after this.

"We'll come up to see him. It's not that long a drive."

"Not yet," Connie said quickly. "In fact, don't even contact him in any way that reveals you know this news. He won't be happy I'm making these calls."

"Got it," Mo replied.

Connie was glad they knew her husband so well. Those early connections are special. "Here is the thing. Josh is out walking along the shore, his favorite place to wander and think. I can almost get inside his mind."

"Women are like that," Carla, Mo's wife, added. "It must freak men out how easily we see through them."

"I know I'm freaked out," Mo added and grunted when Carla poked him.

"I will wager, and we Chinese are good gamblers, that Josh will decide to go back to England, at least for a while. He made some deep contacts there in recent years, and there's some work he will want to complete. He has colleagues here, but few real friends. The ones he cares about are those from his youth, like you, and the recent connections he made after coming out of his shell." Connie momentarily reflected on the arc of Josh's life as she knew it. He had passionate connections from college, including a love she knew she could never match. And then he had these recent connections. All the decades in the middle were lost. He was funny, successful, and even influential during this period but detached from others, as if it were too painful to be involved. They seemed like his lost years.

"But we want to see him," Carla sounded hurt.

"No, listen, I'm not being clear, sorry." Connie took a deep breath. "Wait for things to clear. I'll know more soon. If he does head to Oxford, I want those closest to him to be there, when it matters. You know when it really counts."

"You want us to head over there?"

"I know it is a lot to ask. You have your bookshop and … I can cover any costs."

"First," Mo said evenly, "we are not destitute. More importantly, we would travel to the end of the earth to be with him. Do you understand that?"

Connie was abashed. She had insulted his close friends. "I am so sorry. I … this is all new to me and I haven't …"

Carla came to her rescue. "Don't fret Connie. We all love the schmuck. And, I can say without fear of being wrong here, we will screw up in some way. We all do. There is no perfect way to say goodbye. I hope you understand that?"

Connie's words were laden with emotion. "Yes, I understand … totally. And tell me, who else should be there?"

It was Carla who responded. "Many are gone but surely Peter Favulli and … Bob Wilson. Those are the ones Josh will want to see."

"Bob Wilson?" That name escaped Connie.

"When you first met us, he was in a monastery. We all sought forgiveness in our own way. But he came to his senses and is out now. I think he came to realize it was just another form of prison. We'll get in touch with him, and with Peter."

"Thank you … for being here for him."

"This is no burden. Just let us know when things … when he is ready. We'll keep our distance in the meantime," Carla intoned.

Connie could feel warm tears running down her cheeks. "You are such good friends. He will so want to see you."

"You could not keep us away. We really are family."

After the call ended, Mo and Carla Greenberg looked at each other in silence. Finally, it was Carla who spoke, wiping a tear from her eye. "I was hoping that Irish son-of-a-bitch would live forever. How could he do this to us."

Mo went to the front of his bookstore which now was more of a hobby than a functioning business. He put a closed sign out front and locked the door. Returning to his spouse, he sat heavily as he wiped his moist eyes. "It was like it happened yesterday."

"What?"

Mo looked at her as if surprised she could not read his mind. "The day I was attacked by some Irish toughs, the day he came to my rescue. Didn't know him from Adam and here he showed up to save my Jewish ass, and from assholes of his own tribe. He said later he did it because it wasn't a fair fight. I should have known then…"

"Known what?"

"That he was special. We became friends that day and, later, we bonded in a way that few do. But you know that."

"But you also came to hate him for a number of years. I remember that as well."

Mo sighed. "Not hate, not even close. What would I call it … disappointment?" His wife's comment forced him to a different place. He thought back to that snowy November day decades ago. He called Josh repeatedly to no avail. They had something important scheduled at the time. Then again, everything struck them as critical, that was their world when you were trying to save it from its own insanity. Worried, he swung by his place. No one, but a neighbor mentioned seeing him load lots of stuff in his VW bug. *Going on a trip?* This neighbor asked. *More than a trip* was Josh's ambiguous response. That's what the neighbor recalled at least.

"Seemed like you were pretty pissed to me at the time." Carla persisted.

Mo paused, he wanted to get this right. "I had such an ego then. I thought I was the smartest guy in the room."

"You were the smartest *guy* in the room, just not the smartest person. After all, I was a *gal*."

"Hah, hah," but he was glad she was keeping it light. "The thing is that Josh got to me. I did have one brother, but he went the other direction politically and in terms of personality. He certainly picked different life goals. Haven't spoken in years but the last I heard he was pretty damn rich and complaining about taxes. What a schmuck!"

"We were talking about Josh."

"Right," Mo smiled at her. "He became my substitute sibling, but the one I liked … loved I suppose. Like all sibling relationships, we had squabbles and disagreements and things like that. They were petty. And I thought … at the time … I thought he would be there for me. When things got hard, I believed I could count on him, just like the time in that playground when he bailed me out as my ass was getting kicked, though I'm sure I could have taken those Irish wimps."

Carla let out a laugh. "Sure, tough guy. You probably weighed 140 pounds, soaking wet."

"But I was fast." He smiled back at her. "No, when it became clear he was gone, and it was a while before we even knew whether he was alive or not, I was bitter. It didn't feel like hate. That is what I felt toward my biological sibling since he was, as I said, a selfish prick. With Josh, it was a sense of betrayal, though it ran deep for a while. It took time to think through things from his perspective. He came to his senses before the rest of us, except for Peter."

"It was the times, my dear. They were exhilarating and so cruel. They were, as Dickens once said, the best of times and the worst of times."

"Good to know you've been reading some of the literary works here." He went over and kissed her on the cheek.

Carla laughed. "Nothing like trying to save the world to drive folk over the edge. Tilting at impossible windmills is just the thing to bring people together and then drive them apart. My god, we were so naïve, thinking we could stop a war. And we didn't even do drugs, except for some weed. It was those culture freaks that did the hard stuff while we remained way too serious. My god, were we serious? If we had been high, that would have explained so much."

Mo had an easy chair behind the counter where he rang up his occasional sales. He went over to it and sank into its comfort. This was his spot where he spent hours reading and thinking. He now had the time. People were buying fewer real books, at least not in the usual numbers, any longer. The younger generation was into e-books and audible alternatives. In private, he had begun listening to audible versions of books, enjoying how gifted narrators could bring various characters to life. But he did so in secret, as if he were exploring some depraved porn sites. Still, he had a loyal clientele who loved the feel and smell of paper, who enjoyed chatting with this now aging proprietor. It is true, he thought. There is a smell to these old bookstores, musty and replete with wisdom and adventure and accumulated thought. He had become the books he stored on his shelves, old and redolent of things past. He often settled into this chair when he wanted to reflect on his life, as he did now.

If he had not been caught up in the Vietnam furor of the 60s, he would have gone the route of Joshua Connelly. He would have become an academic, a scholar, a teacher of young minds. He would have spent his life in musty libraries exploring issues of the mind and trying to figure the world out. He mused that he did not have Josh's flare for story telling but he had passion. He was certain he could have elevated his students and opened their minds to new ways of seeing the world. He would not engage in propaganda, which was a favorite complaint of the hard right toward academics where professors groomed impressionable and naïve students toward leftist thought. That was bullshit in his mind. He never recalled his professors directly telling him what to think. They merely opened his mind to information and perspectives not available in ordinary life, not sanitized by a corporate media. Once open and supple enough, the mind could work out a personal world view based on evidence, not given beliefs. And that was the key to everything, being able to think for oneself, not be trapped into conventional expectations. Such a liberation was a joy … and a curse.

For good or evil, he and Carla and Bob and Jimmie and others had been caught up in this hateful war which now was but a footnote to history. For them, it was the bright-hard focus of their young lives. Much like the slow emergence of the conflict itself, it all started out simply enough … with a few concerns. It was the same with civil rights, and poverty, and later feminism, and so many other social issues. Concerns led to doubts which led to anger which, in turn, led to fury and that led to rage. Not being listened to as the carnage increased without end, or any prospect of success could be discerned, was seen as a form of infuriating folly.

It was the same with basic human rights being ignored or trampled beyond reason. Mo sometimes thought it was all a kind of addiction, a trap for the unwary. You believed you saw things clearly, but then all these smart and highly placed authorities saw it differently. In fact, these 'adults' dismissed you outright as naïve, foolish, and easily misled. That was infuriating. They were young but not kids. They simply had the misfortune of growing up in an upside-down world where the kids saw the world as the gown-ups should have. And they had been dismissed. That was the unforgivable sin in his mind. They fought so hard to understand and right things they saw as wrong and they were ignored, then despised and finally, in the end, dismissed.

Frustration upped the ante. Being dismissed pushed them forward. Being ridiculed threw them into an abyss that at first was counterproductive and then evolved into a nihilistic form of masochism. Quiet protests led to angry outbursts which led, in turn, to what were considered acts of sedition by law. Peter Favulli left the group before any illegality occurred and spent his life in the FBI. Joshua Connelly, Mo's best friend, disappeared one November day. Only later did they learn he had fled to Canada where he would spend his life in exile. Jimmie, the Irish kid from Josh's neighborhood, who followed Josh around as a devoted acolyte, blew himself up while building a bomb. Others, less devoted, merely dropped out over time. In the end, only a hard-core group persisted until the inevitable end caught them up. Carla Shapiro (now Greenstein), Bob Wilson, and Mo would be arrested and spend years in jail. When released, Bob would enter a monastery, presumably as an act of self-imposed penance. Mo would never have that opportunity to pursue his childhood dream, he never became the scholar and teacher that had consumed his early aspirations.

Mo realized that his wife was looking at him, expecting him to say something. "Carla, what's your biggest regret about what we did, in the old days?"

"You mean besides marrying you?" She smiled.

"The real old days, when we were revolutionaries of sorts."

"Oh, you mean pre-history." She considered that for several moments. "Well, I never got to become a Rabbi. Back then, there weren't many females doing that, it might have been a stretch in any case. Besides, my father was set against it. Now, they are all over the place. Like doctors and lawyers, women are taking over. I still think about that."

"About women coming to rule the world."

"No, silly, though that is true enough." She was always surprised when her husband failed to follow her train of thought. "About what my life would have been like as a rabbi."

"So," Mo asked slowly, as if he wasn't sure he wanted the answer, "would you do anything differently, and don't say you would marry some rich, handsome guy."

She thought carefully. "No, I would do the same damn thing … we had to do what we had to do."

"Doesn't everyone?" responded her husband.

CHAPTER 4

They Are Coming

"Our prime purpose in life is to help others. And if you can't help them, at least don't harm them."

His Holiness the Dalai Lama

Amooz Aktar sat as the elders had done for centuries, on the heels of his feet with his legs jack knifed in such a way that the trunk of his body was perfectly balanced. That seemed uncomfortable to the occasional Western soldiers and contractors who came through his village. If they were new to the country, they would wonder how a person could assume such a position for extended periods of time. Soon, though, they would hardly notice this habit nor much else in this strange land frozen in time. Oddities became familiar.

It was the time of year when the days were dominated by a sun that seemed merciless as it mutated into a white disc while ascending into the heavens. Amooz had sought the protection of the shade. He was, by the standards of his rather remote village, an old man. Some of the younger villagers thought him ancient. Seven of his nine children had predeceased him by disease, accident, and the fortunes of conflict. His grandchildren and great grandchildren had fared better, but survival remained a chancy thing in the harsh land of sand, rock, and an ever-present blazing sun. He could still recall the days of his youth when he would search the brown landscape for scorpions and snakes. They were hard to see against the various shades of brown in the backdrop. With patience he would seek out his prey, following it patiently when found, and crush it with a rock when the stalking of other game ceased to be amusing. He knew there would be more opportunities the next day.

He often mused on his fate and why fortune had permitted him to survive as so many others had perished. He was now an elder and, as such, considered wise simply for surviving so many journeys of the earth about the sun. Many came to seek his advice, though not all. Several younger men had less respect for his accumulated knowledge. Some could read, while many had access to radios and other sources of information. Unlike prior generations, many dismissed his purported wisdom. Yet, when conflict across families and clans boiled over, his counsel might be sought. It was better than the traditional form of resolving Pashtun disputes which too easily spilled over into violence.

Everyone knew that his watery hazel eyes had seen it all. In his youth, he recalled there was a monarch in far-off Kabul. He knew, or was told at least, that this high man had great powers but they seldom if ever reached him in his village. The struggles in far away cities might as well have taken place on the moon that lit up the rural night when full. Suddenly, this god-like monarch was gone, and the Communists appeared. They reached his village on occasion, preaching what seemed to be nonsense to Amooz and the others who would nod as if they understood and revert to the ancient ways as soon as they left.

When the homegrown Afghan Communists fell into disarray and conflict among themselves, the Russians appeared. They were cruel and angry, governing through force. Though Amooz thought such hostility more a sign of fear and desperation as opposed to strength, they seemed invincible at first, well-armed and protected by tanks and helicopters. The helicopters were the worst. They would be preceded by an unmistakable sound and then appear to rise as if by magic out of the surrounding hills. Initially, they were satisfied to scare the locals. Soon, for reasons Amooz never fully understood, they rained havoc on his and other villages. They had fallen for an ancient shibboleth, that resistance among a captive people could be broken with random killing, including the indiscriminate slaughter of women and children. He had been a peaceful man, except to scorpions and snakes, but this pushed him to anger. Like many of his brothers, he took to the hills with other Mujahadin to fight the occupiers. He still remembers the day when he had been given a weapon that seemed to have come from Allah though someone told him it was from the Americans.

He already had been anointed as a village leader and thus was chosen to use this avenging weapon against the infidels. But no opportunity came at first. Then, one day, another hot dusty day like so many, he heard the familiar sound heading in his direction. He scampered up the side of a hill with his companion, watching the pale blue sky with anticipation. They rose over the horizon, three of these hated beasts lazily rising as if they were untouchable. Amooz had been so ready for this moment, saying a prayer to Allah as he aimed his weapon at the lead copter and discharged its missile. He could see a vapor trail rise uncertainly at first, then straight toward this hated machine as if guided by the hand of God. Shouts of Allahu Akbar arose about him as debris tumbled to the ground and the other machines abruptly turned about and disappeared.

Amooz eventually downed three of these beasts, becoming a hero among his men. Many months later the word reached him that the Russians were leaving. For the first time in his life, he felt driven by hate and wanted revenge. So many of his villagers, his family, had died. It was the Pashtunwali code of honor to avenge all those cut down without mercy or the opportunity to defend themselves. As did many of his neighbors, they quickly intersected the scared Soviet soldiers desperately fleeing his country, but no longer safe in their camps. He killed several as they sniped from afar when given the chance. Yet, it did not make him feel better. His lost loved ones could not be retrieved from the other side. They were gone forever.

Amooz thought that, with the infidels gone, peace would come to his world. Allah, for some reason he could never appreciate, did not permit that. The rhythms of village life were interrupted, often without warning, as various tribes fought for control. Without a central authority, chaos reigned until life might return to a precarious equilibrium, as least for a while. The competing factions saw Amooz and his neighbors merely as sources of revenue and fighters. This was no better than the Russians he had concluded. Finally, one group emerged over all others, the Taliban. They promised peace, honesty, and a return to God's law. Amooz had many doubts, but he was desperate for a respite from the random violence that governed his life in recent years.

For a while, Amooz thought these new leaders might be what was needed. They did restore a sense of order and reduced the wanton theft the warlords used to keep their armies going. Soon, however, he saw that power does indeed breed arrogance, just as he was wanting to believe. These so-called men of God became oppressors in their own manner. Nothing fosters tyranny quite as effectively as unchallenged righteousness. Every blasphemy and sin can be excused when doing God's will, or so they believed. Amooz wept inside as he saw these men trample on his village ways, especially in their treatment of women and girls. Amooz learned to read and spent much time examining the Quran. These messengers of God were violating the teachings of Mohamed, of that he was certain. The Prophet spoke of treating women with honor and respect.

Then, another wave of uncertainty swept through his world. Events in America found their way to his country, mostly in the form of planes crisscrossing the pale skies. Amooz was never certain what had happened but the Taliban in the area seemed frightened, then left in their jeeps and trucks with little warning. In the aftermath, a peace settled on the area. Amooz wondered if a normal world now was possible. After a while, he heard that foreign soldiers were about. Not Russians but British and Americans. They seemed less intrusive than their neighbors to the north, so perhaps Amooz could merely ignore them and continue with life as before. And yet, he knew this would not last. The Taliban were in hiding but had not gone away. They fought back as they had with others who had occupied their lands. Many had come to this land in the past with high dreams, few had stayed. He smiled that this lesson had never been learned after so many failures.

Amooz looked about him. He had seen so much over his life. Yet, he wondered just how much had changed. The dress with which he covered himself, the foods that he consumed, the crops that he planted, the mud and brick houses in which they lived, the animals they raised, and the ancient technologies they yet used had hardly changed in centuries. So many had swept into his life, and over his land, as friend or foe … some allegedly to help and some to exploit. In the end, they had departed, some willingly and some not. A few already had moved on to their heavenly reward or hell, again some willingly and others not. So much turmoil and for what. So much death to what end. This conundrum puzzled him on this day as it had on others. The Taliban, he had heard, would soon return. In fact, they had never entirely left. They simply bided their time, waiting for the infidels to depart, which they always did in time.

His gaze surveyed the fields that stretched out before him. They were small by any standards, large enough for each family to scrape out an existence if they were fortunate. Periodically, men in Western dress had come by who, with broad smiles, explained that they were visiting as friends. Amooz would nod without acceptance of their presence nor belief in their claim. These earnest men would explain how Amooz and the other farmers might increase their yield by using this new seed or by employing some magical chemical fertilizer or doing things in the modern way. Amooz would listen, smiling back at them. When they left, and they always left, he would continue doing what he had always done. He stayed the course less out of ignorance and more out of the rational insight that the downside of trying something uncertain was too high. After all, who would bail him out if this new thing failed.

Amooz knew the following truth in his heart, one of many he had absorbed over a lifetime of struggle. It was a lesson imposed upon him by the harshest of teachers, personal experience. The strangers might be right. If he tried these new things, perhaps his yield might be increased. However, to achieve this miracle, there were so many things to do differently. He would have to buy expensive seed and fertilizer with money he would have to borrow from lenders who would charge much interest. Even if promised free seeds from the government, he could never be sure that someone along the distribution chain would not steal the good stuff and replace it with ordinary seeds. Even with the good seeds, he would have to do things according to a strict schedule … insert fertilizer a precise distance from the seed and water the crop on a given schedule and be vigilant against pests and disease to which these new varieties seemed especially vulnerable.

Amooz recalled doing the calculations on more than one occasion. While he knew nothing about formal probabilities, he was savvy.

The prohibitive cost of innovation, when coupled with the chances of something going wrong, made this brave new world a bad bet. He could do what he had always done, save some seed from the previous year and plant that in the ancient way. The yields were not impressive to be sure. But they were guaranteed, more or less. If he tried these new techniques, and something went wrong, who would save him. It would not be the government and most of his neighbors were less well off than he. His calculus of the pros and cons inevitably led to a decision to stay the course. He had survived this long in doing so.

Then there were others who came to tell the males of the village that it was not good that they had so many children. It was better to have fewer offspring but to provide those they had with more opportunities, especially an education. Again, Amooz smiled at these visitors. In his head, he said to himself that what would have happened had he not sired so many children. As it was, only one male child had survived to care for him now that he was so old. These visitors said such silly things. They did not live in his world, nor face the uncertainties he faced. They lived in places where most, if not all, children survived to adulthood. And while the scourge of some childhood diseases had been diminished, there remained many impediments to surviving to adulthood. No, he thought, siring many children had been his security blanket against misfortune. It would remain so.

Others came on rare occasions, Westerners who brought with them gifts to make life better for Amooz and the others who lived in this harsh environment. With great fanfare, they might build a deep well that they said would replace the existing wells where the water was brought up by an intricate and almost incomprehensible arrangement of pulleys and wooden gears driven by the power of oxen walking in circles. This is how lifegiving water had been secured for centuries. The ancient ways were ingenious, even the wise visitors admitted that but, they argued, modern technologies promised so much more. Let us help you.

Amooz inevitably bristled a bit when these visitors derided the old ways that had sufficed for time eternal. It was certainly true that these new wells went deeper, given the excavation techniques used. Moreover, they would be driven by electricity which would be installed very soon, or so they were told. The old timers had heard such promises before, too many times. In some villages, the promised electricity never came, the money to erect the innovative technology somehow disappearing into unknown pockets. If it did, the electricity was not available with any certainty or was available only if those controlling it were offered baksheesh at critical times in the growing season. Even when all went as planned, the mechanical aspects of these pumps would break down with time. Few knew how to repair such things. Even if they did, getting replacement parts was a difficult undertaking or they charged much for their services.

*Those who came bearing such grand promises soon were gone. They had installed their miracle devices with great pomp and celebration, but no one seemed to care what happened after. The new wells stood unused, adorned with a faded sign saying, '**A gift from the people of the United States**,' sometimes written in a language the locals could not understand.*

Amooz now gazed beyond the fields to the hills and mountains that surrounded him. They were stolid and unmovable. To Amooz, they always appeared desperately thirsty for any liquid that might come their way. When the heavens did offer water, all kinds of bright flowers would erupt along with many flying and crawling creatures. It always amazed him that so much life stood at the ready, erupting with the mildest encouragement. What he dimly realized, from stories often shared by the elders of his youth, that this rugged terrain kept enemies at bay. If that did not work, geo-politics, a term he would never have heard, played a part. For decades and decades, Britain and Russia struggled to a stalemate in the region. Later, it would be the Americans and the Russians playing chess on their lands. In the end, neither gained an advantage, only the Afghans won and, at the same time, lost.

Mostly, Amooz found solace in the rhythms ever present to him. The women filling their clay pots at the well and carrying them balanced on their heads to their modest dwellings. The animals that meandered about, goats seeking shrubs to eat and chickens grubbing for morsels on the ground. There were the men sitting about drinking chai or black syrupy coffee while chatting about issues and concerns that dominated village life. Amooz especially loved watching the water buffalo. They seemed to care for nothing, ambling about as beasts of burden at a pace that never seemed to change. Amooz often thought they had some secret insight into life where they could see through the intransigence of existence to some eternal truth. This afforded them a peace that mere humans could never find.

Amooz's grandson Sayed squatted next to him in the usual manner. "Have you heard; they are coming."

"And who is coming now," Amooz asked knowing the answer.

"The Taliban. The infidels are leaving, and the Taliban is sweeping through the villages. They will take over."

Amooz said nothing for a while, waiting for his offspring to add something that might indicate how he felt on the matter. When nothing was offered, he added, "And what do you think of this, my son."

"Well," his grandson said uncertainly, "it is difficult to say. Some in the clan say that this is a good thing. That to be rid of foreigners is always a blessing from Allah."

"But not all say this?"

Sayed hesitated, hoping Amooz would reveal his feelings. When that did not happen, he ventured forth. "I think the foreigners should go but all else remain the same."

"But that is not likely to happen." Sayed said with a hint of sadness.

His grandson sighed. "No, someone surely will come to rule over us."

"And if that someone is the Taliban. What would you say to that?" Amooz looked directly at his descendent as he asked this question.

"I … I am not sure, only that it is Allah's will."

Amooz smiled. "Confusion is the way of life. What you will learn is that there are few answers and many questions."

"Too many…"

Amooz now laughed. "You are gaining wisdom I see. That is good. Some live their entire lives without gaining much wisdom … if any."

"Well, grandfather, what can you share with me today?"

Amooz looked in the distance for some time without saying anything. It was as if the old man was not focused outside his body but on something within. Sayed wondered if the elder had fallen asleep or had fallen into some preconscious state. Amooz finally broke his silence, talking in a faint voice, as if speaking only to himself. “These men who will come will speak as if they had just communicated with Allah. They will issue righteous thoughts and assert truths which they claim are not to be denied. Yet, in doing so they reveal their own weakness, and descend into their own evil. Do you see?”

“Yes,” Sayed said tentatively.

“Do you?” Amooz looked into his grandson’s eyes.

“No, not really,” the younger man admitted. “I want to, though. So tell me.”

Amooz shifted his position to look directly at the younger man. “A man who speaks as if he is a divine being reveals his own ignorance and weakness. Only the Prophet knew the mind of Allah, all others are searching for that meaning. And that journey must be done with humility, with a searching that is genuine, done in love and with an open heart. The zealots who will come to us will merely assert they know Allah’s mind and heart. But they cannot possibly know since that will only be possible when we are before him in paradise. Here, in our earthly trial, we can only pray and follow our Quran as it speaks to our hearts.”

“But these Taliban say they follow the Quran. Do they lie? Do they even believe that?”

“I cannot look into men’s hearts, but it strikes me that they see God’s word in a most convenient way. That is what ambitious men do, evil men. They see God as a reflection of their will and ambitions.”

“Then they do lie, or at least blaspheme the Prophet’s word.” Sayed said confidently.

"You misunderstand. I cannot know what they mean, only what they say and do. I have lived a long time and I have tried to follow the rules laid down by Mohamed as best I can. Still, the way to truth and paradise is not simple. You cannot do this and not do that, and all then is certain. I think, in the end, our fate is determined by the quality of our treatment of others. Think upon our *Pashtunwali code*. Most of the rules are about treating others fairly, with kindness and honor, especially strangers whom we invite into our homes. After a lifetime of thinking on such matters, I believe that is the path to eternity … simple love of the other. All the rest, all that the Mullahs order us to do, serves their needs, not God's. Those endless rules are to provide certainty to those men who cannot think for themselves."

"Yes, grandfather, I see."

Amooz reached out to touch the young man's face. "And what do you see?"

"What I always see, what you have told me by example."

"And that is?"

"That … that I must find God in here." Sayed tapped his chest several times.

Amooz smiled. "Many years ago, I fought alongside Ahmad Shah Massoud."

"Ah yes, the Lion of Panjshir … he is a legend yet today." Sayed was impressed, not only with the fact but that his grandfather had never mentioned this before.

"He was the greatest man I have known. He was a warrior when he needed to be. But he was also fair with all and kind to all. I fought with him against the Russians and then against the Taliban as they took over the rest of the country. He wanted our people to be free, that is all. No self-proclaimed righteous men of God should impose tyranny over us. He even was kind to the Westerners who came to provide us medical help and educate our children, even the girls."

Sayed looked uncertain for a moment before saying. "Oh the foreigners at the Masoud Center, of them you speak."

"Yes, he had invited them in and protected them until he was assassinated. Fortunately, the Taliban were driven from the land soon after and that camp survived to do good things."

Sayed dropped his head. "And now the Taliban will be back."

"They never left, of course, they merely waited, knowing that this day would come. It is time that new lions arise from this desolate place. The work of Ahmad Shah Massoud is not complete. It is beginning. My grandson, listen to me. You are not a warrior. You are a man of education, of learning. That is good, Allah's gift to you. When they come, do not confront them. That is a job for he who has little to lose and less to offer. You must take your friends and flee to where you can make a difference. Promise me that."

"I …" Sayed could not say more.

"Promise this one thing to an old man." Amooz said in a stronger voice.

"I … promise."

Several days later, Amooz Aktar heard a commotion outside of his home. He paused to say a brief prayer before exiting into the bright sunlight. As he anticipated, there were several jeeps with mounted machine guns and men armed with automatic weapons. The men had dismounted and were already circling the settlement, forcing the women to retreat inside their abodes while rounding up the males into small groups. Everyone seemed compliant, as if expecting what had happened and already agreeing to the new order of things.

The man apparently in charge waived his weapon carelessly, as if he expected some resistance to his words. "We have been visiting all the villages in this area to announce that the Taliban has taken control here. This is Allah's will. The cities are falling to us and to Allah, it is just a matter of weeks before Kabul and the entire nation is with us. Any resistance will be met with Allah's justice. Do you understand?"

Amooz slowly approached the man who was speaking. "And what do you consider justice, the wanton killing of those who refuse your tyranny, the beating of women who refuse to bow down before you."

The leader snapped his weapon in the elder man's direction as the crowd murmured with apprehension. Many were confused about what the old man was doing. Why was he not simply agreeing until these men went away? In that moment, Sayed saw his grandfather glance at him and communicate a message with a tiny nod of his head. A few young men, led by Sayed Aktar, immediately began to edge away as all eyes were fixed on the confrontation unfolding between the elder and the intruders. "And who are you, old man."

"I am Amooz Aktar, merely an old man at the end of his days." His words were uttered with a gentle touch, absent anger or concern.

"Your end may come sooner than you wish." As he finished his threat, another warrior went up and whispered in his ear causing the leader's eyes to flicker with anger. "Ah, you are known to some of us, a man with a reputation beyond these villages."

Amooz just smiled. "I doubt very much that I am known beyond this modest village, at least not any longer. I am a simple farmer, that is all."

"Do not lie. Never lie. You fought against the warriors of God in the old days. We never forget." The leader's eyes were ablaze. "Are you prepared to repent and accept us."

Sayed led several men out of sight as most eyes focused on what Amooz would do next. What the old man did next disturbed most in attendance. He seemed to merely pray silently as murmurs of anxiety rose and people edged toward one another for protection against they knew not what.

"Agree with him." Someone said from the crowd. "Please!"

Amooz saw the man in front of him narrow his eyes as if considering an option. The old man sought to make this other man's decision easier for him. "I cannot agree with those that blaspheme the Prophet and the word of Allah."

"You accuse whom of blasphemy, old man."

"He who uses the word of the Prophet for their perverted purposes, those who violate our women and taint our traditions, those who ground all that is holy and merciful into the dust."

Sayed looked back at his grandfather from the edge of the village. His eyes filled with tears as he realized what the old man was doing ... seeking martyrdom both as an example to his people and a lesson to his grandson. Sayed wanted to rush back and shake this man he loved so, yell at him to stop. No lesson was worth the pain of losing he who was so loved. But that was not Sayed's decision to make. As he looked one last time into his grandfather's eyes, he saw an old man at peace ... believing in his heart that he would soon be in the presence of the divine. A moment had stretched into an eternity when his heart was pierced with more words.

"You are the blasphemer," the man raged as he levelled his gun at the old man's chest.

"Allahu Akbar!" Amooz shouted as a short burst of three bullets ripped into his chest.

Sayed and his companions continued to rush along a ravine that led from the village and which sheltered them from sight of the Taliban. By the time he reached the relative safety of the hills, his shirt was well stained with tears of sorrow ... and of rage.

CHAPTER 5

Celtic Musings

"The best people possess a feeling for beauty, the courage to take risks, the discipline to tell the truth, the capacity for sacrifice. Ironically, their virtues make them vulnerable; they are often wounded, sometimes destroyed."

Ernest Hemingway

Later in the day on which he learned of his fate, Josh walked along the rocky shore along the northern side of a peninsula that stuck out into the Pacific Ocean, providing the promontory on which the University of British Columbia was situated. How many times had he ambled along this path? Too many to count. He could not resist the temptation to look down to find his old canine companion, Mo. But this lovable Pug had passed a few years back, also of cancer. That had been a bitter loss. He had acquired the dog from a colleague whose last child at home had left for college. Josh had no one in his house in those days so such an arrangement made sense. He thought Mo the perfect companion, unlike any human applicant for such a position.

Mo, a rumpled Pug, was affable and affectionate and, most important of all, nondemanding. Of course, a forgotten meal or walk would not slip his attention. Then, a growl or bark would emanate from his rotund body. For a loner who had no intimate human associations, this was the perfect companion for his modest emotional needs. They could meander along this shore as Josh would share his thoughts and concerns of the day, sometimes to his canine companion but mostly to himself. Oh sure, he would see the glances of various neighbors, especially from those who had long concluded that this friendly, yet reclusive, figure was just another of those strange academic types who likely had gone around the bend as so many seemed to do. Those eggheads indeed were odd creatures, they had concluded.

But Josh thought them wrong. His conversations with his faithful pet had served an understandable purpose at the time. Early on, Josh had lost one wife to divorce, even if that marriage were one of convenience, and later a paramour and second real love to a fear of commitment. His only sibling was estranged at the time, had been for several decades, while his associations with colleagues were warm but mostly distant. He had an effortless way about him that made him appear sociable but that aspect of his was more illusion than real. He remained friendly while keeping others at arm's length. Few really knew him or were able to penetrate his protective shell of affable humor and quick intelligence. Those protective devices had served him well he thought. The reviews on this, however, were mixed, especially among those who knew him best.

Only Mo had been privy to the loneliness inside, the regrets still attached to decisions made decades ago in the hubris and naivete of youth. Yes, he had been at the center of a youthful rebellion caught up in the turbulence of his times. He had been infected by the outrage sparked by the Vietnam war and the related social protests associated with America's version of Apartheid and the other 'rights' movements that were soon to burst upon the scene. He had gone through the personal upheaval and transformation that many of his generation endured and survived, mutating from a life of conformity to his Catholic and working-class culture to something akin to an erstwhile revolutionary. His emerging world view metastasized from his intellect to his heart and eventually to all his closest relationships. From the comforting cocoon of his youth, a new personhood emerged, one born of rebellion and hope for a better world. After all, they were the generation blinded by possibility, by this crippling illusion or was it more of a delusion, that a utopia was within their grasp. They only needed to reach out and make it happen. In the end, they sacrificed so much for a false hope.

Realizing that Mo would not be there to listen to his musings, he stopped to look at the mountain peaks across the water to the north, just as he had in the doctor's office. They were the same peaks he had looked upon earlier that day, that he gazed at each day as he trod this familiar path, but they looked more comfortable from this perspective and in this moment. Yes, it was the tableau with which he had become so familiar with over the decades ... the solid mass of rock jutting into the sky that never changed except, and this was critical, for the moods he brought to his experience of them. At times, they were majestic and uplifting. Other times, they were stolid and forbidding. There even were moments when they struck him as flat, static, and uninspiring if not boring. It all depended on his emotional state in the moment. Most days, though, they never failed to move him in one way or another, no matter what. They were his Rorschach test, the template on which to impose his inner self or, more likely, to reveal it.

Reality had proved a harsh and unyielding mistress to his early dreams. As he came of age, the Vietnam War had consumed his attention. No matter what he and his friends did, that conflict went on and on until the U.S. was forced to withdraw in humiliating defeat. Too many of his closest friends died or went to prison or came home from war with visible or invisible scars. For his part, he fled to Canada, losing his family, his peers and fellow revolutionaries, the one woman he loved, and his sense of direction and purpose. And yet, with all that there was surprisingly little regret. What alternative did they have … live a conventional life by forfeiting their convictions? Take the safe route? Shrug his shoulders and pursue a career? Sure, that was possible. But the cost in doing so would have been much greater than the one he did pay. That would have demanded that he sacrifice his soul, his moral compass, his core sense of self. Nothing was worth that. No, he mused as he scanned the familiar peaks, no reward or array of comforts could offset such a compromise.

Where had this sense of conviction and rebellion come from, his need to strike out for some social purpose and a sense of justice? Why the folly of chasing utopian ideals? It had always been there, no doubt of that. He felt it burning inside as the other kids in his Irish neighborhood worried about scoring with the girls in school or upping their status in the local pecking order. His mind had been drawn repeatedly to the struggling families in the Irish ghetto, the poverty and the violence, and too often the hopelessness. More surprisingly, his attentions and even empathy reached out to the Italians on the North End, the Blacks in Roxbury, the Latinos, and newer waves of immigrants filling the area's impoverished neighborhoods, as well as those unknowable faces who struggled and often starved in villages across the globe. This sense of innate compassion seemed inbred, absent explanation and defying tribal definition. It was as if he were hard-wired so. Even as a child, he could never escape some guilt that he was comfortable while so many others were not. He could not evade the anger when he saw that some had so much while others survived on so little. On his occasional treks to Boston's financial center, he would look upon the faces of the elite as they rushed about their business. What do they care about, he would ponder? What, if anything moves them? If nothing but their own interests, where was God's justice in that?

Then again, perhaps this was not nature, but nurture. Could these sentiments have come from his father, Big Jim, who overwhelmed him with tales of Irish suffering at the hands of the Bloody Brits. Or perhaps his ethical center came from his aesthetic mother whose background remained shrouded in mystery though all knew it included unstated sufferings in her early years growing up in Russia, or Lithuania, or Finland, or someplace she never mentioned. This shrouded history went back to the early days of Communism being birthed, nurtured, and ultimately disfigured beyond recognition. His mother remained an enigma … so different from his father yet indecipherable and inscrutable.

Big Jim was less of a mystery. He retained more than his quota of righteous anger. It was always there, bubbling up in the booze-soaked discussions that went on for hours in his Irish bar. Josh was raised on talk of exacting revenge on the Limeys, on the sins of Cromwell and those many absentee English landlords who stored foodstuffs in ships to sell oversees as the native Irish perished in famine or sought escape overseas as impoverished refugees. These were the days of the 'troubles' in Northern Ireland which had spilled over to the sons of Eire in America. Josh was weened on the mythic tales of his people.

Yes, Josh thought, something may well be ingrained in one's chemistry from the preconscious imprints of past generations. There might just be something to that.

He had read not long ago about a Brigid Murphy, an adventurous lass who escaped Wexford in the old country at the height of the potato famine. While almost a million of her peers would die from hunger and disease during those awful times, twice as many would seek escape in foreign lands with the distant North American ports from Halifax in the north to New Orleans in the south being common destinations. No destination, no promised land, was more favored than Boston. Most of these refugees from starvation and neglect by British overlords first made their way to Liverpool and then grabbed some creaky vessel, often known as coffin ships, for the perilous journey across the North Atlantic. In the early years, many of the ships were barely seaworthy and it might take weeks for the crossing during which disease, weakness, and starvation would take its toll. The survivors, weak and diseased, were disgorged on to cities whose native citizens despised the newcomers, labelling the hordes of desperate immigrants as gorillas, maggots, or worse. The most common signs of welcome were those informing them that ***'No Irish Need Apply'*** *for available jobs.*

In Boston, nativist groups like the 'Wide Awakes' and 'Know Nothings' dominated Massachusetts politics in 1854-55. The local natives tried to keep immigrants from voting and holding political office. They harassed the Irish mercilessly, hoping to slow or, ideally, reverse the tide of alien newcomers coming to their city. Even some abolitionists who argued for the emancipation and advancement of southern Blacks reviled the pitiful Irish flotsam that washed up onto Boston docks. The genteel and orderly society of the old order seemed imperilled by this odious tribe that could never be assimilated into a genteel and sophisticated society. It seemed wholly impossible that they could be educated and civilized.

Josh scoured his mind for the details of Brigid Murphy's story, one of the many seeking survival in the new world. She escaped Ireland as the potato famine in the old country had ravaged what she knew. On arriving in Boston, likely alone, she went into 'service' where she worked for an affluent established family, as most young Irish lasses did. She eventually married a Patrick Kennedy, a cooper or barrel maker, who worked on the Boston docks for, at most, two dollars on a good day. Before Patrick died of consumption at 35 years of age, a common fate, they had sired five children. Their first son perished of some common affliction that struck down poor Irish children with horrific frequency in those early days. He was buried miles away, near Harvard University, since the Protestants would not let more Catholics be buried in east Boston where she lived among the growing Irish tribe. The one nearby Catholic burial ground available to them was already full. Her nieces and nephews fared even less well with 10 of 22 dying of disease before the age of six years.

Her second son John Patrick Kennedy, or J.P. did survive and grew up as a street urchin and ruffian showing little promise. Then, as Providence would have it, this would-be hooligan slowly straightened his life out, initially working as a common laborer on the Boston docks, though with even less skills than his father. Somehow, in a miracle repeated in other poor immigrant families, he became a liquor distributor and politician as he worked his way up in society. It was a classic rags-to-riches tale where he would go on to sire the Kennedy dynasty that was destined to rise to the pinnacle of American society. Josh smiled as he thought that J.P.s only surviving son would become one of the wealthiest men in America and his grandson would become the President of the United States in 1960. You just never know, he thought to himself. You just never know. What might he have accomplished had he stood his ground and not fled to Canada? What if he had sought a more traditional life?

Josh reflected on such things often, just as he considered them in this moment of personal crisis. Sometimes he did so for the encouragement he found in their lessons, and sometimes as a reminder of a sense of failure he could glean from these historical memories. He would never replicate such triumphs, would he? Then again, his mountains were less challenging.

His tribe, the Irish, were greeted in most destinations during their diaspora as subhuman and incapable of moral and social improvement. In Boston, where a culture dominated by Protestant Brahmins trained in the rarefied halls of Harvard had long taken root, virulent disgust at the arrival of these newcomers was the most extreme.

Treatment was so bad that even the Irish leadership recommended that new arrivals consider moving inland, away from the city which offered them only disease, penury, violence, and suffocating discrimination. When the public schools demanded that Catholic children say Protestant prayers and learn an Anglophile version of history that, among other things, glorified Oliver Cromwell, the Celtic tribe did not flee. Rather, they stuck together, built their own educational system, including starting their own institution of higher learning in 1863 now known as Boston College. They now were fighting back.

Not only did few of these immigrants leave the city, more kept coming. The tribal instinct to stick together and fight was strong. Slowly, they began to erect their own separate culture that included schools, social networks, hospitals, and even financial institutions. They created a separate and Catholic society withing the dominant Protestant culture. They might be isolated and debased, but they would not be held back, at least not for long. It took a generation, but after the Civil War this despised set of newcomers began a painfully slow climb up the socio-economic ladder. For many, politics was their escape, but others became professionals and skilled tradesmen. The quenching of an Irish fondness for alcoholic spirits, both wholesale and retail, was a common tactic for personal uplift and a gateway into public life, especially through politics and all the associated benefits that route offered. As the final decades of 19th century played themselves out, new immigrant groups, the Italians, Portuguese, Jews, and Slavs partially replaced the Irish on the ethnic pecking order that defined worthiness or, more accurately, unworthiness.

Yet, Josh could not escape this singular thought that repeatedly brought him up short. Some eight generations after the crop failures drove the Irish diaspora abroad into a torrent of hate and abuse, Americans were doing the same thing. They were once again picking on newcomers to blame for all their ills and insecurities. The newest threat had a different skin complexion and were coming from a different direction, but the sense of fear and distrust was strikingly familiar. While the Irish were labelled as drunks, diseased, dissolute, and dirty, the Latinos bumping against our southern borders were seen by many as an alien force that threatened American values and prosperity. Migrants from Mexico and Central America were labelled drug dealers, rapists, and uncivilized by those who treated Donald Trump as the saviour of traditional American values. But in the end, it was the same fears, the same vitriol, and the same sense of rejection. How little had changed. Governing through hate, not hope. Leading through fear and rejection, not inclusion into the county's vaunted melting pot, a promise more mythical than real.

In the 1850s, when the first Nativist movement peaked, and the defense of slavery was at its height, U.S. Senator John Henry Hammonds outlined the principles on which the basis of white protestant privilege was based. According to his pronouncement on the floor of Congress, society was hierarchical. There were those who, by inherited gifts and a superior culture, were destined to lead. Others were on earth to do the nasty jobs, those tasks requiring brawn and the sweat of their labors. Then, the elite could focus on the higher aspirations consistent with their superior talents. To help this Calvinist perspective along, it was easy to identify this elite. They had the correct skin color, came from the same divinely appointed ethnic stock, and believed not only in the same God but worshipped Him in familiar ways. The taint of Popery that was being imported with the Irish scum was a sure sign of Satan's malevolent devices and was not to be encouraged nor tolerated.

In the slavery era and the rejection of all those perceived as outsiders to the dominant culture, a spark of hope was struck, a kind of tentative enlightenment. When Charles Sumner of Massachusetts rose in the U.S. Senate to attack the evil where a class of people were being held in bondage as property, he was physically attacked so severely that he almost died. He had challenged the sacrosanct institution of slavery that, in turn, was the foundation of an almost feudal and authoritarian society in the South. The divide in America was almost complete by the 1850s though Northerners kept moderating their language and seeking compromise in the hope that the Union might be sustained through negotiation and reason.

That proved impossible given hardening ideological positions. In 1856, a partisan of this new Republican Party named Anson Burlingame rose to give his famous ***'Defence of Massachusetts'*** *speech. A Congressman from the Bay State, Burlingame defended a vision of America starkly different from the Southern way of life, one that pushed education, morality, inclusion, innovation, and social opportunity as opposed to autocracy, authoritarianism, rigid social roles, and fixed beliefs. For his efforts, he was threatened with a duel by the same man who nearly clubbed Sumner to death but that never came about. And there we had it, the cultural divide that tore at the fabric of America from its founding and which continues to rip it apart to this day … an inclusive democracy versus an exclusionary rule by a nativist elite.*

Big Jim, Josh recalled, had never been a particular fan of the Kennedy clan. They were too rich, too remote. They had gone to elite schools and consorted with too many of those who had kept what he considered his own tribe in bondage. At the same time, he admired their pluck and success. And they did have moments with which Big Jim could resonate. Josh winced as he thought back to his father's hopes that had been placed upon him. If his dad thought of himself as P. J. Kennedy, Josh was to be Joe Kennedy, P.J.'s only son who would rise to become a famous financier, an ambassador, and a credit to the clan. Josh might not attend Harvard, as Joe had, but surely Notre Dame, which was an elite school … the Catholic Harvard.

Like Big Jim, P.J. Kennedy initially started his ascent up the social ladder with a small neighborhood tavern. This gave him contacts and visibility which served as a springboard to local politics. He was honest and hard-working, leaping directly to a state level political office in 1885, just after the first Irish Catholic had been elected mayor of Boston. From there, he branched out to wholesale liquor distribution, real estate, and banking, becoming one of the more successful of his tribe. Along the way he would work with another Boston pol, John 'Honey Fitz' Fitzgerald. Eventually, P.J.'s son Joe Jr. and one of Honey Fitz's daughters, Rose, would marry and sire a large family that included two U. S. Senators, a U.S. President, and several members of Congress if grandchildren were included. The most promising son, Joe's first born who was named after his father, would die in WWII when he volunteered for a dangerous mission. His plane exploded over the English Channel in 1944.

What saved the Kennedy's in Big Jim's eyes, in part at least, was that P.J. had fought for Irish independence toward the latter part of the 19th century. By the 1880s, that beleaguered land had been savaged by yet another famine. As the native Irish fought to survive, absentee British landlords fought with equal vigor to keep their investments profitable. Rents were raised while the locals were refused any opportunity to buy the land they worked. Almost 90 percent of the tillable land was owned by foreigners with the average holding averaging 2,728 acres in size. As conflicts between owners and farmers rose, so did evictions. Another 100,000 families were thrown off their land during this period. The oppressed tried boycotts to press for their right to claim a piece of the old sod. In fact, Big Jim told Josh that the very word boycott came from the last name of a British land agent who ruled his fiefdom in County Mayo with such a heavy hand that the locals rebelled.

In the British Parliament, Charles Parnell, a member from Ireland, pressed the Irish cause as American emigrees began to work on behalf of the old country and 'the cause.' Land league clubs in Boston and other cities raised money and sent it home. For the first time, the native Irish had resources and backing. A promise of freedom flickered dimly at first but would flare during WWI in the Easter Rebellion before finally achieving success after several years of bloody conflict right after that war, in 1922. P. J. had become a stalwart defender of the cause, working tirelessly to raise money and awareness of what was happening in the old country. His son, Joe Jr., oddly enough, shunned his Irish roots, almost as if he were ashamed of his humble background. After making his fortune as a financier, he became Ambassador to the Court of St, James, America's representative to England, a post his father and grandfather would detest had they been around. It was not until his grandson, John F. Kennedy visited Ireland that the family fully embraced once again their Irish roots. In an event full of symbolism, if not irony, JFK beat the offspring of a classic Boston Brahmin family, Henry Cabot Lodge, for a seat in the U.S. senate in 1952.'

Suddenly, Josh sensed a burning in his eyes. To his embarrassment, he was crying. His musings had reached his heart. They often did. To make matters worse, the chilled breeze touched the salty liquid that was leaking down his cheeks resulting in a sting he could not ignore. Somehow, these ancestral musings never failed to touch him at some primal level. It was all stupid, he would tell himself. Yet, in the end, that made no difference. His sentiments were buried deep inside his DNA, eons of memories and feelings passed on to one generation after another. But it had stopped with him. He had not had issue, would not pass his genes on. Was that some mortal sin, a betrayal of some kind. Did he owe some form of atonement? This was a conundrum he could not sort out in the moment.

He pushed his mind back to his younger days. Everything seemed fresh and monumental then. The world was replete with both possibilities and dangers.

His father was pushing him toward sports and college and celebrity. His mother, when she wandered into his life, spoke to his mind and soul, suggesting a more sensitive and cerebral approach to life. His younger sister remained a constant to him, and a joy when she wasn't being a pest. She was ever present, always asking questions and looking upon him with adulation. He always sought an escape from her attentions yet was happy when he failed. And the Catholic church, which he took very seriously, was his rock which was not surprising for a boy infused with higher moral sentiments. There were many lessons he might have absorbed from his early religious days, but he selected those focusing on justice and inclusion. It was a part of the Catholic panoply of teachings that would be extinguished as the Church lurched to the right in coming decades but was there in a more palatable form for him at this critical juncture in his early life.

And then there was his world on the streets, outside his home. He had been at a crossroads in his early teens. He had to admit there was an excitement to be found on the streets. The Boston of his youth was defined by a set of clans organized roughly around neighborhoods or even settings withing neighborhoods. There were what loosely were considered gangs in the North End (Italians), the South End (Irish), as well as Dorchester, Roxbury, Somerville, among other neighborhoods. The city was a mosaic of tribes. Charlestown was unique, however. Only one square mile, it was the location to a unique brand of criminal, bank robbers. And that was no accident. It had been a prison site and families tended to move closer to their incarcerated family members. Once there, they remained after their loved one's release. Like many family traditions, the family business was handed down from generation to generation.

But to Josh's immature eyes, there was a glamor to these tough guys on the streets. There was the famous Winter Hill gang where Buddy Maclean and Howie Winter fought the McLaughlin brothers for dominance in the city. But that was not the only action during the sixties. The Killeen gang fought the Mullen gang which came out on top, only to be decimated in a horse racing fixing scam that went south. It was then that the most famous of the bad guys rose to prominence … Whitey Bulger. He and his buddy, Steve Fleming, somehow escaped the indictments when the race fixing scandal went down. He also led a charmed life for two more decades, a miracle that was explained when it was uncovered that a top FBI agent was covering for him in exchange for information on the local Italian mafia. Karma eventually caught up with Whitey when, his federal protection exposed, he was about to be arrested. Alas, he was tipped off one last time and fled. After many years on the lam, he was tracked down in California living the quiet life of a retiree living near the ocean. Sentenced to prison, he was beaten to death within hours after being transferred to a less secure facility.

But to a young Josh, these wise guys could be romantic. They had swagger and others gave them their due as a matter of course. That impressed his dad who respected at least some of them. They were tough and took no guff from anyone. That impressed Big Jim who had always seen life as a battle where only the fittest survived. That is how it appeared to his young son. That is how Josh defined manhood early on. The Irish bond enabled many ordinary transgressions, including most sins, to be overlooked. Moreover, at his tender age, getting his father's approval was critical to Josh.

Josh thought back to one Saturday afternoon. He was just beginning to make his mark as an athlete in high school. Still, on some weekends he helped his dad in the family saloon, at least when he wasn't honing his athletic skills. Several local Irish gangsters were at the bar exchanging stories of past scores and adventures to come. At that moment, another wise guy walked in and said, "Sean, some asshole is screwing with your car."

One of the toughs sprang up and rushed outside. There was shouting and then the unmistakable pops of shots being fired. Most ducked for cover but Josh sprinted through the door as his father yelled at him to stop. The young man known as Sean, Josh could not recall his surname in that moment nor now, lay on the sidewalk. Dying, the stricken man said more than once, 'It was a fucking set-up.' His chest heaved with labor as blood oozed liberally from his nose and mouth. Everyone else looked on in stunned disbelief as Josh knelt next to the dying man. 'Stay with me, Sean. Stay with me.' He began to push rapidly on his chest as he once saw done in a first aide class, counting in sequences of 10. 'Hang in there, help is coming.' After what seemed like an eternity, Josh felt strong hands pull him back as the newly arrived medical personnel pronounced him dead. Josh then became aware that he was covered with blood.

"He's gone," Big Jim said. "Give it up, son."

Josh looked at this man he knew from the neighborhood, someone who had always struck him as full of life and excitement. Now, he lay motionless on the concrete, blood curdling around his body, eyes staring into eternity. Josh recalled that tears came to his eyes, for reasons he could not comprehend. He walked back into the bar, now determined that his future lie with academics. Athletics would be his key out of his ethnic ghetto. Yes, his skills on the playing fields would pay the way, or so it seemed to him at the time.

Connie looked up from her computer as he walked back in the door. Josh could see that her eyes were red. "You have talked to the oncologist." He said softly.

"Yes. He called me." She responded flatly. When he said nothing further, she continued. "You are going to ignore his advice, aren't you?"

Josh sighed deeply. "I suspect you'll be incensed with me, you know, for thinking things through on my own, not going through all this with you."

Connie rose from her work desk and walked toward him. "When we were first married that would certainly have been the case. I would have screamed bloody murder at you for shutting me out."

"And now?" He whispered.

"Now I know you so much better. I even get that Irish thing, sort of."

"Shit, maybe you can explain it to me then."

"Ha," she guffawed, "easier to explain the most complex biological interactions in organic chemistry."

"You always awed me with your talent, so much smarter than me."

"Bullshit," she said with a touch of exasperation, "don't try to butter me up." She reached him and touched his face. "My sweet man, you have been my life in recent years as well as a source of infinite exasperation. And I suppose you are partially correct; I am damn smart. Yet, not smart enough to avoid falling for you."

"I had you pegged as a freaking genius."

"No," she corrected him. "I'm just smart enough not to argue with a stubborn Irishman. I know …," her voice caught at this point which irritated her greatly, "that you will want to die on your own terms. No heroics."

"Thank you."

"But you must have been thinking about something out there. You were gone a long time, like back when you and Mo would disappear for your long walks." Now she tried a weak smile.

"He was with me in spirit. I could feel his presence. But yes, I just let my mind wander, as I often do. Earlier, I mused about how insignificant we are in the scheme of things. Funny how that has always calmed me. If I recall correctly, I believe contemplating the stars brought peace to the philosopher Pascal. I suppose they brought comfort to the Neanderthals way before that."

"I suppose." Tears now coursed down her cheeks.

"And then I thought a lot about Boston, about my Irish roots. That's what people do toward the end I suspect. They think of their origins, you know, where they came from. For a while, I imagined going back to where I grew up."

Connie looked sceptical. "Really? You mean Boston."

"That passed quickly enough. Nothing there for me anymore except painful memories. No, I have some time, a few good months for sure. I want to go back to England, to Chris and Kay and Azita and Deena. Usha is still with them. There's work to finish." He paused. "But you must come with me. That's a lot to ask. You have your work, and all your world is here."

"Oh, Jeremiah Joshua Connelly," you silly man. "Don't you get it yet. You are my world." With that, the tears came, and she took him into her arms.

"That proves it." He murmured.

"Proves what," she asked.

"That you are dumber than a sack of rocks." He grunted when she elbowed him in his stomach

CHAPTER 6

Azita's Reflections

"If you feel pain, you're alive. If you feel other people's pain, you are a human being."

Leo Tolstoy

Azita Masoud ambled slowly through the streets of Oxford England. She was on her way to a meeting with her older sister Deena and then with Professor Shahed Al-Hussein, known to all as Ali and the new wife of her adoptive father, Christopher Crawford. She had left for her university office early that morning, long before this normally scholarly town awakened to life and another day in the pursuit of truth or, short of that, at least academic notoriety. She wanted to walk slowly, think upon things.

On her amble through this old town dedicated to education, she noticed some graffiti scrawled on a wall.

"Ishvar Allah tero nam,
Sabko samadhi de bhagavan."
Mahatma Gandhi

She had been by this spot many times. The scribbling surely did not look new. So, why had she not noticed this before? She would have taken it in if she had. She recalled her biological mother repeating this phrase often, before her mother and father were assassinated by the Taliban in the tumultuous days of 2001. And she recalled Amar, her now deceased adoptive mother, also uttering these words on an occasion or two. They were an integral part of Indian lore and a mantra for those seeking religious accommodation.

The thoughts of dear Amar, the doctor from India who had come to work with the Northern Alliance as they held out against the extremists in the Panjshir Valley, always brought a tear to her eyes and a tug to her heart. Amar Singh had worked with Azita's physician father Pamir Masoud after he led his whole family in an escape from Kabul and the oppression of the religious fanatics. Pamir wanted his daughters to have a chance in the world and was willing to risk imprisonment and death to see that happen. Azita seldom brought him to mind without her breast swelling with the deepest emotions.

'Oh,' Azita cried out at the thought of her father before looking about to see if anyone noticed her exuberant expression of emotion. But no one did, the streets were yet empty. Even if someone had, they were not likely to care. Oxford was a college town after all. Eccentricities are commonplace, the weird omnipresent. Now she smiled as she recalled harassing her father endlessly to teach her his medical skills. He resisted at first, believing her interest merely a childish fancy. Besides, he realistically feared retribution from the Taliban morality police for teaching a female such skills. Slowly, though, he could not escape the fire in her eyes and the determination in her furrowed brow as she focused on what he was doing while asking endless questions. He relented, slowly at first and then with more confidence and pride as he understood his ten-year-old daughter was, in fact, a prodigy. Besides, she was too stubborn to be denied.

Now, over two decades later, she stared at the words which loosely translated meant that *Ishvar and Allah are interchangeable names for God since we all worship the same deity.* The Mahatma had railed against the religious provincialism and strife that tore the subcontinent apart during the processes of independence and partition after World War II. For all the great man did, he thought he failed in the end. He could not convince those who freely praised him as a hero and even a demi-god to love one another. That, in the end, is what he really wanted. Separate visions of truth, and the baggage that surrounded the resultant cultures, doomed distinct religious tribes to engage in the most horrendous forms of fratricide. Uncounted numbers, in the millions as she recalled Amar saying once, died as India and Pakistan split in two … a fratricidal friction caused by rivers of people moving across the scorched land to be with their own kind.

Her heart beat faster as she recalled how Amar Singh, the physician who would marry Christopher Crawford and adopt Azita after she was orphaned. They would take her to England where she would pursue her own medical training. Oddly, she afforded Amar more credit for this than Chris even though it was likely his doing. Perhaps that was because Amar, like her biological father, was a medical doctor. That now seemed arbitrary to her as she thought about it but that she could not shake that stubborn thought from her head. Besides, she had seen some of her biological mother in Amar, though she could not escape the possibility that she was imposing this presumed similarity upon them. Chris and Pamir were nothing alike even as she admired her adoptive father immensely.

Some evenings, Amar would share stories that she had heard from her father and grandfather, about the struggles to create a new nation after the world war and, more importantly, the Homeric effort to seek love for others within the blind passions of religious fury. Azita was still a preteen as her adoptive mother, Amar Singh, shared these lessons of trying to shape a country out of so many parts. She also gave Azita some sense of the Hindu culture in which she was raised but which she eventually abandoned for what she saw as the more loving culture of Buddhism.

Azita now wondered if that effort to create a united India had failed. The Hindutva movement had gained popularity in recent years. It was a virulent form of Hindu nationalism that was patterned on the right-wing nationalism ascendant in America and several European countries like Poland, Hungary, and Turkey. Under the leadership of Prime Minister Modi, the BJP Party, or Bharatiya Janata Party, had controlled Indian politics since 2014, anticipating the rise of Trump by two years. They gained favor by attacking and persecuting non-mainstream groups, the Muslims, Christians, Sikhs, Dalits, and other minorities. The BJP, as Amar had told Azita and Deena, were an outgrowth of the RSS, or the Rastriya Swayamsevak Sangh. It was a fanatic from this group that gunned down Mahatma Gandhi in 1948 for preaching tolerance and inclusion. Their hate knew no boundaries.

Azita recently read that an academic at Rutgers had authored a book that painted the old Mughal leaders of ancient India in a more favorable light. Hind nationals were outraged and have threatened her life repeatedly, the same fate that Salman Rushdie suffered though he managed to survive their Fatwa's until hurt in a recent attack. Azita sought out the author's name in his head … Audrey Trushke, that was it. With the Taliban returning, would she and her sister be likewise vilified, threatened, or harmed. In a world wracked by hate, anything was possible. They could become marked women in their native land, or even their adopted one.

Azita pushed out these negative thoughts, returning to those long-ago parental talks so reminded the young girl of the love and wisdom of her own biological mother. Madeena Masoud would instruct her young daughters to never give up on their dreams no matter how cruelly the Taliban extremists worked to stamp them out. Perhaps the stereotype of mothers as nurturers was true but that did not explain her father. She needed to think on this more deeply. In the meantime, she vowed not to be dissuaded by threats or impediments no matter the source. She tried to focus on the present, but her mind had a will of its own.

These two strong women, Madeena and Amar, were gone from Azita's life, the first to assassination and the second to the lottery of death imposed by a worldwide pandemic. She still had Chris, who was her adoptive father. She loved him, for sure, but not in the same intimate way as she had Pamir, her biological father. And Chris's new wife, Ali, whom he married soon after Amar passed was more of a colleague to her than a replacement mother. Besides, it was well known, to her mind at least, that this coupling was a matter of convenience, a way to create an intact family with two parents to raise Amar and Chris's biological offspring … Emma, known as Em, and Elizabeth, known as Liz. The girls were coming into their own and needed guidance.

But did Chris and Ali love one another? Azita had often considered this mystery. They had been colleagues for years and had always seemed close. Perhaps they even had been lovers, who knows, though there was surprisingly little speculation on such a possibility, and romantic speculation ran rife in a hermetically sealed college community. If so, they had been extremely discreet. Kay, Chris's sister, was surprisingly open about her twin sibling. He had been what was known as a 'rake' in his early years, bedding numerous women and acting as if he were allergic to any form of longer-term commitment. Then came Amar, seemingly out of nowhere. It appeared to be an impulse marriage. Azita thought back to when Chris had flown into the Panjshir Valley medical center to take his physician sister out of harm's way and, the rumor had it, to fire Amar for putting her in danger. In those days, he had day-to-day responsibility for the international service program he had started. Now, Karen Fisher was the de facto CEO.

Azita, still a child at the time, who already was doing skilled medical procedures, was left to greet him. Kay Crawford, Chris's sister, along with Amar had found ways to be busy upon his arrival by helicopter. Azita was left with this ominous task since all agreed that the impish and talented young lass could charm anyone when she wanted. It worked. No one was fired and, in a shocking development, Chris abandoned his bachelor life to marry Amar. In short order, he left Afghanistan with a family and a new zeal for the work he was sponsoring. Azita never quite shook the fear that he had settled down for her sake, to bring her and later her sister, to England for reasons she could never quite fathom. And yet, there was no question in her mind that Chris loved Amar. His feelings toward Ali were more of a mystery to her. Her own feelings toward Ali surely were more than confused.

Azita knew that Chris loved her and Deena as if they had been his biological offspring. But he was not Pamir. Chris belonged to the wider world, had too many interests and was spread in too many directions. He was still involved, along with his younger sister Kat, in the family financial empire. With his twin sister Kay and his right-hand person Karen Fisher, he remained absorbed in his international service work. In addition, he managed his academic responsibilities, and occasionally devoted energy to his efforts to forestall what he saw as the coming collapse of democracy in his country of birth … America. He had watched in horror as Trumpism prevailed within the Republican Party even after this political aberration failed to disappear when clearly defeated in the 2020 election.

Chris indeed was fighting many demons and she always approached him with a modicum of guilt when she wanted his time. It was as if she was bothering him in her mind. He never said or did anything to support that feeling but she had it nevertheless. She was jealous of his commitments in the world.

She shook her head at these thoughts, then looked about again to see if anyone had noticed. Why did she need such attachments? Why was she still so dependent on Chris? After all, she was a skilled surgeon who routinely faced danger in some of the most dangerous sites in the world. She, along with her elder sister Deena, had put together a new initiative to seek out young Muslim women, nurture them and, if it were possible, bring them to the wider world where they could pursue their intellectual and professional dreams. That is what Chris and Amar had done for her and Deena. Now this is what they were doing for other Muslim girls, with the help of Ali. That thought suddenly pricked her heart. Ali had become an equal partner in this enterprise. No, increasingly she was calling the shots. Was she being pushed aside, along with Deena? How had that happened. Had Chris engineered it? Would their work become known as Ali's program?

Now Azita stopped in the street as she worked out a puzzle in her mind. Was this her concept, or Deena's? After all, she could not quite recall how the initiative emerged. It involved conversations with Ali, who at the time was just a colleague of Chris's at Oxford and someone Azita admired. In truth, Azita thought, the germ of the concept emerged out of her and her sister's experiences with the Taliban. It was a reaction to the full-on repression of females in Afghanistan. Of that, she was sure. Ali, to be honest, was a product of the educated elite in Jordan. What did she know about the persecution of women, except as an academic subject? Then again, did it matter who pushed the concept in the beginning? Perhaps it did. Azita now spent more time obsessing about who was in charge. Sometimes, in recent weeks, she found herself pushing back against ideas that Ali raised for no apparent reason. Was she being petulant, narcissistic, childish? As Azita slowly continued her walk, she dug deeper into her own emotions.

If honest, she could no longer deny a simmering unease within. There was a resentment against this interloper, one that could not be repressed, and yet, at the same time, could not easily be admitted. It hung in the corner of her mind, taunting her. What was wrong with her? Ali had always been good to her. Chris had come and asked both Deena and her if they would have any objections to the marriage, especially given that it was happening so soon after her passing. Most importantly, Deena and she knew that Amar wanted Chris to remarry. Amar had made that clear as she lay dying of Covid, her body weakened by an earlier bomb blast in Kabul that had taken her husband. At first, she suggested Jules, a flame from Chris's early life lost in a political assassination orchestrated by Chris's right-wing father.

'No,' both siblings had assured Chris when he had asked. 'They loved Ali and surely Chris would need help raising Em and Liz.' It made perfect sense. Even then, though, Azita knew that Deena was troubled, perhaps less so for any dishonor that a hasty remarriage might cast upon Amar's memory and more about Deena's own romantic feelings toward Ali. Deena, the beauty of the family, had always been attracted to women but had never found a relationship that worked over the long run. Frustrated, she had given up on love some time ago, plunging all her energy into work. Yet, Azita could see that her sister was drawn to this comely Jordanian national who had achieved much as a scholar and as an advocate for female rights among Muslims. Azita watched as her sibling had gazed too long at this woman, had smiled too obviously at her witticisms, had agreed

too quickly to her suggestions and, perhaps most telling of all, had played with her hair as they spoke. The signs of affection were all there though Azita could sense they were one sided and considered warning her sister of false hopes.

Then, one day, this almost girlish infatuation disappeared. Deena seemed uneasy in their joint meetings, her eyes often looking away and her participation in the discussions conducted with less energy. Azita kicked herself for not doing something before an embarrassing encounter occurred. Deena must have taken the initiative and been rebuffed. On one level, it all made sense. Here was a lovely, successful Mideastern scholar who had never married and never dated. She never even talked about men or romance even when their conversation strayed from work issues to personal matters. That was clearly not normal for a woman of her age, of any age. What else could explain this behavior? She had to be a lesbian who was reluctant to come out of the closet. As Western as Ali had become, this was always a most difficult step for Muslim females. Surely Deena was aware of that.

'Yes,' Azita said to herself in a half whisper, 'that would have been humiliating, especially for Deena who never quite developed a complete feeling of self-worth.' Her older sibling was vulnerable, Azita had always known that. Despite being the younger daughter, Azita had been tapped as the prodigy. Pamir had tapped her to be the heir to his medical legacy. Their biological mother, Madeena, worked with Deena to get her interested in education but her ministrations did not take for some years. Azita could not figure it out at that age, but her older sister found it easier not to compete with the star of the family. For many years, the two sisters had a tumultuous relationship, often clashing over silly things that too often keep siblings at odds.

Deena, as it turned out, merely was a late bloomer. She came into her own as an independent woman with Madeena's encourage-

ment. This happened later than Azita and in a manner that did not directly compete with her sibling. Deena followed her biological mother and not her biological father's path. She evolved into a champion of education among Muslim women. She got her Oxford degrees in education, started many schools in middle eastern areas where opportunities for girls were largely absent and then pushed those around her to adopt this cause. The more Azita thought on this now, it was Deena that had first pushed this rescue concept among Mideastern female youth deprived of opportunities due to their sex. If the Taliban shut down education for young women, they would rescue as many as they can. Yes, it was her sister who quietly pushed the agenda, made it a practical initiative, and worked though others, including Ali and Chris, to get the University's backing. But was she now being pushed into the background? That was not clear though Azita was troubled.'

As Azita approached her sister's campus office she hesitated, then stopped. Deena must be hurting inside. How could she have been so blind to her sister's plight. It now was clear to her. Ali had turned down her romantic advances and now was inexorably usurping the glory attached to Deena's life work. This could not stand, she decided, but then decided that her conclusion might not even be true. Ali had always been kind and generous to both women, Azita could find no fault with her. Yet, and yet, she could not accept her fully. She was neither her biological mother, Madeena, nor her adoptive mother, Amar. She was some imposter who slept at the side of Chris. Why had he quickly taken her into this role? Had they been lovers in the past?

Focus, damn it! She snapped out of her reverie as she ambled up Broad Street. Access to the quadrangle of Trinity College was to her right, Balliol College was next. She needed to focus on the tasks at hand. Azita pinched herself to stay on task. The issue of the day was what would happen if the Americans pulled out of Afghanistan. Could the government of Humaira Zafari hold on after the U.S. troops left? She knew nothing of military affairs, but the signs were worrying. No doubt that America and its allies had tried hard. They had invested two decades, the longest conflict in America's history to building up an infrastructure and political environment that could stand on its own. But could it?

She knew from reports they were getting from Doctor Singletary in the Panjshir Valley and the Gupta's in Kabul, among others, that the Taliban had been biding their time. The people outside of Kabul, and many within, had no allegiance to the central government that had been propped up by foreign powers. The American's did what they always did. They worked with the elite, the educated, the already powerful. That, unfortunately, was not where the hearts and minds of the people lie. Secular concepts and institutions that had centuries to evolve in the west could not be easily fostered or institutionalized in an ancient culture based on religious affinities and embedded feudal relations. No, a trillion dollars' worth of weapons and technical assistance had not reached the minds of the Afghan people. Azita's heart skipped a beat. It all would be washed away as a sandcastle on a beach when facing the surging tide.

Azita saw that Deena was alone in the conference room. She also had arrived early. *Good*, she thought she might be too early. Now they could talk before anyone else arrived.

The two sisters looked at one another. They had been through much over the years … early sibling tensions, the inevitable competition for the affection of their parents, the ultimate recognition of where they were different and where their commonalities lay. In the end, they had made their compromises and found a zone of affection, even love, at least most of the time.

Azita broke the silence. "Have you accepted Ali as a stepmother," she said abruptly.

Deena looked puzzled, perhaps annoyed. "She never claimed to be such. She's just Chris's wife. Besides, Chris and Amar never legally adopted me, not like you. I was an afterthought."

"Oh no, don't go there. Don't play the martyr card. You were older, adoption wasn't necessary when the issue arrived, but they still treated you as a daughter. They never treated you differently."

"Hah!" Deena sneered.

"My dear sister, it has always been like this. You thought our dear parents, Pamir and Madeena favored me. You think people respect me more because I am a physician of some skill. And you believe that Chris and Amar preferred me to you."

"Did they not?" Deena interrupted.

"No, goddamn it." Azita exploded as he stood up. "Don't make me come over there to slap you."

Silence hung between them as Deena absorbed her sister's strong language. This was not like her at all. She could be temperamental but typically controlled her emotions within a professional veneer. "Please, sit back down dear sister." Deena said quietly. "We are not here to argue but rather to figure out what is happening in our homeland."

"Yes," Azita affirmed as she sat back down, "and whether we can continue our work there as in the past."

Deena brushed her luxuriant black hair back, a nervous habit of which she was unaware. "But I will first answer the question I think you were asking." After pausing as if to collect her thoughts, she continued in a slow, measured voice. "There is much to love about Ali. She is brilliant, accomplished, and seems to care about the same issues we do. And yet, she has not experienced what we have, gone through our trials with the Taliban. How would she really know what oppression is like, that fear which tears you apart? After all, terrorists did not kill her parents. Her brother never died fighting tyranny. She had a childhood of privilege, wealth, entitlement even. So, for her to act as if she is as committed to poor Muslim girls as we are seems to me … as being insincere." She looked away as if seeking a better word. "Maybe put on as a false sentiment."

"For whom?" Azita asked. "Us, or the university, or … Chris."

A pained expression spread over Deena's face. "Ah, there we have it."

"What?" Azita inquired though she well knew.

"It comes back to Chris, and why he married her. We both wondered if this was an impetuous decision. Did this woman take advantage of his vulnerability? Was it not an insult to Amar? She was barely gone when …." Deena stopped.

"When Ali accepted Chris's offer of love while rejecting yours." Azita said the words she had not uttered until now. She expected her sister to reject such thoughts or perhaps fight back. Instead,

Deena remained calm, uttering in a voice so low that Azita was not sure she heard the meaning correctly. "Yes, she did reject me."

Azita rose and mover to sit next to her sibling. "Dear sister, she did not reject you. You must understand that. It turned out we were all wrong. She was not a lesbian despite everything said the contrary. No one who is attracted to women could ever resist a beautiful flower such as you. And men, they cannot take their eyes off you. Did you ever think of how that affected me? I was the ugly duckling."

Deena gently touched her sister's face, "sometimes you surprise me with your gentleness, your kindness, both attributes which typically you normally hide so effectively." Deena smiled so her sister would not take offense. "So, you did know that I approached her to be my lover, partner."

"Oh, I could surmise. We know each other so well. But I doubt others knew and Ali, as far as I know, never mentioned it to anyone. I will credit her with that."

"But that is not why we are here." Deena said with firmness. "We are here to talk about Afghanistan. And one more thing, you are no ugly duckling … ducklings are cute." Deena smiled.

"Absolutely," dear sister, Azita affirmed with her own smile. "However, there is one issue about Ali that remains in my mind."

"Which is?" Deena asked when nothing more was said.

"Who is in charge here? Is it you and I, or Chris, or Karen, or Ali? Sometimes I think Ali acts as if she runs it and that she has the support of Chris in this. Does it matter? Do we want that?"

Deena seemed to think about that question, then said slowly. "Perhaps up to now it was not all that critical. But our homeland is at risk at present, at least it might be. We are at a crossroads."

The door opened and Karen Fisher walked in the room. Karen was now the CEO of the International Service Organization that Chris Crawford started many years ago after he earned his terminal degree at Oxford as a Rhodes Scholar. He started this initiative for both altruistic and personal reasons. He wanted to work out a vision of how an integrated service model might work as opposed to the typical siloed approach to helping people. And selfishly, he wanted to do something that his right-wing father would hate. Helping the vulnerable was a cause that Charles Crawford Senior found laughable and frivolous, preferring to employ his vast fortune to support ultra-conservative agendas, believing fundamentally that human progress would only happen if an elite controlled all things. The masses were too backward for such a responsibility.

The story of Chris hiring Karen was now part of the iconic lore of the organization, passed from new employee to new employee. As the story went, Karen walked into the interview without impressive credentials of the other candidates yet sporting a certain roughness from her Birmingham working class background. Chris was not impressed at first, going through the motions when he asked one of his standard hypothetical questions … *if we were in a meeting and you saw me making a big mistake, what would you do?* Karen, thinking her chance at the position already was toast, answered honestly. *'I would take you outside the room and rip you a new one.'* She rose to leave the room, thinking that was it. But his eyes brightened, and he waved her back to her seat, peppering her with more tough questions which she answered with similar candor. The remainder of the interview mattered not. With that one response, she had gotten the job. Now she ran an operation that had grown under her competent aegis.

"Ali will be in momentarily." Karen said as she sat down. I think she's finishing up a call to Kabul."

"I doubt any of the news will be good." Deena said absently. "We've been in touch with the Singletarys, the Guptas, and others in the field. All warn that the situation is dire."

Karen sighed. "You know, I remember a professor I had at Durham University though I can't even recall which class this was. Anyway, he talked about Afghanistan, which at the time was a place I could barely pick out on a map. But I still recall what he said, at least in a rough way."

"Which was?" Azita asked when she went no further.

"Oh yes, his point was that the Afghan people always won, that repulsed all those who set out to conquer her. I do recall him mentioning the Macedonians under Alexander, the Mongols under the Great Khan, our own British troops who marched on Kabul in 1839 and eventually were forced into a bloody retreat three years later in which most were slaughtered. Of course, we all remember the Russians in the 1980s, who were forced out ingloriously. Why would the Americans believe they would be any different?"

"Inflated egos." Deena offered.

"For sure," Karen agreed. "I've worked with Chris long enough to see it up close and personal but you two know him even better. Americans block out unwelcome news like Vietnam and Iraq. They really have short attention spans."

Azita opened her mouth as if to argue when Ali entered the room, leaving Karen to wonder if she were going to comment on America's military disasters or the personal qualities of the man they all admired.

"Sorry to be late." Ali quickly said as she slid into a chair and opened a notebook on which she had recorded some notes. "That call went longer than I expected."

"But the news is the same, right?" Deena commented flatly.

"Yes. I'm not sure why I keep expecting something different."

"You're not an Afghani." Azita issued in a slightly acerbic tone.

'Neither are you any longer.' Ali said in her head. "No, I'm not," she said with an even voice. "I suspect I'm an incurable optimist."

Karen spoke up, sensing a ripple of tension bubbling in the room. *'Probably just the continuing bad news from Kabul,'* she thought. "You guys are more familiar with breaking news, but the trend has been clear for some time. There were some 100,000 allied troops sent in after 2001 as the Taliban collapsed and went into hiding. Mostly they had come to catch Bin Laden but then the American's started their nation building thing, assuming that would erase the possibility that the country would become a terrorist base in the future. The idea was they would reduce their military presence over time as the Afghani's built up their defenses, their infrastructure, and their national institutions. As usual, they found that winning a military conflict was easier than changing a country's direction or culture."

"Vietnam, being an exception." Ali inserted.

"Yes, they lost both the war and the nation-building effort there," Karen noted absently. "But the withdrawal of interest and personnel has been slow but mostly consistent. The troop level was down to 25,000 in 2009, 9,000 by the end of Obama's administration, and then 2,500 under Trump, who promised to get them all out by now."

"No oil, no profit in Trump's callous heart." Azita uttered bitterly. "Everything is transactional for that bastard."

"No doubt Trump is a complete idiot," Ali said calmly, "but the Americans were never going to stay forever. They had built up an in-country defense force of some 300,000 men. They hoped that would be enough to stave off the Taliban or at least ensure government control."

"They are idiots." Azita was clearly angry. "Almost as bad as Trump."

"What bothers me," Deena interrupted in part to defuse the anger she saw growing in her sister, "is that we were making such progress on the education front. Back in 2001, when our family fled Kabul to join the Northern Alliance fighting the Taliban, there were few girls in primary schools. My sister here was almost beaten to death in a public square for the offense of reading a public poster. Being older, I had to wear a full Burka in public and could only go out in public when accompanied by my brother or father. Mother was banned from her university career and most women were banned from public positions. It was hell."

Azita spoke up with animation. "So true! Our sainted parents were defined as criminals by the religious zealots since mother was teaching us English and mathematics, which she had taught at university in the old days, mathematics that is."

Deena spoke next. "And our papa was training Zita here the elementary skills of medicine. He even took great chances letting her perform simpler procedures on his female patients. That was a substantial risk with Taliban spies everywhere. And now the Americans will pull out completely, letting the extremists likely take over again."

"Perhaps it won't be as bad as we think. After all, there are those 300,000 trained soldiers in the government's service." Karen tried to sound upbeat.

Ali laughed derisively. "I've just finished up a call with Cate Connelly and her partner, Meena Muhaisin. You remember them, don't you?"

"Of course," Karen said, a bit taken aback that they should be forgotten. "Cate is the daughter of Rachel, Joshua Connelly's sister who was killed in the Kabul attack."

"And Meena is also a Jordanian national like me." Ali added.

"And just as strikingly beautiful," Deena said at a whisper she was sure no one heard. Still, people looked in her direction. "Sorry, just thinking aloud."

Karen continued as if she had not heard the last comment. The thing is this. Chris asked me to chat with them. Apparently, Cate has resigned from the U.S. Foreign Service, or at least taken an extended leave of absence. I neglected to ask which.

Not important, they are collecting intelligence for us, easy with Cate's and Meena's contacts. They are getting the story behind the story before they come to England."

"They will be joining us?" Karen was surprised Chris had not mentioned this to her.

Ali sensed Karen's discomfort at being out of the loop. "Yes, but it was all very sudden, something involving Joshua's health, Cate's uncle."

"Must be serious," Karen added distractedly, still smarting from feeling out of the loop. She was in charge, damn it. She should know these things.

Ali continued. "We will find out soon enough, but I suspect so. Connie, Josh's wife, is also coming back. And Usha, Rachel's former partner, has cancelled her plans to return to Canada. It looks as if the Connelly and the Crawford clans are reuniting. Chris has told me many times about how much he misses Josh. I think he sees him as the father figure he never had. We all know full well how dreadful things were with Charles Crawford Senior. Chris never had a real father. Boys miss that." Then Ali stopped, wondering if she was creating difficulties by sharing intimacies her new husband had shared with her.

Karen quickly stepped in. "No shit. When your mother shoots *her* husband, and *your* father, in broad daylight on a Chicago city street because she fears the bastard will murder his own children, one could call that a dysfunctional family. In fact, the family feels that Senior was responsible for several deaths in the family and among their good friends. Makes my clan look like the Brady Bunch on steroids and, believe me, my family left something to be desired. Senior was so evil that Mary was exonerated of all guilt."

At this Ali smiled. "Yes, Chris's sister, Kat told me that part of the story which is still a secret since it hasn't hit the press. Apparently, the bodyguards of Charles Senior hated the man. When Mary Crawford shot her husband in the head, they placed a spare gun in the dead man's hand. They later testified that he threatened to shoot his wife, but she fired first."

"I can't believe that worked." Karen chuckled.

"There was confusion since other witnesses said they thought they saw things differently, but the cops went with the easiest story … self defense. She was, after all, a prominent socialite and evoked much sympathy in the right circles. Besides, Charles Senior was seen as having gone over to the dark side, as a threat to democracy and the American way."

Azita spoke up with irritation. "Yes, a nice history lesson, but what have Cate and Meena to say? Can it be any worse than what we are hearing."

At that, Ali's face darkened. "I wish I had better news to share. But no, their sense of things is as dire as you are hearing from your people on the ground. The Taliban are just waiting until the last American is gone. Deals are being made with the local provincial chiefs. The government will fall like a house of cards. President Ghani will flee and Mullah Abdul Ghani Barader likely will assume power, along with Abdul Salam Hanafi … an Afghan Uzbek political and religious leader. Abdul Kabir is likely to play an important role and there are rumors that Hasan Akhund will serve as acting prime minister while Hibbatullah Akhundzada might act as de facto head of state. In the consensus interpretation of things, it is a done deal though no one in authority will admit to this. Certainly, no one is reporting this to the press."

"Shit!" Karen let out. "No resistance at all?"

Ali shook her head. "Probably not. As I said, arrangements are being struck with current local officials, few of whom are really devoted to a corrupt, secular government. Even if these local leaders dislike what is coming, they have little faith in the current regime. Besides, the Taliban leadership is making promises that they will be less harsh this time, more inclusive. But who around this table believes that? I would bet everything that they will end all protections of those suffering at the hands of men, will detain and punish females for the most minor violations, will facilitate a surge in child marriages, will invalidate existing divorces, and surely will end education and work opportunities for women."

"And think of what will happen when the West pulls out all aid which basically props up the national economy. I would not be surprised if half the population starves. It will be awful. They will need us more than ever. International aid could help but the Taliban is so paranoid. Who knows what they will permit from outsiders, including us?"

Deena sighed with a deep exasperation. "And we were making such damn progress. In 2018, we had 2.5 million girls in primary school. I mean, that was up from a handful less than two decades earlier. The number girls in higher education had reached 90,000 recently, a 2,000 percent jump from when we were girls. There was such hope. We had been identifying the best and brightest to prepare for college and advanced degrees abroad. They would have been the leaders for the next two or three generations. It will all disappear, be gone." She sucked in a hard breath.

"No, that cannot be. We cannot permit that to happen." The words escaped Azita's mouth with a certain amount of venom.

Ali spoke softly. "Dear Azita, let us consider what is feasible."

"No, don't speak to me as if I were a little girl. I was doing advanced medical procedures in terrible conditions when you were still idling away on your damn dissertation in Oxford's Bodleian Library."

Karen saw the anger building in the room. "Zita, I have a sense that the Taliban will permit outsiders to continue providing medical help, they are not that stupid."

"Don't sugar coat this," Azita spit out. "Yes, they may allow the male doctors to continue but what about all the female personnel. And you damn well know they will shut down our schools for girls and refuse to let girls leave the country for higher educations. Those are the very people they fear most, the educated among the very population they intend to persecute the most. They will oppress and suffocate."

"Now Azita, it may not be that ...." Ali never got to finish.

"That bad! Is that what you were going to say. It might not be that bad." Azita paused as if deciding whether to continue. "I believe it will be worse than you can imagine. You two never lived it." She glanced at Karen but focused on Ali. "You cannot really know fear and desperation until you have escaped tyranny in the middle of the night only to see your family perish at the hands of despots."

Karen tried again. "Deena, Azita, I'm going to pull the senior management team together to develop a coherent strategy to all this."

Azita stood up. "Karen, you mean well. But know this. Deena and I are going back there before the end arrives. We will work to save our educational program for girls, or as much as we can. Neither she nor I are prepared to see our life's work in ashes. Come Deena, we have work to do and not much time to do it."

"Wait, you can't do this without resources. I and Chris will have to approve..."

"My sister and I will not wait for your damn approval." Azita asserted in a cold, hard voice,

With that, the two Afghani women left the room.

"Well, that could have gone better." Ali said grimly.

"Oh, I wouldn't be overly concerned. After all, the news from their home is bad, which must be such a disappointment. We'll sort things out soon enough." Karen offered in a bright voice.

Ali did not respond immediately. *She rose and walked to a window, looking out over the tranquil quadrangle below. Students wandered in various directions seemingly absent of any care. She was reminded of her life for so many years, immersed in intellectual questions and, at worst, academic disputes. Though they aroused the fire of the combatants, they were insignificant spates on any objective scale. Wasn't that Henry Kissinger's definition of faculty disputes, virulent arguments by very smart people over totally insignificant issues. Had she drifted toward public, political issues at the expense of intellectual pursuits only because of her attraction to Christopher Crawford? She didn't want to admit that, but she could not refute it either. They would talk often, and she found herself drawn to his simmering ideals and obvious commitments to larger causes. He made her feel selfish while his issues enflamed her. And then, just as she was prepared to admit her growing affection for him, he was suddenly married. While she stuffed her feelings inside, she kept drifting slowly into his professional orbit. Did that happen due to a genuine interest or was it a subconscious attempt to remain close to him. She would have to debate that conundrum another time.*

"I hope you are right, Karen. But there is something deeper going on than the comeback of the extremists in the home country. Yes, that is an unspeakable tragedy but there is something else going on."

"The Masoud gals are not happy with you marrying Chris." Karen said flatly. "They were at first but now …"

Ali looked sharply at her. She saw Karen as a hard-headed administrator, a woman who didn't dally often in human emotions or sense the undercurrents that muddied most interactions. "Is it that obvious? I had no idea … everyone knew."

"Probably not but I do concern myself with more than budgets and logistics. Managing a set of programs like we are doing ultimately involves people, knowing them and keeping them headed in the same direction. And that, my friend, is like herding cats."

Ali cracked a small smile. "You amaze me at times, Karen. Strategic planner, budget wizard, and feline expert."

"Ah, that's my superpower," the other woman said. "I lull people into a false sense of security with my rough exterior. But yes, I am smart and damn good at piecing things together."

Ali looked back out across the campus, the place that had always been her refuge when her own cultural challenges threatened to overwhelm her. "They don't think I understand their world and passions. That's obvious. Just because I didn't suffer at the hands of the religious fanatics, they don't believe I am one of the oppressed. I'm just a spoiled, entitled academic to them, born to privilege somewhere in the Jordanian royal family. But they have no concept of my battles, for independence and for a career of my own. Sure, I could get an education, and the best kind, but I was expected to marry early, have children, and look like a dutiful woman. When I didn't, the worst rumors swirled around me. I could see others look at me with knowing glances … she's a secret lesbian. Why doesn't she marry for convenience and have her lovers on the side? Isn't that what all the entitled bitches do?"

Karen startled a bit at the language. "Okay, excuse me if I am stepping over some line here but why did you wait so long to get married? You must have had many opportunities. Even I thought you were on my team except you never gave me any opportunity to hope. And, in truth, I kept looking."

Ali smiled at that. She had always loved Karen's directness and knew why Chris trusted her so. "I was never going to settle. You of all people understand that. Should I marry to please my parents, my family, my culture. That would be a life sentence. Better I kill myself quickly, much less painful. But I did suffer …"

"Because you were in love with Chris?"

Ali looked concerned. "My god, I hope that was not obvious. I would never step between he and Amar. And there was his relationship with Jules that went back to when they were children. I did not miss that either. It was all so complicated in my head. So, I just stuffed my feelings inside because I could not let them out under any circumstances. I was certain I would remain alone and be satisfied knowing him as a colleague."

"Listen, Ali, I never saw you act in any other way than as a colleague toward Chris. I am positive Amar suspected nothing. But that must have been a bit of hell I would think. I mean, you were around this man all the time but had to conceal your feelings."

"True, it wasn't easy at times, but I was used to it. Anyway, when first Jules was killed and then Amar died tragically, I entertained the thought that maybe love was possible. I quickly stuffed that thought back down. I was shocked when Chris opened up and confessed his feelings. Even now, I'm still not sure of them, whether they are real or merely a convenient way of re-establishing a family unit."

Karen stifled intimate questions that came to her mind. Instead, she went in a different direction. "And now Azita and Deena are, what shall I say, acting out?"

"Precisely! Well. Azita at least. I'm not sure how Deena feels. We had gotten along so well before the marriage. Even right after the marriage, things were fine, or seemed so. But now, when Chris and I have this relationship, they are pulling away. I think everything happened so fast, too many deaths and then too many new arrangements. Is that what you might call them, they are coming to realize that the world they had known is changed and in a way that is permanent now."

Karen looked down at her hands. "I've been curious. This thing between you and Chris. None of us saw it coming. You were good friends, colleagues, but that seemed to be it. Oh, I suppose some thought there may have been a liaison at some point, a secret tryst. In the end, most dismissed that, you know …"

"Because I was supposed to be a secret lesbian or, if not, asexual at least."

Karen looked directly at her. "I won't lie … yes."

"Don't worry, I am not a reclusive academic, though many see me as such. I really am a normal woman. It is just …" Ali sought the right words … "I would not settle. Perhaps that is selfish of me, but I have this pride, or maybe it is a set of impossible standards. I don't know. One thing, though, as I grew up, I saw all these girls being shoved into arranged marriages. Even those who nominally chose their partner did so out of expectations, not their own wishes. Good Muslim girls married and had children. Even as a teen girl I vowed never to do that."

"Your family let you do that?"

"Oh, I paid a price. So many talks, pressures, those sighs and looks of disappointments. But yes! In the end, they permitted, encouraged me in fact, me to run off to England for an education and then suggested I stay. Out of sight, out of mind. I was the lost daughter. Even my childhood friend who clearly married for convenience and had lesbian lovers on the side was accepted by all. She hid her indiscretions. But not me. I wouldn't play the game. I was the bad daughter. Better I live as an exile than bring shame on the family."

"I'm sorry." Karen sought more words, but none came. She had always envied Ali as someone who skated effortlessly through life with wealth and family connections. It never struck her that, like Karen did with her own family, she also had her struggles.

"No reason for pity. I've had a good life. And then, one day last fall, Chris arrives at my office unannounced. I thought something was wrong with him. He talked but didn't seem to say anything which was most unlike him. Not even any jokes, or at least no good ones. Then, after more interminable chit chat, he cleared his throat and proposed. I was speechless. It took him an hour to convince me he was serious. He had all these arguments about why it was such a great idea. Now, I can't even recall them. I was too shocked at the time. His mouth kept moving but I'm not sure I heard anything."

"I never knew this. What did you do? How did you respond?"

Ali laughed. "I didn't throw up, which was my first reaction. But I do recall standing up, trying to decide if I would run for the door. Not sure why I didn't, now that I think on it. I mean … I had always admired him. Before he came back from that sudden trip to Afghanistan with Amar I had lots of thoughts about him, as you know now. Some of them were not exactly proper for a good Muslim girl. But I thought I kept them secret, not even to offer him a hint. That was not me. No, not quite true, I was working my way up to making a pass at him, but it likely would have been so indirect he would have missed it for sure. After that, I pushed all thoughts away, deep where they could not resurface. And they did not, even after Amar's tragic passing, I never permitted myself to entertain the thought. I assumed I would grow old alone. I was at peace with that … I really was."

"So all this came as a shock." Karen was intrigued.

"Absolutely."

Karen grinned. "What did you do at that moment, when he asked that is and convinced you it was not another joke of his. I must know, this is too delicious."

The attractive woman looked embarrassed, "Our secret, right?"

"Of course, I have to keep secrets in my position."

Ali sighed. "I told him we had never even kissed. He would have to kiss me first."

"Wow," Karen issued, "this is better than one of those sappy American Hallmark movies,"

"I suppose you are right. This I remember clearly. A tremor went through my body as soon as he touched me. I was done at that moment."

"This is beyond delicious."

"Hah," Ali half shouted, "now his adoptive daughters treat me as the evil stepmother and I'm not even sure what I did wrong. It is as if they suddenly see me as replacing both their biological mother and Amar, the woman who also was a saint to them. Karen, I am not a saint. I just don't know what to do." She almost broke but held it together.

Karen arose and walked to her. "That, my dear, will have to wait for another day. First things first. Chris always goes a bit ballistic when the girls, why do I keep calling them that, when Azita and Deena go into harm's way. If they were to head back to Afghanistan when the Taliban were taking over, he would have a breakdown. Okay, he wouldn't have a breakdown, but I am sure he would try to break me in two."

"You know how stubborn they are, though."

"No shit. And now Azita has her own daughter to worry about. Kay and I have chatted about what would happen if the worst came to Azita, who would look after young Maddie."

"Karen, it must be difficult for you."

"Everything is difficult in my world but what specifically?"

Ali tried a smile. "Well, Azita's daughter is Madeena, though we all call her Maddie, which was also the name of her mother. Her sister is Deena and Cate's partner, who will be joining us soon, is Meena. Now that must be confusing to you as a Westerner?"

"Absolutely, after all, you all look the same to me," Karen managed a chuckle. "But listen, I am going to bring Chris up to speed. Better I rather than you. I really need to fill him in on what Azita and Deena are up to. That way, I can take any blame if they are upset, and if he goes on the warpath. Taking shit is why they pay me the big bucks."

"They don't pay you enough," Ali smiled weakly.

"No shit. Then I will gather the brain trust, you know Carlotta and Kay and Tomas and Patrick, and Atle and the others. What we do in Afghanistan spills over into our other initiatives. I want the girls to see that, it isn't all about them."

"Karen, I feel better already. You are a miracle worker."

"Not quite." She smiled. "I've never pulled off the best trick of all."

"Which is?" Ali asked.

"Turning water into wine of course."

Ali laughed aloud. "Good party trick."

Karen smirked in response. "Yup, as I get older, I need to up my game to stay popular."

"No," Ali responded. "You have a better trick than the water-wine thing."

"What could possibly be better than that." Karen asked.

"Keeping my husband in line," Ali smiled. "You are better at it than I am."

Karen laughed deeply. "The trick is to treat him like shit."

CHAPTER 7

A Temporary Peace

"Spirituality does not come from religion. It comes from our soul."
Haile Selassie I

Agnes Singletary looked up at the mountains surrounding the Panjshir Valley educational and medical center, officially known as the Pamir and Madeena Masoud Resource Center. It had started as an emergency medical clinic tending to tribal fighters who were conducting a rear-guard action against the Taliban in 2000 and 2001. This geographical area, long dominated by fierce and independent Pashtun fighters was the last stronghold of independence. Agnes was not surprised that the northern Pashtun had held out the longest. One of the larger tribes in the Mid-east, numbering some 50 million scattered across Afghanistan, Pakistan, and India, as well as countries around the world, they were tied together by the principles of *Pashtunwal* … a strict code of honor. Among the chief tenets of this code were *Nang, Wafa, Kheegara* and *Milmastya*. As Agnes has been able to put these ethical principles together, the typical Pashtun must have honor as well as loyalty to kin and tribe. They must also welcome strangers and give asylum to those in need. The one downside, as she saw it, was the need to avenge perceived wrongs, often with violence.

When she first arrived with her husband, she wondered if this voluntary medical venture in their retirement had been a miscalculation. The males of the area looked fierce and warlike. She had trouble connecting with the women, who seemed shy, excessively diffident, and irritatingly subservient to men. She realized that she initially behaved scandalously in the eyes of the locals by treating her husband Archie as an equal. Soon, she learned to correct him in private. Moreover, the food was strange to her taste. Yet, with time, she learned enough Pashto to communicate, which immensely helped the people to open up to them. And they tried hard to obey local customs though she yet missed her evening cocktail and still yearned for a good pork roast. Nevertheless, she learned to love the local cuisine … the kebabs of lamb and mutton, the naan and chai. The kabuli palaw and chappli kebabs became two of her favorites.

It was to this remote valley situated in the mountainous wilds of northern Afghanistan that a group of medical personnel risked their lives to assist the last resisters to Taliban rule. They had come at the invitation of the iconic Ahmad Shah Massoud, the so-called *'lion of Panjshir'* who first found fame as a Mujahadin fighting the Russians in the 1980s and later for holding out against the Taliban. He was assassinated on September 9, 2001, just as the attacks on the U.S. by Bin Laden were being launched. It seemed the high-water mark of the Islamic extremists in the holy war against Western infidels. All of Afghanistan seemed destined to fall to the Taliban.

Among those to respond to Chris Crawford's call to help the beleaguered holdouts was Amar Singh, an idealistic doctor from India and later Kay Crawford, Chris's sister. They were joined by Doctor Pamir Masoud, who had escaped from Kabul with his family and somehow made the journey to this place, which also happened to be his family home. September 11, 2001, brought terror to America and despair to the Panjshir Valley.

There were several moments of despair after Massoud was killed and the attacks on New York and Washington unfolded. Many saw imminent defeat, others resolved to fight back. In the chaos of those days, Chris Crawford flew in to bring his sister out of harm's way and to fire Amar Singh who, in his opinion, had put his sister in extreme danger. As is often the case, things did not go as planned. Osama Bin Laden's surprise attacks on American targets prompted the U.S. and Britain to respond to drive out the Taliban which had given sanctuary to this international terrorist. The original medical staff was modest in numbers. When supplemented by British doctors and medical personnel, the camp grew to become a regional medical center. Later, through the ministrations of the Masoud sisters, particularly Deena, this also became a regional center for the education of Muslim girls and a general resource center for struggling Afghan families.

Agnes and her husband, Doctor Archibald (Archie) Singletary, assumed command of the medical operations when Amar Singh and Kay Cawford left for England after the Taliban threat had been eliminated. The Singletary's were joined by their daughter, Doctor Carolyn Watanabe and her Japanese-Philippino husband, Doctor Kenji (Ken) Watanabe, along with other volunteers from Australia and New Zealand. The camp continued to grow over time both in size and in the diversity of services. In particular, the educational programs for girls helped it stand out as a beacon in the country. Others tried to emulate its programs and its success.

On this day, Agnes looked about her with a mixture of pride and concern. The pride came from all the success they had achieved. They not only provided primary medical care to the sick in the region but also had programs designed to improve nutrition, public health, and instruct locals in basic family planning principles. Once trust had been established, the locals throughout the region responded with eagerness and gratitude. This was not like the American Aid distributed throughout the countryside. A new school building might be built or a well dug and then they would move on. The only evidence they had been there would be a sign saying something about this being a gift from the people of the United States. But there was no connection with the people on the ground. It was the way the Americans now preferred to fight wars, from remote locations using high tech tactics. They tried not to engage their enemies, nor did they often interact with their friends.

Agnes, and her husband Archie, had initially come for a two-year stint. Archie thought this might be a clever way to ease into retirement, mostly to pay back for all the good things that had come their way. But they stayed. And they continued to stay after their daughter and son-in-law joined them. They had fallen in love with the people and the work. Archie would always tell her that they could not leave … where else can you find such grateful people. How else can you make such a difference in people's lives. For a while, their daughter tried to convince them to return to Australia, to buy that retirement house by the sea and enjoy life. 'But I'm enjoying life now,' he would respond. After Carolyn and her physician husband grew curious and joined them for an extended visit, they also fell in love with the work and the people. They were now part of the permanent team.

Now, however, ominous signs were clouding the work they loved. She still remembered the day Archie returned from a call with Professor Shahed Al-Hussein in Oxford. She had told him that things were worrisome. Though they were all happy that Donald Trump had lost his bid for re-election, he was giving evidence of engaging in a scorched earth policy … a time worn tactic of authoritarians losing their grip on power. Just a day or two after the election, he had given orders to pull American troops out of Syria, Iraq, Africa, and most importantly ... Afghanistan. While impulsive, such actions were not unique for this President. In 2019, he had pulled American troops out of northern Syria, essentially abandoning America's long-term allies, the Kurds. Some 160,000 Kurdish families were left to face unspeakable violence. Those around Trump had become accustomed to evading or circumventing his more bizarre orders. Still, Archie worried that the protections from the West were about to end. It had been an exceptionally long conflict, especially for a country not known for its patience.

As Agnes walked toward the school buildings, she recalled that the original one room that was named after Deena Masoud. It had now blossomed into several buildings including hostels where the female students from outlying areas might stay while doing their studies. Already, the school was manned by the early graduates from the post 2001 period who had gone on to teacher training in Kabul and elsewhere. Other early graduates were working as nurses and technicians in their medical facility or as outreach workers in the more remote villages where they instructed villages in everything from early childcare to nutrition to public health to crop diversification and so forth. A few took on what had been male tasks in helping to locate good spots to dig wells for water.

What Agnes, along with her daughter Carolyn, was most pleased about was the newest initiative that both Deena and Azita had developed in recent years. The most promising girls were being identified and cultivated for further education abroad, many in Pakistan and India but others in England, America, and a few on the Continent. They were still feeling their way through this process since rural families resisted letting young females go abroad. Slowly, the success of the first few recruits spawned increasing numbers of volunteers, obviously made possible by generous funding from the Crawford initiative known locally as the Pamir and Madeena

Masoud Foundation. Pamir had been a legend locally for his kindness and his accomplishments. Not far from where Agnes paused to look up at the hills surrounding this valley, a memorial had been erected to honor what was locally considered the martyrdom of Deena and Azita's parents.

Agnes continued to the school complex. Already, she could sense that the level of activity was subdued, that an oppressive tension had filled the air. She sought out the woman who headed the education programs for females who looked up when Agnes entered the room. The younger woman's face was worn with a look of concern that did not sit well with her youthful countenance. "Welcome Ma'am. You come to see how poorly things are."

Agnes could have switched to Pashto but decided to stick with English since that is how she was greeted. "My dear Farzana, I know you are doing your best."

"The girls are afraid. I am afraid. The extremists have not been popular here but still there are many and they are powerful. They looked on what we were doing here from away at first. Now, they are bold. They come to the school room and look in. You can see the hatred. Some girls no longer come. They worry about their families, about their own safety."

"I know. I know. Please continue as best you can." Agnes looked at the attendance records. The number of names listed had visibly declined. What could they do? They could not protect them. They had no weapons, no American soldiers any longer while the British were a mere memory. There were some central government police, but their numbers seemed to be mysteriously evaporating. In the beginning there were the foreign soldiers from several countries but mostly British. Then the Americans took over who, in turn, were sent off to other parts pf the country. Of course, there were local tribal protectors who had fought the Taliban. They would be around in force. Their numbers eventually diminishing as soldiers and police from the central government moved in. Some of these outsiders seemed determined to do their jobs but most, it struck Agnes, were only in it for the pay and the nice unform. Many were not Pashtun and never trusted by the locals. As rumors spread recently about the imminent American withdrawal, their numbers were declining visibly. It was as if they were evaporating in the approaching summer heat. Agnes hugged the educator and returned to see her husband.

Later that day, Agnes sat down with her family and several others who held responsible positions for the running of the complex. None were smiling.

"The school is still at two-thirds capacity, perhaps a bit less."

"That is better than I would have guessed, but these girls hunger for an education, a chance," Carolyn Watanabe said.

Her mother smiled; she had always known her daughter to be somewhat of an optimist. "Let us not celebrate just yet. We see more of the Taliban, or their sympathizers, around every day now. They grow bolder with time, now entering the classrooms and glowering at the teachers and the students. At the beginning they would blend in, try not to stand out but it was easy to see who they were, their dress and beards and hostility are telling."

Ken Watanabe then spoke. "I also fear my wife is an optimist. "At first, these outsiders were unarmed. Perhaps they were intimidated by our guards, the national police. But like our students, the national police are beginning to disappear. In the past few days, men arrive from nowhere sporting their automatic rifles. They parade around as if they own the place. It is so intimidating."

"Yes, these men have no authority, but they do wield power," Archie Singletary nodded wearily. "I fear that if the American presence ends ..."

"When it ends." Ken said firmly. "Does anyone here imagine it is not already decided."

No one argued his point, so Archie resumed. "I believe we must now prepare for a change of regime. I agree with my son-in-law that it is just a matter of time, and that time will be in weeks or months at the most if we are lucky. We all hear the rumors. Various tribal warlords see the writing on the wall. They already are negotiating with the Taliban to save their own skin. A quarter century ago, there were those in this valley that would fight to preserve their freedom. Those days are no longer with us I fear. We no longer have a *'lion'* to lead us. Too many believed the promises from Kabul."

"I hate being so pessimistic," Agnes added. "I mean, I'm too old to be as upbeat as my daughter but still, there are a lot of families in these hills and valleys that recall the Taliban for what they were, and still are. I think many will resist, with their hearts if not with weapons."

"Ooh, I very much doubt whether guns are the answer to anything," the son-in law said.

"You are right, my son. Let us never forget that the man who strikes a blow against another is the man who bereft of ideas." Archie looked about the table. "In any case, let us discuss our worst-case scenario."

"Which is?"

"That the Taliban takes control and that they have not changed over the past two decades."

Carolyn had carefully been listening. Now she spoke. "They will go after the girls' schools. There is no doubt about that."

"Wait," Agnes interrupted, "are you certain? Their leadership has been sounding moderate, not like the old Taliban. They have been suggesting that things will be different this time around."

"Sorry, mother, I don't believe it. I doubt they have waged a low-level war for two decades just to keep everything the same. Once they have control, they will shut down the schools and send women back into some hellish obscurity. Oh, they may let us continue our medical services, they are not that stupid, at least I don't think so. But will they let the female doctors and nurses treat patients, even female patients? They might but we don't know. Will they let any females do outreach work in remote villages? I doubt that very much. Women, in their eyes, are to stay in the home, be subject to their husbands or male relatives. Just about everything we have been doing here will be at risk, maybe except for the medical help we provide."

"We don't have to decide everything now," Archie said with his avuncular disposition. "Yet, I want to get a sense of where we are as individuals. I see two big issues before us, issues that would require advanced planning so perhaps they should be discussed now." He looked around at his family as they waited for what was to come next. "Okay, we have some very smart gals in our educational pipeline. These would be candidates for further education abroad though many are still young. Do we try to get them out now, while we can?"

He paused as if waiting for an answer. "What is your second issue, my dear. I would like to hear both before deciding anything."

"Yes, of course. There is the big question. Do we stay as a family, as individuals? What if they prevent females, you Carolyn and you Agnes and the others, from doing any work here? What if they impose conditions that we find intolerable? Could we ever consider sending all the female medical staff elsewhere? What will happen if only the male staff are available to keep things going, at least until the air is cleared. We simply do not know what the future holds. It could be horrific. I want you to think on this issue more than anything else. However, we should decide very soon. We may not have much time."

Doctor Ferhana Gupta paused from her morning medical chores. She retreated to a small enclosure that was adorned with bright flowers that had carefully been cultivated, a sharp departure from the harsh brown that dominated most of the landscape. It was her refuge. An important meeting had been scheduled and she wanted to take a few minutes to think things through before the important guests arrived. Just the day before, she received a message that Kay Crawford, Karen Fisher, and Carlota Ciganda would be making a quick stop to assess the situation. There was no more information about the agenda though she could well imagine what it would be. The country might collapse in a matter of weeks, perhaps months if they were lucky. What surprised her was that neither Azita nor Deena Masoud were in the visiting contingent. They always came when there were important matters to discuss. Something was amiss.

Whatever the precise agenda was, the outlook was bleak. All around her were rumors that the Americans would soon depart. She could faintly recall, or at least remember the stories, of when the Communists were pushed out by the Mujahadin, helped with American supplied weapons. While there was general rejoicing at the event, the aftermath was not pretty. A power vacuum formed in which competing warlords fought for dominance. The difficulty was that each represented a geographic base or ethnic tribe. None had a broad enough base of support to win outright. As a child she recalled the chaos and uncertainty. Almost anything seemed better than this victory over Russian occupation which had little impact on daily life in the streets. In the aftermath of victory, ironically few seemed safe.

For some reason, Ferhana's mind floated back to those days when she came to know the Masouds, a connection that dramatically altered her life.

She recalled that Deena was almost old enough to consider a friend, but Azita was just a pesky child. Majeed, the eldest and a son, caught her attention for a bit. But she soon lost interest in him since it struck her even then that he was not interested in ideas or education, as she already was. Nor was he particularly ambitious. That attribute seemed to fall to the female Masoud offspring, especially the youngest in those days.

What first attracted her to the Masoud household were the surfeit of books everywhere. Their place was only a block away though the first visits were to seek medical help. It was not long before she found ways to ingratiate herself with both Pamir and Madeena, helping in several ways including organizing patient records and medical supplies. Girls could still attend school in those days, but Ferhana found the pace of learning agonizingly slow. She managed to convince Madeena to supplement her education which, it turned out, was prescient since the rise of the Taliban was not far off. Madeena was willing since she saw her university teaching days ending. As a result, Ferhana's education shot forward.

The Taliban responded to the post-communist chaos and lack of security. Thinking back, Ferhana could not recall whether people responded to their religious message, at least in Kabul, or whether they simply liked the promise of stability. It was the latter, she concluded, but she had little notion of what rural folks thought. She never ventured outside the city, except to travel to visit extended family in other cities, and that did not happen often. Those who lived in what looked like primitive villages normally were available to city dwellers only in pictures found in the National Geographic magazine. Such people might well have been alien creatures from Mars. She had little idea of what they thought about or how they looked at the world. She did recall listening to foreign aid workers as they discussed village life, and the medical challenges they faced with Pamir Masoud. She found the discussions fascinating and, oddly enough, exotic. Someday, she recalled thinking, she would have to discover her own country.

Suddenly, she had a thought. The Taliban offered something all the other tribal leaders could not, a message that was, at least in some fashion, universal. The provincial leaders relied upon personal charisma, or bribes, or ancient clan-based allegiances. Such enticements were strong yet narrow. But a core religious message might well touch those in tiny villages, towns, and even cities across the land. That message was ancient and familiar. Most important of all, it offered unambiguous answers to those who lived on the margins. The message told you whom to fear, and why, and how to achieve glory in some future life since their current life was merely something to be endured. Most of all, this religious message took away the challenge, more like the burden of figuring things out on one's own. When most things in life were capricious, and beyond your control, there was this message, and a set of rigid strictures, that provided one with solace, security, and salvation. Apparently, it mattered little that the message was clothed in hate, division, and violence.

Ferhana recalled that, even as a young child, she loved to read. Since the Quran was one of the few books available in her own home, she started there, laboriously working her way through the flowery language and mixed messages. That would be true of most religious texts, she would later realize, but that insight was not available at the time. To her, the Quran offered many ambiguous lessons so that the diverse beliefs of their readers might be satisfied. Focus on what confirms your own priors and forget the rest. She did respond to those sections where Mohammed talked of treating women with respect and with more equality. How odd, she remembered thinking at the time. That is not at all what she heard from the Mullahs who preached with such conviction. When she brought such questions to her parents, her confusions were dismissed as childish, if not a bit dangerous. She would have to seek answers elsewhere.

Those answers would be in the home of Pamir and Madeena Masoud where she began to spend increasing time as she blossomed into a precocious teen. There she would have access to many books and even the literate conversations. There was this sense of excitement as her world view struggled beyond scripted certainties and was reformed in accordance with her own imagination. That was both exotic and exciting. She would bring her questions, sometimes to Pamir, sometimes to Madeena, and even sometimes to Majeed, the oldest of the siblings who at least knew quite a bit about Afghan and Islamic history. Though her brain was bursting with unresolved issues, she tried not to wear out her welcome, looking for clues that she was exasper-

ating them. However, they seldom displayed that feeling though they would shoo her away on rare occasion.

Yes, Ferhana said to herself, these were the people who started her on the way to becoming a doctor. In her teens, they found a way to get her out of the country and into the home of Afghani contacts who were living in India. There, she might continue her studies. She was not altogether aware of the negotiations among her own parents with the Masoud's and others who would take responsibility for her care and training. She did, however, sense the urgency toward the end of this period and of Pamir's strong support for her. The Taliban had triumphed, dominating all the others except a remnant of resistors in the north. Her departure for India was rushed, almost done in a panic, as the oppressive control over women descended across the nation in the mid-1990s.'

"Ferhana, come in. Our guests have arrived." Bahiri Gupta called out to her in his soothing voice.

That might have been what attracted her to him in medical school. He had this calming voice and easy manner. Most of all, he was not condescending toward women which most Hindu boys were. Too many of her male classmates were paternalistic, or standoffish and uncertain in the presence of an equal female. Bahiri had a quiet confidence that she found appealing. In those days, she often was frantic with fears of failing and disappointing all those who had put such faith in her. He managed to keep her centered. It was not until later that she realized how much he reminded her of Pamir Masoud. No wonder she fell so hard for him.

When she walked into the room they used as a teaching and training area, she was surprised to see a fourth visitor, Professor Shahed Al-Hussein, whom she recognized from video chats but had never met before. "Professor, I did not expect to see you here."

"First, call me Ali. I only expect my husband to call me Professor." It was an old joke with her that, while slightly irritating to Chris for some reason, the jibe inevitably elicited laughs from others.

"Well, nice to have you here, rather an honor I believe. I'm a bit surprised that Deena and Azita are not here. How did you keep them in England?"

The four visitors looked momentarily uncertain before Karen started in her usual brusque and direct manner. "It's like this. Azita, well both women really, are heavily invested in the education program. Chris and I feel they may not be distant enough to make an objective decision." As Karen said this, she glanced at Ali who looked down at the table.

"Yes," Ferhana agreed, "I can certainly see that." She didn't, really, but thought it best not to go down that path.

"Okay then." Karen started anew. "Unforeseen circumstances have pushed this situation to the front burner. The Americans baling out is not much of a shock, they typically give up on their foreign adventures in time. In my job, I must keep abreast of what is happening in other hot spots, and they seem endless. Who knew, when I was taking those courses in politics at Durham, that I'd be using that crap one day. I should have paid more attention in class."

"Me too," Carlota said, "but I'm learning fast. Real life is a harsh, yet excellent, instructor. All is pass-fail with failure way more than a bad grade. I've been looking at other situations. We have similar programs going on in the horn of Africa as you know. There are similarities that are hard to ignore. That is, the loss of Afghanistan is quite like the loss of what we call the African Sahel. The American Special Operations Command Africa, otherwise known as SOCAFRICA has fought for 20 years against violent extremist organizations, or what we call VEOs like Jama'at Nurat al Islam wal Muslimin in Burkina Faso to Ahlu Sunnah wa Jama'a in Mozambique. It has all been at such a low level that most Americans are totally unaware what's going on but there have been commandoes in some 22 African countries. The thing is that violent events are multiplying in the region."

"I was unaware," Bahiri said flatly.

"You are not the only one, most people are," Karen sighed. "This makes everything so hard for us. We are trying to juggle so much, so many crises. But my best guess regarding what is going wrong is that the U.S. always seems to wind up supporting the bad guys, oppressive regimes that say the right things to their American sponsors but screw the people they are supposed to be serving at the same time. Except for the troops on the ground, and they are busy staying alive, Americans interact with the elite in the capitals. They assume that leaders in some of these countries have the same power and supportive institutions as is found in Western nations. Not always a sound assumption. Bottom line, they have no idea about the people. That is left to folk on the ground like us, and we can only do so much."

Carlota picked up again when she saw Karen finishing. "We had our first warnings about Afghanistan last November when Trump issued his rogue order to get out of several hot spots, probably just to piss off the man who beat him. What is a bit disturbing is the suddenness of the move and very realistic fears that the national government simply cannot stand? We've just had discussions with some ranking officials. They put up a front but, when pressed, they wobble. You now, they say we had better plan for all contingencies even though they insist all will be well."

Karen chimed back in. "Yeah, right. Translation, we are all fucked! I mean this is not my first rodeo. I want to tell those wankers to sod off." Then she stopped and looked at Ferhana and Gupta. "I'm descending both into American colloquialisms and my worst Birmingham vocabulary, sorry."

"We understand I think." Bahiri said. "Let me be direct, and to the point. Are you here to close everything, our operations?"

Kay Crawford picked up at this point. "Not everything, no. I am here as head of medical services, Carlota as head of community and social services, Ali as head of the education program, and Karen as head of overall day-to-day operations. And while my brother is somewhat removed from a hands-on control of things, he retains a big say in critical strategic decisions since he controls the purse strings. You see, even if our father hated my twin brother's guts, he never would leave the family money to his preferred daughter. That would be me … if anyone is confused. The family fortune must go to the eldest son … the principle of primogenitor gone amok. Otherwise, I would never listen to Chris," she said with a big smile. "Our best guess, based on what we see and are hearing, is that, how should we put this, any retrenchment of activities under a Taliban regime would be selective."

"Selective?" Bahiri was not clear what was being said.

Carlota spoke up. "Yes, we are guessing at this point. We know what the Taliban leadership is saying but we're listening to others as well. Now we want your input but let me lay out our initial thoughts." She took a big sigh. "We agree that medical services can continue. Not even the Taliban are that backward or spiteful, but the extent to which females can deliver those services is not clear. We also think that community help and humanitarian aid will be permitted though we may have to obscure the source of that aid. I mean, I studied economic development and social work at university. I believe the estimates that a Taliban takeover, coupled with the precipitous drop in foreign aid, will devastate the country. The GDP, as low as it was, will drop another third at least and food insecurity will be severe for at least half of the country maybe a lot more. We face a disaster and those running things will need help. I'm sure we can continue things like nutritional help and early child-care if we tweak the delivery of that help a bit."

"Tweak?" Bahiri questioned.

"Perhaps we can continue to use women to deliver services to women, but they must be dressed, what should I say, appropriately." Carlota almost stuttered as she completed her thought.

"Oh, I cannot bear the thought," Ferhana uttered with despair. "So many years ago, I remember women donning khimars, you may call them hijabs. It was as I was leaving this country. It had been so long for city women, that was foreign to them. Then they were forced into full burkas. I saw Madeena Masoud put one of these blasphemies on, when she left her home. I remember crying on that day. Now I will be …" She could not finish.

"Listen, this is all speculation at this point. We know nothing for certain." Karen tried but did not sound convincing.

Ali spoke up at this point. "Let us not fool ourselves on one point. I cannot imagine that the Taliban will permit the education of females under any circumstances. No way. That is fundamental to their message and their identity, the subjugation of females. They cannot bend on that. I think there are two fundamental issues we must decide on over the next several weeks. The first is how much we can bend those services … tweak them in ways that the Taliban will find acceptable."

"Tweak … whatever the hell that means." Bahiri added, his customary soft voice now hard.

Ali grimaced but decided to be honest. "Yes, for example, I can well imagine that Ferhana will have to wear a hijab when treating patients, maybe a burka. And worse, she may be limited to treating female patients."

Bahiri saw his wife moving to speak but cut her off, not wishing her to make a hasty statement based on the emotions of the moment. "And this elephant in the room, we must end our program to educate females, or at least appear to. That is what you are saying. Of everything, that program contains the most promise for the future. How can we even think of doing that?"

"I fear," Karen opined with voice that suggested sensitivity, "that we may have to make some tough decisions. If we try to challenge them and keep the education programs, we may lose everything. We might have to cut off an arm to save the patient's life."

"And if we forfeit our souls to keep scraps of help going, will we also not lose everything." Ferhana said this so quietly that those around the table leaned instinctively toward her.

"Listen, the real reason Azita and Deena are not here is that they will fight like hell to keep the education program going, perhaps to the point of endangering their own lives. No one wants to lose this thing, and I hate the coming battle with them over it."

Silence around the table persisted as people absorbed what was being said. Then Bahiri spoke in his soft voice. "Listen, if we cannot educate the girl's here, can we not get as many out as possible to be educated elsewhere? There are so many promising ones now. And more in the future. Can we not do that?"

"Damn it, we should give it a shot." Karen spoke with conviction. "We may lose many battles in the short term, but this war is a long one. I, for one, am in this for the long haul. Just look around this room. Except for Bahiri, I see a bunch of strong women, some of whom fought their way to achieve an education and success. We are not going to let a bunch of fanatics break us. But that's me, a tough working-class broad from Birmingham. I can fully understand anyone who says they have had enough, especially those who must stay here and face the insanity in a personal way."

Ferhana raised her hand. "Karen, no need for a speech. I will think on it but, in the end, I doubt I shall run. My husband, you do not have to stay. I would understand."

"We are one, my dear, we are one." He reached out to take her hand.

Karen hoped that no one saw the tear escape her eye. She hated any display of what she considered weakness.

CHAPTER 8

The Crawford Home

"The capacity to learn is a gift; the ability to learn is a skill; the willingness to learn is a choice."

Brian Herbert

Christopher Kelly Crawford opened the door to what he considered his hallowed sanctuary. It was an office in his home that he employed as an escape from the demands on his life which, in his experience, were endless. Here he was surrounded by floor to ceiling bookcases filled with a disorganized array of classics and current works along with journals and reports of various sorts. The floor also was mostly hidden by academic papers, government publications, and more volumes that covered an extraordinary range of topics. The chaos provided Chris with a modicum of comfort as compared to his university office and certainly his spacious office at the International Service Organization (ISO) over which he retained a nominal oversight responsibility as Chairman of the Board.

His academic office was messy by all conventional metrics but within accepted academic standards. One could easily find their way to a chair or the small table when workspace was needed. His ISO space was another world indeed, ordered and well-appointed as befitting the CEO of a major institution. He knew that every time he left it, some anonymous gnomes would sweep in to tidy up while restoring the detritus he left behind back to their proper places. Chris bridled at the sterility of it all. Then again, he knew the purpose was to impress important guests and donors, not a place for serious work. When he did real work there, he typically plunked himself in a vacant desk where he could shout out to a nearby worker if he had a question or needed something. He preferred a world of ordered chaos.

On the other side of the door stood his twin sister, Kristen, or Kay as everyone referred to her. Kay was chosen as a nickname based on the first letter of her name … K. The more familiar nickname of Kris was abandoned when they were toddlers since it was too close to her brother's. Kay realized that when a parent or nanny called out what sounded like Kris, it was usually Chris they were seeking and for some transgression he had committed. She stopped responding to either Chris or Kris altogether. Kay soon appeared to solve the problem. This resolution struck her as prudent, even as far back as her toddler days, that a personal identifier be chosen that clearly distinguished her from her derelict brother. There were times, as they grew into an awareness of the wider world, that she doubted he really was her sibling. He was incorrigible, so undisciplined and attracted to all manner of trouble. And yet, as they evolved into their teen years, she began to detect some talent in this unruly brother, younger than her by some seven minutes and more immature by at least seven years. She even came to admire him on occasion, when he wasn't pissing her off which was all too frequent. She tried hard not to admire him openly, an attraction that both amazed and dismayed her most days.

"Am I permitted in?"

"Of course. I'm surprised you even knocked."

"Really?" Kay seemed slightly surprised. "You have this sign up saying *disturb the inmate of this sacred sanctuary under penalty of a painful death.* Not exactly a warm invitation to unsolicited visitors."

Chris waived a dismissive hand. "Oh that! That's for the riff raff. You know, students."

"And I rank above the rabble? I am shocked."

"Well, to be honest, not by much but yes, you do. Well, it is more like you qualify for the family exemption. I keep thinking that if I get sick, you will treat me at a discount."

"You think that?" Chris's sister said with a malicious grin. "Dearest Chris … you are so desperately naïve. You really should be worried about me putting an untraceable poison in your morning coffee."

"Threats, threats, what would you do without me?"

"My god" Kay uttered in amazement as she looked around. "I simply cannot believe the National Health Service hasn't condemned this dump as a public hazard. I've seen more hygienic toxic waste sites. I hope there are not any bodies of decomposing co-eds buried in here."

"Dear sister, just because you have an orderly but mundane mind, do not criticize we who see the complexity of the world."

"Fine," she said shaking her head, "you have my permission to explore the word's complexity. Just don't live in it. My word, pigs live better than you."

"Your permission?" Chris said mockingly as he retreated to his easy chair. "You do realize that I allowed you to escape the womb first merely as an act of chivalry. If I hadn't, I would have been the eldest surviving child. Even so, as the surviving male I am the patriarch of the Connelly tribe and entitled to all the respect, obedience, and adulation that such a rank demands. There are perks being a member of the superior gender."

"Hah, in your depraved and sexist dreams." Kay meandered to the sofa along the one wall that was adorned with pictures and plaques indicating honors Chris had received. Several of the pictures were of him with various world leaders. "I see you have been busy mastering photoshop." She gasped. "I mean, really, a photo of you with the queen?"

"What can I say?" he smiled. "She's a huge fan."

Before Kay sat, she perused one of the bookshelves. "I must say, from the books you have on display, you look like an intellectual."

"Are you appearing at the comedy club this week?" Chris said as he sat back in his chair, still sporting a broad smile. He loved these moments alone with his sibling and wished there were more of them. Their verbal jousts have been a source of comfort to him starting in childhood. That is when they first banded together against their tyrannical father, despite their own clear differences and ongoing spats.

"You can satisfy my curiosity on one thing," she said with a serious face which told her brother another cut was coming. "Do you still move your lips when you read? I recall mother and I worrying that you were retarded when we were children."

At this Chris let out a small chuckle which he had tried to suppress. "You know, my dear, I really should have drowned you in the tub when our nanny made us bathe together as toddlers. I mean, that would have been perfect. I was too young to do hard time in the slammer and, besides, it was clearly justified. You were an incorrigible shit from day one."

Kay laughed aloud. "As if you could have pulled that off. I could have taken you even then."

"Probably so." His agreement signalled he was about to turn serious. "How are things with Jamie, the family."

"Good." Kay said with a look of relief. "Doing the divorce and remarriage thing was a bit odd I must say. However, Jamie is such a sweetheart, and the girls seem to have forgiven me. I'm still not sure what I was looking for when I split from him. Perhaps I had an exaggerated concept of what love and marriage was."

"I know what your problem was."

"Really Doctor Phil, pray tell … enlighten me." Kay adopted her look of incredulity.

Chris slid into that lopsided smile that was his tell that a joke was coming. "You were trying to replace me in your life and no man, or woman, could do that."

Kay laughed aloud. "That must be it. Past now, anyway, so perhaps not worth too much over thinking. And you and Ali?"

"Surprisingly well so far. I thought she might be set in her ways, but she settled into marriage well. Then again, I'm easy to live with, and no comment from you." He gave her his stern look. "And the girls, Em and Liz, have taken to her which is a blessing. They miss Amar like crazy, but this has helped them adjust. It is Azita and Deena I worry about. Azita mostly."

Kay looked at her brother carefully. "So I've heard. From Karen. There is tension between them and Ali. Maybe it is all the crap going down in their home country. What a potential debacle."

"I wish it were that simple." Chris said thoughtfully. "I … I may have screwed up, moved to marry Ali too quickly. I can see how it might look to others, jumping into bed with someone many thought might be an old lover. And so soon after Amar passed."

"She was not?"

Chris bristled, "No, goddamn it. I mean, before Amar I thought about it, but I never made a move … never. I mean not once! And she showed no interest in me, other than as a friend and colleague."

"Got it!" Kay raised her hands in mock surrender.

"Sorry." He apologised. "Maybe I would have made a move, I liked her a lot, too much to make a casual pass. However, I was still in my anti-marriage period."

"Ah yes, we all recall your early days as a first-class rake and bon-vivant, bedding down a series of bimbos and escort gals. You made us all so proud."

"But I never lied to a single one of them."

Kay laughed aloud once more. "You should work for Hallmark cards." Then she leaned forward. "Listen, I'll see what I can find out. They are talking about heading back to Kabul. I don't think that's wise."

"And you think I do?" The words came out with more force than intended. He softened immediately. "There is not much I can do. I've talked with Karen about not paying for the trip, but they have their own money. You just can't control kids these days, particularly after they hit adulthood." His last words were said with a light touch, but no smile accompanied them.

"Listen, they haven't been kids for a long time. They have a right to make mistakes. And remember this, our father never could control us, thank God! If he could, we would be worshipping at Trump's feet in Mar-A-Lago."

"Good point. I just love them so, but the body blows keep coming. I've lost Ricky, Jules, our older brother Chuck, his wife Beverly, Azita's husband Ahmed, and Josh's sister Rachel. It has been freaking carnage around here. And it's not about to end. We've had the far-right storm the capitol in Washington to overthrow the peaceful transition of power, and now they are still feverishly working to deny reality. I still get death threats from far-right nutters."

"You got that wrong," Kay said casually.

"What?" Chris was puzzled.

"Those threats are from me."

"Hah, hah," Chris laughed derisively, "Attacking the Capitol is bad enough, but people believe their bullshit about stolen elections. Is someone putting stupid pills in the American water supply?"

"Calm down, dear brother." She had a strong impulse to comfort him with a hug but resisted. She knew he would not like that.

"I try but it is hard. If we don't respect our elections there is nothing left, we become just another banana republic with an autocracy doing the bidding of some whacko dictator. We talk about the birth of the American dream, our democracy. Some say it was 1776, or maybe 1783 with the signing of the Treaty of Paris that ended the revolutionary war or 1787 when we adopted the Constitution. But I think the key moment came in 1800 when John Adams realized he had lost the election to his rival, Thomas Jefferson. Did he call out the troops? No, he quietly got in his carriage and rode off to Massachusetts. That was when our country was born, not with words on paper or the conquest of arms but when those in power bowed to overarching principles, the concepts underlying those words put to paper. We became an actual nation of laws on that day."

Kay tried not to smirk. She had heard this story before, heard his political rants for more years than she could count. Suddenly, she was back when they were in their teens, huddled under blankets after they were supposed to be asleep. There, they digested what their authoritarian father had been forcing on to them, hard right messages that struck Kay as wrong, but she was yet too young and naïve to dispute. While she was better than her brother in school, especially in the sciences, he was clearly the more imaginative thinker. Even at an early age, he could see the flaws in the world view offered by their *Pater Noster*. Chris at first led her to believe their father was wrong and later, when they were a bit more mature, that the man was pure evil. That was demonstrated beyond challenge when the patriarch went fully over to the dark side and the family was split apart irrevocably. "I get that," was all she said at last.

"Sorry," he offered with a sheepish grin. You don't need to hear my stump speech. I mean, you were there at the beginning of all my rants."

"Tell me something I don't know! I still have the emotional scars."

Chris looked about him. "That's why I come here. This is my sanctuary from the world. I thought things would calm down after the election, and after our own father was … dealt with. The ISO was on automatic pilot, Karen had taken charge with me acting as figurehead, public spokesperson, and occasional fund raiser. You had taken over the medical services. Carlota had proved a winner in the planning of how to deliver overall services. Ali, with Azita and Deena, would run the new initiative to educate Muslim girls. And we have Tomas, Atle, the team working with Kat, and so many talented folk. They stay because they believe …"

"In you." Kay snuck in. "They like what they are doing but you inspire them."

Chris dismissed her comment with a waive of his hand. He always had trouble with compliments directed at him. "I remember right after our marriages, well our remarriages, I thought I could get back to being a real scholar again. I wanted that. I was tired of the real world."

Kay looked about. "Yes, you fit in here nicely … obsolete and irrelevant."

"Hah, hah! Yup, I should have drowned you in the bassinette. Still, I like this solitude, the chance to think about things. People look at me and believe I like the rough and tumble of political conflict. But I don't. I never have. Left to my own devices, I'd find a cave somewhere and hide from the world."

Kay looked at him sadly. "But you can't, can you? The world won't let you. The tragedy is that you are way too good at what you do even when you don't want to do it. Your personal tragedy is that you care … you care way too much. My god," she winced, "did I just say that?"

"A tragedy indeed, both the fact and that it took you this long to admit it."

Kay looked at him with considerable kindness. "Perhaps long in coming but true nevertheless. And perhaps a tragedy for you, but not for the world. You walk into a room and people respond. Your words bring them together, your vision even sets a few ablaze. I will never repeat what I'm about to say outside this room. In fact, I will deny I ever uttered these words …"

"Which are?" He asked when she paused.

"I am in awe of you." She recoiled at her moment of honesty.

Chris's watch beeped. He looked at it in irritation. "That was a reminder that Kat will be on video momentarily which, of course, is why we are gathered here."

"She's decided then?"

"We'll find out. Oh, and I've gotten more than one email about Josh Connelly returning, with wife and ex-wife, and his niece and her partner. Connie called everyone I think."

"Wait, the whole Connelly tribe? That's great. I love them."

Chris grimaced. Yes, but I wish we were gathering under different circumstances."

"Connie just said he was ill, needed some time away. That's just your damn Irish black cloud speaking. It is seldom right." Kay tried without conviction.

"So you always say. This time I'm not so sure."

Kat appeared on Chris's computer screen as Kay maneuvered to be able to see her. "Ah, my two favorite siblings."

Kay looked hard at her younger sister. Of the children, she most resembled the father, Charles Senior. Early on, Kat had retained a softer look of the youngest child, made even more youthful by a retiring and shy personality. She had been the quiet one who existed almost unnoticed in the background. The eldest boy also was retiring, an aesthetic type, but he had been forced to play a dominant role by a domineering father. It was like forcing a round peg into the proverbial square hole until the mould cracked and the eldest son took his own life in despair. Kat still marvelled that neither she nor her twin saw the simmering ambition and talent in their quiet and younger sister who said little but observed everything. Then, when she was ready, she organized her two older siblings in a family revolt to wrest control of the family fortune and financial empire from the patriarch whom all the offspring had groaned to loathe. "We are your only siblings." Kay chose to suggest the obvious.

"It's a damn good thing you don't have any competition."

Chris smiled broadly. "What is it about you two? Don't you realize I'm the wit in this family?"

"No!" Both women said simultaneously as if it were a practiced response, which it was.

"I miss this so much," Kat noted with a soft expression of regret.

Chris assumed his fake suffering look, "You mean torturing me."

"That too, of course, but I was talking about just being with you guys. Chicago is getting lonely."

"Really?" Chris seemed surprised, "aren't you surrounded by all those super-rich financiers and snobby elites. I always saw you as hobnobbing with the jet set."

"That, my dear brother, is business. Besides, those people bore the crap out of me, for the most part at least. I want connections with people who care about me, and who have interests in more than money and stuff."

"I can't think of a single person here who would do that … care about you that is." Chris deadpanned as he looked at Kay for confirmation.

Kat pursued her thought as if her brother had remained silent. "… and that I care about. Face it, my husband and sister-in-law are gone, along with our elder brother and his wife, and even our dictatorial father, though his demise makes things easier."

"My hopes are rising," Chris said as he looked closely at the screen. He saw this sibling only at intervals. She was changing in appearance, looking older, or should he say more mature. He had wondered after she had assumed control of the family empire whether she sufficiently looked the part. She appeared too young to him, soft of voice, and diffident in manner. She would be swallowed up by the sharks that would circle her in this new role. Over time, though, he saw in her an incisive mind, a penetrating intellect, and a steely core. This quiet one had a will that was not to be denied, and the skills to negotiate the complexities of the modern world of international finance. Looks could be deceiving. Now, looking at her, Chris could see she had drawn much from their father except for those attributes that made him so detestable. And he noticed something else. As she fully lost the physical softness of youth, he could see subtle aspects of the patriarch in her visage. The composition of her face was leaner but with a determined jaw and penetrating eyes. *Wow,* Chris thought, *damn good she didn't inherit father's values.*

Kat's voice broke through his reverie. "Yes, it is a done deal. I'm shifting operations to your side of the pond."

"Great!" Kay enthused. "Will that be difficult."

Kat laughed, "Everything is difficult in life, but this is eminently doable. After all, it is not as if the family owns a lot of fixed assets that need on-site supervision. We deal in cyber-space and relationships, many of which are now in Europe and Asia. I'd be closer to the action over there now that America is being viewed increasingly as politically unstable."

"Good point." Chris added.

"Besides, I have good people who will stay here and mind the shop. And I know Chris will be relieved."

"Me? I doubt that. My life will be a misery when you two gang up on me."

"Bullshit! I'll admit there was some despair when we found out that Father never changed his will and left his personal fortune to you. I went out and invested heavily in escort services, assuming their profits would explode." Kat chuckled.

"Hah, hah, I had already left that life behind."

"I'll admit. You amazed me by turning the bulk of the fortune over to me even though I knew you were nervous that ..."

"Nonsense, I had my closest friend Ricky marry you so he could make sure you never got up to mischief until ..." Chris stopped, not knowing where to go next.

Kat bailed him out by shifting focus. "This move will also help mother out. These months have been a horror for her, wondering if she would be indicted for murdering her husband, dealing with a hounding press that loved this scandal, and terribly missing you guys. I don't have the time to keep her company. She needs to be around the grandchildren and all her children. Even you Chris."

"I'm so pleased to hear this; I'll even overlook the cut."

"And there is another reason," Kat paused as if embarrassed. "We still get death threats. Mother got most of them after father's passing but now, after January 6, they have been targeting me again. The whack jobs are on the rise once more."

"Damn,' came from Kay.

"I know. I mean, every public figure who has taken a stand against Trump and the hard right, who protested the insurrection against our government has been on the hit list of the wacko right. There are so many groups I can't count."

"Is Peter Favulli still providing security?" Kay asked about Josh Connelly's retired FBI friend.

"Oh yes, I wouldn't let him go. It just doesn't help that our father was a patron saint among these crazies. Some of them believe I put out a hit on him personally, as if I would send my own mother to kill her husband and our father. I even wonder if he put out a contract on me before he died and they are just waiting for the right moment, but that is probably the paranoia speaking."

Chris raised his voice a bit. "I don't know. It is not paranoia when they really are out to get you. I think it is clear he had a contract out on your life, for real. Name one person who does not believe that the bomb that killed Ricky was really intended for you. Crap, now the Republican base has bought into the *Big Lie.* They are outraged by the belief that Trump's Presidency was, in their befuddled heads, stolen from him, from them. I watched some nutters the other day arguing that Trump is still President. The Presidential Seal Biden uses is fake, and the military will respond only to Trump's commands. They are delusional authoritarians with no regard for our democracy, and certainly not for human life. And it seems they will stop at nothing to achieve their goals. Hell, they brought weapons to D.C.

and injured or killed police officers within the nation's capitol building. What if they had caught Pence or Pelosi. Does anyone believe that the Oath Keepers would have spared their lives? We are not dealing with rational people here."

"Yes, but father is dead. He was the biggest threat to us personally." Kat tried lamely.

"That means shit." Chris spit out. "You may torture me daily but, Kat, I love you to bits. I've lost too many that were close to me. No more I say."

"We …" Kay corrected him. "We've lost too many."

"Yes … of course, my bad. But just think about this." He said in that slightly elevated tone that suggested he was off on a rant.

"Oh no, I've set him off." Kat grimaced slightly.

Chris was not to be dissuaded. "Shush and learn something for a change. We hear about the Oath Keepers and the Proud Boys and 3 Percenters but there are so many others. Remember that we learned Father was in touch with a group called the Atomwaffers, real nutcases. The thing is that anti-government groups jumped from 149 at the beginning of Obama's tenure to a peak of 1,360 by the end of his first term. Hate is freaking big business in America. There were still over 700 in 2021." He turned away from the screen and returned with a report in his hand. "I won't bore you forever…"

"Too late," Kat interjected.

That failed to stop her brother. "… but the exact number in 2021 was 733. The biggest single category was White Nationalists and Racist Skinheads with 115, and Neo-Nazi followers with 54 distinct chapters. A lot are in response to what are perceived as specific threats such as 65 Anti-LGBTQ oriented hate groups, 50 anti-muslim, and 61 anti-semitic organizations. My point is that there is a lot of hate out there, never mind the Trumpers and Qanon types whose hold on reality is highly suspect. Many are well armed and itching for a civil war. They want nothing more than to strike down what they see as the enemy. And you, Kat, must be high on their list, as is mother. She struck down one of their heroes and you have been identified as the enemy by the right-wing media, along with George Soros among the big money set."

Kay sighed. "I hate to admit it, but my brother is right. I'd feel better if you and mother were here. I … we have lost too many already."

"And bring that ex-FBI guy, the friend of Josh Connelly, with you." Chris added. "I trust his ability to protect people even if they got Jules on his watch."

"I trust him as well but I'm not sure his wife will let him go." Kat said.

"Tell him that his best childhood friend is coming over for an extended visit."

"Why is Josh Connelly returning?" Kat asked. "He seemed so downcast after his sister was killed in Kabul. Connie was vague on her call to me. She only said he was ill and needed a change of scenery. What does that mean."

Chris shrugged. "Not totally sure but I don't like the sounds of it either. I'll just be glad to have him here, a male confidant."

Kat laughed. "If Connelly will be there, I'm pretty sure I can get Peter Favulli to join us. Those two go way back to their Boston days ... very tight."

"I need some sane people around me, not just acquaintances but close friends who worry about the same things I do." Chris said. "You think I overreact sometimes, but I worry about things in America, not that we don't have nut cases here. It is just that we don't have 2.3 guns on the streets for every citizen, or whatever the figure is in the States. Just last week I came across a report out of the University of California-Davis campus. It reported out American beliefs based on a representative sample of some 8,600 subjects. Almost 1 in 4 respondents expressed belief in the worst QAnon theories, things like the fact that Satanic leaders, who also are paedophiles, run the government, and media and high finance. See, they are not totally out to lunch." Chris now grinned. "They have you pegged as a child molester, Kat."

"Oh dear," Kat mocked, "and I have tried to keep my depravity a secret."

"Not totally funny," Chris was serious again. "A higher proportion, 1 in 3, don't believe that minorities suffer any disadvantages. In fact, they believe just the opposite, that minorities have privileges that poor whites don't. This leads to growing anger. They feel they are losing their grip on things. I mean, consider this. More than 4 in 10 believe that our way of life is disappearing so fast that we may need to use force to save it; that having a strong leader is more important than having a democracy. They are driven by an irrational fear that native-born whites were being replaced by immigrants."

"Jesus," Kay remarked cynically, "would that be so bad. So many of native whites are such losers. Have you ever seen who shows up at Trump's rallies?"

"Well, they may be dumb, but they are also angry. According to the Davis study, a full 1 in 4 *patriots,* as they see themselves, feel a need to employ violence to save the country. Moreover, fully half, more than that, believe there will be a civil war in the next several years. It is more than a belief; it is a fervent wish. Politics, from the right at least, has nothing to do with policies or governing. It is fear and hate. How many references do you see to *'owning the libs?'* When is last time you saw anything from even mainstream Republicans that did not label the very policies that even Eisenhower fully supported as *'radical'* and *'extreme'* and *'socialist'* or *'communist?'* You know, Kat, some of your friends in high places, the economic elite, may have a veneer of polish about them. But I fear they are cynical enough to support the growing hate and divisions in the states just to prevent any return of liberal thought or a progressive tax system. They would rather see the whole thing go down in flames than pay a few more percentage points on their tax bill. That is beyond pathetic."

"Now look who's paranoid." Kat retorted.

"You know I love historical analogies. Well, here's my favorite go-to-one. When the recently deposed Chancellor Papen went to see Hindenburg at the beginning of 1933. Papen was a moderate conservative, hoping to save the old order, the business elite and Prussian military. But he worried about the left, real Communists, making inroads on the streets, so he made a bargain with the devil. Make Hitler Chancellor, he recommended to the German President. He is a buffoon and I and the other sensible members of the Cabinet can control him. Once we beat back the left, we can kick him to the curb. Hindenburg hated Hitler but was old. After a brief discussion, he agreed and 50 million dead later, the consensus was that just might have been an ill-advised decision."

"Okay," Kat sighed, "I was never as entranced by history as you. Your point exactly."

"People never think the worse will happen. Evil is something that happened in times past. The world is getting better. We are all more sensible now, kinder. I recall reading a piece where James Tobin, a Nobel Prize economist confidently claimed in the 1960s that poverty in the United States would be eradicated by 1976, the country's bicentennial. And when he made the claim, it was not an outrageous prediction given the progress that had been made in the decades right after World War II. But he was looking at issues logically at the same moment a formidable group of right-wingers was planning to seize control of the political dialogue in America. They were determined to alter the default positions governing how people think about issues. A sustained campaign through new media outlets, right-wing think tanks, and political ads that went for the gut as opposed to the intellect convinced people that black was white, up was down, and your trust should always be put in corporations over government. Corporations? They are organized to screw you by definition. Do you really believe the invisible hand of the so-called marketplace will sort things out to the benefit of all?"

"Oh my, he's on a roll now." Kay managed as her eyes rolled for effect.

"Between 1979 and 1989, the top 1 % saw their share of the country's wealth jump by 15 percentage points. That is a tectonic change, almost unprecedented in history. The elite grew fabulously wealthy while working folks blamed minorities and immigrants and socialists. Wow! And people still regarded the rich as smarter and deserving of their good fortune. Shit, at the time of the 2008 bubble, the financial sector was responsible for 8% of GDP, up from 5% a generation earlier. That's a 60% increase, or $400 billion. Since much of that involved luring investors into risky, obtuse investments that were called innovations, it could be considered waste and fraud. But we reserve those labels for government since the market is perfect. Right?"

"You realize you are talking about my world, dear brother."

"No disrespect, Kat, but the public has bought so deeply into the default positions of the hard right that no amount of evidence to the contrary will change their positions. The private sector can do no wrong and government can do no right. Vaccines will kill you, not save you from a pandemic; cleaning up the environment will take away your job, not preserve the earth for your children; flooding the streets with guns will save lives, not lead to unbelievable carnage where 130 people die from guns every day. In this century, sanity was lost. Paul O'Neill, George W. Bush's Treasury guy, was aghast when he heard Dick Cheney argued that more tax cuts for the rich were okay since Reagan had proved that deficits didn't matter. After all, they had won the midterms and could do what they wanted. O'Neill was to resign. It was an era when pure ideology was in the ascendancy. And this made governing easy since *'you didn't need to know anything or search for anything. You already knew the answer to everything. It's not penetrable by facts. Its absolutism.'"*

'Finished." Kay asked hopefully.

"No! And then, by the time Trump took control, Republicans never bowed to any pretence of evidence and reason. If it was good for their rich backers, that was all that mattered. And when Trump lost in 2020, he just ignored reality. Okay, he is nuts, but a major political party largely endorsed his delusional whims and are working hard to ignore all results of future elections they find inconvenient. I wonder if those poor souls who stormed the capitol because they bought the cult leader's Kool Aid will come to their senses now that they face jail time? Will they see the light? I remember reading about Martin Adolph Borman, son of Martin Borman who was Hitler's personal secretary and a top Nazi. Borman the son almost killed himself when he heard of Hitler's death. But he walked away, and free to think on his own, transformed his life. He became a Catholic priest and fervent anti-Nazi. And here's another thing."

"The last thing, please, please, please." Kat tried.

"You have Republicans, Americans who once hated Russia as our biggest enemy, praising Vladimir Putin only because their cult leader, Trump, called him a genius. Here is a bloodthirsty dictator who invaded the former Soviet area of Georgia in 2008, the Crimea in 2014, and now threatens the Ukraine. Republicans once saw such behavior as inimical to our national interests Now they see it as strong leadership because their so-called cult leader says so. Doesn't anyone think for themselves any longer."

Kat interjected when Chris took a breath. "Kay, you've screwed up."

"How?"

"You were supposed to put Xanax into his morning coffee." Kat smiled.

"My bad, I'll double his dose starting tomorrow." Kay then turned serious. "One thing has always inspired me, and I'm moved by this. During the worst horrors, people still created beauty. As bad as things get, we can always find good."

"What?" Her twin brother was confused.

Kay continued. "Oh, just this. Richard Kattenberg and Sandor Kuti were composers arrested during the second world war, just for being Jews. Both eventually became a statistic, two of the six million who perished in the Holocaust toward the end of the war, one in Auschwitz and the other on a forced march just before the allies arrived. Yet, even in Hell, they continued to write beautiful music. One, I forget which now, hoarded scraps of paper and created moving compositions that are played today. A friendly guard helped to smuggle his work out. In the end, no one can erase beauty, no one can crush the human spirit."

Kat smiled. "This was good. Really! I'm now prepared for what I'll experience when we are together, idealism at its best. I need that after the cynicism and greed I am buried in now. And yes, dear brother, I'm prepared to work with you to fight off Fascism in America. I'm rich as Croesus but gathering more wealth for its own sake has never been appealing. I've always needed a purpose. Leaving the States does not mean I've forgotten the battle. Are we okay on that?"

"Yes," Chris said sheepishly. "Sorry about the rant. I just get so frustrated at how stupid people are … Americans are. I'm not sure I could ever go back. They cannot connect the most basic of dots or figure out their self-interest."

Kat smiled. "Calm down now. Besides, that's a universal truth though I grant you that Americans have turned greed into an art form. I'll be over there more quickly than you imagine, and we'll have plenty of time to plot the counter revolution."

Chris visibly relaxed. "Thanks. It will be so good to have us all together again, a family once more."

"I know, Kay and I will have so much fun torturing you."

"Oh shit!" Chris said with a smile.

CHAPTER 9

Heathrow Airport

[Summer 2021]

> *"Violence is not necessary to destroy a civilization. Each civilization dies from indifference toward the unique values which created it."*
>
> *Nicholas Gomez Davila*

Christopher Crawford grumbled as he found temporary parking in Heathrow airport, near the international terminal he hoped. He was not certain of that. He seldom did his own driving in the London area, usually relying upon his staff for all tedious tasks such as this. This perfectly defined a classic tedious task as he now recalled, though this insight came too late to rectify a decision that seemed reasonable in the moment. True, he had long mastered the skills necessary to negotiate traffic on the wrong side of the road but, residing in the more manageable University town of Oxford, he usually disdained the madness of urban driving in one of the globe's major cities. His hatred of the M-1 ring around the London Metro area remained as fierce and uncompromising as ever. It reminded him of being stuck on the I-94 in rush hour.

Might as well be back in Chicago, he muttered to himself. O*r, heaven forbid, Boston,* he added as an afterthought. The drivers in Beantown are the worst he had decided during several rather short stays in the capitol of the Commonwealth and several discussions with Josh about the comparative horrors of driving in Boston and Chicago. He once ran across a list that confirmed their private assessment. Boston had the worst drivers. In second place was Worcester, only 40 miles to the west. After all, the layout of the roads in both places was incomprehensible and based, as he was told, on the cow paths from colonial days. Moreover, the driving skills of Bostonians were either non-existent or bordering on the intentionally homicidal. *Their roads clearly were designed as a population control measure,* he mused, *probably to offset the effects of a prevailing Catholic tendency to eschew birth control. What else would he expect? Boston is pretty much just a replica of London cloned by British emigres some three centuries ago.*

He usually had staff pick up visitors since he found the effort of surmounting the chaos and crowds around Heathrow suffocating and off putting. Sadly, Thomas Malthus had been incorrect. While technology had permitted the human population to get out of control, there were no effective natural restraints on procreation nor the burgeoning numbers. While it was true that fertility rates had fallen in advanced countries, they remained high in less developed areas. Those places had an inconvenient habit of disgorging their excess numbers onto places like the European Union and the U.S., a pattern that fostered the popularity of rabid populists such as Boris Johnson, Marine LaPen, Victor Orban and, of course, Donald Trump. Malthus had thought starvation would impose necessary boundaries on the size of the globe's inhabitants. And while there were periodic famines and catastrophes like the occasional war, the number of homo-sapiens increased with abandon, exponentially in recent decades, at least in poor countries. The problem, he concluded, was that even small increases in births over deaths resulted in large absolute numbers. The base was too damn large, close to 8 billion around the globe was it not?

It suddenly struck Chris that he was unusually grumpy this day. He was getting older, no longer the idealistic young man who had set out to change the world. 'Why didn't I bring Karen along?' He murmured under his breath as he tried following the signs to the proper location. The obvious answer hit him immediately … she had long ceased to be his personal assistant, now serving as the CEO of his international service organization. She no longer had time for menial tasks. Then he grumped silently, 'anything impacting my personal convenience is not menial.'

He never should have promoted her. He still desperately needed her to manage his own life. His second wife, Ali, was too occupied with her career, as had been his first spouse before she fell victim to the Covid plague. Then again, he also needed Karen to manage his institutional baby. Life really was a series of tough choices. Why couldn't the females close to him be superstars, glittering in their professional lives while keeping him on track in his personal life. He would have to complain to God were he to somehow meet the creator someday.

Something was wrong? He normally was not this grouchy, especially when he was about to be reunited with the man who had become something akin to the brother he never knew, or what Chris had taken as the father figure to replace the original version he had detested in real life? He always loved being around Jeremiah Joshua Connelly ever since looking him up while giving one of his academic talks at the University of British Columbia several years ago. What he had thought might become a conventional and ordinary connection with a fellow academic who happened to toil in the same areas as he quickly morphed into a friendship and now much more.

He had bonded with this man almost immediately and soon embraced several others who were related to him. Despite superficial, yet stark, differences in backgrounds, the two shared common perspectives on those things that mattered in life … values and goals. Their personal bond soon spilled over to others in Josh's broader web. His sister Rachel and her daughter Cate had joined in Chris's international causes. Almost immediately, that connection extended further to Cate's partner Meena, a Jordanian whom Cate had met while working for the State Department at the American embassy in Amman and to Usha, a retired law professor from the University of Toronto who had been married to Josh earlier in life.

The connection between Chris and Josh, however, was more than a mutuality of professional and academic interests. It was much more if Chris were honest. Josh had become a surrogate father to him. His own biological dad, Charles Senior, had been the patriarch of the Crawford clan. Originally of Polish extraction, Senior had been scarred in his early years by rape of his homeland and the loss of the family fortune and sense of place in society first by the Nazi's and eventually by the Soviets. Somewhere in his complex psyche he chose sides and sought a form of revenge on what he considered a hostile world along with the essential philosophy to execute such a revenge. In his mind, only the brutally harsh would survive, should survive. All forms of compassion and collectivism became his bete-noir.

Chris reached the right location and watched as disembarking passengers streamed out. His mind wandered over the past year or so of his life.

In that time, his world had been turned upside down. His dear wife Amar had contracted Covid, and with compromised health suffered during a bomb blast in Kabul, succumbed to this scourge. That same blast had taken the lives of Josh's sister Rachel and Azita's husband Ahmad. As he had been reeling from these blows, things were com-

ing to a head in the American election as Donald Trump fought for another term and made ominous threats about remaining in power no matter what the numbers said. He was already laying the foundations for claiming a rigged election.

In that uncertain environment, his own father seemed to be upping the stakes in the familial and political chess game that dominated relations in the fractured Crawford family. His twin sister Kay and his younger sibling Kat had joined him in opposing the patriarch's plans to instil an autocratic oligarchy in place of a republic. Events seemed to be boiling over as the presidential election approached until Ricky and Jules Jackson, his two childhood friends, were killed. Everyone knew his father was responsible for their deaths except the authorities.

The remainder of the year seemed like a blur. Trump convincingly lost the election though a peaceful transition of power remained in doubt. Chris, in a surprise to others and especially to himself, married his Oxford colleague, Shaheed Ali-Hussein, universally known as Ali. His twin Kay remarried her first husband James Whitehead. And, after an aborted coup attempt on January 6 by the unstable incumbent President, the transfer of power in America did take place on January 20 of 2021.

For a few moments at the beginning of 2021, he thought all was well. His father was gone. Trump was out of power. The work of his adopted daughters and his new wife to elevate the status of women in the Muslim world appeared stable, even robust. The international service organization he formed after finishing up his doctorate at Oxford, in part to piss off his father, was now a mature organization directed by Karen Fisher and managed by a superb staff, hardly needing his input. His academic position was sound. He especially loved teaching and mentoring students. His younger sister Kat, though yet reeling from the loss of her husband, was now firmly in charge of the family financial empire and no longer needed to ward off threats from an estranged and dangerous patriarch. All seemed calm as springtime in the university town Oxford approached. Those days were now long gone.

Chris paused in his musings. He understood that these were the times when a person must remain the most vigilant. Trump was spreading the Big Lie that the election had been stolen, and many were devoted to this fabrication with cult-like adoration. Already, the work of installing devotees in positions where state and local elections might be summarily overturned were taking place. Where they failed in 2020, they might not in future elections, depending on how the 2022 elections went. While his father was no longer in the picture, Chris had little doubt that like-minded oligarchs would carry on his agenda, perhaps including the physical threats to his family.

Chris shook his head, trying desperately to shift his restless mind toward thoughts of the man he was about to greet.

Josh Connelly had played a role for Chris more intimate than mere confidant or colleague. They connected only a decade or so earlier when Chris had stopped to converse about Philanthropic issues with Bill Gates and then was asked to give a talk at the University of British Columbia just over the border in Canada. He agreed to that mostly as an excuse to meet this academic whose memoir he had just read and found fascinating. Chris's instinct had proven prescient, and he soon realized that this older man quickly had become the ersatz father he had always wanted, someone to replace what Charles Senior was meant to be but never had been. As Chris struggled with the uncompromising world view pushed on him by an increasingly tyrannical father, he had few places to turn. He did have the Jacksons, Ricky and Jules. So different from him, black and relatively poor growing up, but from a family that showed what love could be. They were now gone, victims of his father's deranged vendetta. More recently, he had leaned on Karen Fisher at times. But she, as CEO of his organization, technically remained a subordinate to him. That could prove a barrier.

In his early days, he had relied on his twin sister Kay. As children, they would whisper at night to counsel one another as their father sought to bring him into his thwarted view of life and politics. They used one another as sounding boards as they struggled to form their own identities. Mary, their mother, might have been of help but she had been crushed under the sheer weight of her husband's will, finding escape for a long time in alcohol. That addiction ended when she found escape from her marital hell one day. She put aside the bottle and healed her pain in a more constructive way, by shooting her husband in front of a Chicago bakery as he consumed a bulkie lathered with cream cheese. It was one of his favorite Polish delicacies.

Chris scanned the crowd looking for familiar faces. Originally, only Josh was expected. Then he was notified that his wife Connie and his ex-wife Usha would also be arriving. Then another message. It would only be Josh with his niece Cate Connelly and her partner Meena Muhaisen. That really threw Chris and raised alarm bells. After Cate had taken a leave from the U.S. State Department post in Jordan, she and Meena had stopped in Kabul, ostensibly to check things out before heading to England. Why had they detoured to Canada after the Afghan visit? That seemed out of their way and raised all kinds of red flags for Chris. There had been strong hints of health worries for Josh, but he had been told they were not immediate concerns. Chris wondered if this were true. By this time, he was prepared for anything, both in terms of who would be coming through the arrival gate and what news they might bring.

Chris began to muse once again as he realized his wait would continue.

This visit was more than a matter of mild curiosity. Josh was an intimate with whom he could share thoughts and work through the deeper dilemmas of life. He was an alter-ego, the confidant whom he never had, always being surrounded mostly by strong women. The closest males, his father and elder brother and best friend, all were gone. Besides, his elder brother hardly counted given his retiring and remote countenance while his father had been an estranged tyrant. True, he moved in a world where there were plenty of powerful males, leaders, and intellectuals of one sort or another. But that was different than having someone you could trust, could share your insides with. That male bond had been missing for too long in his life.

Why Josh, though? Why did their connection take? They did have that Irish connection, and the dark cloud that hovers over the sons or Eire. They both were academics, but of an unconventional bent. And they both were dreamers and, though it sounded like excess hubris to Chris, both were considered visionaries. Most of all, they both had battled their childhood cultures and domineering fathers. Josh had struggled against a larger-than-life local figure who ran a neighborhood bar while dreaming of a united Ireland and of his son playing football for Notre Dame. It was a suffocating culture of clan and Catholicism and tribal allegiances. Josh had instinctively thought that world too small, too provincial and stifling. It ended when he slid into radical politics and eventually fled to Canada as the Vietnam war went out of control.

Chris had grown up with privilege and wealth. He could have easily sauntered through life with ease, settling into the role of family patriarch after the suicide of his older brother who took his life, as all surmised, when he could not live up to his father's expectations. Those expectations appalled Chris, mostly because they fundamen-

tally violated his moral center. In response, he sought his own path, went to Princeton on a basketball scholarship and to Oxford on a Rhodes Scholarship. Then, partly to spite his father, he initiated an international service organization. It was never part of any formal plan. Still, he had often wondered how his life might have turned out had he enjoyed a father whom he respected and shared a common world view.

What if he had been fortunate enough to have Josh as a father? It was a question he often asked himself. Perhaps he might not have achieved as much as he had. Might not challenge push one to greater heights? That remained one of life's unanswered puzzles, is one spurred on by support or challenges. Now, he was obsessing on another puzzle. Why was he feeling so uncomfortable? Was something wrong? It was that Irish curse rearing its head. He had been so pleased that Josh was coming to spend time with him. He just knew he would pay a price for that pleasure, but what exactly would be exacted from him. Health issues! Just what did that mean.

"Hey, stop dreaming. We're here." It was Cate, Josh's niece. She bounced up to Chris and gave him a big hug. "Meena and my uncle should be along in a moment, I think."

"You always were a bundle of energy, just like your mom." Chris paused. Maybe mentioning Rachel was a mistake. Her death in a Kabul bombing was not that distant and he yet struggled with guilt. She would not have been there, in harms way, if it had not been for him. "I still want to apologize to you for that."

Cate have him *'the look.'* All men know 'the look,' a way that females have of staring that suggests the male's continued life on this planet is in deep jeopardy. "I wanted to catch you first.

Listen to me, no more apologizing for Rachel's death. Yes, we all miss her, but no one blames you."

"But …"

"No, hear me." Her look became deadly. "One more word and I'll separate your family jewels from their customary location. Do you understand?"

"Got it." Chris managed to avoid a smile. He looked closely at this woman who had become part of his extended family in recent years. He could see some of her mother in her, the same soft hair resting on her shoulders and similar bluish eyes that sparkled with life and intelligence. Yet, while Rachel had been intense, focused, and introspective, her daughter was more outgoing and effusive. That's the beauty of genetic evolution, he thought, the chromosomes interact in unpredictable ways to generate such idiosyncratic novelty. Evolution would be impossible absent this genetic lottery. In each of us, there were persistent attributes and unexpected innovation. How marvellous.

"But why did you want to catch me first? You're okay, aren't you?"

"Me? I'm fantastic. I'm so relieved I made a career decision, sort of. I'm thrilled they let me take an extended leave, which makes things easier. I … we, Meena and I, really wanted to work with your project on educating Muslim girls. Mother so bought into that before …" She caught herself and quickly recovered. "I can't think of anything more rewarding."

"Hardly my project but we are all ecstatic to have the two of you." He waited a fraction to see if she would pick up the thread. When she didn't, he said, "And you rushed down here to see me first because ..."

Cate paused while Chris let her create her next thought. "I just wanted to give you a heads up. Josh isn't the same as he was the last time you saw him."

"How bad?" Chris felt his words catch.

"Very, but nothing imminent." She brushed aside a tear. "He's got time, not sure how much and, well, he wanted to spend it here, with you. He's come here to .... Die. I wanted you to know that but keep this to yourself for the moment."

Chris's insides went cold but he fought the sense of doom that enveloped him. He would have to be strong. That is why Cate rushed to see him first, so he would be strong. "Thank you." He took her hand.

"For what?" Cate could see the pain in his eyes.

"For preparing me."

"Well, be prepared for something else. Just remember, I don't acknowledge my biological father and I've lost my mother. With Uncle ... going, you might well become the closest thing to a parent I have left. Lucky you."

"You're right. I am." He hugged her.

The trip back to Oxford was filled with chit-chat, the issue of Josh's health deftly circumvented. Cate went on about the challenges getting a leave from the State Department though her apparent threat to resign outright did the trick. She was valued, given her relative fluency in several languages based on her linguistic training in college coupled with a natural aptitude. Chris recalled that this vibrant young woman had always felt like a failure when she compared herself to her renowned physician mother. He smiled inside since Cate obviously had enormous talent in her own right but the ability to discount one's own accomplishments runs deep. Had he not directed so much of his younger years toward disproving his own Father's disappointment in him. No matter what he accomplished, he felt like a failure. He now could smile at paying for his own education, through scholarships. What was that all about, he might have taken a spot away from a poorer kid who could play round ball well enough to get a free ride at Princeton. But he wanted to shove his independence in his father's face as he broke away from the tentacles which he thought threatened his world view and, more importantly, his sense of moral worth. Even starting an overseas service organization from scratch, raising the initial money to fund it was a way to spit in his father's eye. See what I can do, and it is something you hate. Remarkable things are not always done out of love or moral commitment.

What pleased Chris was that Meena was now quite chatty. He recalled hearing that when Cate first brought her into the Connelly world, she had been a shy, diffident woman … a Muslim who was coming out as the loving partner of a non-Muslim female, a decision that would ripple through her rather elite Jordanian family and culture. Meena's first exposure to Cate's family had been to meet the biological father and his mother, high born American aristocrats who treated her and Cate in a disgusting fashion. She was traumatized at first, subsequently fearing her meeting with Cate's mother, Rachel, and Cate's uncle, Josh. Immediately, their accepting welcome won her over and Meena was soon a member of the family.

Now, in the car, Cate was recounting what they had learned during their stop in Kabul, input that clearly disturbed Chris almost as much as Josh's appearance when he emerged from the runway at Heathrow. He obviously had lost weight and, to Chris's mind, had a grey pallor about him. Perhaps that was his imagination, brought on by Cate's warning. What seemed more alarming was that Meena had her arm intertwined with his, which might have been merely a sign of affection but more likely was demanded by a weakened physical condition. Exploring such things could wait for a more propitious moment.

Upon their arrival in Oxford, Cate and Meena went off to a pre-arranged meeting with Ali, Karen, Azita, and Deena. Chris brought his friend into his office sanctuary. "My god," Josh remarked, "this toxic dump is as bad as I recall, maybe worse."

Chris grinned. "Sure, sure, as if your office is any better. We geniuses respond to chaos, except for the few obsessive compulsives and they are not so much geniuses as bat-shit crazy. For most of us, it reflects our ability to embrace the complexity of life."

"You use the same BS line that I do. Do any of your friends buy it?"

"No one in the family, that's for sure. Listen, you've had a long flight, do you want to rest?"

Josh looked at his friend gravely. "When Cate rushed off ahead to see you first, I suspected she wanted to give you a heads up." When Chris did not reply, Josh continued. "I'm not dying today, contrary to rumor."

"But ...?"

"I am dying." Josh said flatly.

"We all are, my friend." Chris responded wishing he had prepared a more appropriate response, but his friend had caught him off guard with such directness.

"But I am blessed with having a rough idea of when."

Chris still struggled. He knew that any expression of solace or sympathy would be rejected out of hand. Too sentimental, at least among male peers. But he didn't want to go to his normal default position of humor. Not even he could dredge up wit with his heart so burdened with grief, though he refused to let it show on his face. "Answer me one thing. Have you come here just to say good by or to share your good by with us?"

"Such a clever way to put it. Perhaps that is why I am here. Back in Vancouver, even among colleagues with whom I've known for decades, I would have to go through the same dance … the looks of sympathy, the inevitable interrogation of what I'm going to do to stave off the inevitable, and then the disapproval when I indicate I'm accepting my fate."

"I had not reflected on this before but the very thought of you fighting for a while longer on this earth never crossed my mind. I'm reminded of the opening in a Dylan Thomas poem,

'Do not go gentle into that good night,
Old age should burn and rave at close of day;
Rage, rage against the dying of the light.'

Of course, Dylan was talking about his father. Nevertheless, I suspect neither of us will *'rage against the dying of the light,'* but accept it meekly when the time comes. Does that make us oddities among men?"

Josh seemed to relax in his chair, as if some hurdle had been surmounted and he no longer needed to think carefully on his words. "Hah, let's face it. We have long been oddities, even before our easy acceptance of my demise has offered proof to others."

"Yet," Chris put his index finger to his nose suggesting a serious thought, "what makes death, or the prospect of death, so easy for you. Let me help you out on this one with some choices. Might it be the nature of your affliction, your age, or the state of the world."

Josh hesitated for a moment but no longer than that. I suspect you know the answer already. Each of those factors plays a part. I mean, let's face it, infusing your body with chemicals to sustain a terrible quality of existence is the height of folly. Where is the dignity in that, and why do others insist on it, even loved ones? Especially loved ones! For the religious whackos, their insistence on perpetuating life because it is their god's will simply suggests that their deity is a freaking sadist. If you loved someone, you would let them go when their productive time has ended. Of course, age is not irrelevant. Perhaps if I were younger and had decades of possibilities left, I might fight a bit. I'm not totally sure. Glad that is not the case. The warranty on your body is up when it takes you a half hour to freaking straighten up in the morning."

When Josh paused long enough, Chris pursued his thought. "That leaves the state of the world."

"Ah yes, that is the most puzzling question to answer."

"Which makes it the most fascinating." Chris added quicky.

"Yes," Josh responded slowly, "as you know, since I've used this on you before, I've always been confused by the fact that people are joyful at births and sad at deaths but that doesn't seem rational since life is mostly hard and painful, for we Irish at least. If we were objective, we would cry at birth in anticipation of what the baby faces and would express joy at their passing given they are now free from all burdens."

"A bit pessimistic even for me."

"Only a bit I presume. Of course, I'll admit to being conflicted at the situation over the course of my own time on this planet. When I came into it, into my life that is, the world was in terrible shape. A world war that took at least 50 to 70 million lives was in the end stages of its carnage. There would be decades of lingering consequences, more dictatorships, famines, millions of refugees searching for some place to call home, and millions of scores to be settles, often with violence. I would have stuck my head out of the womb and gone back in, but I've shared this with you before. It is not news."

"True, I remember. But now what do you see?" Chris asked with genuine curiosity.

"Ah yes, what kind of world will I leave to my heirs, by that I mean all my students along with humanity in general. As best I can tell, it is a mixed legacy. On the one hand, most people around the world will live out their allotted time in relative security, in numbers not witnessed in human history. They will have food to nourish them, at least for the most part, and sleep at night not fearing a knock of the door. There are local exceptions of course, but nothing like the carnage in the first half of the past century. On the surface, our species has reached a certain level of sanity."

"And beneath the surface?"

"Ah, there lies the rub. Let's see, how to answer that. Okay, there is less running around and killing one another for some ridiculous religious or ideological reason. That is a positive for sure though there is occasional backsliding in that regard. But here is what really bothers me. Our sciences have taught us so much about the world around us, how things work, how to improve our situation, and even what lies beyond our imaginations. The social scientists have opened us to how individuals and collectives work, for good and evil. Our command of historical lessons should have informed us of the folly of past efforts to manage our affairs, lessons from which much should have been learned. For example, we should have dismissed the lure of autocracy and military control after the lessons of Hitler, Mussolini, Stalin, Tojo, and Franco, all recent enough to be remembered. And yet, most seem to see and act as their primitive cave-dwelling ancestors did. Americans yearn for Donald Trump, the Brits for Boris, the Russians for Putin, and I could go on."

"Perhaps," Chris interjected, "but there are more democratic forms of governance around the world today than in most of recorded history. Is that not a reason for optimism? Trust in people takes time. Just take South Korea. We look at them now and believe this is an object lesson in the miracle of democracy. We assume they became like us shortly after they were liberated from the Japanese in 1945 and never looked back. But that would obscure the forty plus years they kept reverting to strong man rule. As in other places, democracy came hard to them."

"Yes, I get that," Josh now looked deadly serious. "Yet even the way you phrase things implies linear progress. Russia's experiment in democracy can be measured in a few years, we see backsliding in India, Turkey, Hungary, Poland, and Brazil. America itself is tottering on the verge of being downgraded from the status of a mature democracy. Every institution that preserves it, the principles and attitudes among men and women that make it work are visibly withering away. The march toward greater collaboration took another step back when your adopted country, England, voted to exit the European Union, surely an act of colossal short-sightedness."

Chris dug in. "Surely, though, you recognize that there are bumps on every journey. Take France. They had their initial revolution in the late 18th Century which became a beacon and inspiration for many American revolutionaries, especially Thomas Jefferson. But soon they were back to an authoritarian military leader, Napoleon, to be followed by a Monarchy and revolutions in 1830 and 1848 and 1870 I believe. It wasn't until somewhere in the 1870s that a fragile, yet stable French Republic emerged. The places struggling now may just be going through growing pains."

"Perhaps, but no situation bothers me more than the country where we were born and which we both fled I might add. We all know the apocryphal Ben Franklin story about when, at the end of the Constitutional convention, a woman asked him what kind of government they had given the young nation, he presumably said … *a republic, if you can keep it.*"

Democracy was never a certain thing. Our founders themselves were uncertain about its merits. They knew they did not want a Monarchy for sure but equally feared rule by the mob, what they saw as the rabble who might well use the tyranny of the ballot box to attack sacrosanct principles such as property rights, or willy-nilly cancel legitimate debts. That was not an idle concern in their day. I mean, Shea's rebellion was an uprising in Western Massachusetts by yeomen farmers who feared losing their farms and livelihoods to Boston creditors. They tried to storm the local courts and attacked officials to keep what they had and fight against what they saw as oppression and exploitation by an elite. Perhaps they had legitimate grievances, I don't know enough about it. The scale and consequences of contemporary insurrections are now more important of course. The so-called MAGA patriots of January 6 were storming the National Capitol to keep power in the face of a lost legitimate election. They were attacking the foundations of our democracy." Josh breathed heavily. "Oh well, I have more to say, but it must wait. I've had a long flight. Perhaps a short nap before we get together with the others."

"Of course," Chris said too quickly when his companion smiled. "Okay, you know I will need you to tell me what you want and need. Don't make me guess."

"Shit, my friend, that would take all the fun out of it. But I will. I did not come to make your life more difficult. I know you have much on your plate. And I will be honest. I did think about going back to Boston for my final days, my roots, but I have only memories there, not all of them good. No, I wanted to come here, to have a chance to spend time with you, and Kay, and Azita, and Deena. But mostly you. We had such great conversations; you were one of the few who could challenge and elevate me. Does that make any sense?"

"Of course, it was mutual. We have always made one another better."

"I'd like to attend a few of your lectures, interact with your students, maybe help you with your political work to save western civilization." Josh smiled at that. "And when the time comes,

I hope you will help me pass on. I'm hoping you won't let me linger on." Josh looked deeply into his friend's eyes.

"I think I know what you mean." Chris said in a very uncertain voice.

"Of course you do. You are a very smart man. I want your help, well Kay's or Azita's help, to leave this mortal coil on my terms." Josh let a tiny smile find his lips "That would be your greatest expression of friendship to me."

Chris nodded almost imperceptibly, as his mind raced through objections and arguments that he knew were feeble and with which he did not agree. Instead, he retreated to the question he did not think had been answered or, if so, he missed. "And how much time are we talking about?"

At this, Josh laughed aloud. "Not to worry, surely I won't pop off before we do another visit to your favorite British Pub, the Hairy Hare."

"Not good enough, a serious answer this time."

Josh gestured an apology. "Of course. In truth, the doctors don't know. Six weeks, six months, a year, could be longer. I doubt six years is in the picture. I tire easily but not much discomfort beyond that. I can help you in your work. I won't be a burden. And I've brought all my followers with me. Connie will follow with Usha shortly. Cate and Meena are here. You can put them all to work."

Chris sensed he was losing his emotional battle. "Josh, even if you were alone, and crawled in here on your hands and knees, I'd be thrilled to have you. I have so missed our discussions."

"And one more thing. Maybe I can get to the coast, somewhere secluded and lonely and not contaminated by civilization. I want to spend some time where I can look at the heavens."

"Really?" Chris seemed amused.

"Oh yes. Do you know the length of a light year?" Josh asked.

"Ah, I recall something about 186,000 miles per second. But that's it."

"Well, that translates into almost 16 trillion miles over a year, the length of a light-year. Now, our galaxy is 100,000 light years across."

"Okay ..." Chris needed more.

"Here's the thing. I am relaxed by sensing the enormity of the universe, and how insignificant we are. All is in perspective."

Chris looked at his friend. "I understand that. I really do."

Josh sighed with satisfaction. "You referenced a poem, so will I. There is a Walt Whitman poem I've liked which, if my mind is yet working, I might recall. Oh yes...

> *When I heard the learn'd astronomer,*
>
> *When the proofs, the figures, were ranged in columns before me,*
>
> *When I was shown the charts and diagrams, to add, divide, and measure them,*
>
> *When I sitting heard the astronomer where he lectured with much applause in the lecture room,*

How soon unaccountable I became sick and tired,

Till rising and gliding it, I wandered off by myself,

In the mystical moist night-air, and from time to time,

Look'd up in perfect silence at the stars.

Thank you, Chris, for taking me in, giving me a final home."

"Josh, you cannot imagine how good it is to have you back here."

CHAPTER 10

The Kabul Airport

[August 2021]

> *"Someone ought to do it, but why should I? someone ought to do it, so why not I? between these two sentences lie whole centuries of moral evolution."*
>
> *Annie Besant*

One could only sense the blush of a new day when the buses rolled out of three starting locations. Each was filled to overflow with some young women forced to sit in the aisles. The passengers were quiet, apprehensive, uncertain of what life had in store from them, though a few chattered with nervous energy. Some yet harbored doubts as to whether they really wanted the vehicles to reach their destination. They wondered if a future in their country was as bad as people were saying and whether the alternative was as rosy as some had promised. It was, after all, a leap of faith for nearly all.

At one departure site, the Gupta clinic on the evening before, Deena reminded the girls of what life under the Taliban most likely would be like. Deena had been old enough to be in school when the extremists took over the first time during the mid-1990s. She told stories of how her teachers initially were apprehensive about showing up for class, then some stopped coming, and then more were frightened away. Not all, though, many stubbornly persisted, even as their pay stopped coming. Those that continued began wearing traditional Afghan dress. At first the classes were enlarged to deal with the teacher shortage but that quickly became less essential as so many students began dropping out of school.

"Each morning," Deena recounted to the girls, "I would count the numbers, look at the faces, and weep inside. There would be another friend missing, likely not to be seen again, and then another and another. I think we all knew it was just a matter of time before we girls would not be permitted to learn. Each morning, my mother would ask if I wanted to go, that it was getting dangerous. She would understand if I chose not to go. She would teach me, she said. Each morning I told her yes, I wanted to go, refusing to give into the threats. Mother … our mother was a highly educated woman. She had taught at university, but that was the first to be shut off to women. Educated females were seen as dangerous, revolutionary. They were a threat to the new regime and to the dominance of men. As the fanatics became more secure in their power, they invaded increasingly into the lives of the people, especially women. One day, it happened. I sat at my desk looked about the class at the few faces that were there and realized that it was past the time for the teacher to arrive. We waited. No one left, not wanting to admit that it was over."

"Was it over?" One of the girls listening asked timidly.

"It was. We knew for sure when a Taliban warrior, full beard, flowing robes, carrying an automatic rifle along with bullets draped over his body, burst into the room. *'Get out he shouted. Go home. You have no place here. Go home.'"*

"What did you do?" Asked another.

"For a moment, we all froze, mostly in shock. But then he pointed his ugly weapon at us. The other girls began to flee."

"And you," the question came from her sister Azita, "I don't recall this event."

"Oh, you were young at the time, too young for a formal education, though already stuck in the books mama had given you. Me, I was in a very early grade, perhaps too young to think clearly. I didn't move from my seat. Later, I told myself it was out of conviction, that I would be like my mother. These men … these fanatics would not stop me from learning. But, in truth, I think I was frozen out of fear. All I recall is that he came at me, his face full of fury, and hit me with his gun as he roared some oath. Things were a bit of a blur after that, but I did run home, crying all the way, hardly able to see with my eyesight blurred by tears and blood. That was the last time I was in an Afghan classroom until we were able to return from England to start building schools and supporting your learning."

"Are you sure it will be the same?" Another girl asked.

This time, Azita spoke. "Only Allah knows the future but let me share one of my stories, one that my sister Deena knows all too well. This was several years later; I was now old enough to do chores but didn't do many since I loved books so much."

Deena intervened with a grin. "The truth is she didn't do any since she was a lazy cow." Several of the girls in the audience giggled.

"Fair enough," Azita also smiled. "My sister is correct. I volunteered to do some shopping that day to show my sister I was not such a lazy cow though, in truth, she might have been right. I prefer to think I loved my learning too much. In any case, my mother sent our brother Majeed with me knowing I was likely to get in trouble on my own. Mother was a wise woman because, of course, I did just that. As Majeed wandered off to a bookshop, I stopped to read a poster in the public square. It never occurred to me that reading was such a crime. Suddenly, the morals police descended upon me and began an unmerciful beating. I must have instinctively fought back since the beating continued, worse even. It was instinct on my part, to defend myself, or perhaps frustration and rage. Only the return of my brother from the bookshop saved me I believe."

Deena sighed. "I still recall him carrying you into the house, beside himself with guilt. He apologised for days. You were so bloody incoherent and making little sense. Then again, nothing seemed off to me since you normally made very little sense." Deena flashed a quick grin. "It is a good thing our papa was a doctor."

"And I recall you surprised me by being a good nurse."

Deena laughed. "Yes, that surprised me as well." She nodded to the audience. "I hadn't liked my sister at the time. I did think her spoiled and lazy and I could not handle blood like she could, but this was her blood. That was different. And we realized something, or I did after that incident. We were different but neither of us was better than the other. We simply had different roles to play in life. Oh, we still argued after that but now we realized how much we needed one another." Deena glanced at her sibling before turning back to the audience. "No, how much we loved one another."

Returning her sibling's affectionate glance, Azita added, "On that day, I think we both realized what life would be like without the other ... unbearable."

Deena flashed an impish smile. "That for sure and also that it was a good thing that you did no chores since you were so bad at it."

"Hah!"

Deena turned serious. "But here is the important thing to remember. While they may talk differently now, there is no evidence that they will be any different now than they were then. And, if we don't get you out now, we may not be able to later, or not as easily."

"Do you understand," Azita added for emphasis?

There were a few vocal agreements and many nods of their heads.

Now, as the sun rose while evolving from a large, orange-tinged globe to a smaller white disc, each bus inched through streets already clogged with cars, people, and other modes of transportation. When they finally had decided on this plan, they thought there was sufficient time to put it into action. Yes, they knew that the Taliban had always maintained some control in the remoter provinces, but the government's control out there had always been suspect. In recent days, their sphere of power seemed to rush inexorably toward Kabul. Surely, many thought to the end, there were enough official police and soldiers nearer the capital to prevent any imminent collapse. How could two decades of effort to build a functioning government with foreign help be for nothing?

Nevertheless, a wave of Taliban successes rolled effortlessly over the country. Local leaders saw the writing on the wall and most made the best deal they could. Others were intimidated, or worse, eliminated in one way or another. Almost immediately, the will to resist evaporated. There was no time left. Desperate people were fleeing in one direction or another. Was this mass of humanity going somewhere or merely running aimlessly in circles? Looking at the faces, the sense of Armageddon across the city, simply the act of doing something, anything probably was preferable to quietly waiting for the end.

Azita sat at the front of her bus. She knew there would be checkpoints, nominally to determine if Taliban were infiltrating the city. Some who manned the posts would do their jobs, or try to, though how was somewhat a mystery. Others, perhaps most, would see this as an opportunity for more baksheesh, the tradition of local extortion that might well be curtailed under the new regime. Make it while you could since who could know what tomorrow might bring. There was a certain zeal among the religious fanatics. They brought misery and a crushing conformity with them but also a certain purity, at least on the surface. That had always been part of their appeal.

The secular-leaning government the Afghanis had enjoyed since 2002 had many advantages, especially for women and those considered minorities such as the small Christian community. Honesty in government was not one of them. Absent a driving ethical purpose, each tribe, clan, family, and individual tended to look out for themselves. Abstract goals such as *'democracy'* meant little to those absent any tradition or experience with self-governance. Securing a public position typically meant more opportunities to improve one's financial position. It takes a long time to introduce the notion of the common good, what might benefit all as opposed to the individual. Even in advanced nations, like America, the concept of the common good was yet controversial and debated between the major parties even today, perhaps more virulently today. The iconic call for *'freedom,'* the *'American dream,'* meant for most Americans getting what they could for themselves, their family, and perhaps their tribe … period. Thus, the appeal of the Taliban to many in an ironic way. They offered something beyond mere personal acquisition. They promised a way to God. It was a form of altruism, but with a high cost.

It soon was clear the normally hour-long trip to the airport would take many hours. None of the planners had realized how bad it would be. At the first checkpoint, Azita jumped from the bus and explained their situation, the guard looked doubtful but let them continue after looking over the vehicle's passengers. No Taliban infiltrating the city in this crowd. After crawling forward at a snail's pace, they reached a second checkpoint. Here, the guards who confronted Azita were more belligerent. No matter what she said, they insisted on checking out each passenger personally for Taliban infiltrators. For a moment she argued the point, then reached in and took out some American money.

"I appreciate your diligence," she said deferentially to the man who appeared to be in charge. "Will this persuade you that such a lengthy interrogation would merely be a waste of your valuable time."

He smiled, took the money, and quickly inserted it inside his clothing. Smiling even more broadly, "Ah yes, sister, please continue your journey and may Allah be with you."

After more agonizingly slow progress, Azita grimaced as they approached a third checkpoint. The students grew ever more restless in the now scorching heat, only partially offset by an air conditioning system that could only do so much as the temps shot past the 100-degree mark. They finally made it to their turn. Azita looked out the front window to see three government guards arguing with what looked like several Taliban warriors. She sometimes wished the Taliban would wear nametags. The government officials were identified easily by their uniforms. She wondered how long it would be before they discarded them to blend into the crowd.

No one seemed to pay attention to the bus. Azita wondered if she should step out as the argument grew more heated. Obviously, the Taliban were here and asserting some control already while these government officials were yet trying to enforce some authority based on a regime that may already have collapsed. Chaos now would be everywhere, and her heart sank as the prospect of getting to the airport dimmed. Perhaps getting on a flight was already beyond their grasp.

Suddenly Azita decided. “Driver, there is an opening ahead. Just go.”

“Oh no, I cannot.”

She took some money out of her pocket and stuffed it in his. “You can. You must.”

He looked at her doubtfully, “You are either very brave, or very crazy.” The driver could see the desperation in Azita’s eyes. Suddenly, he gunned the engine as he muttered audibly “I hope Allah is kind to me when I see him later today.”

Azita looked back but could not see much through the distant back window. The level of shouting increased and then there were shots, two at first and then a few more. "Are they shooting at us?" She yelled to the back.

"We don't think so," came a reply.

"No one is following us," said another.

"I see bodies on the ground." Said a third who started to cry.

Azita collapsed back in her seat, smiling at the driver who was now perspiring and muttering under his breath. She was sitting next to the girl chosen as student spokesperson for this group, one had been chosen for each bus. These leaders were a bit older, multi-lingual, and knew the city. Azita had taken an immediate liking to this girl who had earlier indicated an interest in medicine. Perhaps this one could replicate her journey toward a medical career but shook that thought aside. There were many promising girls. Only time could tell which had the right stuff. Then again, how would she have turned out had she not had a physician father and been adopted by Chris and Amar while being swept off to England.

Once again, they were stuck in dense traffic as they neared the airport. "It was good that you told those stories of the Taliban from the old days last night. Yes, our parents share such stories but sometimes we think they exaggerate to frighten us."

"But you trust Deena and I?" Azita smiled.

"Hmm, you make a good point." The girl seemed to think on it. "We must trust you. You have our futures in your hands now." Azita smiled back but the words made it all the way to her heart.

She had not dwelled on the obvious until this moment. What they were asking of these girls was total trust. They would thrust them into a new world. How many would adjust and thrive? How many would not? How great was this trust they were putting on her? Azita thought of the many medical operations she had done, some in primitive conditions with inadequate resources. In those moments, she went beyond her training and even her better judgment since there was no other options. Those patients had also placed their total trust in her, and in situations where the stakes were higher. She winced at the thought of those cases where she had failed though no one would have fared better in such instances. No physician ever escaped some failure.

This seemed different, however. With a critically ill patient, Azita might face the choice of operating now or the patient might die. At least that often was the prevailing consensus. Here, the choice was to continue into the unknown or go back to their ordinary life except that life would no longer be ordinary. Azita assumed that life in her native country would turn hard and limiting. She presumed that based on her old experiences.

What if she were too pessimistic, what if the Taliban had mellowed? Would uprooting these girls, many of them quite young, be justified? Some of them might well flounder and fail. How would she feel in those cases? She did not know, not really. She was in a zone of uncertainty. She wanted to tell this girl who looked at her with wide, accepting eyes, that the trust being placed in her was warranted. But she could not. All she did was smile back.

The hours had crept by with glacial slowness. Still, the mood on the bus responded to the sights and sounds of planes landing and taking off. They were close, so close. Yet, success could not be assured. Perhaps they would be stopped at the gates. Or maybe the Taliban were already in control, they were too late.

Or what if the planes already had been forced to leave, or their crews taken into custody. She knew they had arrived but had no message in the past hour or so. She looked at her phone but there was no signal. Azita slumped back in her seat. She was exhausted, not having slept much the night before. Whatever energy she had at the start of the had been depleted by the stresses of this agonizing journey.

Azita closed her eyes to shut out the noise and chaos and heat about her.

Her thoughts drifted back to the meeting back in London. She had fought to be here, to be involved. She wanted this. Her mind's eye returned to a day not long after Ali, Karen, Kay, and Carlota returned from their quick reconnaissance visit to Kabul. Azita was simmering with anger even as the meeting started. She could see the events of that day unfold so vividly, as if she were yet there.

Karen took the lead, doing a synopsis of what they had learned from public and private sources in Kabul along with those in the Gupta medical site which, in recent years, had added several new components including family counseling, nutrition programs, and extra tutoring assistance for the more gifted girls. When she finished, Azita immediately spoke out. "We have got to get as many of the most promising girls out. We know who most of them are."

"Wait," Ali intervened, "we cannot go off half cocked. There are things to consider."

"Bullshit," Azita yelled, "I should have gone with you. Why weren't Deena and I there when you visited Kabul?"

"For this very reason," Ali said plaintively. "We knew you two had preconceived positions, that you would rush to judgment. No, I should be precise here. I knew you, Azita, would."

"Not just my sister." Deena said defiantly but was ignored.

Azita looked at Ali coldly. "What you call a preconceived opinion is what I call reality. None of you have lived under the Taliban. You do not know. Deena and I do. We lived through their regime while you grew up in luxury with the royal family of Jordon."

A flash of anger crossed Ali's face, but she pushed it somewhere inside. She kept looking back to find where and when things had gone sour with the Masoud sisters. No immediate answer came, so she let that question drop. Instead, she said in an even voice. "I am a Muslim woman. Never doubt that I care about my sisters."

Azita looked back into Ali's steady gaze for some time as the tension in the room became palpable. When she spoke, it also was in an even voice that struck all as implacable. "We are getting as many girls as we can out know, before it is too late. If you believe I am pressing this issue, it is only because I feel we have no time for argument or discussion."

Karen started to speak but Ali raised a hand to silence her. Instead, Ali responded. "Azita, do not doubt me. Never doubt that I have the best interests of those girls at heart. Don't you think I get the fact that we have encouraged them to dream. I am as aware as you that encouraging dreams can be such a wicked cruelty. Every Muslim girl, whether born in Amman or in Kabul faces a reality in life … that they are a prisoner of their culture." When she saw Azita open her mouth, she pushed on quickly. "Yes, I will grant you that some of their chains are longer and heavier than those that bind others. The prison cells of some are harder to escape but … we ALL know the weight and the burden of those chains, at least to some degree. You look at me young lady and see someone who has never suffered in life, never fought for anything. You see someone who has been handed all on a silver platter. But you know nothing of my life … nothing."

"I …," Azita started.

"No, you listen for a change. I came here today prepared to talk about how we would get those girls out. My only concern was how many, how many were ready, how many we could find places for in other countries and support. It was never whether we would do it but how, when, and to what extent. Reality is that we cannot save them all, and it kills me to admit that."

"I …," Azita tried again.

"Not yet! It may interest you to know that I had discussed this with Chris before coming to this meeting. He agreed to whatever cost was necessary. But he also cautioned that we cannot let our hearts rush our minds. We can only do what we can do and that does not include saving the world. Can you understand that?"

Azita now stood mute in response so Deena spoke up. "Dear Ali, we may seem, how should I put this, excessively passionate about this … about saving as many as we can. Surely, you can understand. I have seen some of these girls grow from wide eyed children to steely eyed young women. They hunger to continue their education. Azita and I see ourselves in them. Sometimes, we can see into their hearts, sense what is there. That inspires us though, we agree with you on one thing." Deena quickly glanced at her sister who betrayed nothing. "We cannot save the world."

The meeting continued, with the substance more on tactics and numbers than anything else. At some point Ali asked whether all agreed. Azita nodded her head and said nothing.

"Yes," Deena said matter-of-factly. "Know this well though. I ... "

"We," Azita corrected her.

"Yes! We will go back and save others when we can. Know that right now."

Azita let the images of that meeting drip away as much needed rest fell over her. But one emotion remained. Chris and Ali had decided things before the meeting. Deena and Azita were not part of that discussion. Had this woman replaced them in Chris's life. That thought burned in the moment of that long-ago day. It still burned weeks later as she sat on that bus.

Hours later, as the sun evolved from a white disc toward the orange ball that would dip beyond the horizon, they all sat on the plane that would take them away from danger. Even now, though, anxiety prevailed. The final couple of miles or so to the airport had been gruelling, with the crush of humanity growing in numbers and desperation. Tears were shed on the bus, some became ill, a few succumbed to temporary bouts of hysteria. But the girls chosen as leaders did their jobs, motivating and consoling until they inched their way painfully to their destination. Even at the last minute, it took frantic phone calls to Afghan and foreign officials to get them on to a waiting-chartered plane where the first evacuees waited for the buses to arrive.

Azita was surprised that the pilots were not Spanish. She had thought that Carlota had arranged for the first flight to Madrid where more sorting and processing would take place. When she asked, a handsome young man told her he, indeed, was not Spanish but Jordanian. All he knew was that there were last minute changes, and they were flying to Amman. He added that any questions should be directed to Professor Shahed Al-Hussein. The pilot then went on to say that this Professor must be an important person since the planes and crews were a last-minute assignment from the Jordanian Air Force.

For a moment, Azita seethed again. Was Ali just flexing her muscle, showing her importance. Why had she made this change so late, and without consultation. She hated telling all the girls that this change had occurred. They were worried enough as it was. But then she calmed herself. *Just get us out of here*, she told herself. *Maybe Amman is better, not such a dramatic first stop to go from a Muslim country to a western one where they would see nothing that made sense. They would have a few days of transition at least.*

She saw her phone had a signal at last. When she checked her emails, she saw several missed messages including one from Carlota ... something about last minute problems with the Spanish authorities. In response, Ali and Meena, with help from Cate and her former State Department colleagues, had arranged this last-minute switch. *At least you all will be safe,* the message ended. Azita was too exhausted to disagree, but her mind still wandered to an unpleasant place. She saw a message from Karen which added little more information other than all would be fine. She ignored the messages from Ali for the moment.

Even now, they sat. Periodically, they would inch further along a runway and then nothing. Hopes raised and dashed. Several times she approached the pilot or co-pilot. Their response was the same. *No problem, the traffic is heavy, and air-traffic control is being extremely cautious for some reason. We must wait our turn.* Azita remained unconvinced. This was not Heathrow. How much traffic could there be here.

When she looked out of the window, she could see the crowds. It seemed as if the entire country waited eagerly to leave at the same time. Small bands of individuals were running across the runways, frantically beseeching random planes to let them aboard. Her heart sank. She wept inside. A world with some hope sinking into fear and despair. Jeeps with armed men began to intermingle with the growing multitude. Were they Taliban, there to stop planes, or remaining government police trying to restore order? Azita stopped looking out the window.

They had two planeloads of young students. How many had they left behind? How many had been too far from Kabul to make it, or their parents refused to let them go, or they could not face the uncertainty because they were too young and inexperienced and fearful? How many future teachers, researchers, doctors, and leaders were being abandoned? No, this cannot be. She looked out and told herself that she would be back.

Then, a final panic. Perhaps they would not make it out. Having fought all this way, what if the planes would not be permitted to leave. Perhaps even at this moment, the Taliban might be taking control of the airport. Her heart seized at the thought. They would be taken as hostages and used as pawns in some international chess game. Now her mind raced in several directions. Would the Taliban remember her father, who had been a traitor to the old regime and assassinated, along with his wife, for his presumed sedition? Perhaps she and Deena would be caste into some hell hole, tortured, and murdered in a public square. They beheaded their enemies. Yes, she decided in that moment. They would force the plane back, take us off, and make martyrs of us. Resistance to their vision could never be tolerated.

As panic rose in her throat, the plane lurched forward once more. This time it turned in a 90-degree angle. She could sense they were now headed toward the setting sun. Her heart, and her hopes, recovered a bit. *Should I pray to Allah*, she asked herself? *It had been so long*, she then thought. Even if God existed, he would no longer recognize her pleas. That despairing reverie was interrupted by the gunning of the plane's engines and a quick command over the intercom. *Everyone be seated, we have been cleared for take-off.* With that, the plane lurched forward and slowly picked up speed.

There was silence on the plane. It was as if everyone was holding their breath. After what seemed an eternity, the plane lifted off the ground and rose steadily into the sky. After another pause, a chorus of shouts and prayers and excited chatter erupted. Azita looked out the window as the city of her birth became smaller and smaller before receding totally from view.

"I will be back," she whispered. "As Allah is my witness, I will be back."

CHAPTER 11

Balliol College

[Fall – 2021]

"Sometimes I wonder whether the world is being run by smart people who are putting us on or by imbeciles who really mean it."
Mark Twain

Josh Connelly had taken a liking to Bodleian Library during his previous visits to Oxford. Since arriving this time, he found himself spending increased time there, collecting his thoughts and considering whether he had time to write just one more book. It would not be another dry academic work even though he had always pushed the boundaries of the academy in that regard. He preferred to publish what he termed crossover works that might appeal to the public while retaining some respect among his academic colleagues. He had bowed to expectations on occasion, co-authoring works which fit well within the rules of the accepted scholarly culture. In those instances, he felt an obligation to his colleagues who cared about such things as promotions, salary, and honors. Such rewards struck him as provincial and had little lure for him.

Josh began to reflect on selected patterns of his life. He had always sought to touch those beyond the hermetically sealed world of his peers. Publishing in the accepted academic outlets essentially meant forcing his thoughts into preformed moulds into which the peer-reviewed journals forced scholars to conform. Yes, he understood the importance for peer-reviews and the exacting standards of science that had evolved over time. He also realized that the rigors of modern science were relatively recent traditions.

As late as 1900, you could enter Harvard Medical school without any science background and might be taught your medical skills by local practitioners who had done no original research. Theoretical breakthroughs might happen anywhere, not requiring expensive labs and teams of researchers. Experts, like engineers, did not easily communicate with one another. When Washington Roebling designed and built the Brooklyn Bridge, he had to work through problems on his own even though European scientists had found solutions earlier. Knowledge was local. Josh certainly had no desire to return to that pre-meritocracy world. But he did remain concerned that the gap between the scientific literates and average people was growing even wider, and that animosity between those in each camp was hardening. In fact, much of contemporary political animus arose as hate between those who knew too much and those who knew too little.

As he sat in his cubicle surrounded by tall stacks of seemingly ancient texts, he realized he belonged to a dying breed, literally and figuratively. He sometimes wondered if he had been born in the wrong period and would have been more comfortable in a different time and place. He mused that he would have been more comfortable some 600 hundred kilometers north in Edinburgh Scotland during the latter half of the 18th Century. There, often meeting in and around the University, a brilliant group of thinkers changed the course of human thinking and action. David Hume reformed our concepts of how society should be organized. Adam Smith founded modern economics with his classic Wealth of Nations. James Black did pioneering work on gases that served as a basis for the development of chemistry as a science. James Watt jump started the industrial revolution by vastly improving the earliest prototype of a steam engine. Adam Ferguson is thought by some as a father of sociology after publishing his Essay on the History of Civil Society in 1768 while William Robertson is credited with advancing modern historical research with his publication of the History of Scotland in 1759. And, finally, there was James Hutton whose peripatetic wanderings and observations of geologic phenomena led him to an insight that utterly transformed our understanding of the age of our world. It was far older than the Biblical suggestion of 6,000 years, a figure accepted even by the brilliant Sir Isaac Newton. Charles Darwin read Hutton's work a half century later aboard the HMS Beagle. It planted seeds in his own head as he observed nature and thought his way toward the theory of evolution.

There was something romantic about doing intellectual work in those days. Even Einstein, at the dawn of the 20th century, could sit in his Swiss patent office when he was unable to find work as an academic, the only member of his small Physics class not to do so. He could use his imagination to consider the physical world in ways no one had before, leading us away from a static Newtonian concept of reality to the newer world of Quantum Physics. Such giants could think big thoughts, try unconventional ways of seeking knowledge, work across disciplines to see things in radically new ways. More than anything, they found ways to get outside accepted convention. Now, science and scientists were so specialized, so provincial, so ritualistic in how we thought about things, how we wrote down our insights, and how we disseminated our thinking. Those in the academy who reached out to the public were penalized for not being serious. To be serious, it was as if one had to be irrelevant in the broader world.

At some level, he knew this was unfair. Science was advancing at a pace that was breath taking. We might reach the singularity in little more than another generation where our consciousness might be melded with artificial intelligence. Who knew what might emerge when that happened? By the end of this century, to be human might mean something totally different. And yet, the divide between the world of the intellect and the world of real people never seemed wider. While we have been peering billions of years into our past through our advanced deep space telescopes while exploring the mysteries about us, most Americans could not connect the simplest dots to understand their world. They could not figure out why a very few now had so much money and others so little, putting any change in the trajectory of our politics beyond our reach. That people could believe the Big Lie of the 2020 election or that Hillary Clinton was running a pedophilia ring out of pizza parlors shocked Josh to his core. Back in America, science was peering back to the origins of the universe while shocking numbers of their fellow citizens clung to the belief that their predecessors rode the backs of dinosaurs. After all, the world was only six millennia old, as an ancient book put together by a committee informed us. How could the species be so advanced and so retarded? So many could succumb to orgiastic passions for their favorite football team as the climate teetered on the edge of irreversible disaster.

"Professor Connelly, deep in thought or fast asleep?"

Josh recognized the unctuous tones of his good friend as he snapped out of his trance. "Why, Professor Crawford, didn't anyone instruct you that it was bad manners to disrupt a genius on the verge of a world-shattering discovery?"

Chris laughed. "In fact, that was the first thing I learned as a doctoral student. My professors were always telling me to go away and stop bothering them. After a while, I realized these so-called geniuses were most likely fantasizing about the sexy new young secretary working away in the departmental office. Thinking big thoughts my ass."

"Oh, no, I wish I knew you could read my mind." Josh broke into his best Irish smile.

"Hah, you are too old for that shit and so am I. Well, you are at least. In truth, I did waste a lot of time in my younger days, excess testosterone can be such a nuisance. But what were you contemplating? You did seem in another world."

"What does a man in my position think about … his mortality." Josh raised his hand as he saw Chris about to comment. "But not in any drab or self-pitying way. No, I was thinking about one last book. Since I'm not passing on my genes, why not gift the world with my thoughts."

"You have already written quite a few, haven't you?"

"Quite right, my good friend. But this time I won't be circumscribed at all by convention, by what my peers might think. That is the beauty of being on death's door." Josh saw his friend wince. "Okay, rule number one. We can't let reality get us down. After all, what are they going to do … fire me? I, my friend, am going out with a smile on my kisser, and you had better have one on yours or I'll beat your entitled ass. Got that?"

"Understood," Chris smiled broadly. "So, what can I do to help with this final *oeuvre?*"

Josh transitioned into a serious aspect. "So glad you asked. Just how many words per minute can you type?"

Chris threw his head back in a hearty laugh. "Why in God's name did I befriend you. You are such a pain in the ass."

"Because we are so much alike. Isn't that obvious?" There was no smile on Josh's face.

"We are both half Irish, me on my mother's side and you on your dad's. That's not much of a connection." Chris looked puzzled.

"True enough, but our other sides came from a similar part of the world with cloudy pasts … Poland, Russia, the Baltic States… who knows. But that is just the start. Think about our childhoods, forgetting the fact that you were a rich, spoiled shit and I a struggling, working-class waif."

"What?" Chris interrupted. "Your father owned a successful bar as I recall."

"Perhaps, but he drank up or gave away all the profits. The more important thing, though, is that we both had bitter falling outs with our fathers. We both struck out on our own and both emigrated to other countries. We both found a way to become academics without absorbing the academic culture. And we both wound up mostly trying to save the world. Come on, get past the fact that I am handsome as sin, and you are as ugly as shit, and we could be identical twins."

"True enough, my friend and after I get through beating the shit out of you, we will pass as identical twins. However, I will stay your execution since I tracked you down for a reason. I'm on my way to seminar. Come along and entertain my young scholars."

"But I haven't anything to say?"

"That's such bullshit, you always have something to say. From what I recall, the biggest complaint about you is that no one can shut you up. Besides, it's the beginning of seminar. We get to know one another at the first session, before I try to drive some out by revealing what a hard-ass I am."

"Can't they tell just by looking at you?" Josh deadpanned.

Chris beamed. "There you go! You can keep them laughing with your Irish wit."

"What wit, I was serious." Josh managed to keep from smiling.

"Enough, spare me. Besides, the discussion will be free flowing. We'll have fun."

"I see," Josh said as if a light had gone off. "You aren't prepared, are you?"

Chris smiled again. "Can't fool you. But these kids are always curious about the States, even more now that America is sliding into the status of a banana republic. You can comment as much or as little as you like. Or you can just sit there and absorb my brilliance."

"But then what would I do after the first thirty or so seconds?"

Bodleian library was adjacent to All Souls College. They exited into the sunshine and warmth of a late summer day. They ambled to Broad Street, turned left, and walked past Wadham and then Trinity Colleges to Balliol where Chris did his intellectual labors.

As they crossed the green quadrangle to a chalky white building adorned with spires and a gabled roof, totally appropriate for this academic cloister, Josh broke the silence. "Thank you"

"For what?" Chris asked.

"For agreeing to bring my friends over, for making that possible."

"It is proving difficult to get everyone here at the same time I find. But when I do, we'll work to make this a big family." Chris reflected why getting everyone together and liking one another seemed so important to him. He arrived at an easy answer, this could be the large and close family he never had as a youth. Was he that needy? He never thought so.

Josh interrupted his reverie. "It will be great to have Cate and Meena and Usha, not to say my spouse Connie all around me. But the biggest surprise has been that Mo, Carla, and Bob Wilson are here. Oh, and Peter. I never thought ..."

Chris sensed his friend was on the verge of becoming sentimental. "There's your problem ... never thinking."

"I'm serious," Josh retorted. "The only times this larger ... family of mine were together were at my retirement. We never had a chance to bond; I mean all of us."

Chris looked thoughtful. "I get it. I do. But listen, they all would be here whether I did a damn thing." Chris said with a touch of irritation in his tine. "I get the self-deprecation stuff. I do a lot of that myself. But you are loved. Just accept that fact. Got it?"

"Fair enough. But let me thank you for picking up the tab for my three old revolutionary friends. They are not exactly swimming in dough."

"Forget it. Don't forget my mother shot my dad before he got around to changing his will. I never would have guessed that in a million years … that he didn't change the will and not that she might knock off the bastard. We all dreamed of doing that. I mean, I think he kept hoping I would see the light and join him on his right-wing crusade. Toward the end, he must have known that was futile. Even an idiot would realize how I would use all his money on the things he detested. He thought he had more time … I guess we all do. So, throwing a few euros toward your informal family support group is nothing … pocket change."

Josh looked toward his friend, "Perhaps nothing to you …"

They walked up two flights of stairs and down a hallway dripping with atmosphere including portraits of past scholars. Josh was breathing harder. "You okay," Chris asked his friend as he recollected stories about his athletic youth and suddenly glimpsed his own future.

"Yes, but I may skip the marathon this year." Josh smiled.

They stopped outside a door that had no outside adornment specifying its function. Chris paused while Josh took a couple of deep breaths before nodding that he was ready. Chris flung the door open to a decent size room crowded with students. At least 20 had found room around an ornate conference table while others had found seating along the walls that were adorned with bookshelves weighted down with scholarly tomes or portraits of long-forgotten scholars. Chris recognized many of the eager young faces but not all by any means. His seminars attracted seekers of his wisdom from other colleges who wished to absorb his insights on political philosophy, world events, and what was happening in their former colonies. The Trump phenomenon had fascinated British students who wondered how the country nominally considered the hope of the free world had fallen into such delusion and self-destruction. They presumed that Professor Crawford could answer their concerns. After all, he was from that fractured land even though he had fled its shores many years ago.

Chris sat at the head of the table in the place reserved for the tutorial head. He signalled someone to retrieve another chair for Josh, which they did from an adjacent room. Josh sat next to him appearing to focus on the spacious windows along one wall. From this view one could see the pristine green of the quadrangle, a magical array of spires collected in a mosaic that looked as if some special effects technicians had erected them. *Yes,* Josh thought to himself, *this just might be heaven, an intellectual cocoon ensconced far away from the burdens of reality.*

"Greetings," Chris started. "Once again, I see we have an overflow crowd. As you may know, I do little to dissuade the riffraff from joining us, but I do give preference to what I consider our paying customers, namely those enrolled in Balliol College. Be forewarned, however, that I will do my best to make this class as trying as ever to drive the faint of heart into a deep coma and hopefully dissuade the usual hangers on from hanging in for long." This classic line of his was greeted by the customary chuckles. "And, let no one forget that I reserve the right to cast out from our company any non-enrolee who fails to demonstrate the appropriate and expected adulation for my genius." Even more laughter rolled through the crowded room. "Finally, you may sleep during the seminar but no disturbing others by loud snoring or crying out after falling to the floor. Are we agreed?"

A hearty affirmation greeted his customary seminar rules. Chris then went on to cover the ordinary and usual overview of the course and other administrative detritus essential to the orderly running of an academic course of study. This segued into the self-introductions of each student. None of the individual colleges within the University system were large, so most returning students from Baliol College were familiar with one another. However, there were newcomers and, of course, interlopers from other colleges. At the end of this ritual, Chris turned to Josh who had been seated silently at his side.

"You are probably wondering who the gentleman at my side may be. Well, I'm not saying this seminar is singularly difficult, but he has taken this course some two dozen times in the past and failed each time. He is a stubborn bloke."

Josh smiled, "I prefer to think of Professor Crawford as a singularly inept educator."

"And right there you can see the core of his difficulties."

A thin woman with a narrow face dominated by oversized glasses and long, straight hair that hung well past her shoulders spoke up. "I don't know Professor; he seems very astute to me."

"Gretchen," Chris knew her well, she had served as a research assistant for him in the past. "How many times have I told you not to let immediate impressions influence your judgments." His remark was accompanied by a knowing smile. "In truth, I suspect this man needs little in the way of an introduction. This is Professor Jeremiah Joshua Connelly, emeritus from the University of British Columbia. I've assigned a few of his articles." Several around the room gave evidence of recognition, having read some of his works in the past. "He is spending time here in Oxford for the next few … months, and may be guest from time to time, if his … schedule permits. As I am, he is an early émigré from America who left to seek more civilized pastures. He, however, resettled in another former colony ... Canada. However, he has spent much time assessing the odd things, political and social, going on in the States."

"Perhaps time to take them back and bail them out." A roundish faced youth with short reddish hair said. "The Americans I mean; the Canadians are doing just fine."

At this Josh laughed. "Excellent thought, but you might wish to start by reversing your Brexit decision."

"Touché," the boy said, failing to hide a mild blush.

"Listen," Chris interjected. "I usually let everyone go early the first day. Those who were counting on this are free to flee. Those who wish are free to stay for an informal chat with our guest. I just ambushed him at Bodleian Library, so he has nothing prepared."

"Then it will be just like one of your typical seminars," Gretchen said with a deadpan look that broke slightly into a sheepish grin.

Two or three made their way to the doors but virtually all stayed. "I was raised in Udaipur, which is in Rajasthan, India," a male student seated close to Chris started in an unmistakable Indian accent.

"I've been to Udaipur," Josh interjected. "A lovely place, very historic. I enjoyed the Lake Palace very much."

The Indian student beamed. "I've been gone for some time now. I did my undergraduate education at Brown University in the States before coming to Oxford for an advanced degree. I was flabbergasted by what happened when Trump succeeded Obama as President. I thought the Americans in New England represented the country's thought and values. 2016 was quite a shock. I was convinced Americans had lost their minds, and now there was an assault on their Capitol earlier this year. Who can make sense of that?"

"Good question, Ashok." Gretchen added turning back toward Chris with an impish grin, sensing that a free-wheeling debate was about to start. "Can either of you gentlemen resolve our confusion."

"That is why you are here, Gretchen, to learn great wisdom from your betters," Chris said with a mischievous smirk.

Gretchen suppressed a witty comeback that she felt free to utter in this class but not in many others. Still, it was early in the year, and she realized some students might be surprised at her presumption of such familiarity. Rather, she adjusted her glasses with a middle finger and smiled. "Yes, that is exactly why I am here."

"In fact, that is why most of you chose Oxford as opposed to that second-class educational institution called, I believe, Cambridge University, though their claim to being an institution of higher learning is decidedly presumptuous." He held up his hand to silence the expected laughter. "We are the intellectual home of those who seek a deeper understanding of the human condition whereas that other place focuses on narrow technical questions." Chris looked at Josh. "Would you care to enlighten us on the human condition, at least in the former colonies."

Josh stared back for a moment. "Not only was I ambushed during my quiet and contemplative time this morning, but now he expects me to wax eloquent on issues about which few can make sense."

"Not to worry," Chris assured him, "it won't take much to impress this crowd." He raised a hand to indicate he was joking but that did not dissuade Gretchen from adjusting her glasses once again in her demonstrative fashion.

Josh sighed, and then began slowly. "This is just a spontaneous rant, so I make no pretence to order or completeness, but these are things on which I've contemplated much of late." From the corner of his eyes he saw Chris smile and lean back. "American politics today are seen as a house divided. There is a red America made up of conservatives and a blue America of liberals. Increasingly, we see little in between. Our national elections increasingly are settled by a few thousand votes."

"Wait," Ashok interrupted, "Biden beat Trump by several million votes. That was decisive."

"It may seem so, but the way we elect Presidents goes back to our electoral college, an artifact built in by the gentlemen who wrote the Constitution and were afraid the bigger and more progressive states even then might dominate national policy. How little things have changed. In truth, a shift of about 60,000 votes distributed correctly across five contested states would have put Trump back in the White House. The U.S. Senate is split down the middle and, though Democrats get substantially more votes for their Congressional Candidates, our House is now back in their control, though barely. We are the *'house divided'* that Abraham Lincoln raised in his debate with Steven Douglas in

1858 during their political contest in which Douglas prevailed by the way."

Gretchen wrinkled her nose. "But we have our Labor Party and our Tories. Aren't most nations similarly divided."

"To a degree, yes, but let me explore the American example for a bit. Perhaps I can illuminate just how deep the American divide goes, why we hate one another with such passion. My native country, when it broke away from the benevolent control of Great Britain, was already deeply divided … clearly by geography. Even the selection of George Washington as commander of the Continental Army reflected the original north versus south divide, the slavery versus free labor split, a nascent industrial culture versus an established agricultural one. The northern radicals for independence thought that appointing a southerner as the head warrior would keep the southern states committed to the rebellion. But slavery was only a surface issue. The underlying cultural divide ran much deeper, reflecting two diametrically opposed cultures, and two visions of both people and our civil society."

"Which are?" Someone from the back interjected.

"Well, there were several fracture points of course, there were Hamiltonians who still looked to England as a model versus Jeffersonians who saw revolutionary France as the guiding light. A key and enduring tension, then and now, is between a culture that values *'opportunity and innovation'* versus one that values *'stability and the protection of property,'* a tension that resounded in your own political battles such as the infamous *'corn laws'* that protected high prices as people starved or when food stuffs were shipped out of Ireland for profit as hundreds of thousands native Irish starved to death."

"I knew you would get that in." Chris quipped.

"Right at the beginning, there was a deep suspicion of democracy. Yes, people should vote but only the right people which, conveniently enough, meant people that looked and thought much like the those creating the founding documents. There were early revolts of the poorer farmers in Western Massachusetts and Western Pennsylvania known respectively as Shea's Rebellion and the Whisky Rebellion. Both were aimed at distant elites whom the insurgents saw as using their power to bury them under debt and/or taxes. Both uprisings were crushed but the elites saw their suspicions validated. If given a real say in this fledgling democracy, the poor might merely vote to void their debt, clearly a disadvantageous move for the elites. That could not be permitted. Not surprisingly, preserving private property was put on an equal footing as a national virtue with the pursuit of life, liberty, and happiness. Consequently, only propertied, white males were permitted to vote, not exactly what we think of as a mature democracy."

"But that limited vision ended about a century ago when women got the right to vote both here and the U.S." A female voice called out.

"Let me continue for a bit more. And I'll try to make this quick, or quick for me at least."

Chis chuckled. "Not to worry, I will have food, drink, and cots brought in for the duration but do notify your loved ones, so they don't panic and file missing persons reports."

"Amazing," Josh responded as laughter circled the room. "I'm shocked that students voluntarily enrol to be in your classes." More laughter drifted through the room as the assembly realized they might be in for an enjoyable session. "As I was saying, a basic cultural split was built into America at its founding. The nominal issue was slavery, but the underling tension was much deeper and more fundamental than even that. How did this tension between opportunity and privilege, or accumulated property, play out? Simply put, the northern states stressed commerce, industrial progress, accessible education, at least relatively speaking, and an ethos that anyone with grit and determination could make it. The southern states developed an agrarian and feudal society that was hierarchical and served the interests of a wealthy elite. This was a society built on extreme inequality with a philosophy to support this view of the just society."

"I hope you intend to explain that." Someone said.

"Yes, a whole theory of society evolved where it was presumed that Providence chose a few to rule, propertied whites of course, while the rest of society was destined to labor and serve. Before our civil war there were more millionaires in the South than the North, a phenomenon based mostly on cotton and enforced human servitude. Of course, this led the elites to gather ever greater power to themselves. The North, fearing that the Union would split, bent over backward to accommodate slavery as a southern institution though, by the 1850s, that willingness was being challenged. The Republican Party was created by disaffected Whigs who wanted to oppose the spread of slavery to new states in the West, facilitate progress through investments in infrastructure, and seek ways to enhance opportunity for all. Resistance to southern dominance in national politics rose in several places. One example, the Wisconsin Glover case, involved a runaway slave who was arrested and was supposed to be returned to his plantation owners. A mob freed him, and the case went to the Wisconsin Supreme Court which ruled against returning him. That kind of defiance made war almost impossible to avoid."

"This does not sound like the Republican Party of today." Gretchen added more as a question than an assertion.

"Glad you picked up on that," Josh responded. "The Republican Party that emerged in the late 1850s were the progressives of that era. Abe Lincoln said that '*we Republicans are for both man and the dollar, but in case of conflict, the* ***man*** *before the* ***dollar***.' During the Civil War, primarily through the leadership of Republican Justin Smith Morrill from Vermont, and with the encouragement of Lincoln, America took its first progressive turn. Morrill once said that '*the property of the people belongs to the government*,' radical stuff in those pre-Marxist days. A whole bunch of radical initiatives followed. A progressive income tax was launched, land grant colleges were formed or expanded to facilitate education, infrastructure investments boomed such as the start of the intercontinental railroad, our currency was wrested from banks and made a federal responsibility, the Homestead Act opened opportunities to small farmers, and so much more, including the ending of human bondage for blacks."

"What happened to that Republican party?" Ashok asked. They were Fascists when I got to America.

"To ensure that Professor Crawford's prophecy of a marathon session does not happen, I will barely touch upon the highlights. For a decade after our Civil War, Republican liberals tried to use their power to govern the South and bring former slaves into civil society. The reaction was severe, including the birth of the KKK, a terrorist group about which you have undoubtedly heard. Reconstruction, as it was called, ended with the Presidential election of 1876. Democrat Samuel Tilden got a majority of the popular vote and was within one electoral vote of victory. The contested election was handed to the politicians in Congress who made a back-room deal. Several disputed electoral votes were given to Republican Rutherford B. Hayes on condition that the federal government evacuate the South and leave the Blacks to their fate. The Republican Party, which had vowed to protect the newly freed Black men and women, sacrificed their principles for power. This proved a slippery slope from which there was no return."

"No doubt." Gretchen inserted with a knowing smile.

"No doubt, indeed! In any case, racial apartheid was imposed in the South for the next nine plus decades. Institutional racism was soon legalized though out the South as a done deal along with the first steps of that Party toward a focus on power as opposed to principles. The second push away from the original principles of Lincoln's party happened in New York State where Republicans realized they needed the support of the emerging class of rich industrialists to win. Lincoln's admonition of man before property was turned on its head and cemented by the election of 1896 when William McKinley beat back Democratic populists with bags of money from the uber wealthy. A pattern was established but it was in no way linear."

"I do hope you explain that." Gretchen asked, obviously engaged.

"Of course," Josh smiled as he turned to Chris, "please order that food and the cots."

"Hysterical," Chris smiled.

"Again, quickly. The two parties were stuck in a time warp for a long time, until the 1960s. Southerners so hated the Republicans for crushing their hopes for secession and a perpetuation of their feudal, hierarchical society that they remained Democrats long after that party drifted to the left. The term *'yellow dog democrat'* became popular where southerners often said they would prefer to vote for a rabid, yellow dog than a Republican. This led to two parties that had an odd mix of liberals and conservatives in each."

A short, stocky youth with a neat beard and a heavy Scottish accent interrupted. "Aye, if I may, I wrote a paper comparing your Civil War with England's and one thing puzzled me. The average white family struggled financially, something not helped by slavery which depressed wages, and yet they died to preserve a system that disadvantage them. Likewise, many English peasants remained loyal to the king, who cared not a whit for them. What do you think explains such odd choices?"

"Excellent question. And Chris, food for at least two days, make that three." A chuckle sifted through the room. "You hit upon a conundrum that puzzles us today, or me at least. I cannot speak to England's ridiculous exercise in fratricide but, in the States, only two percent of southern landowners, you might call them aristocrats, owned slaves in significant numbers. Remember, this was a highly unequal, a feudal really, society. Yet, you are totally correct. What we might consider the serfs or peasants, poor white farmers scrambling to eke out a living from small farms, willingly fought and died to preserve the prevailing culture. The core question is this … why do people blatantly act against their self-interests?" He let the question hang there as he broke into a smile.

"And the answer?" Someone asked.

"I have no idea." Josh responded to audible groans. "Remember the French Socialist Juarez at the outbreak of World War I. Of course a smart crowd like this does. He thought he could prevent the oncoming slaughter by mobilizing the working classes across the combatant nations to strike against insanity and in favor of their own self interests."

"Right," someone said out loud.

"Then you remember what happened to him?" He continued when he saw a few perplexed expressions. "Not only did he fail miserably, but he was assassinated by an extreme nationalist at the start of this conflict that took 20 million lives. To simplify things, some deeply grained patriotic passions drove the multitude of laborers to kill one another at the bidding of the elites. The officer class of the British Expeditionary Forces were graduates of fine public schools like Eton and elite institutions like this while those who went over the tops of the trenches to their deaths came from the lower classes, the people who served on the Lord's estates before the conflict. Likewise, poor southern whites died by the thousands for the privilege of being permitted to feel superior to those of a different skin collar at the cost of their own economic well-being."

A black woman from the back of the room spoke excitedly. "Oh yes, I see that in my African home, lighter skin blacks take immense pleasure in lording it over their darker skin neighbors."

Josh nodded to the speaker. "A universal phenomenon but one that we cannot go into now. Perhaps later. However, I am eager to see any compelling rationale for why people support people and ideas that make their own world a misery and even do so enthusiastically." Josh paused momentarily. "Moving on in America, the first half of the 20th century was a bizarre period politically. You had liberal Republicans such as Teddy Roosevelt and Dwight Eisenhower in the same party with hidebound conservatives such as Coolidge and Taft. In case you didn't know, Eisenhower only ran as a Republican to stop a hard right and highly favored candidate from becoming president in 1952, another Taft. Otherwise, FDR's new deal and NATO might well have been history. Really, Ike once said that *'Every gun that is made, every warship launched, every rocket fired signifies, in the final sense, a theft from those who hunger and are not fed, those who are cold and are not clothed.'* Can you imagine any Republican candidate today uttering such liberal sentiments?

"Not bloody likely," someone said.

"On the other side, we had Democrats and committed segregationists like Strom Thurmond fighting desperately to sustain American apartheid. Strom, a God in his native South Carolina, served into his 90s when he was totally senile. He once ran as an independent for President on the States Rights party in 1948 against his own Democratic nominee. He couldn't yet stomach becoming a Republican, which he later did, but also could not support Truman, also a southerner, who integrated the military and supported minority rights. Our divide was there but masked by historically odd party alliances."

"I cannot imagine such confusion here." Gretchen offered. "How did anything get done."

"Mostly because external threats forced collaboration across the parties … a world-wide depression, a second World War, and an apocalyptic Cold War. But what I call the great *'sorting out'* or what some called at the time the *'Southern Strategy.'* There were several things that happened in and after the WWII period that led to our current predicament. The New Deal expanded the social safety net in response to the Great Depression, a highly progressive tax structure was introduced to pay for the War, President Truman integrated the American military and a 1953 Supreme Court decision struck at apartheid in education. As soon as the entire country was forced to embrace the ideals of inclusion and opportunity, the political realignment took place enabling the forces of destruction to take over the GOP. An oligarchy of the elite used race and religion to advance a less obvious agenda focused on the egregious accumulation of wealth while exploiting a simmering cultural war to divide and conquer. Over time, they perfected the necessary tools including unlimited money, erosion of institutional safeguards, and the tribalization associated with social media to help them. Most of all, they played the long game."

"But is the American battle coming to an end? I mean, Biden won the last election. Trump will soon be in jail or a lunatic asylum, no?" Ashok mildly protested.

"Hah, don't bet on Trump being history. Even if he is, there are Trump clones ready to take his place and without his baggage. It is a long game they are playing and there are blips along the way. By definition, the long game is about keeping at it until the blips pass. The great political sorting out would have happened in the 1950s except Republican President Eisenhower sent federal troops to enforce school desegregation, the new law of the land. His tacit support for this enraged the South and delayed the switch that was coming. In the 1960s, the process of conservative Democrats switching parties and Liberal Republicans being driven out began. By the early 1970s, Conservatives saw that they could take full control of one major party and the country."

"Which they did with Goldwater, am I right?" Gretchen inserted.

"Yes, in the main but there are lots of starting points for a sustained long-term battle for America's soul, many going back to the 1950s. But I always liked the memo distributed by future Supreme Court Justice Lewis Powell around 1972. He laid out a long-term plan for assuming control over the major institutions … the media, education, the Courts, state legislatures, and so forth. He was very prescient, and the strategy has been spectacularly successful. Think about this, a major political party whose agenda explicitly favors a thin slice of wealthy people controls much of government. Since 1988, only in one Presidential election has the Republican party won a plurality of the votes, in 2004. Yet, they have won several national elections, control the courts, often control Congress, and pretty much remain the default position of political values. Even after the Trump debacle, the Dems are only hanging on to Congress by a thread."

"Exactly how do they do that?" The bearded youth with the Scottish accent asked.

"I assume you mean how does the GOP retain such power while being such assholes?" Josh turned to Chris. "Can I say things like that?"

"You just did," Chris shook his head and smiled broadly.

"Good, the obvious tactics are those that go back a long time, voter suppression, gerrymandering, and money. We don't have one-man, er person, and one vote. Nationally, because of the electoral college, the votes in rural America count more. In many states, outright gerrymandering, and we can thank you Brits for the label, shifts success to the Republicans. One example, in Wisconsin, the Democrats have won 53 to 55 percent of all votes for Assembly candidates yet they hold only 36 percent of the seats. The Republicans have worked hard to institute permanent minority rule. The January 6th armed insurgency in Washington, was a desperate attempt to preserve that rule at all costs. That failed but the campaign is not over yet, not by a long shot."

"Why do Americans put up with this? I would be in the streets." Gretchen shook her head.

"Again, we are skirting up to an extraordinarily complex issue but let me give a big and therefore unsatisfactory answer. There is a little bit of self-interest involved. You probably know that the income share of the top 1 percent in America has risen from less than 10 percent to almost 25 percent in recent decades. In the post-World War II era, inequality fell dramatically which disturbed the elite greatly. They saw Franklin Delano Roosevelt as a traitor to his class and his New Deal as rampant Socialism bordering on Communism. Think about it, the top nominal tax rate for the wealthy reached ninety percent right after the big war against the Nazis. The top one-tenth of one percent were exposed to a tax rate of 70 percent as late as 1960. Even I would admit this is about as high as you can go without losing revenue for a variety of reasons."

"Ah, the good old days," uttered a somewhat scruffy looking young man with unkempt and longish hair.

Josh chuckled. "Oddly enough, those are the very days many white rural Americans pine for. Less government and more freedom. While minorities were repressed, women treated as second-class citizens, and those outside the mainstream like gays were suppressed and oppressed, freedom rang in their heads. They forget that the air we took in was often so polluted it was like a constant fog, Lake Erie caught on fire because it was such a dumping ground for industry, and half of all kids never finished high school. Forget about all such trivia, the motivation that drove most of the economic elite was to get more of the pie. They hated the unions which were at their strongest in the 1950s along with the government's increasing reach to protect workers. Economic conservatives saw an opportunity to dismantle the New Deal and return to a government run by an economic oligarchy.

This was the same perspective used by the South to defend slavery in the 1850s. The long march toward the extreme right began with the elite who, as did the aristocracy in the ante-bellum south, saw white men of property as the guardians of culture and those blessed by Providence to rule. Then, they secured compliance merely with race. In the latter half of the 20th century, they relied upon a host of so-called wedge issues, guns and abortion and gay marriage and faux attacks on religion. Well, you get the picture. These wedge issues, and the social discord they generate, are a transparent bait and switch disguise while they rape the working classes. Many hedge fund managers pay less proportionally in taxes than the secretaries who work for them. But culture wars work, too well as we now know. Now a theocracy and white nationalist regime threatens what remains of a civil society in the States. Even the basics of American democracy are in danger."

"This identity politics thing …." Ashok said but never formulated a complete question.

"It is easy to say that the significant issues are identity, values, and culture. Harder to explain that in comprehensible terms. Ezra Klein argues we cannot understand American politics now absent thinking about this mega-identity. Historian Heather Cox Richardson suggests that the American ethos has been dominated by the mythical independent man that matured during the Western frontier days of the second half of the 19th century. The iconic image of the American is the independent cowboy who depends only on himself to succeed in life. Individualism trumped cooperation, no pun intended, which was further tarnished as socialism and Bolshevism threatened the status quo in Europe. That is, partisan identification reflected our deeper fears and became a proxy for our fundamental cultural affinities. People in the suburbs, the South, in rural America feel threatened and thus now hate those they deem as liberal or *'woke.'* Politics is now less about policy and all about tribal hate. Conservatives play on historic fears of crime, of immigrants, of Muslim terrorists, and the list goes on. If there is nothing to fear in reality, they make something up. Our conservative media outlets are 24/7 exercises in scaring the crap out of the gullible and telling them who to blame. It is as if some people are hard wired to be afraid, a hypothesis for which there is some scientific evidence by the way. Being afraid, they look to their tribe, people who look like them and think like them, for comfort. It is a primal response, not an intellectual one. That is why Republican campaign ads have always worked better, they go for simple narratives with an emotional punch. Democrats have long presumed the average voter was a rational person. Big mistake."

"For sure," someone from the back said.

"Yes," Josh smiled. "How one thinks about economics and how one thinks about society mingle in interesting ways. Again, simplistically, some have posited two primary approaches to economic thinking, the *'saltwater,'* or neo-Keynesian advocates versus the *'freshwater'* or neo-classical perspectives. The saltwater types are labelled such since they tend to congregate on the East and West coasts while the freshwater types are found in the heartland. The former are sometimes seen as the *'flaws and friction'* advocates. People are often idiots, pure rationality is a fiction, and markets are not God. I do realize that Smith never said that markets were sacrosanct but that is what the Right believes."

"A conundrum indeed," Gretchen said distractedly as if she were thinking deeply.

"On the other hand, if you start with the assumption that people are perfectly rational and markets are perfectly efficient, you must conclude that unemployment is voluntary, and recessions are desirable, and that government intervention is always a problem. As Ronald Reagan said to great acclaim, government is not the solution but is the problem. Even after the 2008 economic collapse initiated by a housing bubble, smart people like Eugene Fama refused to see the elephant in the room. You know, housing bubbles can't happen since people are careful when buying houses. Yeah, right, and I have some great land in Florida for you. The bottom line is this. Reason, rationality, evidence, and things like that are important, but they are not everything. John von Neuman, it is estimated, could calculate problems at least 100 times faster than a reasonably smart person. He has been compared to your Sir Isaac Newton who once solved two Bernoulli problems in twelve hours while it took the other genius of that era, Leibnitz, the man who independently discovered calculus, some two months to solve only one of the two."

"You're losing me." Ashok looked quizzical.

"Newton was the von Neuman of his era, probably one of the smartest men ever. And yet, he believed in the biblical interpretation on the age of the earth. He accepted that our world was 6,000 years old even as other smart men around him began to have doubts. Newton could push the envelope of our understanding of the universe but there were embedded beliefs he could not abandon … his concept of God for example. We all have limitations to some extent, things we are loathe to give up."

"No argument there," a student uttered, probably to himself.

"One half of America hates the other half … the so-called liberals, because they see those others as threatening their cherished beliefs and the hard foundations of their cultural identity. To challenge ones' core assumptions is to confront their souls. Bringing the two cultures of America together will not be easy. In fact, I often despair it is possible at all. I've said this before often enough, but we spent over 600,000 lives forcing the Northern and Southern cultures together in the 1860s. But a century and a half later, we can see that never happened. It has morphed and evolved in many ways, but the essential divide is still there. Those same states are working feverishly to keep Blacks from voting but under the chimera of a faux legality. These days I wonder if Abe Lincoln, whom I worship in many ways, simply was wrong on keeping the Union together. Better to let two such different cultures go their separate ways."

"Is this a bit like the more things change the more the more they stay the same." Ashok murmured, quite taken with the visitor. "In the end, hope gets dashed by reality."

"Yes, absolutely. Most of us cling to this hope that the future will be better." Josh looked beyond the circle of students who crowded he room. "I can recall when I was roughly your age. I saw all the problems around me, the abuse of minorities, the neglect of the environment, and especially the waging of ill-considered wars. We have always had terrible challenges and, in some ways, things have gotten better. And yet …" He paused, as if not knowing where to go.

"Yet what?" Chris prompted him.

"Well, in the 1960s, as a college student in Massachusetts, I got involved in protests against the Vietnam War, some of which went too far. That's what sparked my emigration to Canada, more like forced it. I didn't go there for an education or a job. I was running away. And yet, at the time, I felt a sense of guilt. It did seem like running away while others protested or went off to fight in a far away jungle. I was left with a taste of failure and guilt that I let people down, my country down."

"Do you still feel guilty?" The question came from Gretchen and snapped him back to the seminar room.

He paused as if thinking hard on her question. "For my friends I left behind, the guilt remains even though they forgave me a long time ago. But I no longer feel a national, or what you might call, a patriotic guilt. You only suffer this patriotic guilt if you had pride in your place of origin or some affinity with your culture and people. You need to embrace the principles for which a nation stands. Think of America, the violations of human rights, the endless conflicts, some for good but too many for dubious reasons, the failure to protect the environment and the unforgivable failures to protect its most vulnerable citizens … especially their children. Just take our gun policies … insane. More guns lead to greater safety? Just look at our freaking numbers, we are the carnage capital of the world. And consider our health financing system. Insupportable, since we suffer at least 40,000 plus amenable deaths per year and pay way more than anyone else for health outcomes that rival those in Romania."

"So, I'm not the only one that believes that." Another anonymous student said.

"Let us face it. What have we accomplished after all this time and effort spent to forge a coherent political culture and civil society? In the end, what have we? We have half a country that yet believes in democracy, civility, community, inclusiveness, and opportunity for all. And we have another half that clings desperately to authoritarianism, division, and a winner-take-all society. There are moments when I believe we recognize our failure to come together as an integrated nation. One side hates the other. I cannot envision a rapprochement. Lincoln, for all his genius and vision, was both right and wrong in the end. A house divided cannot stand and his attempt to unite our hose was doomed from the start. Yes, I repeat what I just said. It is time to split into two or more culturally coherent nations. Now that I'm repeating myself, time to stop."

A hand shot up. "Sir, I have a hundred questions, but I really must go now. Will you come back? Can we pick this up again in the future?"

Chris smiled broadly. "I see I'm being replaced, and here I thought that would never happen. Circumstances permitting, Professor Connelly can be a regular visitor, if he wants."

As they made their way to Chris's office, Josh was still smiling. "Wow, I can't believe what I just did. It was like I had all this BS stored up waiting to come out. But I did enjoy myself. That is the one thing I miss about retirement, not enough interaction with young people."

Chris laughed. "Now there is an example of a selective, and false, memory. You recall the kids you taught as interesting and engaging when, in fact, they were insufferable shits."

"They listened, or seemed to, at least a few did."

"True enough, and there are students who keep me on my toes while others take up space and a few have the arrogance of youth, believing they already know more than we, though they will humor me to see if that will earn them a 1st in their exams. Yet, I will grant you your point. I would miss them."

They reached his office, where Josh found a comfortable seat as Chris reached in a drawer for a bottle of spirits and two glasses. Josh spoke as he gazed out a window toward at the picture-perfect scene that was this ancient university town. "We did wind up in idyllic worlds, did we not? There is something seductive about the intellectual life, especially when you are emeritus and have time to think." Josh handed him a drink. "Remember back when I crashed one of your lectures some time ago."

"Of course, you put my students into a coma on that occasion as well."

"Very funny," Josh rolled his eyes in mock disapproval. "I do recall this young gal who sat in front, gorgeous, and who obviously had the hots for you. Then again, she was young and naïve."

Chis sighed, "You mean the one who had a way of displaying her assets in a most distracting manner."

"Exactly," Josh enthused.

"Glad to know you remain a pervert, even with diminished testosterone. I bet you don't remember my wisdom from that day."

"Of course not," Josh smiled.

"No matter, the female you recall was an Ashley Boyd. She now wears stylish business suits and acts very professionally."

"She's still here?" Josh queried.

"No, but she is a rising star at the BBC, does in depth features. She's been invaluable to our overseas work, especially the program to rescue Muslim girls that my wife, along with Deena and Azita are doing. She is keeping us in the public eye. Hmm, maybe she could interview you?"

"What could I possibly say that would interest a Brit audience?"

"Don't underestimate yourself, you had my kids voluntarily staying after they could have fled. That was a minor miracle. And I have another thought."

At this, Josh broke into a broad smile. "Two in one day, probably a record."

"Seriously, you want to spend your … time writing. The gal with the big glasses and the Indian fellow, the two that talked a lot, are very sharp. They nominally will be working for me this academic year, but I'm spread too thin to use them wisely. They can work for you, do research, organize stuff."

Josh angled his head to one side, a habit he had when thinking on a matter. "I have been noodling this final opus. It is yet a masterpiece in search of an organizing principle which might be useful if I were to employ them more usefully than you."

"Yes, you are right. But, amazingly, I did listen to you in the seminar room. I realize you were speaking off the cuff but there was an underlying theme there, something powerful."

"Pray tell, what?" Josh continued to angle his head in thought.

"The American rift, the cultural divide. That needs more exploration. You … we … can look at this phenomenon as emigres, two scholars who fled and now are trying to explain why."

Josh looked sceptical for a moment. "We fled our fathers as much as we did our countries."

"Hah, don't kid yourself. Yes, we both had deep family troubles, but we rejected where we saw America going. Our fathers are dead, yet we haven't returned. That is true for me, and I would bet my family fortune, which is embarrassingly large by the way, it is true for you. You escaped an intolerable war, for Christ's sake, and spent your career looking at the States from Canada."

"Well …"

"I sense a but coming. Just listen. That theme you laid out about embedded precepts and the cultural divide. Yes, a few writers are poking at it but from a descriptive and contemporary view. You have a unique historical perspective and have not been caught up in the day-to-day political dramas. Besides, your writing is powerful. I think you can give this a sweeping perspective, yet insightful. And more than that, you can dig into the guts of what separates Americans in particular. But here's the thing. I agree that America may be torn apart with a particular virulence but the destructive power of cultural disconnects is universal. That needs examination. See what I'm getting at?"

Josh straightened his head. "Yes, I'm getting a sense of it, and not just that you are a blithering idiot, though that is true enough. The one thing I didn't really touch upon today was the character of the divide. You and I know it is far more than a political chasm. If it were about policies, then we could approach it though evidence. But it is about the deeper ways in which people feel and think that we know so little about."

"Exactly," Chris was now excited. "As you rambled on about in the seminar … "

"Rambled on?"

"Sorry, as you spoke with such eloquence … I was reflecting on what Kat and I were trying to do in the States. We put some of our money and energy, okay the money that Kat has been earning, into research and information distributions designed to thwart the MAGA movement. Yes, Trump lost but, as of today, some seven or eight months after the January 6 insurgency, authoritarianism is still strong. The death of my father did not stop that in the least. There is plenty of money and support out there to end the American experiment. You see that."

"Of course, but …"

"No buts! Kat and I were well intentioned but may have been shooting at the wrong targets with the wrong weapons. We …"

"Stop!" Josh raised a hand. "I get it. We need to get deeper into the core of the divide, into the embedded beliefs that break down any chance of real communication or understanding. You are right about one thing, appeals to the intellect are rather useless. We need to get way down to the emotional scripts underneath, the fears that drive people apart." He finished his drink. "And then we need to rewrite them…"

"If we can figure out how." Chris said as he rose to fill their glasses again.

Josh leaned back in his chair as he took a sip from his refilled drink. Gazing back out the window, he said wistfully, "thank you for putting up with me; I think I know how to end all this now."

"All this?" Chris asked.

"My end days. I thought you were the quick one."

The two men sat and talked for some time.

CHAPTER 12

The Masoud Center

[End of 2021]

"For I was hungry, and you gave me food. I was thirsty and you gave me drink. I was a stranger and you welcomed me."

Mathew 25-35

Farzana Balkhi ended her phone conversation with Deena Masoud and sat for several minutes to think about things. The call had been routine, a weekly communication designed to keep those back in England conversant with how the Taliban rule was unfolding. There were other such communications between the Center senior staff and those supporting their mission based in Oxford and London. Deena liked to supplement those with direct calls to Farzana. She had been one of the first local girls to be identified as promising when Deena pushed to expand local educational opportunities for females a few years ago. After supporting Farzana as she completed her higher education, she returned to first teach and then head the school for girls at the Masoud Center. She had promised to do so and fulfilled that promise. Farzana was grateful for the life she had been offered, and which she earned through arduous work.

Farzana, letting her mind wander, thought she knew why Deena kept calling her directly, kept seeking her input. They had formed a close relationship. To Deena, Farzana was an early success story, emblematic of the promise inherent in their new educational initiative. In many Muslim countries, about half of the nation was suppressed, their talents buried and ignored. How could these places take their place in the modern world when such a form of gender apartheid existed? She recalled Deena talking about her mother Madeena, for whom the original school building on the site was named. Madeena had been a mathematician and teacher at University in Kabul until the Taliban had turned her out.

Most poignantly, Farzana recalled Deena's description of her final chat with her mother. It was at the Masoud traditional family home nearby when the Taliban was being routed after the terrorist attack of 9-11 in America. Her mother had been talking excitedly about returning to the university, to teaching again, and to shedding the oppressive clothing she had been forced to wear in public. She was exuberant and optimistic. Then, early the next morning, Taliban terrorists snuck into their home while Deena and Azita were gathering eggs and, as a violent act of revenge, murdered Pamir and Madeena. The two sisters managed to flee into the surrounding hills and barely escaped with their lives, an event which turned out to be the first of several close calls. Both Deena and Azita were heroes to Madeena, but she had a special tug for her older daughter. While Azita valued female education, she remained focused more on health issues. Deena, however, was a late bloomer herself, and had a more intimate connection with the students, many of whom had to overcome doubts and impediments to find success. Perhaps because Deena struggled more to find her promise, her mother responded to her with some slight favor.

Farzana now struggled with the possibilities Deena laid before her. Despite promises to the contrary, the new Taliban was much like the old Taliban. They first intimidated the girls from attending the school by their hostile presence. Then they segued to outright intimidation and overt threats. Still, many girls came and bravely sat at desks even when their instructors were forbidden to enter the classroom, at least until it was obvious no one would ever come. As centralized group teaching became impossible, Deena and Farzana talked through the possibility of somehow going to the students' homes, of mentoring the bravest and most persistent on a more personal basis. This network of home schooling grew, slowly at first and then certain homes became sites where a few girls would gather, and a female teacher, pretending to do ordinary tasks would sneak books and educational materials to those eager for any scrap of learning. Farzana had despaired in the beginning but now saw a burst of hope in the surrounding gloom.

In her heart, though, Farzana knew that the future was bleak. How much could they teach in such limiting circumstances? For how long could such a deception go undetected? The Taliban were not popular in this area, long known for its independence and fierce spirit. There were even some locals among them who resisted their most repressive rules. Some of the Taliban themselves looked the other way when rules were ignored, even flouted. No one knew how long such lax attitudes might last.

Farzana could see their stares as she walked casually to a village house, bringing books and ideas as she tried to look innocent. The Taliban supporters stared at her, watched her with ominous glares. She had heard the stories drifting in on the winds of gossip from other villages and towns, of girls swept up by the newer versions of the old morals police for dressing inappropriately or acting independently. They had all heard of women being hounded out of their jobs in the bigger cities, especially those positions that had brought them into contact with males. Now, stories of savage reactions were circulating, of the girl beaten to death for merely accompanying a male not from her family in public or the woman dragged from her car for driving on a public street. The vehicle then was set on fire and the girl beaten.

Such things did not happen everywhere, nor was the repression systemic. It was as if they were tightening the screws slowly to see how far they could go. In neighboring lands, Muslim women were beginning to push back against their oppressors, not yet in outright rebellion but in spasms of resistance. In Iran, particularly, the fuse seemed to be simmering waiting for a spark to blaze into the open. Besides, the Taliban were yet cautious about being too repressive. The sudden drop off in foreign aid and commerce already was being felt throughout the land with hunger and desperation rising. The authorities were reluctant to appear too radical if that meant cutting off much needed revenue and assistance. It was a classic trade-off between principles and practicality. Still innate tendencies were hard to hold off for long.

Farzana reflected on such things as she made her way to a home where she knew one of her best students lived. Other students would be gathered there to help one another continue learning. These were the most motivated and the bravest. As she made her way, suddenly a man stood in her way. By dress and demeaner, he was Taliban though she did not recognize him. She went to go around him and he blocked her once more. She trembled but said nothing.

"Where are you going?" he barked.

"To my friends house." She pointed in the direction of her destination. "My female friend," she added quickly.

"For what purpose?"

"To merely visit." She tried to keep her voice steady. "Is that now forbidden?"

"Don't be insolent," he barked. "What is in your bag."

She hesitated. "Gifts."

He looked at her sceptically, then moved menacingly in her direction.

"Is it your practice to harass women in public." She blurted the words out while staring directly at him. "Surely, Allah would not prove of such behavior."

The man grimaced, uncertain. After what seemed an eternity, he spit the following out. "Go, but do not violate God's law. That would bring terrible things upon you … terrible things."

As Farzana moved on, she trembled. How things were changing. Now, even a visit to a student's home was fraught with danger. Simple tasks became laborious efforts demanding forethought and planning. How can one live a life like this? How long could she go on? The tensions were draining away her resolve.

Farzana later found Agnes Singletary chatting with an Afghani man in the main office. She had seen him around the camp in recent days but had not met him. There were so many who were wandering in, looking for assistance or refuge. Most were vulnerable in some way, women and children with distended bellies or the emaciated elderly looking for food or shelter. The Masoud Center was transforming into a major refugee site, much as it had been when the Northern Alliance battled the

Taliban in this area some two decades earlier. Despite the growing numbers, Farzana had noticed this man working with the refugees. He struck her as quite handsome, but it was the way he carried himself that impressed her. He had an aura of authority that stopped short of arrogance. That had intrigued her.

"Oh," Farzana blurted out, looking at Agnes. "I had hoped to have a word, but perhaps another time."

One look and Agnes knew the young woman was much troubled. "Now is good. Come and sit," she said in Pashto, the language she had long since mastered.

Farzana looked at the young man and hesitated. "It is about our … growing problem." She responded in English, assuming the stranger would not understand.

"You mean the Taliban problem?" The man responded in heavily accented but clear English as he gazed directly at her.

That unsettled Farzana. She looked to Agnes for guidance while inwardly detesting her timidity. Agnes spoke. "Farzana, we can speak about our issues freely. This is Sayed Aktar. He has been here for a while now, helping in many ways. He was also an educator, like you."

"Was?" Farzana found a seat, curiosity overcoming her initial reserve. Still, she struggled to relax. How could she trust this man? Might he be spy for the enemy? Then again, Agnes trusted him, so she might as well. It was too easy to succumb to paranoia.

Agnes responded. "Sayed and I were just getting acquainted. He and his friends have been helping to care for the patients, with the refugees, with repairing and expanding our infrastructure, and all manner of things. Quite indispensable. And now I've been learning how he came to us. A remarkable story, really."

"You are an educator?" Sayed asked.

"Yes, though that role is disappearing. I had overseen a large program ..." Even now, she hesitated to say for girls. "Recently, my students ... well ..."

"You can say it." Sayed said directly. "The Taliban is shutting you down, is making the teaching of girls impossible. They are doing this not so much with edicts as with intimidation. But the edicts will soon be here. Make no mistake."

Farzana now relaxed. "Tell me, how did you come to be here?"

"I will try to make a long and sad story short. I come originally from a village where my family had great authority. My grandfather, until recently, was a respected elder who had fought the Russians and the old Taliban. His name was Amooz Aktar, and I loved him dearly." His eyes moistened. "He pushed me to get an education, to think beyond our small world, to learn English. I did all that, believing as he did that our country was ready to move forward. After my education, and some teaching, I was lucky enough to become the head of a school in Kunduz, one that instructed boys and girls. The girls were so eager to learn, to expand their worlds which were so narrow. But I need not tell someone like you."

"No, you don't, but it is good to hear a man who shares my concerns and hopes. Please go on."

"Listen, I have other duties." Agnes said rising. "You two have much to talk about I think." She smiled at them as she exited the office

"I so enjoyed teaching them, directly or through our curriculum, about a new way of looking at out history and culture. I went back to the days when this land was known as Khorasan, and I suggested that some of what they were learning from the Mullahs was ... slanted, especially about women and the role of violence in society. I had his vision of a new land."

"As did I ..." Farzana said softly.

"There are many like us you know. However, they are afraid or in hiding or already dead." He winced for a moment then continued. "It became bad as the Taliban rose up this summer. I knew our school could not continue as is and worried about my village and grandfather. So, I took my wife, also a teacher, and daughter and went there, to my ancestral village." He took a deep breath. "I was there when the Taliban arrived to impose control. It was a terrible day ... my grandfather stood up to them and he was shot down like a dog. He knew he would be and simply accepted it. I ... I and a few other former teachers fled into the hills before we could be discovered." Sayed had a pained expression. "Does that make me a coward?"

"Heavens no! It makes you sensible."

"No ..." he tried but she cut him off.

"Listen to me. Your grandfather knew his time had come. He was ready. But your work is not finished. You are needed ... to create that future in which we believe. You see that, don't you?"

He paused, looking past her. "On some days, in some moments. Then … ."

"Then what?" Farzana said in a comforting voice.

"We did not go far from our village, expecting to return. I feared what I would find. Too many in my family were gone to me, having been dispatched to their reward. My parents and most of their siblings had been lost to war and disease and all manner of calamities. But my wife and daughter remained in the village after I and the others had escaped to avoid who knew what. I had to get them; you must see that."

"Of course," Farzana said, feeling odd that she was disappointed he had a wife, a feeling she quickly dispelled though with effort. "They are with you?"

"My daughter, yes." He said quickly as his voice caught. "When I returned, I found that my wife was dead. The stories varied as to what happened and no one saw it. My guess, they discovered she had been a teacher of girls. Some of them hate educated people, educated women that is. When they could not find me, I believe she was assaulted in a most vile manner …"

"Raped?" Farzana realized he may be reluctant to discuss this so openly.

He merely nodded. "They might have tortured her as well and then killed her to keep their sins quiet. But I was able to retrieve my daughter. At least that … however, the guilt sometimes …"

Farzana suddenly rose, stopping him in mid-sentence. She walked around the room as if giving something great thought. Then she stopped, looking intently at him, having come to a decision. "No more tears." She was taken aback by her own abruptness, was she being too callous? Nevertheless, she continued. "We will mourn later. What we must now do is resist. I came to talk with Agnes about our educational program for girls. Do you know about that?"

He looked quizzical as if he were failing a class lesson. "That you taught them here, yes. Everyone does."

"True, but it was far more than that. With help from England, we were identifying girls of great promise, here and elsewhere, and sending the best abroad for training when the time was right. We were grooming the next generation of leaders. I graduated from the first school here, starting as a little girl not long after the old Taliban were driven out. This saved me and I so wanted to save others."

He rose to face her. "Now they will not permit that."

"Oh, they are not torturing or killing us … yet. They need this Center which provides medical help and aid of all kinds, especially food for those going hungry. Those in Kabul point to us and other programs to show the world they are the new Taliban, more moderate and compassionate."

"That will not last long."

Her face went hard. "I know. In the meantime they make it so difficult for the girls to come here. The girls are afraid, their parents are afraid. Damn it, I am afraid." She saw him wince at her language and smiled. "I am certain Allah will forgive my vocabulary."

At that Sayed laughed aloud. "I am sure he will. Is there something I can do … aside from violence that is? That might make me feel good but … that is something with which I am not comfortable. I would make a very poor Mujahadin indeed."

"But a better man instead," she said impulsively and then wished she had not been so forward.

He paused, staring at her. "You are an interesting woman."

She resumed walking in a circle, then stopped, obviously deciding something. "I had just finished a phone conversation with Deena Masoud, who is back at Oxford University. She is one of the daughters of Pamir and Madeena …"

"The Masoud family is known throughout this area, almost as famous as the *'lion of Panjshir.'*

"Of course! I have been telling her of what is happening here. She … she made several suggestions, one that frankly I found attractive, at least when she first mentioned it." Another pause. "She suggested they get me out, take me to England for further education. I always dreamed of that. And I could help them with the girls that they were already supporting abroad."

He again looked at her in a way that she found disconcerting. She responded as she continued circling so that she did not have to look in his eyes. "Did you say yes. I mean, did you agree to leave. That would make sense. I mean, there is probably little you can do here. Why would you stay? Why would any educated woman stay?"

"What I told Deena Masoud is that I would have to think about it. That is what I was coming here to discuss with Agnes. She is like a mother figure to me, to many of us."

"I should not have interrupted you then. I am sorry."

She waived a hand at him. "No apologies and no tears. No time for such things. But now, talking to you and reflecting on the choice I have, a different thought is coming to me …"

She hesitated as if she might not share her thought. Sayed prompted her. "This thought. What might it be?"

"Well, it is just forming in my head. But here it is." Again, she hesitated, looking for words. "You see, I have started visiting girls who no longer feel free to come here for their lessons. I bring books and lessons and encouragement. It cannot replace this, a real school, but I don't want their learning to stop totally."

"That is dangerous."

"I know. I am being watched; I am certain. And, I have been harassed. That is likely to continue, to get much worse. But how can I stop? So, I am thinking you can help." She dismissed his look of confusion. "We need to talk more of course, but maybe you could act as my family member. And maybe your friends could do the same for other teachers willing to take such chances."

"What? I don't understand."

"Simple really. It will be easier for a female to move from village to village if she were with a male family member. You could be a cousin or something."

"Perhaps your husband," he smiled.

She continued quickly but felt her face flush. "Like I said, perhaps some of your friends could do the same for a couple of the other teachers who have no male relative nearby." She hoped stressing this last point made it sound less like she was asking him directly, even though she was. "We have been talking about a network throughout the area. If they cannot safely come to us, we will go to them. And the older girls can possibly help the younger ones. Where technology exists, we might use that but mostly we must start face to face. Nothing can replace that."

"I have a concern."

"Yes, I know I am putting you in great danger and have no right to ask such a thing. Be honest with me. Is this crazy? Am I desperate? Already I am embarrassed at being so forward. I don't even know you."

"Whoa, you are running ahead too fast. My question was simple. A real education is a long and hard road. What can you accomplish with such a network?"

Farzana breathed heavily. "Yes, I have thought on such matters. For most, the hope is that they will not forget all that they have learned. Perhaps, things will change back. If they do, some of these girls will be prepared to pick up where they left off. Not all will be lost. I especially do not want them to lose hope. That must be preserved more than anything else."

"Yes … hope," he said softly.

"And then there are others."

"Others," he asked simply.

"When the country fell, we were able to get some girls out at the last minute. But there are others who are talented, who have such potential. It kills Deena, and especially her sister Azita, that we were not able to get more out. The most promising cannot be permitted to regress. Perhaps, just perhaps, we can get some more of them out. I know Azita, Deena's sister, keeps talking about that." She grew uncomfortable as he stared at her. "You think I'm crazy, don't you."

"Yes," he said simply.

"Then I should go to England? Is that what you are saying?"

"No," he said firmly.

"Then what?" She had a plaintive expression. "I don't understand."

"You will bring knowledge to your girls." He smiled at her. "And I will help."

That evening, Farzana met with Archie and Agnes Singletary along with Carolyn and Ken Watanabe. They were taking a modest meal while chatting as they often did these days, about their uncertain situation and their even more uncertain future. Everyone had a story to share. Some males harass a female caregiver for attending to a male patient. Another would complain that the female staff dressed inappropriately, and that they were tempting the males. Carolyn said at this point that it took everything in her to keep from saying they should damn well control themselves. Worse, there were stories of men being taken away, for reasons no one knew. The Masoud Center staff seemed exempt, but the growing number of refugees appeared at risk.

The consensus was that, given they were needed by the new regime, they would be harassed but essentially permitted to continue, except for educating the older girls, it would be permitted for the younger ones at present. The remaining on-site activity was diminishing, and they expected an edict to shut it down at any moment.

Farzana grew restless at this discussion but realized she was expected to contribute at this point. This was her program on a day-to-day basis. "I know I have been quiet but there is much on my mind."

She then slowly recounted her conversation with Deena that morning and the offer to come to England. The others displayed little reaction though only Agnes knew that Farzana was struggling with such a decision. Agnes, however, was not aware that Deena had made an explicit offer and had mixed feelings. She had grown to think of the young woman as a grandchild and now found herself struggling to smile in support.

"That is a wonderful offer, my dear." Carolyn said. "With the education initiative struggling so, I'm sure you are tempted No one would blame you for going."

For some reason, Farzana had trouble keeping herself seated on this day. She stood and once again walked about this room as she thought. The others stopped to watch her. "It is a wonderful opportunity. And Agnes, when I stopped at your office, I was fairly sure I might accept it. I mostly wanted to see if you would be disappointed. And then ..."

“Then what, my dear?” Archie asked.

“Then … I talked to Sayed Aktar. You all know him, I presume.”

“Yes,” Carolyn added, “he has become a blessing here as our work has increased, as has those he brought with him.”

“We talked, in your office Agnes, long after you left.” Farzana struggled with the next words. “It came to me how much he has lost, how much so many have lost. How could I go, be safe, think of myself when others are suffering so? No, I cannot.”

Archie spoke again in his subdued, avuncular voice. “My dear, think carefully about this. After all, you cannot save the world.”

Farzana circled the dining table, her face concentrated in thought. “No, you people are determined to stay. Why? You can easily return to Australia, be comfortable, safe, enjoy life. And yet you do not. Is that not what makes humans so odd, yet so special. We are capable of the worst of behaviors, and the best. I will go someday if the opportunity remains. But not now, not when so much pain surrounds me.”

“The pain will aways be here, dear girl.” Agnes said softly. “That is one thing the world will never lack, pain.”

“I have thought of that and yes, this is not an easy decision. But there are too many girls I have worked with recently. I have no children of my own, nor a husband, but some of these girls are like my own. I was there when the hope first was captured in their hearts, first was reflected in their eyes. I cannot leave them knowing, thinking, my absence will extinguish that. You, of all people, must understand.”

There was a long pause when no one said a word. It was Carolyn who spoke. "For a long time, I could not figure out why my dear parents stayed here. They could be enjoying a home on some Australian beach, having cookouts on the barbie with their mates, playing shuffleboard in the afternoon, drinks at sunset, bridge in the evenings."

"Shuffleboard?" Archie burst out laughing. "That would be death for sure in my book. Dear daughter, by now you should know that nothing can replace the look of hope in a young person's eyes."

Carolyn sighed. "Dad, you always were such a romantic."

"As are you my dear," the elderly man said in a wistful manner.

"A gift from you, dear father."

"Or a curse." Archie momentarily looked sad before turning to Farzana. "I think you have more to tell us, a plan perhaps."

At this, the young woman initiated a monologue. She went on about continuing to reach girls in their villages and homes, about using the older girls to mentor the younger ones, how Sayed and his friends could help provide cover and protection if necessary. Then, she overviewed the possibility of taking the most promising to a place where they can be trained as the leaders of tomorrow. "I know I am leaving out many details, and so much is uncertain, but this is what I hope to do … with your permission."

All thought on her words. It was Dr. Kenzie Watanabe, Carolyn's husband who spoke. "Let us all be clear on the dangers in this. We never know when the Taliban might come down on us. This might be a provocation which they cannot ignore. Think carefully about that."

A long silence as Farzana stopped pacing and looked at the table. She knew that Kenzie was making sense, that the others should pay heed to him.

Archie spoke to break the silence. "Let us finish our meal and then work on Farzana's plan some more."

PART II
2022

CHAPTER 13

The Hairy Hare

(Winter 2022)

"Rivers do not drink their own water; trees do not eat their own fruit; the sun does not shine on itself, and flowers do not spread their fragrance for themselves. Living for others is the rule of nature. We are all born to help each other."

Pope Francis II

The evening was frosty with a light dusting of snow to remind all that the dark and gloomy winter yet embraced this university town. One by one they made their way to Chris's favorite English Pub … the Hairy Hare. It was not so much his favorite watering hole, he no longer had one, but it had an odd sentimental value for him. It was the first such venue he frequented as a young Rhodes scholar, mostly because it looked authentic to him at the time even though the locals tried to disabuse him of this ill-informed opinion. He stubbornly refused to bend on his choice; He was Irish after all.

Back then, there was a certain barmaid that had attracted his attentions though she diligently ignored his advances. Her daughter, or was it granddaughter, now had part ownership in the establishment. The Hare, as he called it, had the further advantage of being inexpensive at a time when he was trying to downplay what he saw as the embarrassing fact that he came from extreme wealth. Over time, it became home even though other similar establishments were judged far more authentic by real Brits, and certainly offered superior food and beverage. The more abuse he suffered for his selection of preferred venue, the more he dug in no matter the mediocrity of the fare offered. It had become a matter of pride to him. Over time, he convinced himself that it was a superior establishment. The mind can play remarkable tricks on us.

Chris Crawford thought it was time to bring everyone together in some light and fun conversation, a get-to-know one another better gathering for some at least. It had been some six months since Jeremiah Joshua Connelly had arrived. In those months, the critical members of what he considered his affinity group had come and gone and then returned, some several times. Connie, Josh's spouse, had travelled back and forth to Canada finishing up some of her research as she prepared to spend time with her husband as he entered his inevitable decline. Josh's first wife, Usha, did the same. Though her marriage to him had been one of convenience, to give cover for her homosexuality, she had grown to love him as a brother. She knew there was no other place for her than to be at Josh's side when his time came.

Josh's niece Cate and her partner, Meena Muhaisin, travelled throughout the Mideast with Deena Masoud. On occasion, Ali would join them to visit programs where promising girls were being identified and groomed for additional education in the West. On other occasions, they visited the secondary schools and universities where those in the program were being trained, to make sure all was well. Azita Masoud travelled less, caring for her daughter, and doing clinical medical work in NHS areas serving Muslim communities. Azita also mentored those girls who had been taken out of Afghanistan as Kabul collapsed in the Taliban resurgence. She paid the most attention to those she thought might pursue careers as physicians, nurses, or medical technicians. Kay remained fully involved with Chris's international service work by overseeing the medical component of the ISO model for her twin brother.

Kat Crawford juggled several responsibilities. She ferried back and forth between London and Chicago as she shifted operation of the Crawford family empire to London. Besides keeping the Crawford financial empire intact and growing, she helped raise additional funds to support Chris's work. She was especially fond of his vision of turning back America's slide toward authoritarianism … the conservative vision fanatically embraced by Charles Senior in his later years. While some of her wealthy associates shared her liberal views, she labelled too many of her colleagues in the financial world as provincial troglodytes with narrow interests who, in her mind, astonishingly believed they were worthy of their wealth and deserved even more.

Josh Connelly's oldest companions also decided that they would join their college companion in the denouement of his life. These rather odd connections had been forged when they were young would-be revolutionaries trying to stop what they considered an insane conflict halfway around the world in Vietnam. As they often discussed among themselves, connections forged in such a heated manner are special and, in their case, unbreakable. Mo and Carla Greenstein along with Bob Wilson and Peter Favulli, had taken longer to settle things in the States and come to Oxford but now they were here and enjoying their time with old friend, Josh. Of course, Karen Fisher and the senior ISO team were always busy, often traveling, as the programs they oversaw continued to expand.

Then, one day in January, it struck Chris that everyone would be in town at the same time. That small miracle didn't even occur over the holidays since family ties pulled some away. Now, however, the stars had aligned, and everyone was around. As he called or texted people, there were the usual groans about meeting at the Hairy Hare. Why not a decent venue at long last? Insiders knew, however, that no other place would do. Then there were the moans about being busy and so on. But Chris was determined. Partly, he was motivated by simmering tensions such as the continued coolness between his wife and the Masoud twins, especially Azita, which bothered him greatly.

Chris was cognizant that Mo, Carla, and Bob felt a bit awkward. They were happy to connect with Josh and his family but felt as strangers within the broader network. Chris decided it was time to break down that social distance a bit. Mostly, he felt that they were all getting too busy, that the older days of sharing laughs and tears were being lost. He did not want the laughter to end. Laughter was life itself, he thought. And then, there was Josh. He had been showing signs of slipping. He had less energy, slept more, walked at a slower pace, evidencing discomfort and even pain despite his efforts to conceal this from others. When asked how he was doing, he always responded that he was fine. Despite such assurances, all knew the good times would not last much longer.

Upon meeting resistance to his proposed getting together as a large social group, he used his younger sister as his trump card. She had been moving to London, which was now mostly complete. Many of them did not know her well but Chris thought it was time they should. *She's the talent of the family*, he stressed, *even more so than Kay*. All agreed with him that she had to be better than the surviving male issue. No one disputed Chris's self-deprecatory assessment of his personal worth. Now he wanted the others to judge for themselves whether Kay or Kat was the best of the Crawford clan.

If others still hedged on attending his gathering, Chris would play his last and best card. Don't forget, he could tell them, a great deal of support for their work comes from the Crawford Family Foundation. That money, in case they have conveniently forgotten, comes largely though not entirely from the business genius and managerial efforts of Kat who now ran the financial aspects of the family businesses. What he never bothered to mention is that his father's will had never been changed to reflect his bitter feelings toward his offspring. Charles Senior left Chris with the bulk of his estate and a substantial say over the entire family fortune. His father was a believer in primogeniture with virtually all going to the surviving male heir. If his mother had not dispatched her husband before his time, all knew he soon would have changed his will, likely leaving his considerable fortune to those conservative causes that dominated his life in later years.

Money had always been a double-edged sword to Chris. He loved that it afforded him such freedom, enabling him to do good as he defined that good. At the same time, he never could escape the feeling that wealth shaped how others saw and reacted to him. He wanted to be liked, or not liked, on his own merits. That was always his preference, though it was never possible to know. He hid his wealth through school as best he could, trying to pay his own way. Yet, in the end, his family background would be revealed. He never could determine whether others were responded to him as a person or the possible heir to a fortune.

Now, on this instance, he had no problem playing the wealth card. His calls, or texts, typically ended with the suggestion that they better get their behinds to the Hairy Hare on the evening indicated if they wished their luxurious lifestyle to continue. This would be a genuinely nice way of officially welcoming Kat to England. Besides, they were all too busy. They were not doing enough social things together.

Chris walked into the larger back room he had reserved. It could easily accommodate the expected crowd with all sitting at the same conference table. He was accompanied by his wife, Ali, his twin sister Kay, and her husband James Whitehead. Looking around, he nodded in satisfaction. *Yes, we will get off to a good start as I am excoriated once again for selecting the worst pub in Oxford.* He smiled.

"Why are you smiling?" Kay asked.

"I'm anticipating great praise for my selection of the venue." He responded to her with an exaggerated smile.

"Hah," Kay guffawed. "You will be lucky if no one spikes your warm beer with arsenic." She turned to her husband, Jamie Whitehead. "By the way, dear, I hope you remembered to steal some poison from the dispensary."

It had taken Chris's new spouse, Professor Shahed Al-Hussein, some time to be comfortable with the back and forth among the siblings and those close to the Crawford clan. Such irreverent banter was less common within the Jordanian royal family to which she was loosely associated. Her world had been more formal and polite. However, she quickly was getting there. "Be careful, Kay, it took me a long time to land him. I want to keep him for a while." She then kicked herself silently, realizing she had stumbled onto a sensitive topic.

Kay saw her discomfort and put an arm around her. "Dear Ali, never doubt that Kat and I are thrilled you have taken on the thankless task of keeping our brother in line. We remember what he was before he married Amar. Not a pretty sight." Kay chuckled to keep everything light. "Kat and I shuddered at the thought of what he would have become *once again* if he had remained unattached after Amar's passing. A depraved lech for sure, probably something even worse if that can be imagined. You should have seen him during his young and disgusting bachelor days. No, better you not."

"You have always been kind to me." Ali said with sincerity. "It also has gotten better with Emma and Liz; they are warming up to me. Losing their mother was not easy of course. Even Deena and I have worked out a working relationship, but our personal connection is not yet as warm as I would like. Azita is the one that remains distant. She has gone back to medicine, mostly working with the poor Muslim population in London through Luke Geoghegan's outreach work, though she remains devoted to her work with girls in Afghanistan. She is somewhat less involved in the outreach work we are doing with Muslim girls in other countries though, which surprises me. Perhaps it could be her way of distancing herself from me. Still, she is dedicated to reaching Afghani girls. That has become her focus and her passion. But what can we do for them now that the Taliban is in charge, other than work with the ones we got out at the end?"

"Perhaps the new regime can be bribed? Can you get more girls out with money?" Jamie offered.

Ali shrugged. "The Taliban are not like most regimes. But we can wait and see. They are having trouble governing. They need money desperately. Who knows?"

Kay turned to her brother. "It looks like you have not assigned seating. Lost opportunity?"

"I could have put certain people next to one another. I thought about that. But no, I want to see where people sit on their own. That tells a lot."

Ali smiled. "Excellent thought. I think I'll sit on the opposite end of the table from you my dear." She then leaned in to kiss her spouse on the cheek.

"Good idea, I'll join you," Kay added enthusiastically. "Ali, you are getting so much better at giving my brother a bad time. My lessons are working."

"Hah, hah!" Chris responded, "If Jamie and I sit together, we will be sure to have an intellectual conversation; no chatter about office romances and menstrual cycles."

"Such sexism." Ali tried looking horrified as she poked her spouse on the arm.

"If we can't come up with a great intellectual discussion," Jamie nodded toward Chris, "we could complain about our wives all night but, as I think on that topic, one night probably isn't enough time."

"Don't you mean ex-wives?" Kay retorted as she punched her spouse on his arm with considerable vigor.

"Ouch," Jamie said as he kissed his wife on the cheek. "I need that arm as a doctor."

"I've seen your doctoring," Kay said with a hearty laugh, "I'm doing your patients a favor."

"Ouch," Chris put his arm over Jamie's shoulder, "we guys must stick together."

They continued to arrive in small groups. Chris felt relieved when Kat arrived from London, where she had relocated, accompanied by Karen Fisher and Carlotta Ciganda. The primary offices for ISO were in the Capital city, though a smaller, operational base was maintained in Oxford.

Karen walked up to Chris and deadpanned. "Carlotta and I have been going over the books with Kat. She is a financial genius and we've found some places we definitely can save money, you know, by clearing out some obvious deadwood. So, we've emptied out your office. I mean, you were hardly using it anymore as far as I can see. Besides, dragging me back to this hole pretending to be an authentic English pub was the last straw."

"Karen, Karen, Karen, I found you when you were nothing …" Then he stopped.

"And now?" She fell into his trap.

"You are still nothing," he laughed at his own humor. "Kat, you sit near me. Karen, I have a bar stool for you out front."

She gave him the finger as all in the immediate area laughed at the expected banter.

They found seats as a larger contingent including Josh, Mo, Carla, Bob, Connie, and Usha came in the room. Chris greeted them personally, thinking that Josh looked better this evening, quite certain that he had rested well to be on better display. Next came Cate, Meena, and Deena, probably from a work meeting. Others floated in, filling the seats further from head of the rectangular table. Chris worried, *was Azita not coming?* Had her isolation become complete.

Chris drifted back to the time he and Amar had gotten married in Afghanistan on an impulse. The ceremony was conducted by the British commander of a temporary base established as the Taliban were being routed after 9-11, an officer who didn't know he had such authority until that moment. After, they put this young prodigy, Azita, on a plane to take her to England since her parents had been assassinated and other more remote family members saw this as an opportunity for the young savant. The Taliban struck them down in retribution as their hold on power disintegrated. She was a precocious child, no more than eleven years old but going on thirty and already proficient in many medical procedures.

They had been stopped at British Immigration. Entrants to Britain were scrutinized carefully in the aftermath of the 9-11 terrorist attacks and the campaign to drive the Taliban from power for harboring Osama Bin Laden. Not surprisingly, the first officials they met after landing at Gatwick airport in a private plane grilled Chris and Amar. Who was this Mideastern child with no passport and questionable paperwork saying her family had given her over to the care of this couple? Chris had made frantic calls to many people in power as they left Afghanistan but, in that room facing sceptical officials, worried that the magic had not worked.

Finally, a senior official arrived. She looked at Azita and asked. 'Well young lady, you have created quite a stir. There are a lot of people, important people, concerned about you. Tell me. If we let you into our country, will you give me your word that you won't cause any trouble like blowing up Parliament?

Azita looked directly at this high ranking official with her large brown eyes that screamed innocence. 'Oh no, ma'am. I am here to learn to be a doctor and heal people.' That is how Chris now remembered the exchange at least.

He recalled the immigration official smiling. 'Yes, I am quite sure you will, quite sure indeed. Welcome to England, my dear.'

Where had that innocent girl gone? Could he get her back? He had looked at his watch and decided it was time to begin. The seats were now about full, and people were chatting in many separate conversations. The door opened one last time. In walked Azita. She found a seat at the other end of the table, sat without acknowledging anyone, and then kept looking at her phone. For a moment, he wished she were still eleven years of age. He would be tempted to put her over his knees and give her a proper spanking. Then he realized he never would have done that, no matter what. But she did frustrate him so.

Chris tinkled the glass in front of him with a knife. He was always amazed how well that worked in bringing people to attention. When all eyes focused on him, he suddenly realized he had not given any thought to what he wanted to say, not even a joke to start off the proceedings. On clearing his throat, he went with an old one. "It is my privilege to bring you to one of England's oldest and most revered establishments." A groan went up.

Josh threw his head back in a laugh. "Oldest, really? I saw a sign out front saying established in 1969."

"Scoff if you must. It is a known fact that Oliver Cromwell and Charles the 1st broke bread here before they had their falling out and Charles lost his head as a result."

"Yeah," Karen interrupted, "Charles died here all right … he croaked after eating one of their shepherd's pies. That beheading thing was a rumor spread by the owners."

"Right," Kay added. "To cover up their crimes of poisoning their patrons with what they call authentic English fare. Authentic my ass."

Chris did not miss a beat. "Damn, I could have sworn I told management to seat the two of you out by the bar … I suppose the other patrons complained though."

Karen seemed about to respond when Carlotta interrupted. "As much as we all enjoy the Chris and Karen show, let us spare our guests."

Chris appeared chastened. "Of course, Carlotta is right. Besides, I can always punish Karen later, when no one can hear her screams. But to business. I've wanted to bring everyone together for some time. Over the past few months we have gathered in smaller groups on occasion but there was never an opportunity to include all. We are busy people after all. Besides, there is another purpose tonight. Not all of you know my younger sister … Katerina, or Kat. She is the family financial barracuda."

"There goes your allowance for next month, dear brother."

Chris moved on quickly. "And next to her is the matriarch of the Connelly clan, our mother Mary Kelly." Chris was happy to see his mother there. She had recently joined Kat in England, arriving with her on the most recent flight back.

"Yes, as long as my children have emigrated, I thought I might as well too." The sprightly woman said in a strong voice with eyes that twinkled. "They are not much but they are mine."

"Why mother, that's the nicest thing you've ever said about me." Chris looked pleased.

Mary added with a dramatic sigh. "Dear Christopher, if only I had spanked you when you misbehaved."

"But I never misbehaved as a child."

"As a child? I'm talking about this morning." Her eyes twinkled even more as she looked around the table. "And yes, everything you've heard about me is true. I shot my husband on a Chicago Street. He was eating a Polish delicacy at the time. The man was a son of a bitch, the worst mistake of my life … except for the children. You also heard that it was self defense. That's baloney. I intended to kill him. However, three good things did come out of that marriage, and they are sitting around this table. Thank God they took after me, not him."

Chris looked discomforted. "Well, then, that is not how I would have introduced you mother, but you can see where we got our spirit and …" he hesitated a moment, "where I got my wicked wit. Listen, let's go around and have everyone share something about themselves. Things like, whom did you murder or whom would you like to knock off. Except don't mention me."

They went around the room. People kept their remarks short, and mostly on the light side. Several suggested that Chris was an excellent candidate for elimination and asked Mary if she were up to the task once again. She laughed heartily but said she would need the money up front. However, her advice on how to off him and, more importantly, get away with it was free of charge. Then Chris segued seamlessly into asking several people to comment on their work at present. Karen did an overview of the major program areas, Kay spoke to the medical initiatives, Carlotta chimed on various service programs, Tomas, a newer team leader originally from Africa by way of the London School of Economics, weighed in on community development efforts, Ali on the education undertakings, and so it went. For an impromptu session, Chris was pleased. They prided themselves on not being siloed into narrow areas of concern but that was always a temptation. He made a note that they would need more sessions where an exchange of ideas and initiatives took place.

They continued to talk as food and drink was served and consumed. Two more times Chris took command, once to ask Kat to say a few words about her plans. And secondly, to ask Josh if he would talk of his work and comment on the friends who had joined him in Oxford. Kat made an efficient presentation of her work, stressing that she hoped to keep the ISO funded at a reasonable level, though some expenditure cuts might be necessary. Then she threw out her oft used joke that firing her worthless brother, mere deadwood in her eyes, would make balancing the books so much easier. It always got a good laugh.

Josh ended the formal part of the evening. He reminded the crowd why he had come to England, including an update on his health about which he gave an upbeat report. Then he thanked Chris for several of what he called gifts he had received. He thanked him for providing access to his students and how much he enjoyed sparring with them on the great social and political challenges the world was facing. He so missed that as an emeritus faculty member. Then he thanked Chris for lending him the specific services of three highly competent students … Gretchen Willingham; Ashok Kaur; and Ashok's younger sister, Amandeep. Josh went on to describe the work they had been doing, plumbing as best the could the deeper roots of the political chasm that had ripped America apart. He made a special note that it arguably was easier to explore what was going on in the States from the perspective of those who did not live close to the situation. Perspective was essential. He ended that part of his presentation by noting some practical applications his work might contribute."

"I'm not that giving." Chris hastened to say. "I'm getting something back, and not just your lame insults of me. The work you are doing will contribute much to the work Kat and I plan on doing back home in America. We are even on the scorecard of life my friend."

Then Josh turned to face Chris. "No matter his protests to the contrary, I want to thank this man, and his family, which includes many around this table. He took me in during these days which, as you all know, are dwindling down for me. He has reunited me with the people who have meant so much to me. It is easy to despair about the world and our fates. Then someone like Christopher Crawford comes along and shakes your scepticism and pessimism to the core. Thank you, my friend."

Chris was not expecting that and found himself unable to generate a witty response.

In time, people began to drift out, Azita being one of the first as Chris and Ali noted. Those that were reluctant to leave changed chairs so they could be closer to one another and ordered more drinks. They had not finished whatever was on their mind or perhaps they did not want the evening to end. Most had found some sense of community that they recalled was present when the organization was smaller and more intimate. They did not regret growing in size to become more impactful. Yet, something had been lost … a certain intimacy and familiarity which they had recaptured that night.

"So, they won't kick us out." Cate asked as she and Meena moved closer to those who remained.

"Are you kidding?" Chris responded. "This place is still open because of me. Don't quote me on this but it really is mediocre."

Kay deadpanned. "I hope you are not saying that as any sense of an accomplishment … keeping this dump open is not a public service."

"Hilarious dear sister, I've always regretted not getting rid of you while we shared a womb or maybe when we were stuck in the same crib together."

"I am so looking forward to joining my older sister in making your life a living hell." Kat also deadpanned. "That's what I missed by remaining in Chicago, the daily opportunities to prick that ego of yours."

"Ego? What ego? I have the humility of a Thomas Merton." Chris looked at Mo and Carla. "For our Jewish visitors, he was a Catholic aesthetic of some sort."

"I know." Mo responded. "I have his works in my bookshop, even tried reading him once. It was torture. You Catholics are sick with all that self-denial. No wonder you are so neurotic."

Chris nodded. "He was torture for me as well, if I'm to be truthful."

Kay chuckled. "You read Merton?"

"Sure, back when I still wondered if there was a God, as a teenager. Or maybe I was still in my crib."

"That would, in fact, be your teenage years." Kat quipped.

Oh, dear brother, surely you jest. I checked out your preferred reading as a teenager … nothing but pictures of naked women." Kay added.

"I'm glad mother left earlier. She still thinks I'm a saint." Chris knew this would not work as soon as the words were uttered.

Kat laughed aloud. "No way, she got over that delusion after I showed her where you stashed your weed back in high school."

"It was you? I wondered what happened to my good stuff." He tried looking cross at her. "I was grounded for a freaking month and mother threw away my stash."

"Oh please," Kay intervened. "It wasn't mother taking your drugs, it was me. I was too good to go to drug dealers myself, so I told mother I'd get rid of them. All I did was shift them to my room where I did a little experimentation. Thanks much for the opportunity but, to tell you the truth, I never saw the attraction."

Chris shook his head. "You were always such a nerd. Science was your high I bet."

Before Kay could respond, Carla Shapiro-Greenstein made a sound that drew everyone's attention in her direction. "I have a semi-serious question."

"Thank you," Ali said. "I was afraid we were descending into another Crawford squabble."

"In fact, Ali, my question is for you. I've always been curious about the clothing restrictions imposed on Muslim women. What's with that, if I may ask."

"Of course you may ask, I'm always ready to educate Western infidels. I've been working on my husband for the past several months to no avail but I'm sure you are better students." Ali paused momentarily wondering if she had been insensitive to her Jewish guests, but they were smiling. "Let me start with definitions. There is the hijab, basically a scarf pulled over the head to cover the hair. That is most common throughout the Muslim world. In more conservative areas we have the niqab and the burqa. These are full coverings with the first having an opening for the eyes and the second a mesh covering, which is the most restrictive."

"Sounds perfect for my sisters, to protect the public from having to see them." Chris was already protecting himself as Kay threw an uneaten dinner roll in his direction. "Especially in the morning before the makeup routine, which takes literally forever." Another dinner roll flew in his direction, this one from Kat.

Ali shook her head. "Alas, there is always food thrown at Crawford gatherings. It is good they are seldom accurate. But let me be clear on Muslim female dress codes. The Prophet never imposed such restrictions, specifically on women. He preached general modesty. If I recall correctly, he said something like … *'to the believing men, they should cast down their looks and guard their private parts … and say to the believing women that they should lower their gaze and guard their privates; that they should not display their beauty and ornaments except what {must ordinarily} appear thereof.*"

Cate exclaimed. "Mohamed was spot on about male private parts. I mean, before I came out as a lesbian, a couple of male colleagues tried sexting me pics of *'you know what.'* Really, I'm not sure those pics ever worked on my straight gal friends."

Meena poked her partner. "Cate, shush."

Ali spoke up to end the moment of embarrassment. "There is one place in the Quran where the Prophet speaks directly to women. '*O Prophet! Tell the wives and daughters as well as all believing women that they should draw their cloaks over their bodies so that they should be known and not molested.'* To be *'known'* I believe means to announce that one is a follower of the true faith."

Carla interrupted. "Do you consider yourself to be a follower? Is that too personal?"

"Not at all, but my answer would be too long, another time. Back to the dress code. Personally, I've always believed that female dress restrictions in the Muslim world were a male power play though I also prefer some modesty. And I might point out that Christians went through a similar era of enforced female modesty. Look at Victorian styles, all but the face was covered in layers of clothing. There are several passages in your Bible on the matter, one that comes to mind is from Corinthians … *'but every woman who prays or prophecies with her head uncovered dishonors her head – it is the same as having her head shaved.'"*

"Damn Catholics still won't let women be priests." Kay sputtered.

Ali spoke as if a thought had struck her. "Oh, what separates Christians from Muslims mostly is time, which gives me hope for the future. Christians have around longer and started toward secularism earlier. Religious absolutism is a dangerous malady. I just thought of another Biblical passage that has stuck with me. It is Timothy 2:11 … *'Let a woman learn in silence with full submission. I permit no woman to teach or to have authority over a man; she is to keep silent.'* Now, how is that any different from Taliban 101."

While looking increasingly weary, Josh spoke up. "Interesting, I remember, as a kid, seeing girls put scarves or even just handkerchiefs. That was a time when females were no longer wearing hats but the tradition of covering the head in church remained. The opposite was true for men, they were to take any head covering off."

Ali picked the conversation up. "This whole issue has become so complicated. As you know, customs and laws vary wildly across Islamic countries. Now, where cultural traditions clash, politicians don't know what to do. France banned burqas in some situations which caused many to protest what they saw as a retreat from personal freedom. Recently, in a place called Karnataka India, they have issued a ban on religious dress directed at Muslims. India is undergoing a Hindu nationalist revival, a sorry affair if I must say. Muslim women challenged the ruling saying such a law forces them to choose between their religion and getting an education."

"I had no idea," Carla said thoughtfully. "We must talk more another time."

"By the way," Bob Wilson broke the temporary silence, "I was a big Merton fan later in life during my monastery phase."

"That's right," Cate examined Bob with interest, "you also started out as a revolutionary and went to jail with your friends, most of your friends that is …" she glanced at her uncle with an embarrassed look.

"No problem, dear niece, I came to terms with my checkered past a long time ago." Josh smiled though he was not certain he was being truthful.

Cate went on but continued to blush. "Then you went into a monastery. What was with that? No one was doing that by the time you entered."

"A few were still entering. Just before I left, there was a millionaire business guy who gave it all to charity and joined us. You never know what's inside a person." Bob then smiled in a way that reassured Cate. "How does one answer that. Only unexamined lives are linear and unidirectional. For the unlucky of us, we wander endlessly as we explore new dimensions and opportunities."

"And what were your explorations." The question came from Meena who had been listening silently.

"Hmmm …" Bob paused. "Good question. I did seem to go in several directions. Early on, I was your average Irish kid growing up in a 1950s working class neighborhood. You know, I couldn't decide if I wanted to be a gangster or a priest. In the end, I read a lot … probably to help me decide. Somehow, I chose to go to a decidedly secular college where this lot of Reds you see here led me astray," he waived toward Carla, Mo, Peter, and Josh.

"The hell we did," Mo protested with a smile. "You had already publicly burnt your draft card and then sought us out."

"No, I like my story better. Surely, I'm not taking responsibility for my own mistakes."

Josh looked at him quizzically. "Mistakes, Bobby? Is that what they were?"

Robert Wilson paused as if trying.to get the next words right. "No, I misspoke. Perhaps I overreached in trying to bring down the entire establishment. All I ended up doing … was killing our good friend Jimmie." He looked at Josh. "I'm not sure I ever got a chance to apologize …"

Mo broke in. "That wasn't your fault. It was all our faults and the fault of none of us."

"Mo is right, Bobbie. It wasn't your fault at all. It was mostly mine," Josh interrupted with words said so softly the others had to process the sounds to ensure they understood.

Carla quickly broke in, sensing they were headed toward a set of sad reflections in front of others who might not care nor understand. "Bobbie, you were giving us a tour of your life. Please continue."

"Right … and I'll keep it short. Our aborted revolution landed me in prison for a while until the authorities decided they needed the space for real criminals. Then one day, I was out after serving half my sentence. What to do? Here I was, an ex-revolutionary of sorts with an almost completed BA degree in Philosophy, a prison record, and no practical skills. I did what any rational guy would do, I joined a cloistered religious order."

"No shit!" Cate issued in surprise. "Ooops, sorry."

Bob laughed. "That's the common response, even from those that knew me. But that was not such a big leap if you were inside my head.

"Now, there is a strange place to be I fear." Peter Favulli said.

"No doubt. But it made sense to me. Think about it. For a while, I wanted to be a priest as a young kid."

"So did I," Peter interjected.

"But Bob had a freaking chance of becoming one." Josh said said with a laugh.

Bob nodded his agreement before continuing. "When I got a job to support my education, I worked in a hospital because it helped people and I majored in freaking philosophy … who does that if they want to make some money in life?"

"Clearly someone who doesn't want to work for a living … nor care about money. I thought about it." Chris added.

"But you never had to worry about working for a living." Kat added. "Go on, Bob."

Bob took control again. "It was perfect for a while. I was at peace, away from what seemed like a frantic and insane world.

We worked and prayed and reflected. I did less praying than reflecting. I loved it all … for quite a few years."

"And then?" Josh asked.

"I realized one day that God never answered back, not that I expected him to. I was in my own private echo chamber which isn't bad but, in the end, not enough. Frankly, my own brain was too restless, I needed more stimulation. You bounce around the same thoughts, getting deeper into circular labyrinths with no exit. When there is no divinity, this reclusive life becomes a dead end. So, I left, and Mo and Carla were kind enough to take me in, let me work in their shop."

"We Reds stick together." Carla said with a smile.

The thing is, no matter what I did, the quest was always the same … trying to figure things out. What does it all mean?"

Josh soon tired and suggested it was time to leave. Another larger group departed with him. As midnight approached, only the Crawford siblings along with Ali, Cate, and Meena remained.

Chris turned to Cate. "You know your uncle quite well."

"Of course, he was my real father since my biological father, along with his whole family, were total jerks. You know those rich, entitled people."

"Cate!" Meena uttered in horror. "Think of who is here."

"What? No, not these rich. I was talking about the others who are spoiled, entitled people." she blurted out but could not refrain from blushing.

The Crawford siblings all broke out in laughter. "When the shoe fits." Kay offered.

Cate continued to make herself understood. "No, really … you should have met the Ballentine clan, utter snobs. Total narcissists."

"Oh," Kat piled on, "like my twin siblings you mean."

"No!" Cate continued to stammer and blush. "You have no idea what they were like."

"Oh yes I do, I work with many of them." Kat raised a hand. "It's okay, you can insult us. But seriously, I noticed that you don't use your father's name. That says something. I heard you once did but then changed to Connelly."

"Yes, I switched to mom's name when Dame Ballentine, and her worthless son, refused to admit the existence of Meena or our adopted Mid-eastern girls. That was the last straw. They remain racist to the core. I cut all ties. Well, in truth, it was mutual. They also cut me off, especially out of the will. In truth, I always preferred my uncle to my real … I mean … biological father. Josh has always been my real father, such a loving man."

Chris sighed. "I know, I know. Truth is, Josh has been more of a father to me than my biological dad, a truth my sisters will affirm. Of course, Jeffrey Dahmer might have been preferable to our biological dad."

As Kay and Kat nodded, Cate cocked her head as if absorbing his words. "Yes, I think I can believe that. On the other hand, that would make us related."

"Oh my, that would make him a much, much older relation to you … like he is to me. Rather ancient in fact." Kat was pleased with her quip.

Chris looked serious. "Tell me, Cate. Just how is your substitute dad doing? He puts on a brave front for me, but he seems to be struggling more of late."

Cate looked off in the distance toward a wall adorned with pictures of English hunting scenes and bucolic rural settings of a bygone era. "He misses his sister, my mother, desperately. For most of their lives, they were semi-estranged, he the émigré up in Canada and she focused on her medical career in the States. I was the glue between the two of them during their … what shall I say … separation. Not a happy task at times. When they finally bonded as he retired, I thought we would have a real family for a long time. My dream of those two becoming functioning siblings was becoming real."

Chris winced. "I never forgave myself for Rachel's passing. She wouldn't have been in Kabul if it weren't for me."

Kay stepped in. "Bullshit. That's like saying Josh was responsible for his friend's death during the protest years. I can't recall his name."

"Jimmie," Carla offered.

Kay continued. "Right, Jimmie. We all were in Kabul because we wanted to be there. It could have just as easily have been me."

Cate nodded to Chris. "Josh doesn't blame you, not in the least. He might blame God, or Providence, or himself but he doesn't blame you in the least."

Chris switched gears. "What about his health? I get reports from Kay here but that is medical jargon, tests results. How are his spirits."

Cate paused. "As long as his mind is sharp, and he can work and write, he will continue. At some point, he will hit a tipping point where the important stuff is behind him, or so he thinks. Then he will go rapidly, and I will die a thousand deaths."

"So will I," Josh murmured.

Another silence ensued before Ali spoke. "I want to raise one last thing before we break up. I'm worried about Azita."

Meena nodded. "Yes, I have seen this as well. She is not herself. We used to talk a lot, now she is withdrawn, even angry."

"Is she missing her husband even more as time passes?" Kay asked.

Ali seemed to think on that. "Perhaps, I'm sure that is part of it. She thought they would raise their child together and suddenly, like Rachel, he was snatched from her. But I think she is also feeling another loss. Her vision is slipping from her."

"Her eyesight?" Kat sounded alarmed.

Ali raised a hand. "Oh no, her life's vision of saving Muslim girls like herself. She had a dream as a little girl of what escaping the Taliban might mean for her. By extreme fortune and lots of challenging work, it happened for her. She became a physician. She wanted to bring that opportunity to others, especially Afghan girls. And she saw it happening only to see the promise evaporate and go away … and do so quickly too. I think … I think it is one thing to grow up in a place where so much is possible. Then, life seems a matter of choices. It may not be so but that is what it appears to be. When you have few options, when things are denied you, they are valued so much more … even the little things. Goals become futile aspirations. That is what has happened to Muslim girls. Oh, not all by any means, many accept things as they are. Still, there are many who feel crippled, who know there is a bigger world out there they cannot access. They are the ones who ache for an education, the ones who tasted possibility for a while and then it was gone. Azita feels their pain most of all."

"And does she assume we do not." Chris uttered with frustration.

"Oh, I suspect that's not the only thing bothering her, is it?" Kay asked gently.

"No. She so misses her adoptive mother. Amar was the only one who could replace Madeena, her biological mother, in her heart. I think … I think she resents me. Not so much at first but now … it finally is real to her that Amar is not coming back."

"And Deena?" Kay asked.

"She is cool toward me, but we still work cordially. No, Azita is struggling on more than one level. What I fear is that she will do something rash."

"Suicide?" Chris was alarmed.

"Oh no, I think she will go back to Afghanistan, put herself in harm's way. She cannot let those girls go without trying to rescue as many as she can."

Chris stood. "Well, I'll tell Karen she cannot go, we won't support it."

Ali looked at her husband. "Oh my dear, that would be the worst thing you could do. We cannot clip her wings."

"Yes, I can," Chris looked frustrated. For Christ's sake, I'm still the fucking head of this organization. At least, that is what it says on the foundational documents. Can't I do this one thing. Is that asking too much?"

Ali reached out and guided Chris back into his seat, then said. "You can kill a person in two ways, by taking their life or destroying their dreams. Both are fatal, but the latter is way more painful."

As he sat down, his anger ebbed. "But I love her so. If she was killed in some hopeless venture, I would never forgive myself. I've barely recovered from losing those who died in the Kabul attack."

Ali took her husband's face in her hands. "Look at me." When he tried to twist away, she forced his face to look at her. "We do dangerous things at times. We can either stop doing them to be safe or continue doing them knowing the risks. In the end, I know what you will choose." She saw a small tear form in the corner of one eye. She leaned up and kissed it away, not caring who saw this public sign of affection.

CHAPTER 14

A Discrete Visit

"A teacher affects eternity; he can never tell where his influence stops."
Henry Adams

The truck made its way toward the Pamir and Madeena Masoud Medical and Service Center. On its side was painted the emblematic Islamic icon for the International Red Cross. This partly was a mere subterfuge, one normally used to run medical supplies on a routine basis from Kabul to the ISO medical sites still operating in the country. The truck was authentic, as were the medical supplies it contained. The occupants who accompanied the regular driver included Bahiri Gupta while, in the back of the truck with the medical supplies, were his physician wife, Ferhana, and Doctor Azita Masoud. Both female doctors wore the full Burqa, as prescribed by the new law of the land. The new law was yet to be universally observed but it seemed safer to comply than to oppose. Azita posed as Ferhana's sister who was traveling under the protection of her brother-in-law. Rules governing the lives of females under Taliban control were not being uniformly enforced yet, but they did not want to take any chances.

Before setting out, the three had discussed whether Azita should simply be herself, a visiting physician traveling to a medical camp to bolster a staff increasingly overwhelmed with those seeking help. That was rejected as risky in the end. Especially in the north where they were headed, the Masoud family were heroes to many, yet had an unsavory reputation among the new leaders since they stood against the Taliban in the old days. Archibald Singletary and his physician daughter, Carolyn Watanabe, were at odds over the honorary name that had been given the camp. Carolyn wanted to change it to accommodate the new regime and lessen prevailing tensions. Her father flat out rejected the idea. He had served this area and the people for many years now, knew the reverence with which the name was seen, and stubbornly refused to yield. Carolyn was the one to yield, knowing her father could not be budged once he had decided on something. It was a trait she loved in him, even as it frustrated her.

Though it was technically winter, the season was transitioning to Spring and the daytime temperatures were quite warm. Azita realized she had grown overly accustomed to the temperate weather of England. She found herself quite uncomfortable in the back of a confined truck. She would throw off the full covering when the vehicle was moving, and quickly don her covering when it slowed to a stop, fearing a checkpoint and perhaps a visit by Taliban thugs posing as officials to check out the claims of the driver. The two times those manning the checkpoint looked in the back, they seemed satisfied with Bahiri's explanation that he was traveling with his wife and his sister-in-law who now was widowed as her husband had recently perished fighting the infidels who were yet resisting the Taliban. The subterfuge worked.

Ferhana looked at Azita after the second stop. "You are trembling. Are you ill?"

Azita yanked off her covering, throwing it to the side. She could not quite decide whether she was furious at having to submit to this treatment or worried that this tactic would fall apart at some point. "Not ill."

After an awkward silence, Bahiri pursued what was nagging at her. "But something is bothering you." When Azita remained silent, she continued, addressing her with her familiar name. "Zita, I've known you since you were a little girl following your father Pamir around his clinic. You were the inquisitive one, the world your playground and everything to be understood and conquered. I don't see that girl any longer."

Azita looked at her sharply. "I'm no longer a little girl." Then she looked away. "Besides, I've discovered the real world."

"What, and you are now rejecting that world? I never thought I would see that day, not from you of all people."

Azita said nothing. They travelled in silence for another 30 minutes until the truck stopped once more. Ferhana and Azita could hear the voices outside though the words were muffled. It was clearly another checkpoint, given the gruff character of the unfamiliar voices. "Why do they always sound so angry." Azita had finally spoken as she donned her burqa quickly.

The back of the truck opened as a man jumped up, clearly dressed in classic Taliban attire, and sporting the expected full beard and fully automatic weapon. He looked at the women for a long time as if trying to decide something. Then he turned his attention to the boxes and crates that took up most of the space. Was he going to open all the boxes, just to make sure nothing forbidden was being transported? That might take forever.

Ferhana spoke. "We are nurses, going to help my husband treat the sick in the north. These are medical supplies."

The man's eyes flared with surprize and anger. "Did I ask you to speak?"

"No," Ferhana said in a way that sounded like a reluctant apology.

"Mind your place then." Again, he looked at them as if uncertain what to do next. Then he grunted and jumped off the truck.

There was more discussion, now with raised voices. Even Ferhana, becoming used to her new role in her country, betrayed her uncertainty. Would she hear shots ring out next? Such things did happen now, a harmless dispute escalates amidst the tensions inherent in a new regime yet uncertain of its hold on power. Unwarranted violence can be excused when even the most minimal standards of justice do not exist, especially in the countryside. Ferhana closed her eyes, suddenly seeing a life without her husband. In that moment, she realized how much she loved him.

The voices died down, the engine of the truck roared to life, and the women again threw down their cloth prisons. When the two women looked at one another, both were trembling.

Azita spoke first. "You love your husband very much, don't you?"

"Of course, as you loved Ahmad."

"It is not good to love so much." Azita said in a whisper.

"And why is that?" Ferhana asked in an equally shallow voice.

Azita looked at the other woman as if she was stricken by the senselessness of the question. "Because of the hurt it brings, something beyond physical pain."

Ferhana considered where to go next. "Yes, I fear losing my husband. It would be like losing half of me. But I am not certain why you were trembling earlier. It cannot be the fear of death, you have faced that before, several times. Something else I suspect."

Azita leaned back and closed her eyes, saying nothing for so long that the other woman thought she had fallen asleep. Then, to Ferhana's surprise, she began to speak in a steady voice that suggested her intended audience was herself.

"It is not the fear of death that causes me anguish, this trembling." She paused to collect her thoughts and shift her focus. "Earlier, in this truck, I felt as if I were eleven-year-old again. I was with Pamir in the cab of one truck with our belongings. My brother was driving the family car, with mother and Deena as passengers. We were fleeing Kabul and the Taliban. It should not have been such a frightful trip, father had papers saying he had permission to move north to help treat the regime's warriors battle the Northern Alliance."

"But papers mean nothing when sanity is in short supply." Ferhana said quietly.

"Less than nothing. But that was not what reached my heart that day. I watched my father lie and even grovel before men who were nowhere near his equal."

"But surely you cannot fault him for that. He was merely trying to protect his family. His actions were that of a brave man."

"Oh yes, that is what our reason tells us. But reason is such a weak master. Here was this man who never seemed to have the smallest fault, at least in my eyes. I had him on this pedestal, above all other mortal men. He was my divine presence, the source of all wisdom and courage and love. I recall thinking at the time that I would never marry since no other man could possibly match his stature in my heart."

Ferhana tried to suppress a smile but could not. "Oh, my dear, you were not the only one to worship your father. When I was only a bit older than you at that time, in my teens, I worshiped him in the same way. You were a waif at the time. He was a man to be admired."

"But you found Bahiri."

"And you Ahmad. The men we find for ourselves are not gods but can be good and decent. That is enough. Besides, I am sure your mother found faults in him on occasion."

Azita became animated. "Perhaps, but all I found was perfection in my father, who seemed so commanding to me, and so wise. Then I saw him struggle with these men who held such power. I can still recall siting next to him in the cab of that truck as he shared jokes with these men, as he flattered them and their beliefs, as he offered them bribes. This was not the man I admired."

"But you survived, as did your family." Ferhana offered. "He did what he had to do."

"Yes, we survived. I thought about our experiences in those days many times in the coming years, the conclusion of my thoughts was never pleasant. He stepped off his pedestal for love, for love of his wife and for his children. It was as if he sacrificed his principles for …" Then Azita stopped.

"For something greater. Remember that. Some throw away their values for nothing, or something as meaningless as money. That is not what your father did."

"I know, I know that so well. And that is why I trembled earlier. He violated his core for a greater good. The inescapable truth is that life sometimes leaves us little choice. That has been such a horrific lesson. Some childhood memories can never be pushed aside. They remain with you. It … it is not good to feel things so fully, to believe, to love. No, it is not good to feel such things. They betray you and leave you with a bitter rage."

Ferhana thought of several responses but uttered none of them. She would consider her own thoughts for a more appropriate moment. Instead, she moved closer to Azita and put an arm around the woman she considered a younger sister.

After arriving, Azita walked about the center named after her parents. So many changes. The medical facilities were now larger, supported by the addition of Afghani doctors and nurses under the direction of Archie, his nurse wife Agnes, along with their daughter Carolyn and son-in-law Kenji, also physicians. As government sponsored medical services struggled, privately funded efforts under foreign sponsorship became more essential, and in greater demand. The old refugee facility, which had fallen into disuse after the Taliban were routed after 9-11, was back in business. She saw large numbers of emaciated women and children wandering around aimlessly. Hunger now stalked the land. How had this been permitted to happen? Foreign benefactors would not aid the new regime. *But who did that hurt,* she asked herself? *Surely it does not cause discomfort to those rul-*

ing this agonized land. They are well fed. Anger flushed through her body.

She eventually wandered to the first schoolhouse now stood empty, forlorn. It had been named after her sister, Deena. To Azita, her elder sibling had come to represent all the best in Afghani women and the promise they represented. Deena had been a late bloomer, seemingly concerned too much with frivolous things to amount to much. Then, almost without warning in Azita's eyes, she blossomed into an advocate for female education. Now, it was as if she wanted to replicate her journey of a life discovered with other Muslim girls ... a promise fulfilled for an entire nation.

Now, Deena was not with her. How different they were as children. How intertwined they had become as adults. Azita reflected on this puzzle.

They had discussed at length whether she should come on this trip. In the end, they decided the risks might be too great. While Azita had a reputation as a healer, her sister had made a name for herself as an educator. Worse, from the Taliban perspective, she was considered an advocate for female education, almost as famous in some circles as Malala Yousafzai. Perhaps the Taliban were not that organized, would not put together who she was or why she had returned. If they did, however, at best she would not be permitted to enter the country. But far worse eventualities were possible ... imprisonment or even death. Stories of hangings and beheadings were now common, though none yet formally sanctioned by the central government which was struggling to appear moderate. Perhaps some rumors were exaggerations but clearly women were losing their lives for what seemed like small infractions such as being in the company of a man not her husband. There never appeared to be any penalty for the male.

Besides, she had slipped away without telling many of her colleagues. She had travelled to ISO headquarters to inform Karen Fisher of her plans and ask for institutional support. Upon seeing Karen's face transition to a look of horror, she immediately regretted putting the administrative head of the operation in such a delicate position. Azita felt she had no choice. She had to go back home to Afghanistan as she first promised on a plane out of that country. Yet, she could not disappear without informing anyone of her plans. If she left suddenly and mysteriously, they would start a massive search for her. How humiliating would that be?

She recalled the confrontation with Karen. They had gone back and forth with Karen stressing just how crazy and futile this venture would be in the end. When that failed, Karen played the sympathy card, how Karen permitting this wild scheme to continue would infuriate Christopher and jeopardize her position. Azita paused momentarily at that plea but quickly responded by asserting that she would be going in any case, with or without program support. Having the backup of ISO would, if Karen thought about this clearly, reduce the risk of the worst happening. Think about it, helping her would reduce the risk of tragedy.

As their debate wound to a close, Karen knew she was defeated. She looked at the woman opposite her with an aspect of total disapproval. And yet, she knew inside that she was looking at a mirror image of herself, the feisty working-class lass from the mean streets of Birmingham who fought her way through Uni as an outsider before moving to the top of the international service world. You don't do that by playing safe.

"Go, but for Christ's sake, don't get yourself killed." Karen said with a hint of desperation.

"You won't tell anyone until I'm gone."

"No, I'll handle the paperwork myself." Karen grimaced. "My god, you will be the death of me yet."

Azita smiled and turned to leave. "I am sure that Allah will look with great favor on you."

"Perhaps," Karen said to the retreating figure. "Just go and, for Christ's sake, Allah's sake, and above all my sake, keep yourself safe." When the door closed and she was alone, she placed her head on her arms resting before her on the desk.

'Chris will kill me, for sure this time. I should have listened to my mother and just gotten married,' Karen lamented.

Azita moved disconsolately among the empty rows of desks. She knew that some classrooms had been converted into living space for refugees forced out of their homes by renewed violence or famine. But this original room had been kept as a teaching center though without any students at present. Now it seemed a hollow tribute to her sister, with a layer of dust covering the desks and the few books remaining in the mostly empty shelves that had been erected for that purpose. It might have been converted for use by male students, but their numbers also had decreased as hardship blew over the land like the persistent winds. It had been kept available for the day when the female students would return.

She was taken out of her reverie by a soft voice. "Doctor Masoud."

Azita turned to see a familiar looking woman standing uncertainly in the doorway. "I hope I am not intruding. I was told you wanted to see how things were on your own. But I hoped for a private word."

Azita's initial look of irritation softened. "Wait, I do know you. It is Farzana, am I right? But I forget your last name."

"Farzana Balkhi."

"Of course, you were one of Deena's favorite students in the early years. I am so glad to see you."

Farzana felt relieved as she entered the room. "I am thrilled to see you. And yes, your sister often asked me to come to England to further my education. But I could not."

"And why not. Deena spoke so highly of your potential."

"Several reasons. At first, I was engaged and thought of having children. After my husband was killed, I considered her offer. But then I could not leave the school children. I think Deena understood. When you look into their faces, especially the young female faces, it is something you do not forget, ever."

Azita walked over to the woman and hugged her. "Deena has conveyed that feeling to me many times. I yet remember when this room was dedicated to her, all the students singing songs and showering her with such praise. I was jealous of her that day, foolish of me since I had my medical career and many awards. Still, the joy on those young faces …"

The other woman smiled. A wise woman once said, '*if you want to end war, then instead of sending guns, send books. Instead of sending tanks, send pens, instead of sending soldiers, send teachers.*'

"Did my sister say that?"

"Oh my," Farzana giggled with embarrassment. "No, that was a favorite quote of mine from Malala."

"That is good. I will tell my sister that she must author a book so that she can be the source of so many inspirational quotes. The only words of her that stick with me come from when we were young girls when she called me a lazy cow for avoiding my household chores." Then Azita shifted topics. "Balkhi? Why does that name sound familiar?"

Farzana gently laughed. "It is famous but for nothing I did. There is a respected character in Afghani literature. Her name is Rakia Balkhi. As the story goes, she was a princess way in the past. But she was not like other girls. She liked to read, to write poetry, and to dream openly of a better life for all females. Her brother, the king, was most displeased with her. It all came to a head when he told her she must marry another prince whom she detested. She refused, saying she loved a servant in the palace. For her disobedience, her brother had her killed. But her spirit lived on, at least in this popular story which was embraced by the free-spirited women in this land."

"You imagine yourself to be a modern-day Rakia?" Azita asked with a smile.

"Why, of course. With her surname, what choice do I have." Farzana laughed, then turned serious. "You know what I have been up to these days, now that the female students have been driven away."

"Not all the particulars, but in general ... yes. You have been going out to the villages and working with the girls on their studies, in their homes. I cannot believe your bravery and foolishness."

"Foolish for sure, though I am not sure it is brave. More like necessary. Besides, I heard from Deena that you almost died at the hands of the old Taliban just for reading a notice in public."

Azita was surprised that Deena had shared that story. "No matter, how is this campaign of yours going? That is partly why I am here, and to fulfil a promise to myself." She half whispered the final words.

"Let us walk outside, this empty room now depresses me." Once outside in the sunshine, Farzana continued. "It is all exceedingly difficult. The Center has an uneasy truce with the Taliban, who realize how needed these services are. These men are great at revolution but know little about governing. Still, they make allowances for us. The female staff must wear a hijab but not a burqa. They look the other way when males medically treat females, or the female doctors treat males. I must believe they know what I am doing. I, and the other teachers, take precautions but still. Every day we wait for ... the end."

"What precautions are taken?" Azita asked.

"We bring a male along whom we pass off as relative. I have a man named Sayed Aktar, a former educator like myself. He is a saint as he passes as my husband when I am out of the center traveling to villages. As you know, it is frowned upon, forbidden in many areas, that women travel unless accompanied by their spouse or a male relative. He can also help since he is very educated himself."

"Does his own wife not complain about him passing as your husband."

"She has passed, killed by the Taliban … for speaking out, as was his grandfather. Sayed barely escaped himself. We have several former teachers of girls doing this work. Most bring their own husbands as protectors but some of Sayed's friends have stepped up when that is not feasible."

"And this is working?" Azita looked sceptical.

Farzana looked about her, as if checking to see if anyone was listening. The two women had walked away from the former school buildings toward the surrounding hills and far from prying ears. "That is why I am glad you are here. I fear I am too optimistic when speaking to Deena and even the administrators here, like Doctor Singletary."

"Archie."

"Yes, Archie. The truth is that we are being watched. The truce that exists between the Taliban and us is fragile. Who knows when it might end? I can see them watching me when I venture out. I am hearing that some of the girls, their families at least, are being visited and warned. I doubt we can continue much longer."

Azita stopped walking and looked at Farzana. "It is as I had feared. Let us continue and talk more. I have been thinking about something."

The two women continued to walk, linked arm in arm, as they engaged in a heavy conversation.

Later, they all gathered at the home where the Singletary family resided. It was a larger accommodation situated on land that sloped up toward the surrounding mountains. From the veranda, they had an excellent view of the entire complex and the mountains to the west. They were seated in comfortable chairs around a table that was arrayed with hummus, kabuli pulao, chapli kabab, aush, and korma, along with an assortment of pickles and vegetables. The food offerings were accompanied by sweet tea and juice offerings. Archie, Agnes, Carolyn Watanabe and her husband Kenji, along with Bahiri and Ferhana Gupta had started to eat when Azita, Farzana, and now Sayed arrived on the veranda.

"Oh my," Azita exclaimed at the sight of the table. "It has been so long since I have seen such a table. What a treat."

"Surely you have Afghani delicacies in Oxford." Carolyn suggested.

"Yes, but I fear I am remiss in not frequenting those places often enough. I will make up for it upon my return."

Agnes smiled. "Well, this is a special treat for us, we do not eat this well every day. Your visit gave us an excuse for a party."

Archie sighed. "We could eat this well every day. It is not a question of resources or a deficit of food, not for us. The problem is that we are living among such poverty. This country has never been wealthy, but things are getting worse weekly. So much of the economy was supported by foreigners. Now they have gone. Few business types trust the Taliban so whatever supports the economy enjoyed are drying up. The farmers are going back to opium, the cash crop the Americans tried to erase. It is hard to imagine that two decades of effort can unravel so fast. One certainly cannot blame the impoverished farmers. They must do something to survive."

Then Agnes spoke. "We hire many locals, more than we need. Where else can they go? And we are doing more community development work, helping farmers when we can. We have been discussing things with Carlota and that newer African man back in London, Tomas. I think they understand but it is difficult to communicate the reality of things when all changes so quickly."

Carolyn looked directly at Azita. "We do our best to communicate with the leadership back in England, of course, but perhaps a first-hand report will help ... bring the desperation of our people back to the leadership in a more dramatic way."

Azita looked at this doctor intently. Carolyn was Australian by nationality, married to a Japanese-Filipino man, and living in a rural Afghanistan valley. Yet, she called those around her '*our*' people. How did such things happen, where people could embrace others so different from themselves and with such fervor? Azita found her eyes moistening. It was fortunate that the cool and dry evening air so easily evaporated the tears struggling to the surface of her cheeks.

Archie spoke, "I have prepared in writing what I think we will need to respond to the growing crisis. What I have written are the details. What we need is someone who can deliver the message in a dramatic fashion. You understand I hope."

"Of course, I will bring the message back. I am certain we can bring more supplies and food and medicines in; the supply planes and trucks will come in a steady flow which, she then smiled mysteriously, might help accomplish what I have in mind. But I must confess something. I am not here in any official capacity." Azita looked uncomfortable. "It is worse than that. Almost no one back there knows I am here."

Archie lifted an eyebrow. "Ah, where do they think you are?"

"I told people I was asked at the last minute to lecture at a medical conference on the continent. No one questioned it. Karen Fisher knew and agreed to give me cover for a few days. By now, she might be telling the others what I'm up to. If you hear a huge growl from the north, that would be Chris, and Kay, and Ali all exploding in rage at me."

"I see," Archie said quietly. "I did wonder when I got no advance word from London that you would be coming. Bahiri called and said you were in Kabul and wanted to come north. I just assumed the cloak and dagger stuff had something to do with security."

"And Deena not being with you made us wonder." Carolyn noted.

"Deena, of course knew. She and I talked at length about this but decided to risk only one of us on this venture. She is known as the advocate for girls' education, not as famous as Malala, but still she has this reputation. It seemed more likely I could get in and out as a doctor."

"Exactly why did you come, my dear?" Agnes smiled, as always.

Azita took a deep breath. "When the government collapsed. You may recall we evacuated many girls out at the last minute so that they might continue their educations elsewhere."

"Of course, we all applauded that."

"It was so few." Azita's voice caught with emotion. "My heart broke as the plane lifted off the runway … so many were being left behind. I've returned to get more out. Not today, of course. But Farzana and Sayed and I have been chatting about some possibilities. We have a plan."

"A plan?" Bahiri said dubiously. "Does this plan involve these transport planes and trucks you spoke of a few moments ago."

"Yes," Azita smiled enigmatically. "I do have a plan, indeed … assuming that Christopher and Ali do not kill me upon my return to England."

Then she laid out her thoughts.

CHAPTER 15

Connections

"Our worst enemies here are not the ignorant and simple. However cruel; our worst enemies are the intelligent and corrupt."
Graham Greene

"So, this is how the one percent live." Karen Fisher walked into the spacious office that Katerina Crawford had rented for her London center of operations.

"Are you kidding," Kat rolled her eyes in response. "You should have seen my Chicago haunts. This is a toilet in comparison. Things are so bloody expensive here."

"Tsk! Tsk! Too bad, so sad." Karen did not look impressed by her complaint. "Think you have it bad. This is the first time I'll be in the same room as Chris since the Azita escapade. You've heard of her secret trip back home?"

"Of course. You don't see my brother's Irish temper often but…"

"Exactly," Karen rolled her eyes. "So, do you have a place where I can escape just in case he loses it again?"

"She's back, right? Unharmed? Isn't all well."

"Well," Karen shrugged her shoulders, "the last time I talked with him on the phone he did not crack a single joke, did not insult me a single time."

"Ooh, that is bad, very bad. Perhaps I can ask Peter Favulli to join us. He's in charge of security and packs some kind of concealed weapon, just in case my sweet sibling goes around the bend once more."

"You are a funny lady. But seriously, tell Peter to aim for a leg if he must shoot. I just want to slow down the sot's attack a bit, not dispatch him to his reward."

Kat broke into a big smile. "Why I believe you now can officially be considered one of the family. He usually reserves his Irish temper for us sisters."

"Temper? That I can handle. It's when he goes glacially silent. That's when I start to worry. And about being a member of this family, I've been there for a long, long time if his ire is the ticket to joining this exclusive club."

Kat was about to respond when the door opened. Kay, Josh, and Chris entered. Kay and Josh greeted Kat and Karen warmly while Chris sat quickly and silently into a chair. Everyone noticed. The room suddenly was bursting with tension that momentarily rendered all silent as each person groped for place to begin.

After some desultory chatter, Karen took the lead. "Okay Chris, no more fucking silent treatment. Scream, yell, throw something at me. I'm guilty. I enabled her to go. I put her in harm's way. I'm guilty. But tell me this. What else could I have done?"

After what seemed an eternity, Chris responded in a muffled voice. "You could have warned me about her intentions. I could have stopped her."

"Wait, are you listening to yourself? That's ridiculous. Stop her! She was going … period. If she had to walk over your fucking prone body, she was going. After all this time, you still don't get her?"

Now Chris's voice flared. "She's my daughter, my responsibility. If she had been arrested or, God forbid, been killed, that would have been my responsibility. Not yours."

"Are you somehow suggesting that I wouldn't have been torn apart with guilt had harm come to that woman. You cannot possibly be suggesting that I don't love her because, if you are, you have sunk to the level of the most moronic bloody sot in Oxford. No, in southern England. Sorry, in the whole of the U.K."

"Bullshit," Chris's face had turned a shade of red, "there is a difference between liking someone and loving them, between friendship and family."

"Yes, family you are stuck with while friends are those you choose." Chris opened his mouth, but Karen continued in a low roar. "Wow, sometimes even smart people can make terrible choices. Years ago, I chose the Crawford clan to be my family, even at the expense of my own. Damn, I have been offered several top positions the past few years, most would have paid way more than you. I'm now hot property in case you haven't noticed. But, for some inexplicable reason, I never even considered them. Okay, maybe a couple. That was MY stupid choice to stay, so no complaints. But you know why, don't you?" When she got no response, she repeated. "Don't you?"

She saw his face relax a bit. "I assumed because I'm a sweetheart," he said sheepishly.

"Hah! Because I was stupid enough to think I had become family." Karen paused, realizing that she may have won this one.

"You are part of my family." Kay offered with sincerity.

"Thank you," Karen said to Kay though taken off guard by her comment. "Having family is everything. And being part of a family is not some accident of birth. So, don't you ever doubt my feelings for all of you, even if my feelings for the Irish male SOB who's in charge of this family occasionally go south."

"That's not true." Kat interjected in a softer voice.

"What?" Karen sputtered, looking confused.

"That Irish male SOB to whom you refer is not head of the Crawford clan. Kay and I are … and now I think you. After all, that guy who thinks he is the top dog is burdened with a Y chromosome, a huge impediment to overcome and surely a challenge to rational thought."

Chris sighed. "I know I've been an ass. I just get … so afraid sometimes."

Josh raised a hand. "If anyone is not part of the Crawford clan, it is me."

"No …" Chris started.

"Let me finish." His voice had a steady authority to it even though his pallor had grown slightly more ashen in recent weeks. Several times, Chris had been on the verge of seeking a medical update from Kay or Jamie but always backed off. Still, they all had noticed this apparent change in his body even if no one verbalized their individual concerns. It was as if expression of their fear might make it real or hearing any evidence of his decline might hasten it in some way. At the end of the day, they were consoled by the fact that his mind seemed unaffected by his flagging body. He was still Jeremiah Joshua Connelly.

"Go ahead, Josh." Kay prompted him.

"I lived much of my life without a family, a functioning family. That was a self-imposed exile I imposed on myself. What an idiot I was. Then, I was bludgeoned into feeling again, mostly by Connie and my sister Rachel. I found I deeply loved both. And I have suffered the inexpressible pain of losing my sister. There is not a day that goes by that my heart does not break at her loss." He paused to collect himself. "But let me say this. Each moment I had with Rachel, really had with her, remains a treasure. That is what love is in the end … the knowledge that loss is inevitable yet irrelevant since you must accept the end, whether in the short or the long term. You simply store the good moments up for what must be endured after the loss. And no matter what scale you use, nor how you calculate things, love is always worth it in the end. Fight among yourself if you must, but never overlook the love that binds you together."

Cate and Connie spent the afternoon fixing up some delicacies for their guests expected that evening. They had decided to take a chance with an odd combination of Jordanian and

Chinese offerings, this after a long discussion about whether it would be safer to just bring in Indian take-out. That, after all, was Josh's favorite but he would not be there. No, they decided in the end to make this a personal affair according to their own tastes. With Josh spending a couple of days in London with the Crawford clan, this was the time, it was thought, to get to know the people to whom Josh was so attached. An evening of food, drink, and conversation was just the ticket, if the choice of cuisine did not put an early end to things.

Josh, Connie, along with Cate and Meena and their two adopted girls had rented a larger, rustic home on the east side of Oxford, not far from the Botanic gardens and Magdalen College. From their front porch, they looked over a green pastoral scene though the urban center of New Marston could be seen in the distance. Cate and Meena in particular thought the arrangement and setting perfect for them. Their girls could be looked after by Connie and Josh when they were sent off to sites in the Mideast to look over ISO projects or help develop the growing emphasis on female education. So far, they were elated to have joined the Crawford world.

As the women fretted about whether something had been overlooked, the doorbell rang. In marched Morris Greenstein, his spouse Carla (Shapiro) Greenstein, Bob Wilson, and Peter Favulli.

"Nice digs," Peter observed as he checked out the appetizers on the dining room table. "Ah, not Indian food I see."

"Is that bad?" Connie asked concerned.

"Hell, no! That's always what Josh forced on us."

Meena beamed. "It's a combination of authentic Jordanian and Chinese dishes."

Peter opened his mouth but said nothing.

Connie stepped in. "Peter, you will eat everything and like it."

"Yes, ma'am," the retired FBI man mumbled. "Wow, you sound just like my Italian mother … and my Italian wife. Frankly, I could never tell them apart."

Mo Greenstein laughed at this point. "Yup, I would bet that Italian, Chinese, and Jewish mothers have a lot in common."

"Yeah," Carla interjected. "They raised useless sons though, in truth, I cannot speak to Chinese moms on that score."

"I can," Connie laughed.

Cate interjected. "Come on. The food's ready. And I have arranged the EMTs to be on call. And if anyone bitches, we can whip up some Irish delicacies … fifty ways of serving potatoes."

They all picked up plates and circled through the offerings. They selected small portions of each to begin, especially the Jordanian offerings. Then, Connie and Meena noticed that they all went back for seconds. The two women laughed out loud when Peter went back for thirds.

"What?" he said defensively. "At least this isn't more of that Indian crap. And besides, you can't get good Italian food in England. Now, come to the North End of Boston …"

"Here we go." Mo sighed. "Anyone have a more interesting topic?"

Cate put down her dish. "Yes! I do. We have an agenda for tonight, beyond torturing Peter that is." She paused as she considered her segue. "We really know so little about you, other than you are Josh's old friends. Sometimes, we get to hear all of you reminiscing, but that just gives us glimpses of a world we know so little about. I don't at least." She paused again. "Here's the thing. My uncle had many colleagues and acquaintances from so many years in academia and the political world. He spent much time with some of these men and women. In the end, though, he wanted to be with you, to share what he has left. But some of this confuses me yet. You knew each other so long ago, and then lost touch for decades … a break that hardly was harmonious. I can't quite figure it all out, the intensity of the attachment."

"Me neither." Connie added. "When I first learned of his medical condition, I wracked my brain about whom he would want to be informed about this. Sure, there were some colleagues but, by that time I knew where his heart lay. I realized that when he talked about people he cared for, it was you guys. So, you, Mo and Carla and Peter, were the first to be called. I missed you Bob because I thought you were still locked up in some monastery. And then, when finally I got around to asking him, the first suggestions out of his mouth were all of you folks. He wanted you to be with him when …"

"You can say it," Cate assured her.

Connie smiled. "When my husband buys the farm." She looked embarrassed at her language, but no one seemed to notice.

"Why does that strike you as strange?" Carla asked.

"Strange?" Connie asked quickly, happy that no one seemed to notice her flippant language.

"That he would want to see us again." Carla added.

"Well, I'm thinking of my own experiences. I can barely recall my friends from back in college." Connie asserted firmly.

"Connie just nailed it," added Cate. "I can recall a few, maybe exchanged a few texts or Facebook posts with some. But there is not even one that I would seek out if I were … in my end days. No, there is something else here. Besides, everyone knows the 60s were the best decade ever, especially if you really got involved in the decade. By that I mean not just doing some drugs and listening to some music. Just ask anyone who lived through it."

Mo and Carla and Bob and Peter looked at one another. It was Bob who started. "Listen, I can say without fear of contradiction that it was not the best decade ever. It did, however, stand out for people like us. It was raw, emotional, tempestuous, and unforgettable. But what is a mystery to me is whether what we recall so vividly was unique in some fashion or whether most experiences of the young are somehow special."

"No," said Meena who surprised herself by speaking out, thinking she had the least to contribute to this conversation. "I mean, think about what was just said. You people bonded in a distinct way. None of us did with the people we knew at a similar age, at least not with the same intensity. I get together with school mates on occasion. They are nice events, but nothing terribly special."

Carla made a noise that drew attention to her. "I think I get it. Listen, I had an uncle. He fought in World War II. His unit was in the Battle of the Bulge, with Patton's troops that relieved Bastogne. Then they fought their way into Germany. Once, only once, did he mention liberating a couple of concentration camps. Both of us being Jewish, I was curious about what he saw and how he reacted. I would ask him. But he would never talk about it … at least with me. And yet, he would get together with other vets from time to time. I knew they talked about such things. And I challenged him … *what can you share with these strangers that you cannot share with me, your family?*"

"And?" someone asked.

"You must understand. He was my favorite uncle, always friendly and smiling. But when I pushed him on this topic, he would look at me with eyes that were focused on something far away. *You could not possibly understand. You should not have to understand.*"

"Wait a minute." Peter said with a mild tone of protest. "We in this group were not at war, not a real war. Okay, I bailed early on you guys but the kids who fought and dodged bullets went off to Asia. We did everything we could to avoid all that, to stop it in fact."

Bob Wilson smiled. "True enough, Peter, but there are the equivalents to war."

"Yes," Mo affirmed.

"You need to explain this, I'm just a WOP that played football with Josh, or against him that is, in high school."

Mo responded quickly. "Not buying that BS, you are damn smart for a WOP and are much more to him than an athletic opponent. Besides, we have talked about this many times before. Why did the protests transform our worlds like they did?"

"Is it any surprise," Bob broke in. "How many kids do something so profound that it disrupts their education, sends them to prison or into exile, and changes their subsequent lives forever."

Peter rose and seemed on his way to bring his plate to the kitchen. "Okay, fair enough, then explain this. I ran away from you guys to a very comfortable middle-class life. Josh never could quite figure out why you forgave him. I could ask the same question. In fact, I will. Why have you forgiven me?"

Peter stood there, frozen halfway to the kitchen as no one filled the silence.

Eventually, Carla spoke. "Well, if you must know we only came to England as part of a plot to do you in. We thought we had a better chance of getting away with it on foreign soil."

"Be serious."

Carla seemed frustrated. "Listen, you moron. None of us knew what we were doing then or how to do it. But that aside, you never abandoned us when we got in trouble for things. I mean you defended Josh from your DOJ buddies who wanted to string him up by his balls. You were so helpful to us when we were caught. Come on, we know you wrote to the judges and prosecutors on our behalf. I mean, you said stupid stuff …"

"Stupid stuff?" Peter queried.

"Yeah, saying crap about us being confused kids but with good hearts, that you knew us, and blah, blah, blah. We could have gotten longer sentences. You did your best and never said a word to us."

"Oh," Peter looked embarrassed. "Shit, there goes my tough guy image."

"Besides, you were one of us. You saw the world as we did. In the end, few others did. Many mouthed the right words, but few had real convictions. And the thing is, we were right, goddamn it. We were."

Suddenly, Carla turned to Connie, Cate, and Meena. "Is this all babble to you? What do you want to know about us, those days?"

Cate cocked her head. "Not babble at all. I've wanted to unlock what is inside my uncle's head for a long time and this is a start. I'm reminded of this movie. It already was a classic by the time I first saw it. What was the title … *American Graffiti*? What struck me was this sense that the characters were living through a period of momentous change, both societal and personal. It was like 1962 or 1963. Some would stay where they were, the Ron Howard character for example. Others would be transformed like the Richard Dreyfus character, or at least be open to new possibilities. The thing was … our college years were a tipping point where little would be the same in the future. Perhaps it is more accurate to call that era an inflection point where both we as individuals, and society at large, went in new directions. Am I right on this?"

"Spot on!" said Carla. "You nailed it. We went through this transformational point in time, which only happens every once in a great while. There is nothing like having your world view challenged, uprooted, and then replaced with something new. It's a breath taking and unsettling experience. You never forget those whom you shared it with."

"For once my wife is right about something." Mo said as he inched beyond Carla's reach.. "Do you have more questions?"

"Oh, just a few dozen more." Cate said. "Just one for now. Did things really change that much, or did you simply imagine they did."

The others pondered her question.

Ali looked up as Deena and Azita entered her office. She embraced a passive aspect, the demeaner associated with a disinterested bureaucrat. As the two visitors sat in chairs on the other side of Ali's large desk, she continued writing on the document in front of her. Azita was about to speak when Ali finally put her pen down and looked up at her visitors. Silence hung between the three until Azita spoke.

"Are you not going to welcome me back?"

Ali remained passive. "Have you been on a trip?"

Azita's expression clouded. "You damn well know where I have been, and what I've been doing."

"How would I?" Ali's face was tinged with anger. "Did you tell me what you were up to? Did you email me, send a memo, text, call, anything? Let me answer that for you … no. I had to hear of it from Karen after you were gone."

"You would have tried to stop me." Azita protested.

"You don't know that." Ali shot back.

Azita paused a moment before speaking "Well, your husband would have, and you would do his bidding. Of that, I am sure."

Ali laughed without humor. "Clearly, you have no idea of my relationship with Chris."

Azita was stung by her use of his name. It struck her as too familiar. "I know my father." The words came out defensively, and Azita chastened herself for not maintaining control.

"And I know my husband." Ali allowed her own composure to slip a bit. "Remember this, we are both related to this man by a legal arrangement. Neither of us is biologically related to him." Ali spoke louder as Azita opened her mouth to speak. "And we both have known him for the same amount of time … actually, I have known him longer since he and I were friends before he met Amar." Again, Ali continued to speak as Azita tried to interject. "Chris, my husband and your father, is a complex man. He has been through a lot in life. Even before he met and fell in love with Amar, he shared some of his trials with me. Don't forget, we were colleagues and, as I said, good friends." Now, Azita made no attempt to interrupt, wondering what the term *good friends* meant. "He told me all about his tyrannical father, the suicide of his older brother who succumbed to the imposing will of the so-called patriarch, the suspicious death of his sister-in law, Kat's coup in taking over the family financial empire, and then the patriarch's irrational revenge that led to the deaths of Richard Jackson, his lifelong friend, and Julianna Jackson, his first real love. He hid all his pain behind that Irish wit of his. You could never tell where he was by looking at him. He would make others laugh over and over as he died bit by bit on the inside."

It was Deena who responded at this point. "Wait, did you love him all those years?"

"That is not the point," Ali's voice rose in irritation. "The point is that the man we all love has lost so much. He seems blessed from the outside, with looks and wealth, and charm. But inside, where few can get to him, he is often a bundle of pain."

"I know ..." Azita tried.

"I am not sure you do." Ali struck back. "If you had, you would not have run off like you did. He was sick with worry when he found out and I mean physically sick. Do you have any idea how much he loves you?"

"Of course..." Azita started.

"Bullshit!" Ali started at her strong reaction. "Sorry about that. Listen Azita, you could have come to us with your plan."

"Our plan," Deena interjected. "I knew all about it. I pushed Azita on. The only reason I didn't go was that my reputation as an education advocate might tip off the authorities there, it would be too dangerous, and that other reason."

"Other reason?" Ali looked at Deena.

"Yes, if things went bad, really awful, only one of us would be ... gone. Less pain for the survivors and, you know, someone to carry on the work and to care for Maddie if her mother was gone."

Ali shook her head slowly. "That was ... thoughtful of both of you."

Azita pushed on. "But we couldn't tell Chris, that is for sure. He would not have let me go and you would have backed him up."

"Think for a moment. You are an adult. You don't need his permission, certainly not mine. You simply didn't want to face him." Ali leaned forward. "And just to set the record straight, I don't know whom I would have backed. In the end, I probably would have taken your side."

"I don't understand..." Azita looked doubtful.

"Saving Muslim girls has become your dream, right? Turning at least some of them into medical professionals has become your guiding vision. I'm right on that, am I not Azita. And you, Deena, you want to create the next generation of Muslim female educators."

Both women responded affirmatively, but their words were low and indistinct.

Ali pushed on. "You realize that you can only heal and save just so many with your own talents and hands. But finding hidden talent and giving others the greatest opportunity imaginable can have exponential effects over time. You see that, feel that, breathe that. Damn it, that is my dream as well. Sometimes I am ashamed by how easy I had it growing up with all kinds of resources and privileges. But that makes it even more important to me to lift those who face real hardships. I've never understood those who have been successful mostly because they started closer to the finish line and then conclude they did it all on their own. How naïve! No, how self-delusional. I think … I think that some of us are drawn to the notion of equality, that we should have a similar place at the start of the race. That cannot be in any absolute sense, of course, but we can make the race just a little less uneven. All I can do is live that dream vicariously, just helping along the way." For the first time, she smiled at Azita, who remained silent as one tear found its way down her cheek.

It was Deena who broke the awkward silence. "Let me ask again, you did not answer the first time. Did you love Chris all those years ago … when you were colleagues?"

"That, my dear, is a very impertinent question … but I will answer it." Ali had a sad look. "No, I don't think so but I'm not sure. It was not for lack of interest, that's for certain. I thought about it a lot. I even considered propositioning him, or at least making a pass. Now that would be outrageous for a good Muslim woman who was being pushed by her family to marry. But, in the end, no, I could not do that. I worried he was too much of what you call a 'player' who could not love a woman seriously. I could never encourage him in any way. I made sure I did not fall for him, not all the way that is."

Deena cocked her head. "I'm still not sure I understand. You were already away from your parent's control, living in a land where no one would possibly care …"

"That sounds naïve to me. I had these doubts about him. Besides, if I struck up a public affair with such a prominent man, who could keep such a thing secret."

"But you could have kept it discrete." Deena persisted.

"I would know. Listen, I may not have been a model Muslim woman, but there are embedded cultural affinities one cannot easily shed. I could never share my body unless it is mutually shared with my heart. I think he understood that. While we both were tempted, at least I was, he kept that part of him aloof. We shared much about our lives but never crossed that physical intimacy line. To seal the matter, he came back from that trip to Afghanistan with Amar and you, Azita. That window was closed to me after that. It simply would have been wrong and, more importantly, I grew to love both of you so much. Amar was such a good woman, so special, and good for him ..." She seemed about to say more but could not.

A second tear made its way down Azita'a cheek. Deena noticed this while chastising herself for leading them down this path. "Perhaps we better listen to what Azita has to say based on her visit. We would need your blessing, Ali, before proceeding."

Ali looked at Azita for several moments without anything being said. It was difficult reading her expression but clearly it had softened from where they had begun. "Yes, I want to hear what you have to say. Never doubt that. But let us not tarry. I have another appointment in an hour, a visitor from Cambridge University.

After Azita and Deena had left, Ali sat while decompressing from what had been a draining meeting. What had happened to her quiet life as an unmarried academic. Then, her only personal burdens came from her family who pestered her about her choice to remain unwed. They had long concluded she was a lesbian though decided silence on the matter was preferable to bringing the issue out into the open. Now things were so complicated.

From her office, she could see the spires and ornate carvings that adorned the roofs of the ancient colleges around her, and the pastoral countryside beyond. Yes, she could have remained sheltered and comfortable in this paradise. But would she have been happy. She had loved this man from afar for so long. Now, he was hers. But was he? His proposal after Amar's sudden death from Covid had surprised her, shocked her. Her dreams of being wedded to this man, born when they were young colleagues, had seemed over for so long … buried under years of repression and neglect. When Amar first passed, the common rumor was that Chris would marry his old flame, the lovely TV personality Julianna Jackson, or Jules as she was universally known. He had grown up with the African American beauty, and it was well known that he had asked her to marry him when both were young. More than that, as Amar lay struggling to breathe at the end, she apparently asked Chris to marry Jules as a personal favor to her. She wanted a woman to take care of Chris and her young girls, Emma and Liz.

Ali had once considered the possibility that Amar apparently never considered her as a suitable mate for her husband. That bothered her at first until she thought on the matter with some objectivity. She held her feelings in check, never displaying what lay in her heart. Amar never had an inkling that Ali walked about with that heaviness of unexpressed love. She felt pride in that, along with some wonder that her display of inner control and discipline came at some unknown price. Of course, Amar must have thought that she was a lesbian, as so many in the college community did. That gave her com-

fort. And now, Amar's brother would be at her door. Ajinder Singh, known as Aji, was an astrophysicist at Cambridge, moving there after several years at the University of Toronto.

Why didn't she mention to her recent visitors that Aji was her next appointment? She had listened intently to Azita and Deena as they discussed the situation in their homeland and possibilities for saving what they could. Ali was sympathetic but kept wondering if they could accept reasonable limits on their dreams. She had also kept an eye on the clock. When the time for his arrival approached, she uttered encouraging words and set up a planning meeting, saying she would need to think on things, especially about how to approach Chris.

Now he was 15 minutes late. She checked her phone, no text or email. She was about to text him when there was a knock on her office door. She felt anxious for some reason.

"Aji, so good to see you again."

"And you, Ali. I have not seen you since the wedding. Sorry about being late, my damn meeting with my colleagues went longer than anticipated."

Ali laughed. "No problem, we all know you can't get academics to shut up, they love the sound of their own voices."

The two spent several minutes exchanging pleasantries, summarizing their research though Aji lost her for a bit in his summary. Then they moved to family and common acquaintances. "In fact, Deena and Azita were here earlier."

"Oh my, I would love to see them."

"You are here for several days I believe. I will make that happen. But there was something Deena asked me earlier that caused me pause. It is a bit delicate, but I hope I can still proceed."

"Of course, anything."

Ali paused but realized she could not back out now. "Okay, Deena asked me if I had loved Chris."

"I assume you do, you agreed to marry him."

"No, back when he was married to your sister, and even before." When Aji said nothing, Ali went on. "Here is what is bothering me. Did your sister ever talk to you about me, about being jealous or having any suspicions about me and Chris? Please be honest. This is extremely important to me."

Aji didn't hesitate. "Yes, she talked about you quite often."

Ali's heart lurched. "In what way?"

Then he smiled, it was a warm, disarming smile. "Often, she would say that if I were not already married, she would have matched me up with you because you were such a wonderful woman. To be honest, she never liked the choice I made all that much."

"But was she jealous? Did I give her any cause for concern? If I did, I had no …"

"Calm yourself. She was confident in Chris's love and affection for her, even if she knew of his wilder early days. They had a good marriage. But she did share some interesting views if I may share them?"

"Of course. I will not let you leave until you do."

Aji smiled again, as Ali considered what effect he must have on his coed students, having that combination of looks, intelligence, and charm. "My sister did talk about you. She could not understand why the two of you had not married early on, before she met him. In her mind, the two of you were perfect for each other, so suitable. You were both academics, in the same general area, sort of. You had similar temperaments, and likes, and she would go on. It was a total mystery to her that he was single when he showed up that day in Afghanistan to, in her words, *fire her ass* for endangering his sister. But not once did she ever, for a moment, express a shred of jealousy toward you. You can trust me on that."

"Thank you, Aji." Ali sensed tension draining away from her. "With the sudden remarriage, I've found myself wondering. Who thinks we had been lovers? If not lovers, does anyone believe I had not been plotting to steal him away from her. I would never, you must …"

"Perish that thought from your mind. "You were nothing but kind and a good friend to my sister, and I thank you for that. I still miss her so much."

"As do I. And dear Aji, she loved you. Many a time, she would look to the evening skies and point out constellations or talk about galactic phenomena. She was proud of you, her younger brother who was so brilliant."

"Odd, I considered her the brilliant one, breaking stereotypes to become a physician." His smile faded a bit. "I just hope that I can be kept as part of the family."

"On one condition, that you spend time with your nieces, Emma and Elizabeth, teaching them about the mysteries of the heavens."

Aji flashed that smile of his one more time. "Try and keep me away."

CHAPTER 16

Farzana

"Education is the most powerful weapon we can use to change the world."

Nelson Mandela

Farzana Balkhi rose well before dawn. She found it difficult to sleep in any case. Too many thoughts swirled in her head, especially on this morning. She would start her quest today. Yes, she had meant to do so on several recent trips into the villages but always hesitated. How could she look into a parent's eyes and suggest that their daughter escape to an unknown world, where they might not see their child for a long time, if ever? She put herself in the parent's eyes. Would she be able to let her child go, even if she believed it would open a new world to them? Then again, how would she know? She had never married, nor had any children of her own. What mothers felt was a mystery to her. That was her starting point for this morning's musing.

Her train of thought often took a circuitous route. This morning was no different. She now thought about her lonely personal life. There had always been excuses for waiting on marriage after a brief engagement early to a man who tragically passed away. After that, she had her schooling, and then she wanted to focus on her teaching and the increasing responsibilities she had been given in the educational programs the Masoud Center offered. She had embraced the education of Muslim girls as passionately as Deena and Azita. Then one day, she realized suddenly that she was too old for marriage by Afghan standards, too educated, too independent. Perhaps if she were living in an urban area, her prospects would not be so bleak. There would be educated men willing to marry a non-traditional woman such as herself.

But she was here. There were educated men for sure, but all were married it seemed. The traditional village males looked upon her as some alien creature. It might be fine for the western women to act like males, but it put them off to see one of their own acting that way. Had she made a good choice? She had the normal curiosities and yearnings of most females, but she could get by without that nonsense, so she had convinced herself. But not having children. That always caught her up. There the emptiness could be felt. That is why she became an educator, to be around the young and give them the same kind of opportunities she was fortunate to enjoy. What could she do with a child of her own?

Then the image of Sayed forced its way into her train of thought. She tried to push it away, she always did. Why? But she knew, it was no mystery. He just might meet her lofty standards. He was educated but never displayed the arrogance that some university men displayed. He was good looking in a somewhat aesthetic way, though she usually dismissed that as unimportant. He was easy to talk with, an advantage they both seemed to enjoy as he accompanied her on their long treks to the villages. These were the journeys where he pretended to be a family member, usually her husband, to give her cover in case Taliban true believers stopped them. She enjoyed their talks, especially about his journey from typical village boy to a university education and popular teacher. The stories about his grandfather, Amooz Aktar, especially intrigued her … the village elder who had fought with the Lion of Panjshir against the Russians and then against the Taliban back in the old days. She recalled him shedding quiet tears as he told her how Amooz died when he stood up to the new wave of Taliban that had swept into his village. What moved her most in that moment was that he was not ashamed of his tears. He had feelings which she found unsettling in a positive way.

Then, she shook her head. She was thinking like a schoolgirl. He was widowed with a daughter to raise while she had been engaged once, but only briefly and very early on. But her betrothed had been a young man she barely knew, nor cared about. More to the point, Sayed had never intimated any interest in her, never once. He was friendly but … so why was he in her head? He had plenty of opportunity, on their long ventures in the countryside as they drove from village to village. It struck her that he had veered their conversations away from what might be considered delicate topics.

NO! It was clear. He had no interest in her. Perhaps he had his eye on another prospect for a future wife. There were many in the camp who had lost husband or were just coming of age, at least if he were interested in a younger wife. And why wouldn't he want a young one. Isn't that what all men wanted. Yes, she was thinking like a romantic schoolgirl, and that thought bothered her. She was past that, was she not? Perhaps, just below the surface, he was like all men, only interested in sex and someone to cater to his needs.

She pushed him out of her thoughts and back to the girls she would see today. She had run through various narratives in her head, some she had rehearsed with Azita when she was here, and they discussed what seemed like a wild and improbable plan back then. Azita had admitted that she had not cleared it with the people in England and this could never work without their support. While she sounded confident, Farzana had her doubts and kept waiting for word that the whole thing was off. Now, today, she would test the waters. If no one could be found on this end, it mattered not what England said. It would be off.

⁂

Sayed also stirred early. He had trouble sleeping ever since the day he was forced to flee his village. His waking hours were troubled by waves of guilt and regret.

He constantly asked himself whether he should have stayed, fought for his grandfather and his family. Then he would reason that his grandfather, Amooz, wished to die on that day, knowing full well that living once again under the Taliban was unacceptable. The warrior who had gunned him down had done him a favor. Yes, Sayed was sure of that. Amooz might well have consciously baited this man to give his grandson time to escape, knowing that educators and so-called intellectuals were seen as enemies of the new regime, particularly out in the countryside. Sayed was known to be critical of the Taliban and their potential return to power.

But what about his wife? Had he not abandoned her to her death? That was unforgivable. Yet, there had been no time in the moment. Nor was there any reason to assume she was in trouble. She was not a threat to these men. She had briefly educated young girls but did not stand out in any way. He had been critical of the new leaders, not her. He assumed he could slip away and come back in a day or so, a week at the latest.

He never did discover what went wrong, or why she was assassinated? Was she shot, like his grandfather, or beheaded or hanged as if she had committed some unspeakable offense? In his worst imaginings, she had been taken by one of these men, maybe several. When she refused to let them have their way with her, she was beaten before being raped several times. Sayed could imagine her calling out for him, but he was nowhere around. Then they would take her somewhere to shoot her, better not to have a witness and who amongst the browbeaten villagers could object. Even if he were there, what might he do? He was no warrior. He was a man of intellect and sensitivity. What could he have done, useless as he was? He had never fired a gun in anger. Perhaps that is why no one from the village confirmed or denied his worse imaginings. They might not really know, or they might be silent since that seemed the kinder path to take. Perhaps it was a conspiracy of compassionate silence … since telling Sayed the truth would break him, his guilt and despair might overwhelm him.

Was he not broken already? Telling him the truth would merely put an end to his restless mind searching over and over about things he could not prove or disprove. That is a special agony. Especially at night, during his fitful bouts of sleep. He could see his wife searching for him, pleading for his help. He would cry out to her, 'look my dear, I am here.' But she would never see him, even as the shadowy woman looked at him, through him. Why couldn't she see him. Perhaps it was conscious on her part, more rejection than a failure of sight. Perhaps she wanted to punish him for his lack of courage, his abandonment of her to a fate worse than death. Is it not a man's duty to protect his wife? And what had he done, fled under the rationale that he could always return for her. His sense of shame would rise until his throat constricted to the point where taking in oxygen was impossible. As he approached unconsciousness, he would spring awake gasping for breath. He regretted the fact that he was yet alive.

He checked his phone as the dawn suggested itself over the eastern hills. He noticed a text from Farzana. He sensed a frisson of excitement course through him. He noticed such a reaction of late and didn't like it. He needed to discipline himself better. The message merely asked if he were awake yet. *Did she sleep even less than he?* Still, it suggested she was thinking of him, even at this hour of the day. He poised over his keyboard but didn't press any of the buttons. To do so would be to engage with her. That was easy in the beginning, when he was asked to accompany her as she visited female students in the villages and towns throughout the valley. He felt useful doing so, and it gave him a purpose again, an educational purpose now that he was torn from his life's avocation. It was less easy now. He knew why, yet tried to suppress that realization?

He recalled feeling awkward around her at first, his efforts to interact coming across as stilted and forced inside his head. But she did not seem to mind and easily kept their conversation going as they moved from one household to another on their mentoring tours of the Panjshir Valley. It was not long before they knew of each other's pasts and future aspirations. Both were struck by the similarities of what had been, other than the fact that Sayed had been married and had a daughter. It amazed Sayed how comfortable their interactions had become except for the one line he could not cross, nor fully admit to himself. He could not verbalize his growing interest in this woman. To him, that felt like a sin. It was too soon after the death of his wife, which yet felt raw to him and for which he felt so much guilt. No, he could not go there now. Could he ever?

An hour later, he pulled up to Farzana's living quarters to begin their day. The sun had almost peaked over the hills now, the overhead sky a continuous distribution of color from light blue in the east to deep purple in the west. The air was fresh yet dominated by the brittle chill of the high desert night. The debilitating heat of summer was still weeks off, but it would come with inexorable certainty. Already, the semi-arid land to the south toward the capital already showed signs of torpor that dominated summer.

Farzana emerged carrying two boxes. Both were labelled with the Muslim version of the Red Cross symbol to suggest that medical supplies were inside. She nodded to Sayed in a way suggesting there were more to retrieve. Farzana arranged the boxes strategically, placing the educational materials in places where access was more difficult. The ones containing real medical supplies went toward the top. This was a *'just in case'* tactic, if they were stopped by Taliban officials or, more likely, those working with them to earn some money. As the rural areas became more economically desperate, villages were turning on one another to survive. This had worked so far. When questioned, they told inquisitors that they were from the Masoud Center and distributing basic medical supplied to smaller villages so that those experiencing minor ailments might avoid a long trek to the Center for help. Farzana had been around the Center long enough to convincingly chat about what they were delivering and how the materials could be used. Two or three times, a *'donation'* proved necessary. Both Farzana and Sayed wondered for how much longer their subterfuge might work.

Farzana checked the vehicle, now overflowing with materials, one last time before speaking.

"Listen Sayed, let us chat before we leave."

"Of course."

Farzana hesitated. "We start today."

"Start?" He asked, knowing the answer since she had shared her secret earlier.

"Yes, with some of these girls, the best ones, the ones with families who might be … willing, I am going to bring up the subject, the possibility, that Azita Masoud discussed with me, with us."

Sayed made a sound that was not a sound. "When we talked about such things when she was here, it all seemed exciting. Then again, I suppose I never considered we might try it for real. It seemed to me too far-fetched. Besides, you told me she was here on her own. The people in England in charge of the Masoud Center were not on board. It seemed more like fantasy to me."

"I'm still not sure it will really happen, but she wants me to try as a test case. Just me, and that means you as well of course. She wants to know if any of the families will go along with this. There is a price to pay, and a risk. Perhaps the alarm will be raised. And if no one is interested, willing to take the risk, this crazy dream will be at an end before it starts. And we might end up in prison or worse for a lost cause. If lucky, we might only get off with a beating, but this could result in something much worse." She need not fill in the details.

"And if they, the families I mean, are … interested?" Sayed already knew the answer.

"Azita and Deena believe the top people in England will go with this … this crazy idea of getting more young girls out of the country. Already, some parts of the larger plan are starting. Did you notice the helicopter landings? It has been arranged, with the usual bribes, that medical supplies will be brought in this way, directly from Pakistan, not by laborious trucks through Kabul. The local Taliban has been convinced that this is in their best interests, more supplies are needed to meet a growing demand for help. More than medicines will be delivered, food and other essentials to keep body and soul together. I mean, they have reservations, but they are okay with things now."

Sayed looked puzzled for a moment until it fell into place for him. "Ah, loaded helicopters arrive that should be empty when they return, but they won't be."

"Exactly, and while our vigilant overseers might check the first few flights, it should be routine by the time we start moving our special cargo." Then Farzana's demeaner turned ominous. "All this sounds fine on paper. But I must be honest with you, Sayed. The risks are great."

"For all of us, but for you especially." He protested.

She reached out and took his hand. "I long ago prepared myself for the worst but I have only myself to look after. You have a daughter. She will need you." Farzana took a deep breath. "Once I start talking to the families, anything can go wrong. I am trying to select families very carefully but who knows. I may guess wrong, or word may spread no matter how careful we are. My worst fear is that a desperate family will turn us in for money."

"Wait, are you asking me to stop helping you?"

She looked steadily into his eyes. "Yes, in a way ... yes, of course I am. I have no right ..."

He cut her off. "You really believe I would go away and have you do this craziness on your own?"

She wanted to say yes, unequivocally. She wanted desperately to protect him, keep him from harm's way. Instead, she said weakly, "No, I don't want you to go away." She gripped his hands with more force. "But I cannot tolerate the thought of any harm coming to you, of leaving your daughter an orphan."

He pulled back from her, disengaging his hands. "Listen to me. Listen carefully. I love my daughter more than anything in life. But don't you see, that's the very reason I also must do this … for her. Think about it. Do I want her to grow up in a world where she is forced to be ignorant, perhaps beaten into submission as a second-class citizen, barely even that if these monsters get their way? I don't want her buried in suffocating clothing every time she leaves the house. I certainly don't want her being totally submissive to some man who can oppress her and abuse her without consequence. No, never, I shall not leave her to that kind of world. Do you understand." His eyes were fierce, emboldened with a fire Farzana had not seen before.

"I understand," she said quietly, now embarrassed by her pathetic attempt to *'save'* him. That was so presumptuous of her, even arrogant. But another feeling suffused her body, leaving her equilibrium unsettled. He was stronger than she realized. He had always been diffident toward her, she had to work to get him to open up. He would share facts about himself but not feelings. Moreover, he seldom questioned her decisions which was nice in one way, and not so nice in another. This was a new and bolder side of the man.

"You can order me away, of course. I would never force myself on you" He caught what he had just said, hoping that it would not be interpreted in the wrong way. "Otherwise, I am in this to the end, no matter what that end might be."

Farzana exhaled, unsure if this was really a pyrrhic victory. "Thank you. Frankly, I'm not sure what I would have done had you listened to me … you know, when I told you to go away."

Sayed smiled back. "Well, I support treating women with dignity and equality. That means rejecting what they say if it is stupid."

"Stupid!" Farzana was about to protest when she caught his broad smile and merely wagged a finger at him while smiling back. "One more thing. We may go far afield today. I am starting with a few select girls, the better candidates, at least in this direction." She pointed north. "I cannot guarantee we can make it back by nightfall."

Sayed wondered if his face betrayed any reaction as he understood what was unstated in her message. "I understand," is all he said.

The main road was easy enough to traverse. They travelled in silence, each focusing on their own thoughts. The air was warming quickly, and Farzana shed the blanket she had thrown over herself. The hills about her were becoming more pronounced, the more distant mountains more distinctive. Spring flowers could be seen, adding color to the normally drab environment. Still, her land was never drab in her eyes. She had read somewhere that people come to love what is familiar to them. English people are passionate about their bucolic, green countryside. Arabians and Persians find great beauty in the sweeping desert landscape. The Swiss cannot imagine anything but majestic mountains. Islanders find serenity in water and waves. Perhaps that is why she loved this land so, why she had trouble imagining leaving. It had been imprinted on her soul when she was so young.

"You are going to tell me when to turn off?" Sayed's voice broke into her reverie.

"Yes," she snapped to, looking about for some sign that would indicate their location. In half a mile, we go to the left."

As they made their way over secondary roads, Sayed continued their conversation. "I came across an article about some brave teachers during World War II. What you are doing reminds me of them, at least in some ways."

"Really?" Farzana was curious. "How so?"

"In Norway, after the Nazis took over that country, they put a puppet ruler in charge … Quisling was his name I believe. Anyway, the new government ordered all teachers to pledge their allegiance to Hitler and then teach obvious Nazi propaganda. Some 10,000 teachers refused to do it, almost all of them. After the schools were shut down in response to their refusal, many continued to teach in private homes, just like you and the others have been doing."

"What happened to them?"

"Ah, it wasn't pretty." Sayed now sounded reluctant.

"No, tell me." She insisted.

"The regime arrested most of them and sent them to camps where they were abused and tortured. The regime tried to break them. As I said, not pretty."

"I see." Farzana said quietly. "Definitely not pretty."

"But it didn't work. That is the good part. They were released after a year or so and permitted to return to their teaching positions. Not so bad … in the end."

Farzana said nothing, simply thought on his story. Eventually, they pulled into an area with several larger farms. Most villages were poor, primitive, but these holdings were more affluent and established. Sayed wondered if some of the owners were professionals who dabbled in farming as a sidelight.

"Perhaps we should have discussed this earlier, but should I remain with you? You will talk with the mother, correct?"

"Yes, and the selected daughter." Then she paused a moment as if first considering this though, in truth, she had thought this through more than once. "I will start alone, first going through our normal lesson. But I will shift quickly enough, feel my way toward suggesting a different path for this daughter. In truth, I have no idea how they will respond. But, if it goes well, we must involve the father. If you can, spend time with him, talk about his crops or livestock or whatever men talk about."

Sayed laughed. "I'm an educator. I know little about such things, you know … practical things."

She smiled at him. "Oh, you are a clever man. I'm sure you can fake it."

He smiled back. "You would have a better chance at faking it. Aren't women better at that."

Farzana found herself blushing in response but was saved as the student in question bounded out of her house, excited to see Farzana. She was about 12 years old, with a roundish body, large eyes, and a nose that seemed a bit small for the rest of her face. She still sported her baby fat, also a sign of affluence, but was exuberant and inquisitive which made her an attractive candidate and a delight to be around. Farzana thought that if she failed here, perhaps the entire scheme would quickly unravel. She had picked this family for a reason.

"Moska, how good to see you." She gave the girl a big hug. "You reflect your name; you must realize that. You are a huge smile wherever you are."

"You have told me that before," the girl giggled.

"And it remains true. Let us see your mother."

Inside, the mother brought tea and cakes for her guest. The three chatted about general things for a while, a custom that should not be overlooked. Then Moska's mother said, "I fear I am taking too much of your time. You must have many visits to make but I love your company."

Farzana took a breath. "Yes, I do have several visits." Another pause. "I am not just here for Moska's lessons, though I do have some materials for her. "There is another matter, an important one that might require a big sacrifice of you. For that, can I speak to you alone. Moska, can you leave us for just a few minutes while I chat with your mother."

The mother was confused but sent her daughter off with some new reading materials to keep her occupied. "This sounds important."

"Important and confidential. What I am to share with you must remain between us. I cannot stress the importance of this. You will see how big a problem this is if the wrong people were to find out." Farzana watched as the mother's eyes narrowed.

"Tell me what is on your mind."

Farzana took a deep breath. "I want you to consider permitting your daughter to leave."

"To leave the village? That has always been my hope, to send her for more education in the city. It will be painful for me but such an opportunity for her. She loves learning."

"No," Farzana said softly, hoping that Moska was not listening just outside the door. "I mean leave the country." She waited as the woman's eyes now widened first in disbelief and then in an expression difficult to interpret. "You might not see her for a long time."

"Perhaps not ever." The woman said as if speaking from far away.

Farzana thought about lying at this point, or at least obfuscating things. She could not. If there was a time for honesty, this was it. "Yes, perhaps not ever … it all depends. We hope not but I cannot lie to you."

There was a long pause, seemingly an eternity went by as Farzana waited for this woman to order her out. It suddenly struck her with full force what she would be asking of these families. How could she have been so arrogant, so self-interested. How dare she ask a woman to make such a sacrifice? Did only her needs matter. She was about to beg forgiveness and flee when the woman spoke. "Speak to me more about this."

Farzana laid out what she knew about the scheme, which mostly focused on how they would get the chosen girls out of the country. It was not long before it was decided to bring in Moska and her father. Sayed also joined the larger discussion, happy not to be faking an interest in agriculture any longer, a subject about which he knew little. He was certain his deficiency of knowledge had been detected immediately. The family raised many issues, where would Moska go, who would take care of her. And how could they afford such a venture. They also raised concerns such as Moska's limited English. For most, Farzana could fall back on the example of previous girls who had gone overseas and, to the extent that Farzana knew such details, where some had gone to school, their living arrangements, and how they were doing. Farzana kept looking at Moska who stared back with apprehension and excitement. The things being discussed were beyond her imagination yet part of a world about which she had long dreamed."

Finally, the father said that they must bring others in on such a decision. "No" Farzana insisted. "We must keep this discussion among ourselves. I beg you. Our lives, Sayed's and mine, may rest on secrecy. I am sorry but I must insist."

"I understand," the father said gravely, torn between wanting to provide his daughter a better life yet wondering how he could send his offspring into the unknown. This was a decision beyond his experience. Could he make it on his own? What would the others say? How might he explain it? What consequences would fall upon them."

For several long moments, no one said anything. Farzana hesitated between talking more and forcing some indication about their reaction. This was taking longer than she anticipated. There was no way she could visit the number of families she had on her list in one day. The awkwardness of spending a night with Sayed probably was unavoidable. The obvious now was clear to her. How could she have expected anyone to respond to such an extraordinary and unanticipated suggestion so quickly. Farzana realized she had lost track of how much time had passed in which the father and mother whispered to one another.

Their side conversation was interrupted by Moska's clear voice. "Mama, Papa, I want to go."

"But my dear..." her mother started.

"No, you have always told me to be brave. You have always said that I was worth something, that I was special. Do you think I have any chance showing that I am such now that the Taliban is in control? No, I must go."

In her heart, Farzana knew the decision had been made.

Farzana shared more information before moving to depart when the mother asked her to speak privately. "Where do you go next." The mother asked. When Farzana mentioned another settlement nearby, the mother raised her hand. "Wait, come with me to the home of my friend. She also has a daughter who has been to your schools at the Masoud Center. Her daughter is younger, so perhaps you do not know her, but we all know she is very gifted. Yes, Allah has blessed her for sure."

Farzana hesitated. She knew this girl, had heard she was a quick learner, but had never taught her personally. Should she go with the list she had carefully prepared beforehand or go where Providence might lead. She made a quick decision. "Show me the way."

Sayed had grown increasingly uncomfortable as Farzana pushed to visit one more home and then one more. Finally, when she suggested one final visit, he expressed his concern. "It soon will be too dark to return. You have us well off the main roads. Travel at night would be dangerous, if not robbers then the Taliban. They will be very suspicious of travellers in this part of the country at night."

Farzana replied with more confidence than she felt. "I have thought of that. There is a place not far from here, for travellers. We can eat there, and they rent rooms."

Sayed grunted. "I am famished, that is true."

Farzana laughed. "Just like a man, thinking of his stomach."

"And how would you know about men, you have never been married." His words were meant to be light, a way to break the tension he felt, but they came out with more of a bite than intended. He wanted to apologize but was not sure of the right words. He remained silent.

Other than giving directions, they said nothing until darkness fell as they reached their destination. "Before we go in, understand something. We are supposed to be man and wife, so we must get only one room."

"Oh, I had not thought of that." He mumbled.

"That is hard to believe. I thought you were a man. And I know about men because I have brothers, messy and smelly creatures that they are." When he tried to respond, she talked over him. "About the one room, you can have the bed, I can sleep on the floor. I have a sleeping bag in the back, two actually."

He said nothing in the moment but went about arranging for a room for him and his *'wife,'* as well as food to be brought to the room. When casually asked about his journey, he vaguely said something about travelling to see an ill family member to the north and having trouble with his vehicle on the way which slowed them up. He tried to look normal throughout the transaction but could not help feeling he was betraying his inner guilt. *'They must see I am lying.'* If the proprietor had, he revealed nothing.

They ate in silence for a while. Finally, Sayed said, "You did a wonderful job today. I was sure no one would respond to this crazy scheme. But there were several. Perhaps some will drop out but who knows? When some agree, others may find the courage."

Farzana already was chagrined at her reaction to his earlier comment about her never being married. That was small and petty of her but his observation, while clearly made in jest, did hit home. She pushed herself to get past her hurt. "Yes, *we* did well today. You were exceptionally good with the fathers. They likely would not listen to me. Thank you."

"No, all of this is your doing. I am a follower."

She hesitated, then spoke her mind. "You are not like the men I've known at all."

A pained expression briefly crossed his face, then he burst out laughing. "I was very wrong about you. You are a quick study of men."

Her laughter came a moment latter. "It is not such a skill. Men are simple, easy to understand."

Instead of responding, Sayed checked his phone and smiled. "I can't believe we still get a signal here. The British and Americans did leave us with one thing, a good communications infrastructure."

“That undoubtedly served their interests,” Farzana noted. “But you are smiling.”

“Yes, my daughter is doing well tonight. She is old enough to miss me.”

“Wow, I am embarrassed, but I don’t even know her name. Tell me about her, about your wife whom you have lost, and about yourself. We have been together much, talked much, yet I know so little about you.”

Sayed paused until Farzana was certain he would say nothing. Then he started, focussing on his daughter. “Her name is Esrin, such a beautiful girl.”

“Esrin?” Farzana echoed. “Does that not mean an inspirational woman?”

“Yes. And she will be if she has some opportunities.”

“And your wife, is it painful to talk about her. Her loss must be so great.”

He paused, “It is painful mostly because I feel such guilt. I will be honest. I loved her in a way, but not completely. I think something was missing. You see, it was an arranged marriage. Oh, I was an educated man, at university in Kabul, so my family sought out a beautiful girl for me and educated to a modest extent. She could teach the younger girls starting an education and they loved her. She was extremely sweet.”

Farzana thought, *‘sweet? Not like the sarcastic harpy I am.’* What she said was, “she sounds quite lovely, but you were not happy. Is that what I’m hearing?”

"Not so much unhappy as … unfulfilled. That is why I … like being … around you," he stumbled over his words. "You are quick and understand so much."

"For a woman?"

"No, no!" He was flustered so she decided to end his discomfort by remaining silent.

"Hah," Farzana exclaimed, "that is not such an excellent quality in a woman. You have wondered why I have never married. Think on it for a moment. It is not such a mystery. I am too independent, too picky, too outspoken. I would never marry just to have a husband, nor have one selected for me. My stubborn nature caused such a rift in my family."

"I find that a positive thing."

"Then you are a minority of one. I would rather die than marry just to be married. I would need a man who shared my values, my vision in life. Such men are not so easy to find. When I was in university, there were couple of possibilities. But I had been around the women at the Masoud Center too long, they spoiled me. They trained me to value and protect my independence. For me, that meant waiting until I could be my own woman and knew what I wanted. The western women did not marry early. Then, one day, it was too late, or so it seemed. The good ones had already married, and I was back north, doing something I loved but alone."

"But' Sayed said carefully, realizing he was treading in dangerous waters, "you seem happy in what you are doing."

"I love the Center, the teaching, the girls, all of that. But now the girls are mostly gone, banished to their villages. And I have … none of my own." Farzana could not believe she revealed this to this man she was only now getting to know. She quickly changed topics. "I am genuinely concerned. Today went well, much better than I expected. At the same time, this creates more risk. All vowed to keep our secret, but how likely is that. If nothing else, the girls will share the most exciting thing in their lives with their friends, even with the risks. From now on, we live on borrowed time. The Taliban kill for so-called sins much less extreme than what we are doing. I am ready, I assume you have thought this through, but I am thinking of Esrin. If you were not in her life …"

"I have given this thought as well. There are family members …"

"I want to suggest something else." Farzana cut him off. "I talked with Deena about this, thinking ahead, before I even asked you to take these risks."

"You did?" He looked at her with open admiration.

"Just listen. If the worst happens, they will get Esrin to England. They have already discussed this possibility with a woman named Cate and her partner," Farzana was reluctant to say the partner was a woman. "Cate has worked in the middle east and her partner is a Muslim."

"Go no further," Sayed said. "You have taken a great weight off me."

They continued to talk about themselves and what might be in their immediate future until they could no longer put off the issue of sleeping arrangements. Farzana spoke first. "You take the bed; I will use my sleeping bag."

"Never," he responded with unusual authority. "I am the man here. You take the bed. See, I was right, you know nothing about men."

She reacted for a nanosecond before seeing his broad smile. "Yes, my master," as she laughed aloud.

Later, she lay in the bed hearing him turn over and over trying to get comfortable. She weighed her options, and her conflicted feelings for several more minutes. Then out it came, perhaps without a real decision inside her head. "Get up here."

"But," he stammered.

"For Allah's sake, get up here now. Or neither of us will get any sleep."

Sayed slowly rose and slid into the bed next to her. He kept himself as far away from her as possible, clearly risking a fall and injury. She lay there, thinking through how she had managed to get into this situation. In truth, she knew even if the truth were obscured by much cultural baggage.

Slowly, she reached across in the total darkness and found his hand. She expected him to pull his away. He did not … and then she knew.

CHAPTER 17

Conversations

"Do a good deed and throw it in a river; one day it will be given back to you in the desert."

Rumi

Kristen *'Kay'* Crawford entered the small café patterned after coffee shops that are ubiquitous in the States. *'That is the problem with the modern world,* she said to herself, *everything looks pretty much the same no matter where you go.'* That was not precisely true, but it seemed so to her. Looking about, she saw Professor Shaheed Al-Hussein at a corner table. They exchanged waves before Kay went to the counter, ordered a sweet role and beverage, and made her way to the same location.

"Oh Ali, I blame you. You are the occasion of my sin," Kay said as she settled in.

"What sin?" Ali asked, confused.

Kay looked longingly at the plate in front of her. "Look at this sweet roll. It must have 1,000 calories. And will I enjoy it?" She paused for half a second. "That was a rhetorical question. No, I won't. With each bite, I will feel my hips expanding, my thighs exploding, and my bum becoming grotesque."

Ali laughed, reminding herself that all the Crawfords had this wicked wit. Chris might be the worst of them, but Kay was not far behind with Kat rushing to catch up. Ali surmised that the female members of the clan sharpened their verbal jousting skills in a desperate attempt to hold their own with their surviving male sibling. It was fight back or be devoured.

"You exaggerate. You still look marvellous ..." Ali said and meant it.

"For a middle-aged woman you mean." Kay grimaced. "However, we are not here to chat about my fading beauty and figure. You had something on your mind I believe."

Ali was taken aback by the abrupt shift in the conversation. She had asked Kay to join her and suddenly doubted that decision. Her concerns seemed so trivial while she knew Kay was a busy woman. Suddenly, Ali wished to disappear but that was not possible. All the opening lines she had practiced while waiting were gone. The only thing she could come up with was the topic most on her mind, "Do you think your brother loves me."

"Chris?"

"Do you have any others?" then Ali cringed slightly as she remembered that there was an elder male sibling who had committed suicide many years ago.

Kay seemed not to notice Ali's discomfort. "Of course he does ... I think ... has he said anything differently ... he's not cheating on you, is he?"

Ali raised a hand. "Hold on, I started this badly. I even practiced beforehand and still am making a mess of it. I'm much smarter than I'm showing right now."

Kay laughed, "when it comes to matters of the heart, we are all idiots. This comes from the mature woman who married a man, then divorced him and took up with a woman, only to realize that was a mistake and then remarried the same man. And you are coming to me for advice?"

Ali smiled at this. "True enough. I did not think this through. But you are here, so let me try to get this out, and this is just for you. Understood?"

"Of course." Kay leaned in as this had taken an unanticipated turn.

Ali sighed. "I was the woman who was whispered about in my family. You know, the one that they were sure was a lesbian so it was good she lived in England where she could not be an embarrassment to everyone. But I was not … a lesbian that is. It was more like I would never settle and was into my career. Time passed and one day I woke up and found the few interesting men were married … except one."

"Chris."

"Yes." Ali looked embarrassed.

Kay repressed a smile, but not completely. "I'm sorry. I have a bit of a problem thinking of my twin as George Clooney."

"Some days, I have the same issue." Ali chuckled, trying to keep her tone light. "We crossed paths often, perhaps intentionally on my part. On occasion, we would attend lectures together, had a few casual lunches, but it never progressed beyond friendship. The thing is, I wanted more, and there seemed to be a lot of tension."

"Why didn't you approach him or jump his bones?" Kay caught herself. "Wait, was that too forward?"

"Not at all but you must know that is impossible. I could never, not even hint as much. And as far as jumping anyone's bones …"

"Bad choice of words," Kat stammered, "sometimes I forget you are from a civilized culture."

Ali smiled. "You can't shock me. I just never heard the expression before though I can surmise the meaning."

"OMG!" Kay said as if experiencing an epiphany. "Then Chris suddenly married Amar and you have been suffering since."

"Oh, please know that I loved Amar as a sister and was happy for him, but yes. Still, there was this silent sense of loss, maybe a missed opportunity for these many years. I assumed it was the last opportunity."

"You are good at hiding things. I doubt anyone ever guessed. But I'm not seeing your problem. He proposed to you very soon after Amar's passing. We all were a bit taken aback but not shocked. We all could see he was very fond of you though no one guessed it might be reciprocated. We considered you too sophisticated to fall for his so-called charms." Kay flashed her own impish charm.

"I'm surprised. I felt everyone was walking around assuming that we had been having an affair all those years, something I hoped Amar never believed."

"She did not, that I can say with certainty."

Ali looked relieved. "What keeps nagging at me is why did he propose when he did. There had been so many opportunities in the past, before Amar. I cannot recall us even holding hands. There were moments when our hands would touch and neither of us pulled away."

"Wow, that's hot." The words escaped Kay as she raised her hands in a half apology.

"No, it is more sad than funny, G rated for sure. But I can't … I can't help thinking he proposed only for the children's sake or some other reason that has little to do with me. Kay, I don't want half a man. Can you understand that? I have too much pride."

Kay sat back, realizing she would have to respond with care. "The short answer is … yes. He loves you, at least in my humble opinion. But you want more than that." She collected her thoughts. "My brother seems simple on the surface, always with a quick joke. The real man is much more complex. If you had grown up in our dysfunctional family, then you would begin to understand. I always thought he was so scarred by what he saw in our home that he could never imagine having a loving home himself. You should have seen him as a young man. He ran away from commitment like it was the plague, going from one woman to another but always feeling guilty afterward. He started using escorts at one point, easier he said, easier to walk away after, he clarified. I wasn't very close to him during this period, but I could feel his pain from afar. Then again, the whole family was in pain. We all used humor to hide things, he most of all."

"I'm not sure that answers my question," Ali interjected.

"I know but listen to me. Chris was beginning to find himself, what he was all about, here at Oxford. He came into his own as he put together his ISO and found, to his surprise and my shock, that it worked. He had already separated himself from his father, we all had but especially Chris. In fact, setting up his organization was partly driven by his need to do something his father would hate. When it succeeded, I think he felt he could be a whole man, a complete man. My guess, more a strong feeling really, is that he might have been working his way up to proposing to you. I'll bet you were his first choice, but he had to get past all his negative feelings toward the seductive illusion of domestic bliss. He had never seen any of that in our home, and he just could not believe it could be real. Let's face it, he was damaged goods."

"I think you're just making this up, to appease me or make me feel better."

"No," Kay said sharply, "I wouldn't do that. And then, the trip to the Panjshir Valley happened. All my fault, I had joined Amar and Pamir Masoud, Azita's dad. This was during the worst days of 2001 when the fighting between the Taliban and the Northern Alliance was at its most intense. Chris went crazy with worry for me. He may insult me all the time, but he loves me fiercely."

"That is not a secret." Ali interjected.

"Anyway, he flew in ready to read me the riot act and fire Amar, whom he had never met in person. We will never know what happened, other than it was a miracle. Circumstances, a seminal moment in time, the playfulness of the gods, but he wound up marrying Amar and adopting Azita. He went from rogue bachelor and *bon vivant* to married man and father in an instant. And I think … I think he also fell in love with the work he was supporting. I'm guessing here, but up to that moment it had all been an intellectual exercise to him, could he pull this initiative off and piss off his right-wing father, the patriarch and autocrat of our dystopian family. Then, in that moment, he knew why he was really doing all this, what he was meant to do. It may have been the first time he really felt genuine passion."

"And love … for Amar."

Kay looked away for a moment. "No, well perhaps. But not just that. He found his larger purpose in that valley, something beyond torturing his father. Amar just happened to be there. I'm not saying he didn't love Amar, deeply, but I now sense he may never have stopped loving you, though I doubt he ever was conscious of his feelings. It's all so complicated and men … they can be so shallow. Can you understand?"

Ali looked at Kay across the table. She said nothing.

Chris walked into the main offices of his international organization. He was shocked by the number of unfamiliar staff and new faces that were helping run his program. He stopped to look at a large map on one wall, different colored pins were placed in a host of places across the middle east, South Asia, and into Africa. He quickly determined that the colors represented the array of services being offered in each site. He was startled. He had started so small, and now look at what it had become.

Carlota Ciganda appeared beside him. "Are you lost sir? I don't seem to recognize you."

"Hah, hah, but I'm worried. Looking at this map, will I have any money left to support my debauched lifestyle."

"Not after you pay for the wild parties we have at your expense." Carlota smiled broadly.

After Karen, she had always been one of his favorite managers. She was quick, yet competent, attributes he valued in staff. He was losing touch, stretched too thin. This bothered him more these days. He needed to spend more time here, reconnect with his staff.

Then he noticed Luke Geoghegan approaching. "Are you taking my money as well," Chris greeted him.

"Of course," Luke had a sheepish, somewhat sleepy smile that belied his intelligence, "but not too much. I'm still with Toynbee Hall, only here to coordinate services for the London Muslim community."

"I've got to have all of you down to Oxford soon, so we can all get reunited. But now, I've got to see the big boss. Is she in?"

Luke smiled. "Good that you don't confuse yourself with the 'big' boss."

A moment later he was entering Karen Fisher's private office. "I'm just here checking on my troublesome employees."

She looked up in surprise. "I have mirror around here someplace, look into that and you'll find him." Then she smiled. "This is a surprise. How did you know I'd be in and available?"

"Did you forget, I have access to the calendars of all senior management."

"That?" Karen scoffed. "Hell, we keep that filled in just to fool you into thinking we are working hard. Wait, are you here to yell at me again?"

Chris did not answer. Rather, he walked around her desk where she rose to give him a big hug. Releasing her, he said, "I can't believe how far you have come. You were little more than a brash and uncultured shit when you walked in for that interview way back when."

She raised a hand. "Stop there, we are not revisiting that interview when you were on the verge of chucking me out the door until I stunned you with an honest answer."

"Fair enough, but I worry about you. I know others are trying to steal you away and I keep going off and yelling at you. That makes me a class A dummy."

"Sit," Karen said. "I'm sure you didn't stop by to state the obvious?"

Chris smiled weakly. "Obvious or not, I have an important question. I want to know if you are you happy here, with the organization, with me, and with yourself."

"That's four questions."

He looked at her seriously. "Let's start with yourself. Sometimes, I wonder if I've robbed you of a life. You are alone. You work 70 plus hours a week, or that's what your calendar indicates."

"Ah," Karen laughed, "the fake calendar is working."

Chris remained serious. "I still recall way back when I had to go to the States when my brother died, err, killed himself. You were just my PA then and I dragged you along. Somehow, that was a final straw that broke up your relationship with your partner at the time. I think that was the night you stayed with me in bed, you said you couldn't be alone. I never forgot that. You must have been hurting badly. You've had other relations since then, including my sister Kay but, in the end, you are alone. I cannot think that the demands of this job are robbing you of a life."

"Wait, with all the crap going on, this is your worry … my love life?"

"Yes, because it is more than just a love life. We both know that." Chris looked at her steadily.

"You are right about one thing. I have been offered more money, quite a bit more, and for work that is less demanding. Some of these philanthropic places run themselves. What's the old joke about working for a philanthropic foundation?"

Chris laughed. "You never have a bad meal, and everyone laughs at your jokes."

"But that is not what motivates me. The money I mean, though I do like good food and making people laugh." Then she stopped.

"Go, on," he urged her.

"I see you are not going to let this go." She drew a deep breath. "Fine. Here's the thing and you know it already or should at least. You held me that night so long ago, when the woman I thought I loved dumped me. Your expression of affection was nothing sexual … it was like a brother consoling a sister. That's what it felt like to me. Ever since, when we have squabbled, fought, got angry with one another, I think back to that night. It reminded me that we had a kind of love … no, have a kind of love. You had become my family. You know, the brother I never had. I mean, the competition wasn't much since all you had to do was replace my worthless biological siblings. They were half a step above rutting pigs."

Chris blushed slightly with embarrassment. "I take it they didn't set the bar very high."

"None of your usual self-deprecation shit. Just listen. Well, first it was you, but then the family grew with Azita and Deena and Kay and Amar …" She brushed her cheek with a hand. "Pathetic, isn't it. Then again, you know what my family was like back in Birmingham. Even now, the only time I hear from them is when they want money. The crazy thing is, I keep sending it to them. At least it keeps them from showing up at my freaking door. Monetizing love, somehow that never is the same as the real thing."

"I suspect not." He said weakly.

"Anyway, that's it. I never should have confessed all this because you won't believe me when I threaten to quit for more money."

Chris fought against a strong urge to walk around her desk and give her a deeper hug. He knew, however that would generate a kick to the region of his body he wanted to preserve. Instead, he decided to rescue Karen by moving in a different direction. "Listen, I have a question about love and family. It is one of the things that brought me here."

"I assumed it was not my pretty face." She wiped a bit of moisture from the top of her cheek.

"Deena, and especially Azita, have been ignoring me. Azita has been downright cold, especially to Ali, which was not the case at first. You talk with them more than I do these days. What the hell is going on? I mean, what have I done wrong?"

Karen rose and walked over to a large window generally facing northeast. She looked across the Thames toward St. Paul's Cathedral for a few moments. "I've never considered human relationships my strength," she issued a laugh that came out more as a crackle. "Still, obviously I've noticed and have thought about it. I think one cause is obvious, the other not so much."

"Start with the obvious."

"They are afraid you love them too much. It's that simple, really. They fear you will shut down their efforts to save Afghan girls from the Taliban. This had become their prime mission since the Taliban takeover. It is all just too close to their own experience, and they believe … they know … you will try to save them from themselves and their passion."

"Am I wrong." Chris asked.

"Yes," Karen replied curtly. "The other cause is deeper, and I think it affects Azita more. They … she … have been consumed with this abandonment thing."

"Abandonment?"

"Come on … think about it. When Azita was something like eleven, she lost her brother, and then her father and mother. Deena was older at the time and perhaps able to handle the loss better. Now, they both look like mature adults, Azita can work around the human body as a physician better than anyone I know. But that loss as a child never leaves. And now …"

"She loses Amar, her replacement mother."

"Yup, I think that is harder for Zita. And don't forget she lost her husband just after getting pregnant with Maddie. I slept through my psych course, but I don't think she dislikes Ali. My guess, she really liked her until Ali became, in her eyes, mother number three after Madeena and Amar. She, and maybe Deena, might be pushing Ali away in anticipation of more pain. She's been through a lot. A person can only take so much and, let's face it, she feels deeply about things."

Chris rose and joined Karen at the window. "Thanks Doctor Phil."

"We'll see if you still want to thank me after you get my invoice."

They continued to talk as he put an arm around her shoulder.

Katerina Crawford found her way to Mary Kelly's private area where she spent most of her time now that she was in England. It had been intended as a private retreat for Kat when she wanted to escape people and pressures, but she had other options for that. Kat chose to live closer to London as opposed to Oxford, with her living suites in the same building as her new corporate offices. She reasoned that this kept her closer to the financial markets, though she was never sure that was necessary. After all, Warren Buffet lived in Omaha Nebraska and that did not keep him from becoming one of the richest people in the world.

Nevertheless, Kat was pleased with the arrangement for now. Mary's private space was next to her bedroom and had a great view to the east which included Big Ben and that large Ferris wheel, the so-called London Eye, which rose from a position adjacent to the Thames. Kat could keep close watch on her and there were plenty of staff members from both her and Karen's shops to stop by and keep her company. The one downside to the arrangement was that Chris and Kay were in Oxford but that was not far away, at least in physical distance.

"Mother, did you have an enjoyable day? I'm having some food brought up."

"Katerina, you fuss too much. I could get my own food. After all, I don't need much." Mary put down her book, glancing to the window. Dark already. I sometimes forget how far north we are. But London is pretty by night, so there is that. Not as foggy as I had been led to believe but there is that drizzle."

"It wasn't fog in the old days; it was smog like Los Angeles used to have. Now, though, they no longer have all those coal-fired stoves. And I fuss, mother, because you need to keep your strength up." Kat walked over to her and took her arm. "I think you have lost more weight. That's not good, no. I should have Kay look at you."

"I won't hear of it. Don't you go bothering your sister, she is busy enough."

Kat smiled. She knew that her mother could never quite figure out what she did in her work. Her twins had real jobs … Kristen was a doctor and Christopher was a professor, though he did that other stuff that confused her a bit. What Katerina did was a mystery to her, just as what her husband, Charles Senior, did with his life remained beyond her understanding, in part because he preferred her ignorant. *'Men's work,'* he would say. *'No need for you to worry about it.'* His mysterious work did make them ever richer, though, and she was called upon to host dinner parties on occasion. On those social occasions, she was expected to be the beautiful and silent adornment. That peripheral role grew to rankle her, almost as much as the unsavory character of the men with whom her husband associated.

"I'm busy too, mother, but would drop everything to make sure you are well. Believe me, she would do the same."

"I'm such a bother," Mary grunted. "And what exactly do you do? When I visit you, I find you surrounded by computer screens, typing on a keyboard, with voices coming from speakers. It all seems chaotic. And you can't fool me, Katerina. When you finish with me here, you will go back to it immediately. You have no life, my dear. I worry."

Kat kissed her mother on the forehead. "I have the life I want, that's all that counts. Someone needed to wrest control of our fortune from father. He was doing such terrible things with all that money." Then she laughed. "Now your offspring spend the family fortune doing good, but there is such a lot of good to be done in the world that the money goes out pretty fast. That keeps me at the grindstone, making more so that we don't run out."

Mary looked alarmed. "Should I speak to your brother. If he is making it hard for you …"

"No, no mother, he is not making things hard for me. I'm joking about running out. Just the opposite in fact. He and Kay, Kristen I mean, are making all this finance stuff worthwhile. I would not do it just to make money. We are using the financial empire Charles Senior created for a good purpose … finally!" Kat paused to consider that she still had trouble calling him father or dad. Would that reluctance ever end?

There was a knock on the door and a woman wheeled in a cart with food for the two of them. "Look at this feast, such a waste. I can't finish all this."

"Do what you can mother." Kat looked at the frail woman in front of her take a few bites. She willed the woman to take more but food obviously no longer appealed to her.

A cold sensation coursed through the younger woman. She was losing her mother, bit by bit, day by day. Of the children, Kat had remained closer to home, running under the radar in the familial conflicts. While Chris and Kay ran off to far away schools, she studied economics at the University of Chicago and did graduate finance studies at Northwestern, the coursework expected of the eldest brother, Charles Junior, who had no aptitude for such things and struggled so in his studies as Kat sailed through with honors. Junior tried to appease the patriarch but crumbled under the pressures and eventually committed suicide. That was his escape. Charles Senior never noticed his youngest daughter's accomplishments, females didn't count.

Since Kat was not expected to succeed, her father focused on bringing Christopher into the role as heir to the throne. Chris fought desperately to carve out his own path. As this dance between father and son continued, Kat watched and learned. When she was ready, Kat brought her siblings into a coup that wrested the family empire from their father. She had bided her time, learned all she could by observing, and struck when she believed the time was right, while he was fully distracted by his right-wing causes and before he realized how dangerous his younger daughter was. Still, she needed her siblings and was not sure they would trust her technical skills or management abilities. She was, after all, the baby of the family. They did trust her, though, and the coup succeeded. After that, the infighting and violence and hate escalated. Mary Kelly ended the family fighting by shooting her husband on a Chicago Street, an act which was justified as self-defense. 'This woman is the bravest of us all,' Kat said to herself, 'and soon I will lose her.'

"Katerina! Are you listening to me?"

"Sorry, mother. I was daydreaming."

"I was merely recalling that your father never used computers, not until late in his career. It was mostly paper and the telephone. That's how I remember it."

"Mother, did you …" Kat stopped, suddenly unsure if she wanted to continue, "did you have good days with our father."

Mary smiled. "Do you think I would have married him otherwise? You do know my parents did not approve. He had prospects but no fortune. My father was sure he was after my money and my mother simply did not trust him. But I was in love, and he was nice to me in the beginning. But I learned a great lesson from that."

"Which is?" Kat asked.

"Always listen to your mother," Mary smiled.

Kat laughed. "I fell into that one. I have another question. Do you have any guilt or regrets or anything stemming from …"?

When Kat stumbled over her next words, Mary finished for her. "Gunning him down on a public street? The answer to that is yes."

"What are they?"

"Only one … that I didn't do it years earlier." Mary smiled. "Listen to me Katerina, these are the questions a daughter begins to ask when time is short."

"Oh, no … no."

"Oh yes, I know my time is running out. And I'm good with that. However, I do have a regret about you. I neglected you when you were young." Mary saw her daughter begin to object. "Don't deny it, it is true and, by the way, you should never disagree with your old mother. I was so worried about Charles Junior. Your father killed Junior even if society thought it was suicide. And Christopher, he also was targeted by your father, especially after Junior was gone. And maybe Kristen to some extent. You were younger, quieter, seemingly safe from the battle lines. I hate to say this now, but I sometimes forgot you were even there. By the time you came along, that other 'problem' of mine had arisen, my drinking."

"Mother, you never …"

Mary spoke as if Kat had not. "Remember this. I love you deeply and passionately. And what you have done, accomplished. I am so proud."

Kat burst into tears. Mary followed. Both were embarrassed, the Irish never betrayed feelings. When they recovered, they ate in silence, reflecting on their lives.

Carla Shapiro Greenstein was walking down Broad Street in Oxford when she noticed a familiar face going in the opposite direction. It was one of the late winter days that spoke more of spring than anything else. The sun was yet low in the sky. It was out nevertheless, and the air had a suggestion of the coming warmth. *'Thank god for the nearby gulf stream,'* Carla thought to herself. She had read somewhere recently that palm trees could be found on the west coast of Ireland near the cliffs of Moher. She quickly angled her trajectory to intersect with Cate Connelly who was lost in her thoughts.

"Cate!"

"Oh, Carla," Cate stopped abruptly. "Sorry, I didn't see you."

"I didn't mean to interrupt you; you look as if you are on a mission."

Cate shook her head. "No, really, I'm just wandering but I suppose I'm obsessing on something. I tend to lose myself when that happens." When Carla cocked her head as if hoping for more, Cate obliged. "Well, the thing is that I'm worried about my uncle. You and the others have been with him more than me.

I'm traveling a lot in the Mideast and see him only occasionally. Has his health deteriorated recently?"

Carla debated whether she should lie, or at least obfuscate the truth but that was not her style. She usually went with honesty, even when brutal. "Well, I'm no doctor so take this with a grain of salt."

"Please, tell me what you see."

Carla sighed. "He's declining. There is little doubt. We all, I mean my husband and Bob and Peter, have talked about it a lot over the past two weeks. We are so glad to be here and yet so torn..." She seemed on the edge of saying more but didn't.

"Listen, I know a delightful place nearby. I'd love to chat a bit. Do you have time?"

"All the time in the world." Carla chuckled. "I'd love that, but not the Hairy Hare."

Cate laughed with gusto. "Of course not. Why in god's name does Chris drag us there?"

Some ten minutes later, they were seated in a cosy bistro. For a few minutes they talked about Oxford, about the generosity of Chris Crawford in letting them spend time here and be with Josh during this period and touched further on what might they expect soon with respect to the man they both loved. Then Cate paused in that way which signalled a change in topic.

"I'm glad I've got you alone, not with the other revolutionaries." Cate chuckled slightly to convey that the word revolutionaries was meant affectionately. "I want to find out more about uncle from his old days, when you knew him best. You know he was my surrogate dad when my relationship with my loser biological father went kaput. And I spent much time alone with him when my mom and he were not getting along. They avoided one another. Oh, how I hated that."

"Spending time with Josh?" Carla was confused by that.

"OMG! No! I hated the rift between the two people I loved so. Here's the thing, though. I couldn't get uncle to talk much about those days. He always had this terrific way of making a joke or changing topics and I was afraid of offending him. But you knew him from those days as well as anyone, right?"

Carla smiled. "You might say so. Did he mention we were lovers back in the day?"

Cate's mouth dropped. "Ah, no."

"I thought not. It was never serious, for him that is. I tried not to feel anything. It's just sex, I said to myself. I know it was just sex to him … a typical guy. When I think back to how I threw myself at him, but only my body since sentiments like love and affection were totally bourgeoise. I convinced myself I was beyond all that. What bullshit." Carla looked at Cate whose mouth was still open. "Wait, am I shocking you."

"No, no," Cate lied, "just a bit surprised."

Carla wasn't convinced by her denial but decided to continue. "I knew he would never be *'mine,'* as they say. He was so anti-commitment then except for this one girl whom we knew about but never got to know at all. He kept her away from us. Her name was Eleni. I know he loved her deeply."

"And ..." Cate prompted.

"Who knows, not something he talks about. He ran off to Canada. She didn't follow him, or he didn't ask her to. I believe it was the latter. Then he suffered that loss for decades."

"How tragic. He never mentioned her to me." Cate looked pensive. "Not quite true. Her name came up, but he didn't reveal much."

"No surprise there. The damn Irish are a secretive lot but I do know they found each other via cyberspace after several decades. The little I was able to pry out of him is that they recognized how much they loved one another."

"Wait, was this before Connie."

"Certainly, well before Connie lost her senses and married the lug." Carla smiled.

"And he let her get away a second time, this love of his life." Cate was enthralled.

"There were two problems this second time around. First, she was married. Second, not all that long after they reconnected, she came down with cancer and passed away."

Cate absorbed this news and made a mental note to push her uncle on this lost love. That might explain a lot. "Let me get back to what he was like in college. When I got to know him, he always struck me as so gentle and kind, so laid back and witty. It is inconceivable that he lived as an exile for fear of going to prison, that he could ever have done anything outside the law."

"Unlike the rest of us hoodlums."

Cate blushed, "No, not that … I"

"I'm just pulling your chain." Carla laughed and took a sip of her drink. "Know this, it was more than an unsubstantiated fear. The rest of us did get sent to the slammer. Even in Canada, it was a close-run thing for him for quite a long time. We all protected him, especially Peter. Thank him for keeping your uncle safe, or at least out of the slammer."

"I still cannot wrap my head around the fact that this man I love so was a wanted man."

"But you can see the rest of us being criminals." Carla laughed.

"Damn, I can't stop inserting my foot into my mouth," Cate said blushing once more.

"Just kidding but let me see if I can make sense of this for you." Carla looked toward the ceiling for a second and began. "We were all very smart. I was told I could read by age three and do numbers and basic arithmetic a year later. I don't recall all that clearly, but I was considered somewhat of a prodigy of sorts. My parents were deep into Judaism so, not surprisingly, there were a lot of religious texts around. I ravaged anything I could get my hands on. Did you know I wanted to be a Rabbi as a young girl? I was taken with the old stories about how Jewish scholars kept the Torah alive after the diaspora when the Temple in Jerusalem was destroyed and Jews were scattered around the world. Most cultures would have disappeared or been absorbed by others, but not this tribe. That inspired me as a little girl."

"No, a Rabbi?" Cate said thoughtfully. "Wait, perhaps I did hear something … "

"No matter, my dream was not to be. Thing is that my family was conservative. Rabbinical studies were for males, which my brothers were not into. So, no Rabbis in our family. When you think on it, most of us were religious in some way, the core of our group at least. Bob dabbled in the seminary and later a monastery, Peter thought of the Priesthood for a while. My husband had a certain kind of religion, a radical humanism along a passion for saving humanity. Even your uncle had a religious calling of sorts."

"What? I never heard such a thing." Cate said.

"It was not conventional by any means. But I could see it."

Cate was curious. "What do you mean?"

"For one thing, he read philosophical stuff a lot, and some religious texts. He was an enthusiastic fan of Pierre Teilhard de Chardin, the Jesuit Priest and evolutionary scientist. What struck me was that he could have had any girl in college. He was handsome and witty and smart. He had been quite the athlete until he gave it up. Yet, he avoided most girls."

"Really," Cate was surprised. "He talked a different game."

"Mostly BS, and I think I know why he turned down opportunities. He never wanted to hurt any of them, and he thought he might. He told me that females wanted relationships while guys wanted sex. It was a mismatch that was bound to lead to disappointment at the least, real hurt in most cases."

"But he and you had sex, right?

Carla chuckled. "Oh, did we ever. I still blush at the thought of it. But I had him fooled into thinking I was the exception, that I was into sex without all the emotional baggage. He bought it; I think. Then again, I never gave him much choice. He would call me the *'wild Valkyrie'* as I would jump his bones. Poor guy never had a chance."

"Wow, that's …" Cate struggled for words.

"Hard to see now that I'm a grey-haired old grandmother. We change."

"Apparently!" Cate agreed.

At that, Carla screwed up her face as if thinking hard. "No, that's not right. I mean, some things change. I shed my wild ways, sure. But the things that mattered don't change. They don't. Ever wonder how we could reunite after decades and pick up where we left off. Think about the fact that we, of all Josh's colleagues and acquaintances and so forth, are the ones with him here. Have you thought about that?"

"Yes," Cate said, "a lot."

"Some of that, what shall I call it, deep connection might be attributable to our age when we were together and the period in which we met. Emotions run hotter in the young, everything is fresher and more intimate. And then, it was the 1960s, need I say more. But that does not answer it all, not by a long shot." She took another look at the ceiling. "We came together for something we felt deeply about. It was a cause, our cause. We felt we had no other choice, that to walk away was to compromise our moral cores."

"But wait, Josh did walk away, that was his guilt all those years."

"But listen carefully if you can get him to talk about those years. What's important was that he never walked away from us … from what we were fighting for and against. He walked away from the path we were on, the one leading us to do the same violent things that those on the other side were doing. He was right, the rest of us were wrong. We eventually saw this, perhaps he was even more spiritual than the rest of us."

"I can see that, that you all were spiritual." Cate nodded.

"Remember this, though." Now she looked directly into Cate's eyes. "The love we had for one another never flickered. That love kept him away for so long because he thought he had failed us. But it was there, always there, and that's why we are here. Do you understand."

Cate merely nodded. She found it hard to speak.

Azita looked lovingly on Madeena Amar Zubair as she put her daughter to bed. "Sweet dreams, Maddie," she whispered to her daughter.

She occasionally considered changing her daughter's last name to Masoud, to honor her parents, but always dismissed that thought. She yet loved her late husband, and this was his legacy. Then she joined Deena in their living room. The two sisters had shared a house since shortly after the birth of Azita's and

Ahmad's child. His sudden death in the Kabul attack left Azita as a single parent. Given her busy schedule, having her sister available proved a blessing though they were times when neither was available. Fortunately, there were many available individuals to take care of the child when she was gone, but she preferred her sister when possible.

"I think Maddie has fallen to sleep." Azita said on entering the room. "Tell me, now that she is growing, does she look more like me or Ahmad?"

"Oh, Ahmad for sure. Allah would not be so cruel to give your looks to your daughter," Deena said without cracking a smile.

Azita slumped into her chair while glaring at her older sibling. "I have prepared an ad for the net. It reads *'looking for a nanny for a beautiful and precocious child. The successful candidate will replace my obnoxious sister in this task. The only qualification needed is that the candidate does not believe herself to be a great wit.'*"

"There is a point here." Deena said in a way that sounded like a question but wasn't.

"Isn't the point obvious?" Azita asked. "You are deluded into thinking yourself a great wit."

"Not that point. Over the years, we have become like our adoptive father, using so much sarcasm. We were once good girls."

Azita considered reminding her sibling that Chris had never formally adopted her since she was approaching the age of majority when the issue arose. But that was a moot point as they both realized. Chris had considered them both his children, as had Amar until her death from Covid. "I was the good child. You ...?"

Deena had her serious look that suggested she needed to move away from their common banter. "I've been communicating with Farzana."

Azita straightened a bit in her chair. "And ...?"

"Things are falling into place. I mean, progress is being made."

"Tell me." Now Azita was fully alert.

"Recruitment of girls in the Panjshir Valley is going better than expected, though they are frightfully worried that such a thing cannot be kept secret. Bahiri and Ferhana are having success in Kabul as well. So one worry is past, we are getting willing recruits."

"Now the trick is to get them out."

"Even on that score we are making progress. There is a continuous movement of medical and emergency relief supplies between Kabul, other sites, and especially the Masoud Center. It will be easy to smuggle the girls being first gathered in the Capital of Kabul north to the embarkation point in the Panjshir. Things are looser there. In addition, we have also begun to fly helicopters into the Center on a regular basis. That is becoming so routine that the Taliban no longer checks them. They are just grateful someone is taking care of the suffering that has been unleashed given their incompetence. When they do check, it is always when they arrive, not when they leave. While they are waiting, the girls are getting intensive English training and being prepared for what is to come."

"I so worry about how these girls will adjust. It was easy for us, well pretty easy. But many of these girls are quite innocent, naïve. They know nothing except village life. The changes will be massive. Such culture shocks!"

"I have the same fear though we are doing what we can in preparation, the Afghan families lined up, the mentors and tutoring they will receive at the beginning, the counselling, all of it. And they have been selected with some care. We can only do so much." Deena tried to sound confident. "I will say that Karen has been fully on board, a great supporter."

"And Chris?"

"He is not happy but hasn't shut the operation down as long as we stay in England, though he worries about problems for the Afghan staff if all this leaks." Deena said matter-of-factly before adding, "And so do I."

"Ali?"

Deena squirmed. "So far, she is going along with it. She has done nothing to impede things from moving forward, but I'm just not sure where she stands. You should reach out to her, talk openly with her. It hasn't helped that you have shut her out." Deena waited for a reply but got none. "Farzana did make one strange request."

Azita responded to that. "Oh, what?"

"Well, she has been working closely with a man named Sayed Aktar. He provides her with security, more like cover, when she travels to the villages. He is a widower with a young daughter, and he worries about what will happen if ... if the worst comes to pass for him. So, I was thinking that we can get his daughter out in the beginning. Cate and Meena can adopt her. They already have two …"

"No," Azita said firmly. "I will adopt her. Rather, we will … in practical terms if not legal ones."

"But Cate and Meena were married in Canada, we are just sisters."

"Just sisters? Just?" Deena realized her error as Azita continued. "We have argued and fought most of our lives, but we love one another desperately. Is that not like a married couple? I know you will look after Maddie if I'm gone."

"You mean die?" Deena's words sounded harsh. "That will not happen."

"It might," her sister protested.

Deena raised a hand. "I will not permit it.

"Besides, she should have a sibling to love like we have one another." Azita would not let the issue drop.

"But Zita, you are likely to remarry …"

"No, I won't."

"Really? Why not?" Deena asked even if she was not surprised.

Azita lay back in her chair, now looking directly at the ceiling with her eyes closed. Deena waited patiently until she concluded that no response would be forthcoming. As she was about to rise, leaving her sister to what she assumed was a nap,

Azita spoke. "I won't remarry for the same reason I have acted like a child around Ali." She now spoke quickly to prevent any interruption by Deena. "Yes, yes, I know I've been acting out lately … I'm not an idiot. I mean, some of my tension with her is real. I … I have always thought she was less committed to Afghanistan than we were, that she shared Chris's reluctance to let us take risks for what means so much to us. But I'm not sure how real they are. Yes, I should talk these issues through with her like an adult, not let them fester."

"And the real issue…" Deena prodded.

Azita looked away from the ceiling so that her eyes met her sister's. "It is just that there has been so much death. There was Majeed, our brave brother, then papa, and mama, and Ben, my first love, and Ahmad, my true love. When Amar was taken from us. Even Rachel. I thought … I thought … enough, just enough."

"I think," Deena said softly, "that we were not put on this earth for comfort."

"But why so much pain?" There was anguish in Azita's voice. "Now Ali has taken this role as my new mother … our new mother. See, I refer to her as I did our biological mother even though she is more like an older sibling in age."

"Sister, don't …"

"Say nothing, just listen." Azita leaned forward. "I know. I know that I'm pushing her away because I'm afraid to love her. Damn, if Chris had just found some anonymous woman on a dating site, or in a bar. Then I would be fine. But he selected a woman that I admired and with whom I felt such a closeness. The worst thing was … Ali has always reminded me of Amar. There even is a physical resemblance, no?"

"Well, yes." Deena managed. "There skin color is similar."

"The reasons are unimportant. I'm protecting myself. I'm the child again, pushing away the loved one simply to avoid possible pain. I find myself struggling against pushing you away … it is all just like the child I was when I lost …"

"*We* … lost our family." Deena corrected her. "But I understand, you were several years younger than I. Besides, long ago I realized you were the sensitive one, even as you dived into bloody bodies to heal them. You revealed nothing as you did this work while I tottered on the verge of vomiting. But you felt everything, inside, you felt their pain and embraced it." Deena rose and walked back and forth. "I have been thinking. It is likely one of us will have to go back, especially if something goes wrong. That will be me."

Azita jumped up. "No, it is too dangerous for you. You are almost as famous as Malala now, as an educator. You are a marked woman among the extremists."

Deena looked at her sister with cold eyes. "This is not a matter for debate. Once upon a time, you could dominate me with your intellect, your reputation, and your will. No more. I am the eldest and I will go. You must stay with your baby. And who knows, perhaps you will have another one from our homeland." Deena's eyes softened a bit.

Two or three times, Azita opened her mouth to argue. Nothing came. She walked to her sister, embraced her, and finally said.

"Dear Deena, I have been a shit to you so often, but I have always loved you beyond measure."

"Oh, I know. Look at me … how could you not."

Both siblings laughed.

Jeremiah Joshua Connelly and Corinthea 'Connie' Chen sat at their dining room table. Before them was a simple meal Connie had prepared. She had cut back on the portions recently, mostly in response to her reaction to seeing how much food remained on Josh's plate when he finished. This was her secret measure of his decline, an inevitability that drove her into denial and obfuscation. Though she realized that any such stratagem was foolish, the tactic enabled her to delay the acceptance of the unacceptable. Her husband was dying.

How had she fallen so in love with him? She was a scientist and a scholar, a hyper-rational person. She was, or thought she was, beyond the needs of ordinary women. At first, when they went out, she saw him as a diversion, good enough for a night at a play or visit to a museum. But slowly he wound his way into her head. How did he do that? It was that damn Irish wit, he made her laugh. Humor is the ultimate aphrodisiac. But that wasn't all of it, not the entire reason for her aching heart. He was a decent person, if highly flawed. At some point, she realized she wanted more from him, a basic human need that drove her to distraction. She then discovered that he could not easily go beyond his affable humor and his eclectic intellectual interests. There seemed to be nothing inside the man, at least nothing he was willing to share. She drifted away, almost with a sigh of relief.

It wasn't until the week of his retirement from the university, when his sister and his college friends gathered for the event, that his isolation was challenged, his shell cracked. Connie recalled his sister Rachel telling her that Josh had erected personal 'shields' of the kind seen on Star Trek, the show that first hit the airwaves around the time he disappeared to Canada. Somehow, those close to him managed to penetrate those shields to find a deep and sensitive man of infinite complexity, the nice and interesting guy long buried by guilt and perhaps shame. *'The Irish have so much of those things,'* she whispered to herself.

"Did you say something?" Josh asked.

"No, no," just thinking to myself. Connie looked at how much food he had left on his plate and winced. She fought against pushing him to take more. He would just see such an effort as trying to make him take some experimental drug. He would just dig in, those damn stubborn Irishman.

As she started clearing the table, she realized he was speaking. "I'm moving over to my favorite chair. Forget about the table, join me."

"But this won't take long …."

"Join me." He insisted, in a way that struck her more as a plea than a command.

"Alright," she watched him move to the living room, looking unsteady to her eyes. She almost rushed to support him but restrained herself. *'Not yet, not yet,'* she thought. *'He won't like that.'*

Once in his chair, he looked over at her as she settled in her own recliner next to him. "Well, I can say one thing. You could have done much better than marrying a hard-assed Mick."

She thought of several witty comebacks, the kind that had made their marriage of a dozen plus years so full of laughs and joy. She ignored them, instead saying, "marrying you was the best thing I ever did … maybe second to having my daughter Erica."

"Hey," Josh smiled, "I made the top three. Good for me."

"Not so fast, I'm still thinking …" She stopped when she realized he had turned serious.

"Connie, you see it … you must." She opened her mouth, but he continued. "It won't be that long now. Then again, I've lasted longer than many expected so who knows. But I need to know one thing, maybe more than one but I'll settle for one. You understand why I'm not fighting this, don't you?" Connie nodded as Josh continued. "Sometimes I think I'm being selfish, that I should try all this crap they suggest since the people around me want me to hang on. But don't you see, that's what it will be, just hanging on. You, and the others, would just be fussing around this wasted body. You would be conversing with someone who is not Josh Connelly. You must see that. You must see that would be Hell for me."

"I do." Connie's words came out more as a croak. "And you must see that even half of a Josh Connelly is more than most other men."

He chuckled. "Thank you. The thing is that I am half a man today, right now. It only gets worse from here. I cannot bear the thought of looking into eyes filled with pity and sorrow. If it were up to me, I would …"

"Don't say it." Connie shouted, before recovering and hoping to change the direction of the dialogue. "Do you have any regrets?"

"Other than not nailing you earlier?"

"What are you talking about? I gave it up very quickly." Connie protested. "I couldn't resist your damn Irish charms."

Josh smiled. "We have different notions of quickly. But yes, I have a few regrets as you know. My sister Rachel … I wasted so many years without her, avoiding her in fact. My friends, who are with me now. I should have gone to them decades ago, not waited for them to find me so late in life. And I suppose not saving mankind from itself is on the list."

"Oh," Connie laughed with effort, "you still have time for that."

"Oh wait, my father … Big Jim. That's another hole in my life. You know the story of course. You've heard it enough. He centered so much of his life on me as he got older. I was going to Notre Dame, play football for the Irish. He would brag to everyone about that. You could see the pride in his eyes …"

Connie said softly. "And then you stopped. It was after you hurt a kid on the field."

"I crippled some poor bastard, not intentionally of course. But it happened, and then I walked off the field for good. He never forgave me; we fought all the time after that. Then I went to a non-Catholic college, got with the radical students, and the rest is history."

"Well, where you ended up is great. So …"

"But I never got a chance to make amends with him, or mother. I left them with piles of misunderstanding and badness and disappointment. Maybe it could have been turned around, maybe if I had made a fucking effort …"

"And maybe not. Some things cannot be repaired. The differences among some of us can be chasms that are unbridgeable. She wanted to say more but decided to shift to another possibility that had always intrigued her. "Children, what about not having children. Everyone I know says you would have been a good father, a great dad in fact. Cate adores you, while my Erica, even though she knows you less well, thinks so highly of you. She kept telling me I did such a great job in landing a guy like you. More than once, she has remarked that I married above my station, the little shit. Wait til she sees how little I'll leave her in my will." At that, Connie chuckled.

Josh laughed out loud. "When people praise me as a potentially good father, I think of Lincoln's old saying … you can fool way more people than you ever imagined. Well, he said something like that. But no, I never had any doubt about that. I can't think of a more difficult job and, to be honest, I never felt up to it … way too selfish. Besides, I would have felt bad bringing someone into the world I saw about me. It's not like they have any choice in the matter, do they? Besides, I had my students. They were like children in a way." He paused as if thinking about the past. Do you realize that I still get emails and texts from some of them, even now? I guess word is spreading that I'm checking out. It is odd, I can't recall some of them, what they look like, even as they share what I meant to them. Some say I changed their lives; can you imagine?"

"Yes, I can." Connie thought he was missing the obvious. "Hey, there were so many of them and only one of you."

"We can thank God for that ... only one of me." He chuckled as he often did when he wanted the listener to know he was joking. "But there is a lesson there I learned over and over. You can never know when you are touching someone else. A dialogue with a young person that you forget about within a few minutes is something they just might recall and treasure. That's a blessing and ... a responsibility you don't soon forget."

Connie smiled at him. "Yes, I think you are right but somehow teaching kids about chemical reactions doesn't transform their spirits."

"Nonsense," Josh asserted. "I met some of your grad students. They spoke about you with awe and reverence."

She dismissed his comment with a wave of the hand. "They had too. I had their future in my hands. I had them sign a pledge when I agreed to take them on as doctoral students where they promised undying fealty to me."

Josh threw his head back in laughter. "And this is what I'll miss. You, my dear, are the funniest and wittiest Chinese broad I've ever met."

"Chinese broad? Good thing you never called me that on campus. I would have had the women's study department on your ass."

"Hey, I'm not the brightest bulb on the marquee but the light is still lit. I knew if I said anything like that on the politically correct campus, my decomposing body would next be floating in Burrard's Bay, unrecognizable after the beating I'd received."

"And I would have struck the first blow. But don't be naïve. I know ways to get rid of your useless carcass so that it would never be discovered. You know, with help from the miracle of modern chemistry. For example …"

He looked at her in such a way that she did not complete her thought. "Connie, I love you beyond words. I never thought I could … love anyone, after Eleni. Actually, I never thought I would want to. Well, you know that story. But here's the thing. Those regrets, the one's we just talked about, are real enough. But here's a big one. I will miss your kindness and wit and intelligence. You have meant the world to me. I only hope I … go fast enough so that you don't see me as …"

"Stop it. Hear me. Stop it."

"Yes, yes … but sometimes I hope there is something beyond this mortal coil. I doubt there is but therein lies one benefit of passing on, finding out what might be next. Just think, you might be listening to my sparkling wit for all eternity."

"Oh, spare me Lord, I'll make a reservation in the other place, heaven that is since you will be in the toasty alternative."

She rose and managed to slide next to him on his large recliner, he didn't take up much room any longer. As she cuddled next to him, her head on his chest, he massaged her temple. "Thank you, Connie. Thank you for being part of my life."

CHAPTER 18

Ominous Signs

> *"The world is a dangerous place to live, not because of the people who are evil, but because of the people who don't do anything about it."*
>
> *Albert Einstein*

Doctor Archibald Singletary got through to his counterpart, Doctor Bahiri Gupta, on the third try. Tensions were rising within the Masoud Center, and he needed a sympathetic ear with which to discuss matters. He agreed that this scheme to smuggle girls out of the country to further their education was all well and good. However, what will happen when it unravels which, in his mind, it surely will at some point. Then what? He had difficulty sleeping at night, his imagination running wild in the dark. He saw the Taliban sweeping up the senior staff, torturing his wife and daughter, before beheading them in a public square. He did not mind what he might suffer but could not bear any harm coming to them. *'Calm down,'* he told himself. *'They haven't started beheading people yet, not that we know at least.'* But how long would their restraint last. This scheme would be treason to them. *'They found unforgivable sin everywhere and in everything, just like so many of the early Christians,'* he muttered under his breath.

"Bahiri, my friend, how are you doing?" The two men first discussed medical supply issues and making combined pleas to England for more supplies and staff. They chatted about the rising demand on their services, the growing poverty and despair among the population, how to best prioritize needs, and how to efficiently allocate what they did have between them. Eventually, this discussion of practical matters diminished, and they moved to what was becoming a salient issue to both of them. As in the past, they realized they should be circumspect but were not used to being careful about language.

"Archie, you must be worrying about the same thing I am."

"That education scheme I assume." Archie responded.

"Exactly," Bahiri affirmed. "Ferhana is so supportive of it, as am I, but I keep thinking of the risks. When I bring them up, she dismisses them. I cannot understand that. She undoubtedly recalls what the Taliban were like. After all, she fled to India to continue her education the last time they were in power. That was a blessing for me since then I met her."

Archie sighed. "Don't you see, my friend, that is exactly why she is such a supporter. She remembers. The same with Deena and Azita Masoud. Those two have hatched this scheme because they saw what happened to their own mother and how, had they not been rescued as young girls, they might have spent their lives as married slaves to some brutal, overbearing husband. Those two, can you imagine?"

Bahiri laughed, "I would pity the poor men who married them."

Archie continued. "The staff member who managed the education program here," he was going to say *the one for girls* but didn't, "is so enthused about his as well."

"Farzana … no?"

"Quite so. She has been remarkably successful in recruiting … subjects. I never really thought it would work but … she has found volunteers. I admire her zeal. She saw her … special program diminishing in size and that hurt her deeply. And my wife is also a huge fan."

Bahiri chuckled again. "My friend, we joke about what might have happened if Azita and Deena were married off to dominating husbands. How different is our situation?"

"You mean being dominated by our wives? Yes, true but with one key difference."

"I'm not sure I see one." Bahiri tried.

"No? You don't?" Archie responded with incredulity. "We, on the other hand, love our wives."

The two men continued chatting about sundry topics for a while until they circled back to the topic that had dominated their thinking of late. Bahiri sighed and said in a faraway voice. "Is this not always the case?"

"I'm not sure I follow." Archie responded.

"Sorry, that life poses for us these untenable choices. Do we play it safe so that we can keep doing our good here but at the cost of so many futures among young girls? Or do we help them and risk everything? How does one resolve such a conundrum?"

Archie thought a moment. "I am no longer a conventionally religious man though I yet find comfort in the concept of a deity. And yet, I still have a faith in some unseen Providence that helps us decide when a decision is demanded. Perhaps it is no more than our individual conscience, but it is there. We will know the answer when we must, but we must also prepare before any choice is thrust upon us."

Farzana and Sayed had gone toward the west on the latest journey into the countryside, toward Faizabad. They visited several homes on the way, but their destination was Badakhshan University in the city itself. Faizabad had developed along the Kokcha river which ran out of the surrounding peaks and had gouged its way through the rocks after centuries of ceaseless geological effort. A city of some size, it had a hospital, a variety of government services, and Khamchan high school, an excellent institution that had provided several girls capable of advanced education in the past. Most important of all, it had an airport which might be useful, no essential, if things became dicey. It could accommodate larger planes.

Faizabad not only was isolated from the rest of the country but normally was a fiercely independent region. Many Mujahadin who had earlier fought the Soviets and the Taliban were from this rugged outpost situated amidst the country's rugged northern frontier. There no longer was any organized resistance in the region, no *'Lion of the North'* to motivate and organize a functioning army or execute tactics that might have some prospect of success. Perhaps a leader would emerge, but none had so far. Nevertheless, Farzana had originally come from this area and sensed that many resisted the new regime with understated resolve.

Farzana and Sayed continued posing as a married couple, finding accommodations with old acquaintances of Farzana who were doubtful of this sudden marriage but said nothing. More than once, Farzana was mortified by doubtful looks and what she deemed as reproachful glances. Perhaps, however, she was being overly sensitive. *'No,'* she concluded, *'they know her sin but are willing to forgive her, even if she were not sure she could forgive herself.'*

They made their way to the university campus which struck them both as less active than normal. The depletion of female students was marked but not as universal as might be anticipated. Numerous students, male and female, had been driven away by economic necessity as circumstances deteriorated throughout the land. Other females succumbed to the dictates of the new regime and returned to their homes and traditional expectations. Many continued to resist, however, though they did obey the more restrictive dress codes expected of females. The remaining female students generally refrained from behaviors prohibited by the new rules, no fraternizing with males nor anything that might be considered imported or influenced by the infidels, like western music and dancing. Even public laughter was done cautiously. They bristled under the restrictions but paid the price willingly to continue learning. They did worry that their stubbornness might hinder their professional prospects if there were any.

Farzana had taken classes here before finishing her advanced degree in Kabul where the academic standards were higher. While she had loved her work as an educator at the Masoud

Center, part of her wanted more, more learning and more intellectual challenges. She saw herself teaching at this level one day, an aspiration that had struck her as a pipe dream. Once, she screwed up her courage to mention her aspirations to Deena Masoud who responded by sharing her own experiences. Deena talked about how she had lagged behind her sister, how she was a late bloomer, and how she finally came into her own. In the end, the early despair imposed by the first Taliban regime could not deter either Masoud sister from finding themselves. It was a story Farzana had embraced and kept with her, though the prospect of achieving similar success remained unlikely to her.

Sayed kept watch outside a campus building as several females made their way inside. They had been recruited by word of mouth, some known to Farzana but a few not. Each meeting, each home visit, each conversation that she knew to be treason to the new regime caused her heart to beat faster. Some days, the tension was unbearable. But what else was there to do.

After some general introductions and discussion about what the Taliban crackdown had meant to the women in this area, the dialogue turned more specific as Farzana segued into the topic of greatest concern to her. "All of you know the Masoud sisters by reputation. A few of you are acquainted with them personally. It is no secret that they were able to get a few girls out in those last, chaotic days as the Taliban swept over the country."

"Yes, word reached us of this. Many of us wished we had been on such a plane." A tall young woman in her late teens said. "Are the ones who made it out doing well?"

Farzana could never quite decide how open she should be, but now shrugged at her inner doubts. She had already committed indefensible sins in the eyes of the new regime. '*They can only kill me once no matter how many crimes I commit,'* she said inside before speaking out loud. "I do not know the details. In general, they have been placed with sympathetic families. Many, though not all of these, are earlier Afghani emigres. Those helping us are working hard to place each girl in the right educational setting or having them tutored personally. Some, I believe, are still as a group getting prepared for the Western culture."

"But how are they doing emotionally? I mean, are they coping, being in such new circumstances and away from all that is familiar?"

Farzana tried for honesty. "That is beyond my knowledge. I cannot believe that there are not some problems. However, I do believe that virtually all are glad they took this chance though some may well wish to return home after things change here … if they ever do change. Perhaps I simply want to believe that, but I am hopeful."

Another girl, shorter and with a darker complexion spoke, "Some problems are to be expected. Still, I would give my right arm to be one of them. Each day, the new regime makes it more difficult for us. They harass the teachers and our parents. They harass us. I feel so selfish for putting the others in such a bad position, perhaps a dangerous situation, but I cannot give up on my hopes. I cannot."

"No one should be forced to confront that," Farzana continued. "Let me ask this, have you heard anything, any rumors, about getting more girls out of the country?"

The attendees looked at one another. Finally, one said cautiously. "There have been whispers but everyone is reluctant to talk. We thought it just fanciful wishes. Besides, no one knows whom to trust. Would the person with whom you shared your dream not be a true friend?"

The tall girl spoke up again. "I also have heard some mentions about what you are doing. I had discounted them, however, since there are so many rumors. I assumed, or hoped, that is why you are here. But there is such danger in all this."

"I know," Farzana said.

"Do you?" The tall girl replied. "This has never been a Taliban stronghold, far from it. And when they first took power, they tried to sound reasonable. It would not be like last time they said. But from what our parents say, it is not so different, and certainly won't be different in the future. The beatings have commenced among those defying the new regime. We all walk in fear that we will be accused of something and punished, or worse. Are you prepared for the worst?"

Farzana looked at the girl as a cold shiver coursed through her body. *'Was she prepared?'* What she said was this. "Before we go further, I want each of you to decide something. No one should stay unless they are prepared to pay a price, perhaps the ultimate price. I bring great danger with me. Yet, I bring what I hope is an … opportunity, though I cannot guarantee anything except considerable risk. Believe me on that. No one will think the worst of you if you leave now. It is perhaps the wisest of moves you can make. I will leave the room while you discuss this, since I will only reveal more to those committed to assuming these risks."

Farzana left and walked around the campus for a while, breathing in the feel of a campus once again. Yes, she wanted this in her future. But how? Then she kicked herself. She should have told them how long she would be gone. They might discuss this for hours. But curiosity overtook her, and she returned in about a half hour. As she approached the room, she wondered if it would be empty. She saw Sayed at his post but decided not to ask him anything. *'Did he see all the girls leave?'* That, indeed, would be mortifying. He smiled at her. *'Was that encouragement, or an expression of sympathy?'*"

As she entered the room, her heart beat faster. They were all still there.

"Where were you?" One of the girls said. "We thought you had abandoned us."

Farzana fought a tear back, not wanting to show emotion. "Listen to me. I have thought on this hard. I am certain I could get out of the country and save myself. But I cannot be so selfish as to think only of myself. I cannot save everyone but perhaps I can save a few before … they catch up to me." She looked out over the eager faces. Yet, in the back of her mind she could not dispel the thought that one of these girls belonged to the other side, was collecting evidence that would be used at some sham trial before her execution. She pushed aside this thought.

"Are you still trying to talk us out of this. That would be futile." It was the tall girl who cut her off. "And don't talk like a martyr. This land is covered with the blood of martyrs. Some of us are ready to go. But you must also go. The danger is real and there maybe little time left."

Farzana nodded, she had come prepared to argue them into her scheme and now found they were ahead of her. She tried not to let her emotions show.

Agnes Singletary found her daughter Carolyn as she was finishing up with some late arriving patients. There was nothing medically serious among them, so she left their care to the nurses on that shift. Obviously, her mother Agnes wanted to chat. Otherwise, she would never interfere with clinical hours.

"You know," Agnes started, "this is a beautiful place if one discounts the politics. I mean look about you. There are springtime flowers blossoming on the hillsides. The high peaks are still covered with snow. The air is crisp and the sky an azure blue. Yes, indeed, this place can get into your soul."

"Hmmm," her daughter grunted. "You are beginning to sound like a tourist commercial or maybe that Lebanese poet Kahlil Gibran, one of my favorites. Can you imagine having that job?"

"As a poet?" Agnes queried.

"No, the job as head of the Afghan national tourist agency." Carolyn then eyed her mother curiously. "What's on your mind?"

"Can't I just have a walk with my daughter?"

Carolyn remained suspicious. "Of course. It is just that you never, almost never that is, interrupt clinical hours. So, fess up."

"Well, I know your father is worried and so am I."

"We all are," Carolyn was not sure she wanted this conversation now, or ever.

"I've been watching things carefully, very carefully. Suspicious strangers are mixing in with the influx of villagers seeking help. They question the staff and those in need. These surely are Taliban seeking out information about us. Some of them wish to close us down no matter how much good we do."

Carolyn took her mother's hand. "Why would they do that? This land is hurting so. Does it make sense to attack those bearing good things as gifts?"

"Oh my, I thought I was the optimist, the one with rose-colored glasses. Today, my dear, you may be wearing them I fear." Agnes smiled but her normally twinkling eyes remained dark. "The men who keep watch on us are controlled by hostility or perhaps it is paranoia."

"Yes, we make it hard for them to paint all infidels as the tools of Satan, which is true." Carolyn's expression remained doubtful. "But that has been the case from the beginning. Remember the hostile visits, the searches they did, for God knows what."

"Yes, true enough. They did back off grudgingly, though they were not comfortable with how many females were in positions of authority, or the way we dressed, or our attitudes, or much else. I think we often fail to think like them. It is just a world so alien to us. At least the world into which you were born."

"I was born?" Carolyn was puzzled.

"Oh yes, so much changed from when I was a girl and when you were raised. Do you think I would have been satisfied at being a nurse, though there is nothing wrong with being one? I've enjoyed my work very much. Still, had the world been different, I could see myself working alongside your father as an equal. But it was not easy then. It was not that someone told me I could not become a physician. At least I cannot recall anyone saying such a thing. It was more that no one ever encouraged me in that direction, even though I was tops in my high school class in the sciences, by far. I vaguely recall my school guidance counsellor, my family, my neighbors all singing from the same hymnal … you will make a great nurse. Perhaps it might have been different had we lived in Sydney or Melbourne, but I grew up near Perth. That was such a remote and a conservative area."

Carolyn screwed up her face. "How could I never have thought about that? I mean, you encouraged me to go for my dreams, ever since I can remember. I'm so stupid. It never occurred to me you might have wanted to be more than you …"

"Hold it there. I achieved what was possible in my world and I married the best man in the world. I doubt many women are happier, after I get Archie fully trained that is."

Carolyn laughed at her mother's old joke. "I almost understand what you are trying to say. See if I have this right. We all have … what shall we say … understandings of how the world should be organized. We see the Taliban as primitive and extreme, but our own society was like them not all that long ago."

Agnes nodded. "I knew many women being shamed for showing their legs, elderly women back then who had been beaten for trying to vote or for acting like men. We had fewer legal rights when I was young."

"Wow, mother, you did have it rough."

Now Agnes laughed. "Don't go overboard. We never had to wear a full burqa, but I faced many restrictions that did not seem so out of the norm to me then. Now, I cringe at the very thought."

"They would have driven me crazy." Carolyn interjected.

"And if the menfolk tried to reimpose those rules now back in Australia, their womenfolk would rise up. And that is the point, is it not?" Agnes stopped walking to look at her daughter, "I have tasted freedom and possibility, while you have experienced so much more than I. Don't get me wrong, I'm not blind. I know you faced discrimination and sexism along the way. It hasn't always been easy for you, but all it took was a little moxie for you to get what you wanted. Now, the women coming behind you find it easier. I think … I'm sure that's what drives Deena and Azita. They have seen the repression first hand and then they were permitted to reach the mountaintop. They cannot go back. And they cannot watch and do nothing as their country slides back toward a primitive society."

"I understand their frustration, but it is all so futile."

"They will not … cannot admit that. Remember the old river metaphor. No matter. The sisters are starting by plucking out a few girls who are drowning in the river right now. They will first get them ashore and then take them to dry land where their lives can be resurrected. And then, they will prepare them for what it will take to change things."

Carolyn nodded. "If I recall the metaphor accurately, the saved ones, the ones plucked from the river, will take the long view. When they are ready, they will be sent back upstream to ensure that the supply of girls falling into the river is stopped, or at least slowed."

"It seems improbable now since changing such encrusted traditions and norms seems impossible. However, you never know ... you just never know. Look how much our homeland has changed in a generation or two." Agnes sighed. "Right now, though, we are plucking a few willing to get out of the river that will sweep them along if they do not resist. But the risks are great. Your father and I have talked at length. He is beside himself with worry and I cannot blame him. But what else can I do, we do?"

Carolyn hugged her mother tightly and let her go. "I'm with you. We must try, is there a choice? However, we also must have a plan if things go awry."

"When they go awry, my dear. When! Tomorrow, pay more attention to the men who loiter in the camp without families or apparent purpose. They are looking, searching for sins real and imagined. What is happening cannot be kept secret for long. "Let us continue our walk and plan. I'm sure our menfolk are talking but doing nothing useful."

Professor Shaheed Al-Hussein's mobile phone rang. She saw it was Karen Fisher calling. Ali looked at her watch, it was 10:15 in the evening. Not terribly late but certainly not during normal working hours. Then again, Ali knew that Karen worked long hours, sacrificing whatever private life she might have developed for the work she loved, or was it a devotion to her husband Chris. Ali never considered that any romantic spark ever existed between Chris and Karen, but she had little doubt that a deep bond was there. She saw them as siblings, the kind that fight all the time but would give their life for the other.

Ali put down the report she was reading to pick up her phone. "You are working late," she started off.

Karen seemed startled. "Wait, what time is it." Then a pause. "Not late at all. You freaking academics don't know the meaning of work unless I interrupted some amorous activity in the bedroom."

"You are hilarious, Karen. The longer you hang around with my husband, the more you sound like him … and that is *NOT* a compliment. No matter, what's on your mind?"

Before Karen spoke, Ali could hear a chair being adjusted or turned as if the caller was getting ready of a longish telephone call. "What's on my mind is the new Afghan project?"

"You mean Azita and Deena's project to spirit promising Afghan girls out of the country before the Taliban can crush their souls?" Ali asked though she was sure of the response.

"What else? It has been keeping me up at night and, believe me, I cannot lose more beauty sleep."

"Me too," Ali noted.

Karen sighed audibly. "I am just torn. I love the idea. Don't get me wrong on that. But I am so afraid the sisters have a case of tunnel vision. This is too close to them, so they can't see the bigger picture. They aren't able to appreciate the blow back we might get if this goes awry. You see the dangers, no?"

Ali put the caller on speaker phone. For some reason she could never fathom, this enabled her to think more clearly, and she was sure no one could hear the conversation. "More than you can imagine. I mean, I have never been oppressed personally by religious extremists. Not in any total way that is, not like what is going on in Afghanistan or Iran or Saudi Arabia. My home, Jordon, has been spared the worst of all that. But I am aware, as all in my extended family are, that the extremists have plotted, and in the past, tried to kill members of my royal family. True believers are everywhere. I've been close enough to see first-hand, and certainly through my studies, how rigid perceptions of the world can distort thinking and behavior. It's a disease I call monotheistic absolutism."

"You eggheads come up with fancy terms for everything," Karen said with an exaggerated Birmingham accent she used for effect. This made Ali smile.

"Do you realize you sound more like a Birmingham working girl when you hear something you consider rubbish."

"No I don't," Karen shot back. "Okay, maybe a little. So, what does this term *absolutist monotheism* mean?"

"Monotheistic absolutism," Ali chuckled very lightly as she corrected Karen. "Nothing more than something we have covered many times at the Hairy Hare … essentially *'my god is better than your god.'* This is a debate that has been going on forever. Remember Moses competing with the priests of the Pharoah to see who had the strongest magic or to prove that the Israelites really were God's chosen people, which was their only hope for survival. And when they were dispersed, or beaten in battle, did they question their God. No, or not often, they questioned their devotion to God. No matter how often disappointed, they stuck to their belief system."

"You are losing me, professor," Karen interjected with a bit of irritation.

"Simple, really. The world is populated by people who are distributed across a dimension we might call subtle thinking. I just made that up, but it means something like this. At one end of the spectrum, people see everything in black and white terms while those at the other end engage in nuanced and subtle thinking. Some can even entertain contradictory thoughts as they incorporate dissonance within their world view, and not be afraid to struggle to come up with a new coherent view. Where a person lies on that distribution, from rigidity to subtlety, is determined partly by genetics and a lot by experience. Think about it. If you grow up in a small village in Afghanistan, how much contradictory input will you be exposed to. And where are most Trump supporters in America, in white communities in more rural states or rural areas in more populous states. Get the same message consistently and you begin to treat it as sacrosanct, a given from God. My worst example would be a working-class girl growing up in Birmingham."

Karen chortled. "Now that last cut is a classic Chris line. I will have to rescue you from him."

Ali went serious. "This is just a guide, not a predictive theory."

"Heaven forbid that an academic would say something definitive," Karen responded. "But I get what you are saying, and even agree with it."

"What the Masoud sisters are doing is salvaging younger girls, so they have a chance to experience the broader world while their minds and personalities are elastic enough to profit from the experience of seeing things in a larger context. They want to stretch them so that they can be the activists and visionaries of tomorrow. What they fear is that people like Malala Yousafzai will pass on or be forgotten. They worry that there won't be enough dedicated or talented followers to carry on the fight. They see this as a long-term struggle. Never doubt that."

"I'll grant all that. But I am also stuck on the immediate picture thing. When the Taliban figure out what is going on, they likely will be furious. This would be like spitting in their faces. They will shut down the Masoud and Kabul operations and perhaps the few other sites we have in that country. It's not that this would put a huge dent in our worldwide operations, but a lot of innocent people will suffer. Like we have said repeatedly, these extremists are great at pontificating and riling folk up, but they stink at delivering basic services."

"Karen, I know you are in a tough spot. Maybe that's why you get paid the big bucks."

Karen interrupted, "wait, before you shove this back toward me, which is where you are headed, I need a straight answer or two. I never saw you as fully backing this Masoud sister's scheme. I'm right on that, am I not."

Ali paused before answering carefully. "You are correct, but only in part. I have never wanted to shut down this effort. I have, however, often wished they would scale things back. I'm so afraid they will push so far that the regime will have to make an example of them … of us. Perhaps I lack their courage."

"Now that, I do not believe. More likely, you are afflicted with common sense. However, time is running out for me. They have some girls prepped and ready to leave. We've been running supplies at a higher level directly into the Masoud camp for some time now. Either this increased activity seems routine by now to the those spying on them or has raised all kinds of red flags. Azita and Deena are pushing me to give the green light. If they complain to Chris, he will turn to me. Frankly, I think this is one time he cannot decide. He sees the horrendous consequences to going ahead and he won't want to alienate the two women he considers as daughters by shutting their dream down. Men are freaking weak, you know."

"Wait, you want me to be the bad ass now? I'm supposed to say no since Azita already hates me and Deena is no longer my biggest fan for reasons I cannot figure out." Ali's voice broke a bit. "No, scratch that. I've figured it out."

"Ali, I'm on the fence here. We've all been letting things develop mostly by default. No one wanted to be proactive. If it were clear on one side or the other …" Karen paused. "If I saw this scheme as being without merit, or something of benefit only to the Masoud sisters, I'm strong enough to pull the plug and take the consequences. I've had everyone mad as hell at me in the past. It goes with the territory. But, in my eyes, this is a close call … "

Ali broke in, "Give it the green light."

"Really?" Karen was taken aback.

"Yes, we can overthink everything. Bottom line, there is no right answer here, just options with unknown consequences. And believe me, I've lost many hours of sleep wrestling with these issues. It was so much easier when I was just a scholar."

Karen chuckled, "that ***is*** a cushy job, no doubt about it."

Ali ignored the cut. "At the end of the day, I've come to believe the sisters are right. Yes, we can heal and feed some people now, perhaps many. But I cannot get around the notion what we would be doing is patching on temporary band aids over massive sores. It would be little more than easing the pain somewhat as the infection spreads."

"I see where you are going, the river metaphor once again."

Ali's voice suddenly came across as more confident. "We go back to it because it taps a universal truth. We won't make progress until we go back to the source of the problem. That means developing role models that shatter the stereotypes thrown about by the extremists. We need a cohort of smart, and aware Muslim women who had been rescued from the clutches of those who would keep them in bondage. Does that make sense?"

"Of course it does." Karen responded softly. "I just wish there was less of a price to pay. But life is not easy. One last thing. Do we need Chris's okay?"

"I'll take care of my husband," Ali said with more confidence than she felt.

"Okay then, I'll give the green light."

"Good," Ali then added, "Oh, and make sure you have an exit plan for the foreign staff if things go wrong."

"You mean when the shit hits the fan?"

"Precisely."

Karen gave one last hollow chuckle. "What the hell will be my exit plan when Chris comes to dispatch me to my eternal reward?"

CHAPTER 19

Connelly's Vision

"As long as there is unreasoning bigotry instead of understanding and tolerance, our nation will fall short of its full power and greatness."

John. F. Kennedy

Corinthea 'Connie' Chen met Christopher Kelly Crawford at the door. She hugged him in a desultory manner as if fully preoccupied with other things and gave him one of those forced smiles that fail to conceal the grief lying just below the surface. "Thanks for coming Chris. He wanted to see you before the others."

"Of course I'm here." He could not fully control a tinge of exasperation in his voice as if to say, *'where else would I be.'* What he did say was, mostly concerned by the request that he stop by, "Has he declined a lot recently?"

"Oh, nothing dramatic, at least not to my non-medically trained eyes," she wanted to reassure him. "Of course, he has his own clock, his own way of assessing … things. I suspect he knows when another threshold has been passed." Her voice caught slightly though she forced herself on. "All I know is that he wanted to see you, and several others. But you are the first. He insisted on that, as I said. There is one thing I have noticed, on his … decline. Sometimes there is a sharp change, or sharp to my eyes, followed by a stable period. I suppose there will come a time when the decline is … precipitous."

She led the visitor to a room that had been converted into a working space. Josh seldom went into the office he had been provided at the college. He found that too taxing these days, preferring to save all he could to focus on his work with the students Chris had provided him as assistants. Chris notice that this area of the house had been transformed into an intellectual's man cave with books and reports and articles piled everywhere in no discernible order. It was quite a large area, and Chris immediately saw that this may well have become his world, with bed for sleeping and an adjacent toilet, since this had once served as a master bedroom. Yet, it now had become an intellectual's lair with the clutter expected after decades of academic use. *'Perfect,'* Chris thought, *'this is what I want when my time comes.'* He made a mental note to bring Ali by to see this so she would know what to do for him when his time came.

Josh looked up as Chris entered the room, his eyes brightened for a moment before assuming a relaxed, satisfied aspect. "Welcome to my lair. I suspect the last time you were here it was used in a more conventional manner."

Chris whistled. "I see you have commanded full control of your world. I must ask your secret. If I proposed something similar to Ali, she would point out that I have at least three or four official offices scattered about. Damn, I'm not sure how many any longer."

"No big secret, just convince people you are dying. Works every time."

Chris looked at him sharply. *'Was he not really dying, just faking it for effect?'* What he saw dispelled that moment of hope. Josh was thinner and lacked color. Though the room was warm he had a blanket over his lower body which perhaps disguised to some extent the ravages of the slow-moving disease. Pace in such matters clearly was subjective, with the observer oft seeing what they wanted to see. Yet, his eyes were bright and animated. Chris wondered, *'how much would this demonstration of energy take-out of him?'* Josh would exit on his own terms. "Josh! You have the best scholarly man cave I've run across."

"Yes, I admit it. Everyone is being so kind. Perhaps I should have exited this tedious world decades ago."

"Chris, talk some sense into him." Connie rolled her eyes as she exited. "Oh, I'll leave you two miscreants to your mischief."

Josh looked directly at Chris. "Others will be joining us, but I wanted to see you first. My internal clock tells me it is time to get my shit together." He spoke louder when he saw his friend try to object. "No time for useless evasions of reality."

"Quite right." Chris muttered.

Josh leaned back. Many years ago, I ran across a poem my Ralph Waldo Emmerson. The damn thing stuck with me. It is still in my head …

> *"To laugh often and much;*
>
> *To win the respect of intelligent*
>
> *People and the affection of children;*
>
> *To earn the appreciation of honest*

Critics and endure the betrayal of false friends; to

Appreciate beauty, to find the best in others; to leave

The world a bit better, whether by a healthy child,

a garden patch or a redeemed social condition; to know

even one life has breathed easier because you have lived.

This is to have succeeded.'

... The thing is that these last few months have had me thinking hard on what I am leaving behind."

"I think about that a lot for myself, even now. I keep coming up with nothing." Chris smiled.

Josh smiled. "You will consider it in a far more immediate way when your time comes. Believe me on that one. I guess we all ... no, all of us who think hard about stuff ... try to figure out what we have learned in life. I suspect none of us comes up with anything original, except for a few like Newton, Darwin, Einstein, Hawkings, and the like. But some insights and lessons strike us as worth noting. Long ago, as an ersatz revolutionary, I was struck by this image of transformational change. The pace of change was exhilarating, suggesting something brand new, but only if we could shed our self-destructive instincts and habits."

"Including useless conflicts, such as Vietnam."

"Exactly! Then I was struck by simple insights, those things we all know in retrospect but fail to appreciate at the time. Think about this. In the year 1500, we could still have renaissance men who commanded most knowledge available to us. Consider Da Vinci for example. Yet, two and a half centuries later, it took groups of scholars to gather extent knowledge into the first encyclopaedias. Dennis Diderot organized one of the initial efforts. It was only a little more than a century later that the academy realized that an educated man needed more than four years of advanced study to command even a single subject in any adequate manner. So, graduate schools were founded by the 1880s, at Johns Hopkins first and then Clark University. And now, it is axiomatic that the vast majority of all scientists that have ever lived are alive today. The smartest scientists in select fields are experts only within a narrow subfield of their study focus since the accumulation of knowledge continues to proceed exponentially, at lightning speed. Academics in the same University department can no longer talk with one another."

"And yet, we seem to be dumber than ever." Chris interjected.

"Spot on," Josh enthused. "Some seven or eight decades ago, America embraced vaccines to eradicate polio and other devastating viruses. Jonas Salk was a public hero and turned down opportunities to profit from his polio cure. The public good was a virtue then, and scientists were heroes. Recently, many Americans drank bleach or some such rot when their scientists came up with clinically tested vaccines to stop a global pandemic. Some on the right want to put the scientists who stopped the pandemic in jail."

Chris groaned. "You are right, the nutjobs want to put Doctor Fauci in jail. Talk about a freaking regression."

"Exactly," Josh said with some animation. "We could argue that our failure to advance is the result of old vices, like greed. You know, the same old stuff about one-third of wealth is owned by the top 1 percent and some 40 percent of new money goes to the top 1 percent. Or we look at factoids like in 1989, the middle class controlled twice as much of the wealth as the top 1 percent. Now the top 1percent has as much as the entire middle class. And if we take a more global view, we see 17 percent of the world's population living in just 35 OECD countries command 62% of world's GDP while people in the other 160 countries make do with the remaining scraps."

"Which means ... though I know my bottom line on all these trends."

"Same line, I presume. Resources and advantages, when accumulated in such egregious inequality, give the privileged few such enormous power. It leaves so many others excluded, suspicious, and hostile."

Chris interjected. "I still remember a classic witticism from Will Rogers, something he said during the great depression in the 1930s. *"Ten men in our country could buy the world, and ten million can't buy enough to eat."*

"Will was a classic, I visited his homestead in Eastern Oklahoma once, not all that long ago." Josh mused. "Anyway, the question now becomes, how will the privileged use their advantages, excluding those few who think of the common good? In the old days, they might oppress people by force, with mercenaries whose loyalty they buy. Now, I would suggest they employ, for the most part, subtler means. Oh, we yet have the usual array of authoritarian regimes from the nominal left in China, North Korea, and so forth. And we have the usual array of wanna-be Fascists like Putin, Matteo Salvini, Jair Bolsonaro, Eric Zemmour, Marine le Pen, Victor Orban, Modi, and now Trump or, more likely in 2024, DeSantis.

"Subtler means?" Chris queried.

"It would prove embarrassing to be seen as opposing democratic principles, unless you are from an area where there is no tradition of such, like Russia. In most other areas you must appear to support the will of the people even as you systemically go about dismantling democratic protocols step by step. The thing is to manipulate grounded beliefs in such a way that ordinary folk vote against their interests willingly, enthusiastically, even in the face of overwhelming evidence to the contrary. You know the drill. We have all those naïve voters going into polls to vote for Republicans whose only explicit goal is to enrich the few at the expense of the many."

"That never ceases to amaze me." Chris groaned.

"The Republican base, mostly less affluent white working stiffs, still believe that party does better at managing the economy and representing their interests. There are decades upon decades of evidence to the contrary but that is part of the default position of the American society. Worse still, America is a lighthouse site. If that country can be gaslighted to willingly give it all over to a few uber wealthy individuals at the expense of the many, that tactic will likely work anywhere. Orwell's nightmare will be realized where slavery is freedom, war is peace, power is right, and poverty is moral turpitude. Trump is an idiot, but he still had a major political party doing his bidding in pushing the totally false and discredited proposition of *'the big lie.'*"

"I suppose that is what the founders most feared about a Republic, that ordinary people would not be capable of governing their own affairs, that an elite had to keep them in check, thus the electoral college and non-elected or appointed senators … in the beginning at least." Chris agreed.

"Absolutely, but every safety feature has a flaw. The passions of the mob can be dangerous, populism run amok that can easily slide into despotism. But the so-called elite is very likely to shift the rules further to their advantage. Why do the one-percenters, on average, pay less taxes proportionally than working folk? That's a rhetorical question … because they can. Astoundingly, they have convinced working folks that this is fair. Easy to do when you control much of the media. Then, distracting the masses, or enough of them at least, is child's play."

"I sense you are moving toward a proposition here."

Josh smiled. "Can't fool you. But let us wait for the others. I wanted to have a moment to thank you again."

"You have done that enough already."

"Perhaps." He spoke more softly now. "I never wanted children. However, I can't help thinking that it would have been nice to have one like you. That would have been a fine legacy to leave. But that not being the case, I will leave you to oversee my legacy, gifts of a more abstract nature."

Chris was about to ask what he meant by his final words when there was a light knock on the door. Connie peered in, "Ashley is here. Ready for more company?"

"Absolutely," Josh beamed, as an attractive, professional looking woman in her early 30s walked into the room.

Chris looked, pause, then did a double take. "My word, Ashley …" then he paused.

"Boyd. My word, professor, you don't watch the BBC news much do you?"

"Of course. You are a star now. But give me a break. You look so different. When you were in my class you looked quite …"

"Don't say it." She interrupted. "I looked like a harlot, probably behaved worse. I cringe at the thought of those days, a highlight of which was that one class that Josh here, and your black friend from America, visited back in my day. I cannot imagine what they thought of me. I think, at the time that is, I was seduced by the attention my looks got me. That happens to a lot of young girls. Some never get past that and are stricken when it all goes away after a few extra pounds or a couple of kids. I was lucky. I looked in the mirror one day and had an epiphany. *'Get by on your talents, not your body.'* That's what I told myself."

"Good for you." Chris said. "And I must be honest, I've seen enough of you on TV to witness this Pygmalion like transformation. Still, you look different, better I mean, in person. That happens all the time. You see someone in an unexpected place, and you cannot place them. Most embarrassing. But good for you, your success I mean. And you are here because …?"

"Oh, the network has enough faith in me now to do a few side projects. No guarantee it will get airtime, but Josh's story has appeal, an exile for his beliefs and how he has evolved. I think we can sell it to the top brass on the Trump phenomenon. Brits are still fascinated by that character. It is like our obsession with Hitler, how did a sophisticated people fall for that nutcase."

"Now we know, look at America" Chris said. "It is way too easily done."

Josh interrupted. "This lovely young lady hasn't figured out that what I'm telling her is all BS."

She laughed. "Oh no, I check out your claims. It is the BS that Professor Crawford dished out in his seminars that remains highly suspect."

"Wait," Chris protested, "you lapped up my genius."

"That's because I had a hopeless girl-crush on you." Ashley blushed. "Oops, I shouldn't have confessed that even though it is ancient history."

"Wait," Chris protested. "I thought men got sexier as they aged."

Ashley chuckled. "You keep thinking that. But I suspect a few naïve co-eds yet have the hots for you. Young girls are so impressionable."

Chris had a retort, but the door opened again. In came Morris Greenstein, his wife Carla, Bob Wilson, and Peter Favulli. Chairs were secured and all settled in place. "We came by to see if you were ready to join the revolution once again." Mo said with a straight face.

"I'd be most happy to. However, my loyalty record is suspect. Are you sure you want me?"

"We voted. Carla was a hold out," Mo gasped when his wife's fist caught him in the midsection. "Oh god, when will I learn," he managed.

Josh chuckled. "We never learn. That's why males are an evolutionary dead end."

Once again, the door opened and in came Chris's two siblings, Kristen and Katerina.

"Kay and Kat made it." Josh beamed. "I was dubious about them when I sent an invitation out."

"For you we would come," Kay said. "For our brother, not so much."

"Not a chance." Kat added for emphasis.

Josh continued to smile. "We are only missing the students Chris loaned me for my work. They are very smart, but you know students. Not like in our day," he nodded toward his old college mates, "we kept our noses to the grindstone, studying all the time."

"Study, my ass," Carla snorted. "We were too busy getting ourselves educated and trying to save humanity to waste time on our courses."

Bob Wilson snorted and then apologized. "I recall how naïve we were. I remember getting excited by the Narodism movement."

"What?" Chris interjected.

"Oh, we fantasized that we were early revolutionaries, like the early Bolsheviks before Stalin ruined everything. The Narodists were Russian intellectuals who would live among the peasants and freed serfs to bond with them and incite revolutionary fervor. Didn't work then, seldom worked anywhere in fact."

Mo smiled. "Yes, I saw myself as Vladimir Ulyanov, Lenin to most of you … trying to create a new world or maybe Lenin was just attempting to avenge his brother who was hung by the Okhrana in 1884."

"You do look a lot like Lenin, the same baldhead." Carla said with a smile before turning serious. "Yes, we had our childish role models. I think I patterned myself more like the Boyeviki, the pseudo revolutionaries who were more like romantic, rogue gangsters causing the old regime all kinds of trouble. That's how Stalin started along with other characters of revolutionary legend like Kabo and Kamo."

Peter smirked, "I always knew you clowns were a bunch of freaking Reds."

"Now you have to be a Republican to be a Red," Josh added. "George Orwell's world has arrived, maybe a bit after 1984. Words and concepts are reversed … black is white, up is down, freedom is slavery, and so on. You know, the word Bolshevik comes from the Russian word bolshinsto which means majority. However, the word emerged as a label for the more radial element of the party at a London conference in 1903 when they were, in fact, a distinct minority. All is illusion. Today, psychologist would call it framing but the notion has been around forever … language matters."

"As do values," Carla added. "I think we all suffered from an advanced case of '*tikkun olam.*'"

"What?" Peter asked.

"That's an old Jewish tradition associated with wanting to repair the world. It is rampant among Hebrews though I've noticed that some Catholics are so inflicted." Carla looked at Josh.

Josh pushed on, apparently wanting to take hold of the dialogue. "I'm hardly a model for Catholicism. But there is another point we absorbed back then."

"Which I'm sure you will share with us." Peter prompted.

At that moment, the door opened one final time and the three students entered and found room in the background. "Ah, my brain trust. For those not familiar with them, I give you Gretchen Willingham, Ashok Kaur, and his sister Amandeep. I could not have carried on without them. But I digress."

"We always thought that the best part, your digressions." Peter slipped in.

Josh gave him the finger and continued. "The other obvious point is that change takes time. Most Americans saw the conflict in Vietnam as if it were captured by the political contest of the day. What they failed to appreciate was the historical context of things. They saw some Communists challenging us Americans. Few knew the French background, how missionaries first went to Southeast Asia in 1802, and how today's Vietnam, Cambodia, and Laos was usurped into French Indochina by the 1880s. The colonial masters played the divide and conquer game. The blowback by native nationalists also took time. Ho Chi Minh, the George Washington of his country first went to Paris in 1920 for studies and took up with the Commintern there between 1924 and 1926."

"Not surprising," Mo interjected. "They likely were the only ones talking an anti-colonialist line."

Josh nodded and continued. "Eventually, he returned to Vietnam to begin the protracted process of national liberation. But in

1940, the Japanese replaced the French. During those years, Minh and General Giap created the Vietminh with American help from the OSS, today's CIA. When the Japanese were defeated with much help from the Vietminh, Ho Chi Minh believed that his country would be granted independence. After all, he fought for the allies. Yes, he was that naïve. But America did what it always did, it betrayed indigenous allies and sided with the European Colonials, in this case the French. That led to more conflict that lasted some three more decades. Like our revolutionary patriots, the Vietnamese nationalists would not give up despite how bad things got. And the Americans, like the British in the 1770s and 80s, found it too expensive and hopeless to continue. We would also get on our ships and go home."

Kat interrupted in her incisive, professional voice. "I suspect the point is now coming, though the history lesson is fascinating."

"Yes," Josh responded, "I see why they put you in charge of the family fortune. You have a bottom-line mind. All this is to segue into my main points which involves where we should go with our work to save democracy in America. Listen, I am very aware of the work Chris and Kat and the others in your organization have done to push back against the rise of authoritarianism in the States. And I know the reasons behind this passion, aside from values. I had enough discussions with Chris to see how deeply the family was affected by the work of your father, an ideologue of the worst and most despicable sort. My father was similarly blinded, by the Irish Republican Army and a united motherland. But he didn't have the money to create much havoc, nor was he as despicable as the Crawford patriarch. Charles Senior did have the money, a narrow obsession, and a black soul."

"No shit." Kay uttered before apologizing.

"I guess my first point is that the lessons we learn in our early years never fully go away, though we employ them with more care. Think of Ronald Reagan. He had been a Roosevelt democrat until he earned enough money in the post WWII era when we still had a progressive tax structure. When he saw his tax bite, he became a Republican and never looked back, eventually helping spark a political revolution that created the winner-take-all, inequitable society we now have. We also learned a few immutable lessons."

"Which are?" Chris leaned forward.

"You and Kay and especially Kat poured a lot of the family fortune into fighting off your father's political agenda in the runup to the 2020 election. You supported background research, political ads, gave money to key organizations like the Lincoln Group. All that was fine and necessary. In fact, you did help stave off the worst outcome, the re-election of Trump, though that pathological narcissist will not admit to his loss. Did any of us ever think things would go so far as they did on January 6?"

"That was a wake-up call." Kat noted.

Josh pushed in. "Then, as I've listened to the chatter since I've gotten here, it struck me you are without a direction. Are you still focused on going after Trump and the other denizens of the hard right? Perhaps you will shift your focus to the next wanna-be authoritarian in line, probably DeSantis? The right, now embodied fully in the Republican Party will not back down from the pursuit of power by any means. If we think the threat to American democracy ends with Trump, should he really go away, that would be a huge mistake. Where they are now is the product of a decades long campaign which has altered the fundamentals of America's political dialogue, and that is key." Josh paused, looking around the room. "I've been using Gretchen, Ashok, and Amandeep as sounding boards for my thoughts. They really are smart kids. They remind me of us," he looked at his old college friends, "but less impetuous."

"You mean less foolish." Carla added.

"Perhaps we were foolish but, as we have discussed more than once since we reunited, we were right. Here's the thing, though. Being right is not enough, nor is knocking off the autocrat *du jour*. You must focus on two larger ends." Once again, he paused, signalling something important. "You must transform the underlying political and social narrative that dominates public discourse. To do this, you need to take a much longer view. Before you jump on me, let me babble a bit while I've still got the energy."

"You have the floor, my friend." Chris said gently to Josh.

"I mentioned the importance of semantics or framing issues a moment or two ago. Well, that seems an inconsequential or perhaps obvious point, but those approaches are extremely critical. What the right learned so long ago, a point we have noted earlier, is that values and policies arise out of underlying gut narratives. Oh sure, the nerds and some of the elite stress evidence and analysis but as real people know, the best story wins the day. Even some policy wonks realize this. And the right has the best stories." He caught himself. "That's not quite correct. They tell the best stories. They tell people what to fear and whom to blame. More importantly, they tell it repeatedly and simply. Above all, they don't bury their message in academic journals and government reports. Thus, they have established the default position for the American dialogue. Too many people embrace their world view without knowing it."

Kay interrupted him. "As Chris keeps telling me, I'm just an overpaid mechanic of the human body. Can you explain this in another way?"

"I can try. Basic narratives are the premises we rely upon to assess right and wrong, good and evil. They precede our judgments of policies and politicians, which partly explains why voting patterns shift so little despite the mountains of cash spent on elections. Minds are locked in. On one level, we have specific policies we argue over. Is welfare good or bad? Are taxes too high or not? What should we do with migrants at our border? Do vaccines kill or cure us. Is being pro-life about protecting the pre-born or helping vulnerable children after they are born? But there are more fundamental beliefs that inform and shape how we see these obvious choices."

"Such as," Mo asked.

I'll suggest just a few here. We have all heard of the *'social contract,'* a principle that replaced autocratic rule, often monarchies, with governments that were legitimate only if they somehow based on the consent of the people. But what is the basis of such a contract? Is it founded on the *rights* of the governed or the *obligations* that people have to one another? How one answers that underlying question goes far to determining what form of society one sees as being legitimate and responsive to the governed. It informs the kind of society in which you want to live."

"How so?" Mo asked.

Josh wrinkled his forehead. "For example, from that basic choice flows our notions of *control* or *oppression*. Locke stressed vertical control or the tyranny of the elites. Hobbes focused on horizontal oppression or the universal struggle among ourselves. The hard right sees freedom as being liberated from most government regulation, a vertical perspective. But is that freedom? To my mind, that merely exposes us to an oppressive onslaught from so many of our grasping, self-interested peers who would abuse us and trick us in ways you cannot imagine, and which government is best equipped to counter or control. Caveat emptor is nonsense, especially in markets where information is imperfect and power is distributed unevenly. Look at how Americans are being scammed by the most expensive health care system in the world that delivers sub-par help. That take is more based on a Hobbesian view of things."

"Spot-on." Kay interrupted then raised a hand to apologize. "I mean the American health system sucks. I'm not sure about the Locke and Hobbes thing,"

"Our system of law also reflects our foundational concept of what is good. We, the British and the Americans, rely upon a sense of justice that is adversarial. We pay attention to the rules of the judicial game and then let the contestants battle it out in what is presumed to be a fair contest within an objective arena. Please, so much depends upon the resources each side has. Justice is easily purchased."

"And the alternative" Gretchen asked from the back of the room and then looked embarrassed for speaking out.

"Good question. The French, for example, pursue an inquisitive form of justice where both sides seek the truth. It is less about winning and more about getting things right. How unamerican, Socialist even. The same goes for our policy debates. I cringe when our economists reduce all to zero-sum games where every loser must oppose a policy no matter how much good it does."

"I have always hated that." Chris uttered with some passion. "You see these analyses all the time pointing out who will win and lose given a change. Sometimes you must sacrifice things for the common good, damn it."

Josh went on. "We assume that we have protocols for assuring that the will of the people is represented when, in fact, money is the driving force behind who wins and loses in that arena as well. Campaigning is almost exclusively determined by money raising activities these days with only a few contests determined by ideas. I counted the number of emails and texts and snail mail I got asking for political donations during one day in the last election. It was over 200 when I stopped counting. Not long ago, there was a Wisconsin Senator, named William Proxmire, who spent less than a thousand dollars on his re-election campaigns. You can't run for County Coroner on that kind of money today. We now care little about decent governance and more about instilling irrational hate for the other side and stoking unreasoned fear among our own base, hardly a prescription for a positive and productive public dialogue."

"It is beginning to come, what you are trying to drive through my thick skull." Kay was listening hard. "I think you are saying that most of what we have been doing with our political work in the states has focused on the wrong level. Is that it?"

"Precisely," Josh seemed animated. "One must think of the challenge in layers. There are the surface layers where specific policies are fought over, this direction or that. Then there are the underlying layers where the basic normative narratives lie, what is good and bad. They shape our decisions. Perhaps there is even a deeper layer where the foundational structures of our values lie, where we determine and embrace the absolute necessities for a decent society."

"Like an onion?" Ashley Boyd broke her silence. "I can't believe this, but I still recall a paper of yours, Josh, that Chris assigned to our seminar. It approached the stagnant policy debate about the public dole with the onion metaphor. It just hit me that you wrote that paper. We all loved it."

"Guilty, and I now can see why you are so smart. You read my work. But seriously, we could argue about which elements go where forever. For me, a foundational choice lies in how we differentially value competition versus cooperation. Do we see our individual and collective futures depending on who wins and beats the others, or on how best we collaborate for some larger benefit or societal goal?"

"I can guess your choice," Carla smirked.

"I bet you can. The American and British economic systems, our legal systems, our political systems, almost all are premised on competition and winning. Rewards inevitably go to those that scramble to the top of the heap, which justifies their accumulating all the goodies. That is how we have defined excellence, and fairness, over time. Many believe that is how progress is made. That is why people acquiesce to tax schemes that reward the winners of society at a price paid by the average Joe. With a straight face they argue that it is fair when Bezos and Musk and Trump get another tax break because they earned all those billions by hard work and superior talent even if they sucked at the government trough to get it. They argue it is efficient in an economic sense, since it drives the economy forward. Even if the American economy always does better during Democratic administrations. It is the John Wayne obsession, the tough man doing it on his own, without government or any other help. About half of America adores that view. They see Democrats as helping the losers of society and worse, rewarding indolence and failure while spiting their most valued virtue of self-reliance."

This time Kat spoke up. "In terms of what we should do in the future, where does this lead? Despite being a member of the filthy rich elite, I am eager to help."

Josh emitted an embarrassed chuckle. "It is okay to be a member of the filthy elite if you support me with your ill-gotten gains."

"I'll second that." Mo asserted.

Josh pushed on. "Well, the students have brought some reading material for you all. But I can say this now. The other point I made when I started is that change takes time. Few revolutions, for good or evil, happened overnight. The right laid out a rather specific plan in the early 1970s, perhaps disappointed with Nixon's performance as President, too liberal in their eyes."

"He was a big spender." Chris threw in.

"The thing is, they stayed with this strategy over the next half century. They managed to alter the underlying narrative sufficiently to establish a new default position for what constitutes the good society. I can remember when policies were assessed by the litmus test of *'what does it do for the poor.'* Hard to believe but that this was true. Now, it is what *'how does it benefit the top one percent'* or, more accurately, *'the top one-tenth of one percent.'*"

"And you think we can chip away at these fundamentals, as you call them?" Chris asked.

"I am saying that is our only hope. I was most impressed by the Lincoln Project. Being former Republicans, they went after the gut, not the brain. They knew from experience that was more effective in moving the masses. Now, we are brainiacs so we cannot eschew what we do best, focus on rational arguments. But we should learn from the other side. Repetition and simplicity are the key, along with taking the long view. As I have hammered away at so often in the past, the hard right took decades to shift the default position of American politics away from a more cooperative and collaborative foundational underpinning. You know, where we are in this together, the attitude that prevailed in World War II. For at least a half century we have had a foundational premise that idealized grabbing all you could get no matter the cost to others. But that core value or understanding is not immutable. If they could change it, so can we."

"You believe that, don't you?" Bob Wilson said in a voice tinged with more admiration than doubt.

Josh nodded to Bob before looking directly at Kat. "My dear, you better bring some of your rich friends on board since this would take even more lucre than the Crawford family has." Josh then winced slightly, as if in discomfort. "You know, when I was young academic and policy wonk, I suffered terribly from the famous imposter complex. You know, I was just a working-class kid from Boston who didn't belong in a world class university or the halls of power. I kept waiting for the adults to throw me out. That never happened and, when I fooled them for years, I gradually recognized that I belonged, that I made sense when I talked and authored papers and reports. But now … now I almost feel I'm on the backside of things …"

"What are you saying?" Chris asked softly.

"That I'm babbling to all of you but not making any sense. I feel I've lost my edge, not as sharp as I once was." He took a deep breath as if there was not enough oxygen available. "I can't even decide if all this is the ramblings of an old fool."

Gretchen spoke. "That is nonsense. It has been a privilege working with you. Your … mind is amazing, and I've been around some good ones."

"Absolutely, she studied under me … the best." Chris uttered with his lopsided Irish smile.

Gretchen considered a few retorts but remained serious. "Professor Connelly … Josh. You make connections that very few others can. And this plan you have authored is … remarkable. I know Ashok and Amandeep feel the same."

"Now I'm embarrassed. I didn't mean to force any praise out of you, except maybe from Chris and I'm not quite sure why. What would it profit me to seek adulation from such an inferior mind?"

"I should throw you out on your Irish ass, except you are so popular around here. I just don't get it." Chris deadpanned.

"The rest of us do." Kay responded wit an equally straight face.

Everyone now laughed at this exchange, which pleased Josh much. Taking another deep breath, he continued. "I'm running out of steam here. But take what we have written. It lays out more fully the concepts I've started to articulate here and begins to suggest a campaign. The thing is that there will be so many individuals and organizations fighting over the individual political contests and policy battles. That arena will be overrun. But with your resources, you just might start waging a different kind of war, one aimed at where perceptions are formed, and values affirmed. I have ideas for that kind of war, as you will read, but I'm afraid you will have to work out the detailed strategies. Sorry."

Chris found his voice crack as he said. "Hey, you Mick, no apologies. We won't fail you." He wanted to say more but found he could not.

Kat bailed him out. "In some ways, this is a godsend, I think, though I will have to study it more. I have this staff that worked hard on the election cycles, but we are in a lull right now. We could use a new direction, get their juices going. Exceptionally talented people need a vision more than anything, a challenge. This might be it."

Josh smiled briefly. "Before you all go, and I get more beauty rest, one more thing. In the old days I would have memorized this but now I'll read it. Just a passage from one of Ray Bradbury's works, *Fahrenheit 451* I believe. In any case, this selection has always stuck with me. He picked up a piece of paper that seemed aged:

> *Everyone must leave something behind when he dies, my grandfather said. A child or book or a painting or a wall built, or a pair of shoes made. Or a garden planted. Something your hand touched in some way so that your soul has somewhere to go when you die, and when people look at that tree or that flower you planted, you're there.*
>
> *It doesn't matter what you do, he said, so long as you change something that's like you after you take your hands away. The difference between the man who just cuts lawns, and a real gardener is in the touching, he said. The lawn-cutter might just as well not have been there at all; the gardener will be there a lifetime.*

"Now, time for you all to leave and get to work." For some moments, no one moved. "For Christ's sake, I'm not going to die today. You will have plenty of time to mope about me. Well, some time at least."

Each person shuffled out, first saying a word or two directly to the man they loved before exiting. Carla kissed him on the forehead, Mo exchanged their old revolutionary handshake.

The students distributed the documents they had brought. Chris noticed that Gretchen had tears flowing down her cheeks. As she was about to join the others outside, he leaned into her and whispered. "He has touched you deeply."

She looked at her academic mentor. "I love that man," she said in a barely audible whisper.

"So do I, so do I." Chris walked to where Josh rested, his eyes now half closed. "I'll be back after I read this. But for now, can I borrow that Bradbury piece."

Josh handed Chris the wrinkled piece of paper. "And Chris, one last thing."

"What?" Chris leaned even closer.

"Don't fuck this up," Josh smiled broadly.

Chris laughed loudly as he straightened up and exited the room as Josh closed his eyes to rest.

CHAPTER 20

Intimations of the End

> *"We know they are lying. They know they are lying. They know that we know they are lying. They know that we know they are lying. And still they continue to lie."*
>
> *Alexander Solzhenitsyn*

It was a bright sunny day as the helicopter took off and headed east over the adjacent peaks toward an azure, blue sky. Ever more supplies were needed as the swell of refugees from the area surrounding the Masoud Center increased in numbers and need. Supply flights in and out were a constant reality these days. Many were malnourished, some ill from untreated ailments as many local public medical facilities suffered loss of personnel, resources, and essential supplies. As Farzana watched the aircraft disappear into the cloudless sky her heart fluttered. Another handful of girls were aboard, on their way to a new life.

As the airship escaped her sight and hearing, Farzana considered her journey so far. It had started modestly, with a few carefully selected girls, and their families, being approached with caution. After a cautious start, she ranged further and further afield, from Pyawusht to Shalzor along the route of the Panjshir river, and so many other communities that stretched in the low places surrounded by the rugged Kush. At first, she sought out only the families she knew and the girls who had studied at the Masoud Center. It was planned as a modest initiative where caution would prevail to keep things quiet.

That was a fool's endeavor, and all engaged in it realized as much even as they refused to accept reality. Slowly, with glacial inevitability, the modest beginning picked up speed and grew beyond the control of those who thought they were in charge. Farzana should have realized that in the very first few days as she witnessed target families sharing her vision with others in their small communities, others they thought could be trusted. But who could be trusted in these times, especially as the economy became more desperate? Yet, there was little that could be done to control things. It had to be stopped altogether, or let the thing run its course to whatever consequences would arise.

While a significant number refused her offer in the early weeks, that trend shifted as the new reality of a second Taliban rule sank in, not only in terms of oppressive regulations but also of economic disaster. For a nation so dependent on foreign aid, the cessation of western help proved disastrous. Beyond that, talented women were driven from public positions and zealots proved less capable of governing than they were at rousing their devotees to religious fervor. It was a hard lesson to learn, that competence trumped passion in the affairs of society.

It was not so many weeks before Farzana noticed changes as she visited new and old villages. Families whom at first resisted her entreaties or who refused her offer outright now welcomed her. They saw her as a way out of an increasingly hopeless situation. New families with whom she had no previous contact approached her, often traveling many miles to offer their daughters, and even sons, for exile to places they could only dimly imagine. She knew vaguely that girls were seen as less essential in many of these families. Sending them away lessened the imploding financial crisis within the home. This put Farzana in a bind. This was not a humanitarian project per se. It was an educational effort. She wanted girls with a thirst for knowledge, and with some promise of intellectual talent. But that was not always obvious at first. She knew that some never had an opportunity to shine but, with help, could rise far. It was the hidden treasure problem.

The opportunities for exit were limited. Only a few at a time could go while many waited and pleaded their case. Her educational assistants, teachers when they were free to educate girls openly, worked with girls who had never been to the Masoud Center school. Were some of them raw talents? Could they be educated if given the chance? How could one possibly know? Every day she looked into eyes wide with hope, or was it fear? She had to deny most supplicants, her words increasingly felt like daggers into those whose entreaties could not be honored and to her own heart. She knew that some supplicants saw this as a possible way for the whole family to escape, believing that once the child was in another land, the rest of the family might easily follow. Her doses of reality often were ignored. It was a painful exercise and each night she would cry herself to sleep.

Making the situation worse is that more girls were coming from Kabul. The families were more sophisticated there, with more of them eager to send their young girls abroad for any semblance of hope, no matter how vaguely understood. While it was easy for Ferhana and Bahiri to identify the most promising candidates, getting them north to the Masoud Center proved challenging. A few could emigrate using normal travel channels if their families had sufficient resources and family members abroad who could provide cover for a girl traveling out of the country for a so-called 'visit' abroad. But that opportunity was limited and could not last forever. Eventually, it would be realized that these girls were not returning. Security at the Kabul airport was tight. Soon, the better candidates were cautiously shipped north to the Masoud Center, hidden in supply trucks that routinely travelled between the medical facilities. As with the supply flights in and out of the Panjshir Area, they were sufficiently routine not to attract attention.

As the number of girls waiting for their turn increased, hoping that it would not be long and then fearing that their time might come, other tactics were explored. Perhaps the girls from the mountain area west of the Masoud Center could escape on the larger supply planes that flew in and out of the airport serving Faizabad. That would eliminate the dangerous trip to the Panjshir Valley and increase the numbers who could get out. And so it happened that another pipeline to the West was created. As in the case of girls flying out of the Masoud Center in Helicopters, the plan was simple. The girls would dress as males, and seemingly help in unloading the supplies from the aircraft. Sometimes, Taliban officials might check the boxes being unloaded for contraband, but they all contained medical supplies or supplies to operate a medical center and refugee camp. When there were Taliban officials in the area, the pilots would keep their props rotating to kick up dust. The workers, real and fake, would cover their faces to protect themselves and hide their gender. It all appeared chaotic from the outside, though the number exiting the planes at the end of the unloading were less than the number who originally helped. No one ever seemed to keep track. As the planes rose from the airport, many a girl peered out the small windows. The city, and the Koksha river, would soon disappear from their view as tears of relief and loss crossed their cheeks.

Yet, all involved knew that this was a trickle compared to the growing demand to leave. And so, another strategy emerged, one that suggested the desperation creeping over those involved in the operation. For those children who were older, a more dangerous plan developed. Former teachers and their husbands would volunteer to escort small groups by public transportation to Jalalabad, using various schemes that they were traveling to attend weddings or visit sick relatives.

Then they would hire local drivers that would get them closer to the border before hiking around the border posts toward Peshawar in Pakistan. The entire journey was fraught with danger, but the final leg remained the most difficult and dangerous. Suspicious eyes were everywhere but they found the authorities had yet to organize themselves fully. They were still consolidating power, especially in the rural areas outside major cities. Their hold on power in the north and east remained the weakest of all.

None of these schemes were enough. Farzana would communicate her frustrations and worries to Deena and Azita both of whom shared her concerns. All three knew the delicate balancing act in which they were engaged. With each new tactic came risk of exposure and retaliation. Farzana would discuss the situation with Archie, Agnes, Carolyn, Kenji, and other senior staff. By this time, they all fully understood the scope of the operation and the extent of the risks involved. The time to reverse course had long passed, forfeited in those first few weeks when the dynamics of the situation fully revealed the dangers all faced. She thought back to those days. Had she thought everything through? Had she appreciated the dangers? Now she could not reimagine her thinking at the time. She saw the need and felt such a longing in her heart. How could she fail these girls?

At the time, though, she was thinking about the girls she knew and cared about personally. Somehow, the reality of things escaping her control managed to elude her. How could that have happened? But she realized that was such an easy trap. The intense desire to ease the pain of others can easily mask the obvious futility of one's hopes and the inevitability of failure. And so she walked through the camp on this warm day. Looking about at the faces surrounding her. There were so many, and their expressions infused with such despair. It was agony for her. What she could do was so little in the face of such bottomless need. It was in these moments that she despaired of God. She recalled something she had read once in a text. It was a saying that had been scratched on one of the buildings at Auschwitz during the holocaust. She could no longer recall the exact words, but the meaning stayed with her, something like 'if there is a god, he will have to plead for my forgiveness given what I have seen here.'

Farzana stopped. Her reverie was dispatched by the reality about her. She had seen as many distended bellies among the children as she could tolerate on this day and whirled about to walk back to the administrative buildings. What else could she do but what was in her power for whatever time she had left. In her heart, she knew her fate. It was not pretty. The foreigners might get out, but she had no protection. Her fate was likely sealed when all was revealed. Her greatest regret was Sayed. Yes, she had let her heart get the better of her. Now that she had found this man with whom sharing her life seemed a good thing, that life probably was near an end. If she were not beheaded in some public ceremony as a lesson to others, she could imagine even worse fates. But again, what choice did she have?'

She focused on the distant mountains. They always gave her solace. They would remain long after her troubles, and the troubles of her people, were no longer present to her. That gave her an odd comfort in a world that made little sense. Just as her moments of despair were receding, she almost bumped into a man, one of the Taliban who spent much time observing the camp. She knew he was important, at least locally, and thus she had taken great pains to avoid him, but now she had been distracted. She cursed her inattention and tried to walk past him.

"You are the one named Farzana."

She stopped, suddenly feeling dizzy. "Yes." That was all she could say.

"I wish a word."

Her heart stopped, as her mind frantically sought an escape. "I don't think that appropriate." She tried to ease past him, but he moved to block her way.

"Just a moment sister. Besides, whatever I say is, by definition, appropriate."

Farzana recognized this man. She even had heard his name mentioned but now her mind was frozen. What was it? What confused her in this moment was that he sounded educated, even urbane. That was so unlike most of the new rulers who struck her as little more than illiterate thugs. "Of course," was all she could say as she came to a full halt.

He smiled at her, which made her queasy. Yet, his words were not hostile. "Do you miss teaching?"

She froze for a moment. Then it struck her. *'His name is Aalem,'* she said to herself with satisfaction. Then aloud, she managed. "I only do what is asked of me."

At this, the man she knew as Aalem laughed out loud. "You are a clever lass. That is for sure."

"If you say so," Farzana muttered without looking at him.

"I see we are not to have a dialogue. That is a pity," Aalem said with apparent sincerity. "I know you to be a clever and, how should I out this, a devious young woman. Yes, yes, you are a most worthy adversary."

"Adversary?" Farzana said sharply, before controlling her voice. "I think not, Sir."

He seemed to think hard on what he would say next. "I would say one thing. Be careful. We cannot hide what is known to Allah. Yes, sister, pay attention to those around you. You have friends, some that seem as strangers to you. However, they cannot protect you in the end. *Allahu Akbar*, my sister." With that, he strode off toward the administration building."

"Allahu Akbar." Farzana called out as he strode away. A shiver coursed through her body despite the heat.

Aalem strode into the office of Doctor Archibald Singletary. "Doctor, I am so glad you are free to see me. I know you are a busy man."

Archie forced himself to smile. Over the past few months, Archie had come to an epiphany of sorts. While the Taliban seemed unidimensional, that was not the case. Yes, his experience supported his perception that, by and large, they were unsophisticated and incapable of subtle thought. Yet, before him was an exception though he did consider the possibility of the exception proving the rule. The man he only knew as Aalem obviously had been educated and likely held important positions in his prior life. He seemed at ease with the mantle of authority, a burden that suffocates many others or distorts their personalities in ugly ways. More intriguing was the suggestion that Aalem harbored a more complex set of beliefs than the typical Taliban leader, most of whom parroted the usual script absent variation or imagination. "God is great." Archie began, the usual and safe greeting in cases such as this.

"Of course," Aalem said distractedly, "I hope your family is well."

Archie looked at his visitor with curiosity. This man had never embraced the casual hostility of the cause that he now served. Still, Aalem's civility never could fully obscure the fact that he served a vision that most westerners found offensive. Aalem's functioning in this grey area, just outside the bounds of expected discourse proved disconcerting to the doctor. It was always easier if people remained on script. When they did not, one had to think hard on each detail of the interaction. Archie found that irritating in most cases, but rather fascinating in this instance. "They are well," he responded cautiously. "May I inquire as to the well-being of your family?" He immediately wondered if he had been too familiar, and followed up with a more neutral offer, "please be seated."

"You are most kind."

"Would you care for some tea?" Archie asked. When his visitor nodded, he picked up his phone and offered instructions to some unseen person.

Without responding to the physician's question about his family, Aalem spoke in a friendly, yet serious tone. "I have always had one regret since being charged with, how should I phrase this, looking after your operations here."

"Which is?"

"I have regretted not getting to know you better, or your family." Aalem smiled when Archie's expression suggested surprise. "I know, I know, this is not something you expect from an official representing the Taliban." He paused, but only for a moment. "I am sure that my superiors would not be pleased with such familiarity, but I am an honest man. I crave sophisticated company. The people I'm surrounded with daily are … as you might imagine, not very stimulating."

After a momentary internal debate, Archie decided to respond in kind. "I am not surprised. You strike me as an educated and worldly man."

"Most kind of you to say," taking Archie's response as a kind of invitation to further openness. "As a young man, I wanted to be a doctor. I grew up in these mountains and knew the Masoud family. I was familiar with Pamir, even before the medical work he did right here in this camp. I was so disturbed when he was assassinated, it was a crime I never forgot nor forgave. You see, he was a role model for me. I wanted to be him."

"What happened to your dream?" Archie asked sincerely.

"The Soviets happened. At an age when I might have pursued a medical education, I was fighting the infidels. I was there when they fled north, back to Russia, to escape us Mujahidin. I was quite young then but managed to kill several of them, though that left me both proud and confused. You see, I wanted to be a healer, not a killer of men. But what choice did we have?"

Archie wanted to say that we all have a choice but went another route. "Could you not have resumed your medical studies then?"

"Perhaps, but the war had scarred me. I had this affliction common to us warriors, you Westerners have a name for it …"

"Post-traumatic stress disorder most likely, or PTSD."

"Yes, of course. As I think back on it, I sense that my soul had been tainted in the conflict. I did go back to university. I studied philosophy of all things. How impractical! And I learned chess. There came a time when I could no longer hide within the university. I had to decide on a real future. But my country was in chaos by then, the early 1990s. With so many factions fighting one another, it was difficult not to pick a side. I ... I ..."

"Aalem, you can be open with me. If you have heard anything about me, then you know I am discrete and principled." Archie was fascinated with the turn of the dialogue.

Aalem looked at him with an intensity that unnerved the doctor. "Yes. It is just that it is difficult after so many years of living in the shadows." He cleared his throat. "In those days, I almost joined the Northern Alliance."

"Wait, you mean the so-called Lion of the Panjshir Valley? He was a sworn enemy of the Taliban which had ascended to power. He fought them right here."

"I know, I know." Aalem shook his head sadly. "I was confused at the time but that is where my heart lay, with the Alliance. He was such a charismatic person. But so many of my compatriots in the war against the Soviets were on the other side. And back then, before they came to power, I could excuse their ... what shall we say ... rigid views. They promised to bring stability to a land paralyzed with violence. I was naive enough to believe that they would moderate once they got control. So, I caste my lot with them. Maybe it was the right decision. After all, they won, didn't they?"

"My dear Aalem," Archie determined that the man was being ingenuous though he had not real proof of that, "were there not many subsequent opportunities to change course in your life. After all, the Taliban were out of power for two decades."

Aalem looked at Archie with considerable sadness. "You know, I think we endure life under a grave misapprehension … that we are creatures of free will. When we are young, we make decisions in the fog of ignorance that is youth. I did, joining up with those with whom I bonded on the battlefield. You do connect in a special way when you face death and fight for a cause. We were driven to rid the Soviets from our land. That was a sacred mission, our *jihad* or *holy war*. The one thing that Afghanistan had, of which she could be proud, was that no foreign power had conquered and controlled her, at least not in modern history. The Macedonians, the Mongols, the Russians, the British, and most recently the Americans tried but, in the end, they all left in defeat. But I digress. We make decisions based not on logic but emotion. And then, over time, we find ourselves trapped. With the years, other paths in life become unavailable to us. We are … trapped."

"My friend!" Archie caught the appellation he casually employed, which surprised him. Was he beginning to consider this man friend or was this a mere contrivance to put a potential enemy at ease? "Life is a long journey. I believe we encounter many junctures in the road which diverge and offer us new opportunities. I am hard pressed to accept that you, that all of us, are where we are absent some conscious complicity. If choice does not exist, how can we ever determine moral worth. How would any God, no matter the name, separate the worthy from the unworthy?"

"You see!" The bearded man said excitedly. "That is why I have longed to become your friend. I will admit a secret to you." He looked around as if someone might be hiding in the room. "I have desired to play chess with you, to drink tea, and to discuss great thoughts."

"You know I play chess?" Archie was surprised.

Aalem smiled. "I know many things about you and, you see, chess is a vice of mine. Sadly, I have few worthy opponents, not any in fact."

Archie looked upon this man across his desk in sympathy. He had such power in his hands, perhaps the power to end his own days in the land he had come to love, along with his work with the people who sought his ministrations. This man likely had the authority to end Archie's life. And yet, he was lonely, seeking an ordinary human connection. "My chess board is open to you, though I may not be a worthy opponent. I haven't played much in recent years." Archie then wondered if he had made this offer as a tactic to defuse a potential adversary or because he wanted to know more about this man. It was the latter he decided.

"Thank you. I will take advantage of your generous offer. But I came here for another purpose, not merely to secure a chess opponent." Aalems demeaner changed, his face was suddenly pinched with something akin to embarrassment. "What you have been doing … no, what you have been condoning is bringing considerable danger to you and what you are doing here."

"Wait," Archie tried but was cut off.

"No, just listen for now. I am not blind. Really, how long could you keep smuggling girls out of the country without detection or consequence?"

"But …"

"I have known for some time. Such an operation could never remain a secret. We, I mean the Taliban, have informants everywhere. Even if that were not the case, people talk. One could look the other way in the early days. The numbers were few and we are far away from Kabul. But the few is becoming a flood. You and your people have earned much credit even among the hardened zealots, for the medical and humanitarian work you do. They know they need you and what you bring to this land. But, at the end of the day, they are zealots. They would cut off their hands to fix a sore on their fingers. Educating girls is a sore to them."

"But you are not one of them." Archie protested weakly.

"That is of no matter, even if true." His face adopted a sorrowful aspect. "I made my choices long ago, now I must live with them. The reality is that I can protect you, but only up to a point. That point, my friend, is fast approaching." His expression became grave. "In confidence, let me be honest with you. The regime, the leadership, has been restrained up to now. They have moved cautiously in fear of stoking some reaction from the Western powers. But now that fear is receding. Those in the West will do nothing."

"Which means?"

"They will begin tightening their grip on power and become more … obsessive in pursuing their vision of what Allah wants."

"I'm not sure …" Archie started.

"Just think about it for a moment. Mark my words, by the end of the year, they will terminate all higher education for women, closing all university opportunities. They will eliminate by law or intimidation all professional opportunities for women who now will be expected to stay home. Think about that for the moment."

"You mean here, where we serve Afghani patients?"

Aalem looked solemn. "I fear so. Your wife, your daughter, might be forbidden to treat patients, certainly males. I'm not quite certain how far they will go. They may exempt foreigners from some of their harsher rules but there always is conflict within the leadership as factions compete for power. One never knows who will prevail."

Archie looked crushed. "But surely you can intervene, at least here."

"Believe me when I say that I may look powerful to you but that is illusion. You have little understanding of the factionalism and infighting among the Taliban. There is always someone out to benefit at your expense. Power and authority, once seeming invincible, can be gone in a moment. And remember, your attempt to hide what you are doing with young girls did not remain secret for long. Secrets seldom do."

Archie looked at the man across from him for a few moments. A moment of anger passed through him where he pondered asking this man to leave his presence. That was not him, however. Instead, he said the following. "Perhaps now is a good time for a game of chess. And we can chat more about your future, and ours."

Deena read the lengthy statement she had gotten from Farzana. Then she checked her phone to see calls from Ali and Karen. *'It was happening,'* she thought. She frantically called her sister, leaving several messages until she called back.

"Zita, are you still doing your medical rounds with students?"

In addition to her work with Muslim girls being shipped to Western sites for education and training, she also worked with the NHS to train interns and residents. "Yes, but we are almost finished. Sometimes I wonder if I ever was as ignorant as some of these…."

"Never mind that. We must meet. It is falling apart at home. Karen and Ali know but I am holding them off with texts until you and I can chat. But I promised we would meet with them tomorrow." Deena paused to catch her breath. "We knew this would happen. We planned for it."

Azita breathed equally hard on her end of the phone. "Nevertheless, the reality of it is harsh."

Within an hour, the two sisters met back at their home.

"How did you put Karen and Ali off?" Azita asked.

"I basically told them that I was waiting for more information from the Masoud Center and that I had to talk with you before anything else."

"And they were okay with that?" Azita asked?

"No, but I gave them no other option. I suggested that we had been planning for this contingency and would explain everything to them in the morning." Deena then smiled. "Okay, then, *you will* explain it to them in the morning. *I will* be gone."

"No," Azita responded firmly.

"What do you mean no. I'm going and you are staying."

"No," Azita said with greater emphasis. "We both go."

Absolutely not." Deena said just as strongly. "We've been over this a hundred times. We cannot risk both of us and you have a child."

"No," Azita said for a third time. "Just listen. My child will be fine if something befalls me. She will be loved and cared for. I have no doubt about that whatsoever. What is important is that we be together, do this together. What has grown on me recently is that we are one."

"Don't you remember all our fights, I thought you were a spoiled brat for so long."

"Yes, yes," Azita said with irritation. "And I thought you were a hopeless romantic absent vision or ambition. But we grew up. And what did we find … our other halves. We are like complements to one another, different yet fitting together … Ying and Yang. I am quantitative; you are verbal. I am straight; you are gay. I would heal; you would educate. That list can go on. At the end of the day, we a have the same goals. We are a single coin with two different sides."

Deena tried again. "But I beg you. We cannot put both of us at risk."

Azita's voice rose sharply. "Do you honestly believe I will let you go into harms way alone, without being at your side. You cannot possibly believe that. I would die a thousand deaths waiting here. No, I am going."

Deena considered other arguments. In the end, she understood that further debate would be futile. With a huge sigh of resignation, she said, "get ready, then. We leave tonight."

"How?"

"Chartered plane. It is all arranged."

"And the briefing of Karen and Ali?"

Deena pointed to a laptop. "I've already prepared a detailed overview of the operation as I worked it out with Farzana."

"I was going to have you tell them after I was gone."

"And now?"

"I will email it after they cannot stop us."

Azita smiled. "I like the way you think." Then her expression darkened. "But what about Chris. He will be furious."

"I'm not sure. His close friend, perhaps his only male friend, is dying. It will be any day now. He should focus on that. In any case, it will distract him."

"Death," Azita sighed. "I can never decide if it is a tragedy or a release." She paused. "I will prepare a different message for him after I throw some clothes together."

CHAPTER 21

Shadows

"If you want to tell people the truth, make them laugh, otherwise they'll kill you."

Oscar Wilde

Chris Crawford was sitting in Katerina Crawford's new living quarters. She had finally settled on a larger Georgian manor located on the edge of Berkhamsted, a town northeast of London. The structure was of perfect size to accommodate her needs, house her mother Mary, and provide living accommodations for several service staff and younger unmarried personnel who helped manage the financial empire. Mary Kelly loved it because it provided manicured grounds on which she could spend warm summer days and easy access to the countryside which she enjoyed after a lifetime in large cities. The professional staff were attracted to it since it permitted easy access to London and Oxford while avoiding the crushing costs of living in the Capital city.

There were lovely accommodations to be found in the local town which was connected by the tube to the center of London for those who could not tear themselves away from an urban environment. Kat was far removed from worrying about the costs of things or concerned about easy access to bucolic distractions.

Still, she saw several advantages. She could have physical access to her siblings without being swept up in their worlds. Some distance was necessary if she were to focus on the finances that kept everything running. She also found it therapeutic to wander through the town on occasion which had maintained a semi-rustic charm despite its proximity to London.

She recalled how delighted she had been upon first seeing the accommodation, at least until the estate agent went into the pedigree of the property. It turned out the original family had made its fortune in the burgeoning opportunities of the industrial revolution before acquiring large holdings in 17th century Ireland. *'Ouch,'* thought Kat, *'better keep that from Mother.'* The builder of this estate probably made his fortune on the backs of Irish peasants, shipping food stuffs off for profit as the natives perished from starvation or emigrated. Being quick of mind, Kat immediately rationalized away any guilt. Buying this place was like spitting in the figurative faces of the original lords of the manor. They eventually had fallen on hard times while a descendent of a family they had forced to emigrate now owned their legacy. *'Yes,'* she told herself, *'there is justice here.'"*

On this summery day, though that season had technically passed, she was meeting with her siblings about the financial status of the Crawford empire. Occasionally, Chris would encounter pangs of guilt about how much he was spending on his global service interests. Kat had never raised any cautionary warnings, nor complained to him in any serious manner, nor imposed any fiscal constraints other than the usual admonition to avoid frivolous expenditures. Still, Chris realized he was subject to bouts of Catholic and Irish guilt. Was he falling into an easy narcissism that he saw infecting other wealthy people? While he lived very modestly for a man of his fortune, which had grown exponentially after his father's passing, he seldom resisted spending money when it came to doing good for others. He had trouble saying no when suffering was involved.

The three siblings eschewed Kat's office which did not lend itself to more informal, family meetings. In the business part of the house, there was always the distractions of global financial news popping up on several oversized computer screens. A living area was better, more relaxed though there were serious issues to discuss. What had become known as the Afghan Girls Project (AGP) had quickly ballooned into a major initiative though Ali had made sure that other poor Muslim girls from conservative areas of the Mid-east had access to these opportunities. The Afghan part of the project was always reasonable in scope, there were only so many pipelines out of the country. But the flow from other parts of the mid-east grew as news of the initiative spread by word of mouth. Today, among other things, they would talk about quotas and selection criteria to be imposed going forward.

"Wow," Chris said at one point, "the costs of the AGP are rather high. Are we sending them all to Harvard?"

"Karen explained this to me. We will have to bring her back into this discussion soon, but I wanted a family-only discussion first. Anyway, the per-capita cost for those evacuated is not trivial, with housing costs, tutoring, educational fees, and so forth. We also provide a small stipend for the families left in the home country. The staff are good at finding scholarships and local charities to bear some costs, but it adds up. Can you go back to your buddy Bill Gates?"

Chris smiled. "Bill is generous, but he already supports a lot of Kay's extravagant medical spending."

"Hey!" Kay protested.

"But I'll see what I can do. He loves education projects, though his ex-wife might be a better bet. Do you think I can get them to compete with one another as to which is the most generous?" Chris smiled broadly at that thought.

At that moment, Mary Kelly walked in. "I heard that all my children were here. And I was not invited? I should put you all over my knee."

"Mother," Kay said with a chuckle, "you never spanked us when we were naughty as children. It is too late now. Besides, the horse is out of the barn."

"Horse ... barn? What are you talking about dear?"

"I thought my statement self-evident. Just look how bad Chris turned out. He needed spanking as a young brat, which he did not get. Now look at him. Spare the rod, spoil the child."

Mary had a sharp wit, but it ended with any actual or implied criticism of her offspring. "Nonsense, he is a treasure, though I did worry when he was young that he might take after his father. Thank God he did not."

Chris rose and led his mother to a nearby seat. "Mother, I will tell you about the worst secret in the world. We are what we are because of you. Never doubt that for a moment." He then kissed her on a cheek.

"Posh," Mary uttered her denial, but a brief smile suggested she liked that sentiment.

Kat spoke up, "We are chatting about how fast we can spend the family fortune as we, or should I say Chris and Kay, go about trying to on save the world. Let's face it, billions don't go as far as they used to."

Mary now laughed. "Oh how I wish your father was here to see this. It would have killed him dead for sure. I could have saved a bullet, and a lot of hassle by watching him stroke out as he learned his wealth was going to help people as opposed to controlling and exploiting them. He was such a misanthrope as were all his right-wing, Nazi friends."

"You have become quite the leftist, mother?" Kay offered.

"I always was but it was not fashionable among my set as a young girl. My parents were wealthy and believed they earned it all on their own. Common mistake. Yet, they never completely forgot their simple roots. They were good people, really. Perhaps that's how they saw through Charles Senior. I thought him charming, they knew he was a bastard."

"It was lust," Kay said with a hearty laugh.

"Shush you." Mary protested.

At that moment, the door opened, and Karen and Ali entered.

Karen started. "Sorry to bother you like this, but we had to track you down. They've gone off the deep end again."

"Who?" Chris asked.

"You don't know?" Ali was surprised. "Azita and Deena."

“Oh no. What now?” Kay frowned. “I wondered where they were this morning. Weren’t they supposed to get in touch?”

“Guess you didn’t get the memo.” Karen added with sarcasm.

As Chris and Kay looked at their phones, Ali spoke up. “Don’t bother looking now. They left a long message. We can fill you in. They spirited themselves off to Pakistan. According to them, things are collapsing at the Masoud Center.”

“Are they?” Chris said rising, his heart rising to his throat.

Ali took a deep breath, vowing not to lose control or overstate things. “I knew that things were getting worse there. We all did. I had been in continuous contact with Doctor Singletary about matters. I’ve been preparing for this, getting things ready. I just wish they would have trusted me.”

“And I’ve been getting reports from the Gupta’s, Bahiri and Ferhana in Kabul.” Karen added and then turned to Ali, “you go ahead.”

“Well, the good Doctor, I mean Archie, has raised several red flags in recent weeks. He has a friend who nominally is one of them but apparently remains a decent man. He has been filling Archie in, informing him that the Taliban knew about the scheme to smuggle girls out of the country. They have suspected such for some time, apparently.”

“Really, how could they not.” Kay interjected, “They are not the brightest bulbs but still …”

Ali pushed on. “Apparently some of them turned a blind eye given how useful their work at the center was in terms of providing medical services and feeding the increasing crowds of malnourished. But that was ending, the era of good will that is. The regime apparently was becoming secure enough to pursue their original extremist vision. Bahiri and Ferhana had already stopped sending girls north in the pipeline. They realized the game was up. Besides, everything is much more dangerous in the capital. But Farzana, the leader at the Masoud Center, continued despite the warnings."

"They are zealots after all, I mean the Taliban, not people like Farzana." Karen added unnecessarily.

"Apparently something happened, triggering this response by Azita and Deena." Kat, as usual, went for a bottom line.

Karen continued. "Essentially, Archie's source of inside information, the man who warned him that their secret no longer was a secret a while back, tipped him off that the end was coming. This protector can no longer keep harm away, at least not much longer. After he warned Archie, he seems to have dropped out of sight. We don't know if he has fallen into harm's way himself. The Taliban have a history of eating their own."

Ali picked up the tale as she took her place in the group. "Based on what this unnamed insider had told him before disappearing, the authorities would soon sweep in and take control of the camp. They would arrest the females running the girls smuggling program and impose draconian restrictions on operations. Things like Carolyn and Agnes and the female medical staff being highly restricted on what they could do, whom they could treat, what they would be required to wear, shit like that. The specifics were never clear."

Chris looked surprised at his wife's language. "Did you say shit?"

"The word fits." Ali said, not backing down.

Chris recovered. "Has this takeover started, has anyone been arrested or hurt?"

"Not that I'm aware." Ali said. "I just got off the phone with Doctor Singletary "Everything is quiet there but tense. I came as soon as I could."

Karen then noted. "But apparently Azita and Masoud are not taking any chances. They had developed some cockamamie plan to get out as many girls as they can along with the former female teachers who taught at the center. I can't believe all the thought and effort they put into this. The whole scheme is quite elaborate."

"What king of plan?" Kat asked.

Karen emitted a small groan. "They intend to get some out by last minute flights, both helicopters and regular planes. Others will escape by various land routes out of the country to Pakistan using trucks and busses. There is even an overland trek planned if other tactics fail. They did all kinds of backchannel preparations to put this scheme together. It is complex for sure though what they will do with the girls if they get them out is a bit obscure. We will need to do some full court work to ensure it works. I have staff all over this now that no one can stop it. We are trying like hell to make it work."

"How did they plan on paying for all this?' Kat asked more out of curiosity than concern.

Karen shrugged, "They had control over some of the money for the AGP initiative. But let's face it. This is a popular project among the Afghan activist community. They may have been raising money on their own."

"Why the fuck didn't they include us?" Chris exploded. "Now I will have to contact the British Government, especially the British Global Response Agency. Shit, they just might set off an international incident and get some British nationals … oh never mind. Time to call in some chits I suppose. I swear, those two will kill me one of these days."

"That's what you are worrying about?" Kay looked at her brother dubiously.

"Yes, I take my death very seriously." He responded.

Kat sighed. "Don't be so overly dramatic, it's unbecoming."

Chris seemed about to reply to her before looking defeated. "Really, they know how much I love them and yet they keep putting themselves in danger. Why. Explain to me why?" His question was directed to no one.

It was Mary, his mother, who responded. "What a silly question, son. They do these things because they are so much like you. I find it fascinating that they have so many of your traits even though they are not your biological daughters. They take so much from you, from our family really, my side at least. I have no doubt on that score. They have the Crawford heart, and the Crawford sense of purpose."

"Mother, please," Chris tried to divert her.

"No, you listen to me." She said firmly. "Why did you bring Azita back from that country when she was just a girl, take a wife and bring her up as your own, and then later take in her sister as well. Do you remember what you were up to that point, rootless and, I might add, debauched? While I loved you dearly, I was afraid you were becoming your father, not in politics but with women. It looked like you would never marry, simply go from girl to girl. Yes, you were committed to good causes, but you know what I thought about that."

"I suppose you will remind me." Chris surrendered.

"Damn right I will. I thought you were only doing this service stuff to piss off your father. I never could decide if you really believed in anything. Then you surprised me. You brought back these girls from a land that I could not pick out on a damn map, and a wife of all things. And miracles of miracles, you acted like a good father and husband. Suddenly, I had a son whom I could look upon with pride. You do know that I had never cared for all your academic achievements or your fame as an athlete. Others talked about what a good basketball player you were, and that you went to Oxford as a Rhodes Scholar. Those things meant nothing to me. They were baubles, like the bright jewellery that attracted me as a young girl. After Afghanistan, you were a different person, someone I finally could admire."

"I don't see it that way," Chris went with denial one last time.

"Bullshit," Mary cried out as the others recoiled in shock. "You didn't see it because you had zero self-awareness then. You weren't a man until you became a husband and a father, someone of substance. And the difference ...? Well, the difference was you finally had a purpose in life. What you were doing was no longer merely a way to exact revenge on the father you despised, no longer merely a distraction of some do-gooder dilettante. Finally, you saw something you could accomplish

… take pride in. And guess what? You learned all that from two young girls from Afghanistan and a wife from India of all things. The wife thing gave me a hearty laugh, the one thing you swore you would never have. I wasn't at my best in those days, but I loved every minute of all that."

Ali spoke up as he saw Chris about to speak. Her tone was modulated yet suggested a deep concern. "Your mother is right. Wow, now it makes sense to me. I kept you at arms-length for many years because you struck me as incomplete, a man to the outside world but a boy inside … so smooth and accomplished, yet equally flawed. Then you realized what you were doing in this world. The girls did that … and Amar. I never could."

Mary seemed enthused by Ali's support. "The real point of all this is that you learned from those you took on as children for whom you were responsible. They taught you, the child performing as a tutor to the man. They taught you things like being responsible for another being. And they taught you other priceless lessons … that purpose in life is everything. Without that, all is a charade, pointless scripts, and meaningless distractions."

Chris blushed. "That's fine, mother, but what has that to do with Azita and Deena risking their lives again …"

"Everything, you moron." Mary spouted the words as if her son had regressed in age to a two-year old. "Don't you think I didn't die a thousand deaths when you opposed your father or went into dangerous parts of the world yourself. I did every time, but not once did I consider asking you to stop. I especially feared your father, my husband. I knew what cruelty he was capable of. Have you already forgotten what happened to your older brother, to your sister-in-law Beverly, to your best friends Jules and Ricky? Is there any doubt he was responsible for their deaths, and that you were next? But did I ever ask you to stop? No, never"

"True, all you did was go out one day and kill him yourself."

"But you cannot do that to an entire political regime. What you can do is permit those you love to do what they must do. If you take their purpose away from them, you will have killed their spirit. That is a far crueler death than merely losing one's life. This is the hardest lesson each parent must learn … to let go of what they love the most."

Chris looked at her in silence for a long time before quietly saying, "thank you, mother."

Everyone sat for several more awkward seconds before Kay spoke up. "I haven't been paying attention to emails this morning. I just noticed one from Azita."

Karen looked at her phone. "Oh, I've gotten one from Deena. It looks long and detailed." She went off to read it.

Kay raised a hand. "This one is addressed to the three of us … Chris, Ali, and me." She continued to read from her phone for a bit longer before saying, "It is a little personal, but I think I can share this with everyone."

Kay started reading:

> *Dear Chris, Ali, and Kay,*
>
> *By this time, you are aware that Deena and I are off to Afghanistan, well Pakistan to start. I intended to explain why I needed to do this, why we needed to do this. But I found I could not find the right words. There are some things that are inside. You know you*

cannot reason them out with your rational brain but know full well why they must be done. It is as if such things are givens on your soul. I know this doesn't make sense, but it is the best I can do at present. I only ask you to forgive me.

My God, there is so much for which I must ask forgiveness. I have been such a petulant child of late. I knew it but could not quite stop myself. It is as if I had become a little girl again, pouting and lashing out at others for reasons I could not verbalize. I just hurt.

I suppose the foremost thing was losing Amar. It seemed like the last straw after Pamir, Madeena, Majeed, Ahmed, and all the others less close to me. I remember lying in bed at night yelling at Allah in my head. 'Why are you being so cruel to me. Haven't I dedicated myself to doing good things.' Silly now, but I suspect it was all part of the grieving process. As a woman, I can accept that one cannot shortcut the grieving process. Men can, but we all know them to be odd creatures.

Kay chuckled lightly, "Sorry, that struck me as amusing."

I'm now sure that the crisis back home has snapped me out of it. You would think that would drive me further into a depression or mid-life crisis. Do women have those, or is it only men? No matter, seeing others being in such danger got me out of myself. I'm not a child. I'm a physician who wants to help others, not just heal them physically but through hope for a better future.

At some point in the recent hours, a thought struck me. We all die. Okay, that is not the headline. But since our death is not conditional, but an absolute, only the timing is uncertain. It then struck me that we all face a set of choices involving one critical decision. 'Do we guide our actions to postpone the inevitable or do we pursue our purpose in life despite the risk?' To live in fear is not to live at all, I am certain of that. The crisis at the Masoud Center, and Kabul, woke me up again. Some epiphanies must be relearned, over and over. Time to decide. I have chosen purpose over any useless extension of my time on this earth.

Mind you, I have not lost all sense of proportion. I will be careful. After all, I do all kinds of things to stay alive like exercise and eating correctly. I do intend to be around to watch my daughter grow up. But I cannot do that at the cost of what means so much to me. The very opportunity that you, Chris and Kay, gave me so long ago, plucking me from a life I cannot imagine now, is what I must bring to others. It is a form of karma, of paying forward.

And Ali, I am so sorry. You did nothing to deserve the way I've treated you recently. I have acted like a little shit. You never pretended to replace Amar in my life. It has been my narcissism, and childishness to pretend that was the case. You have been nothing but a wonderful role model to me and, more importantly, a loving wife to Chris. And God knows, he needs that. Please forgive me.

Kay chuckled a second time. "Ain't that the truth."

Don't worry about us. When, not if, we return, I want to throw my arms around you all. I cannot express in words how much I love you all. Danger heightens all kinds of feelings, but affection, no love, must be more sensitive feeling of all. And don't forget, Deena and I have been through this before ... we are veterans. All will be well.

All my love,
Zita

Kay wiped a tear from her eye as she put her phone down.

"*Ikigai,*" Chris said softly.

"I'm sorry dear, what did you say?" Ali responded to him.

"Ikigai is a Japanese term. As I understand it, it means the purpose for being here, on earth, in life. How many philosophers have waxed on about this topic? How quickly we forget." He looked toward Mary. "Mother, you are wise beyond your years and your years are many."

Mary gave her son a bemused look. "I cannot figure out if that is a compliment or an insult."

Karen spoke up in her take charge voice. "Time for action. Ali and I should go after them. They should not be doing this on their own."

"I'm going." Chris said firmly.

"No, you bloody sot." Kat shot back. "Can't have the whole leadership off to commit suicide. Besides, I'll take some of the guys … Atle, Tomas, and Luke for sure."

"She is right." Kay said softly. "More importantly, Chris, you must stay back for Josh's sake. I've been paying close attention to him in recent days. His end is near. Only days now, at best. You must be here if he suddenly fails."

Chris looked as if he had been slapped. He simply nodded.

CHAPTER 22

Hegira – Preparations

"Knowledge is of no value unless you put it into practice."
Anton Checkov

The helicopter looked just like all the others that had been flying in and out of what now was generally called the Masoud Refugee Center. The medical services part of the operation continued unabated, increasing in fact. However, the educational, public health, and community development functions had been ratcheted back. A few girls still showed up for classes despite the harassment and disapproval of the local Taliban, but their education was spotty. It was now widely recognized that a nearly total ban on female education was imminent. The other outreach efforts had fallen victim to the chaos introduced by the new regime, largely overwhelmed by a collapsing economy and the loss of female workers now afraid of upsetting the new rulers.

The transformations notwithstanding, the level of activity at the Center, no matter what it was called, never ceased. Families and individuals straggled in daily. They came with vacant eyes lacking focus, gaunt expressions that had seen too much despair, children dragging behind, many with distended bellies and untreated diseases. These were hardened individuals used to deprivation and struggle. They thought themselves as independent and self-sufficient, capable of facing anything Providence might throw at them. But even the toughest of men, the most resilient of women, reach a point where reality could no longer be denied, where pride could only be purchased at the price of death. At that moment, they would begin migrating to the one place where a glimmer of hope remained.

Doctor Archibald Singletary watched the aircraft land, spewing up clouds of dust as the rotation of the large vertical propeller slowly came to a halt. He knew this was a special shipment, more than food and medicines. It also contained a human cargo that brought with it uncertainty and perhaps danger. Yet, he remained remarkably calm. After so many years in this land, he had grown accustomed to a simmering fear that never left him alone. It was little more than a chronic irritation now, perhaps akin to a case of indigestion that could not be shaken. He had learned too live with it. What he could not as easily accept was the sight of desperation about him. That, and the knowledge that his powers to deal with it were so limited, was something that did erode the shell protecting his equanimity on occasion.

He never thought of himself as a particularly reflective man. but he did have his moments. As events swirled around him, he recalled Carolyn, his physician daughter, observing something that stuck with him. 'Dad, are you familiar with the American author John Steinbeck?' After he responded that he had a passing recognition of the name, she went on. 'No matter, he wrote this book that I read in college, for a literature class that mostly bored me. But this one got to me; I've never forgotten it.' When Archie asked why, his offspring continued. 'It was a story about a people in a place known as the dust bowl, a part of America that faced horrible conditions in the great depression of almost a century ago, the one grandfather talked about. Climactic change and economic disaster scarred their farm-

land beyond repair. They were a proud and independent people that reached their limits of endurance, most fleeing their land and farms to find hate and persecution wherever they went.'

'Do the poor wretches who come to us remind you of those migrants in the book?' Archie had asked.

'Yes, very much. But I think that book changed my life. It made me want to join you here. Does that sound ridiculous?'

'No, my dear, not at all.'

'Anyway, I think Steinbeck won a Pulitzer award for it and it helped him get the Nobel Prize in literature.' Archie recalled thinking he would have to find that book.

The good doctor watched intently as side door opened and several individuals jumped off. Others who had been waiting crowded around the open door to help unload the cargo. Surreptitiously, two of the 'men' who had exited the plane worked their way to Archie, each carrying a bundle. He nodded and led them to his living quarters. Once inside, he picked up his phone and made a call while the 'men' exited into an adjacent room. Moments later, the two emerged in more traditional Afghani female garb.

"Welcome," he said to Azita and Deena Masoud. "You two have created quite a stir back in England. I feel I am harboring dangerous fugitives fleeing the law."

"Oh my," Deena exclaimed. "We did not intend to get you into trouble. We will explain everything to them when we get back."

Archie laughed, "You won't have to wait that long. Most of your compatriots are hot on your trail."

"I should have thought of that." Deena said thoughtfully and then asked. "Is Chris among them? Is he coming?"

"No, I was informed that he stayed behind to prepare a suitable punishment for the two of you. Are you familiar with something they call *'the rack?"* Archie laughed at his small joke.

"Then we must do this before the others get here and drag us back for the torture he surely is preparing."

"You can relax" the older man said with a chuckle, "you will be spared the rack. No, sadly enough, Chris has stayed behind for another purpose ... to be with a good friend of his who is dying I understand."

"Oh my, I knew that Josh was deteriorating but I did not know it was so serious. We are adding to father's problems." Azita said as she looked to her sister with a sorrowful look.

Deena nodded to her sister and looked back at Archie. "You said we would be *spared the rack*. I don't understand. They are not coming to drag us home? If not that, what are they up to?"

Archie's face again eased into his gentle, warm smile. "I think you have much less to worry about than you imagined. We are still reluctant to be open in our communications though the Taliban is not nearly as sophisticated in intercepting messages as the American CIA or the British MI-5. But, reading between the lines, they are on the way to help, not to put you in shackles. That is how I read the tea leaves."

Azita looked dubious "Really? Are you sure?"

Archie smiled. "You must trust me, my dear." At that moment, the door opened and in walked an Afghani man in full Taliban dress. He said nothing, merely stared at the two women who instinctively shied away from him. Archie continued to smile. "Do not be alarmed. This is Aalem, the source of information I had mentioned to you. I thought we had lost him, but he was merely off planning for the safety of his family."

"Allah be with you," said the man in clear English.

"And with you," Deena replied cautiously.

Archie stopped smiling "I have one request of you, to take Aalem with you. He has risked everything to protect us for as long as he can. Now he is under such suspicion that, when you do what you intend, his life may be over." When Azita looked dubious, Archie continued. "You are asking yourself if you can trust him. Am I right?"

Azita nodded, "yes." Inside her head, Azita considered what better way to lure two of the most hated women to the new regime than to pretend to help until they fell into his trap. Now they were in his trap.

"Look at it this way. What choice do you have? With one call, he could have us all arrested and worse." Archie could see the two women react to this obvious point. "He will not though. I mean, I've played chess with the man. You get to know someone playing chess."

Aalem spoke at this point, the clarity of his English surprised both women. "Let me say this, every man comes to a point in his life when he must decide who he is, what he stands for. I have taken the easy path for too long. Now I must be true to myself."

Archie then added. “If you leave him behind, I fear I may lose my chess partner … forever.”

“Of course, we will take him,” Azita said, her worst fears about this man beginning to abate. “But let me ask, how much time do we have?

Aalem spoke calmly but with authority. “Oddly enough, they are waiting for my signal before coming in to round up those they consider infidels and enemies of Allah … starting with you two and Farzana.” He nodded toward Azita and Deena.

“But,” Archie added, “if what I think will happen takes place, they might not wait much longer.”

Azita looked puzzled, “I’m not sure what you mean.”

As our population of refugees and desperate people has swelled, so have the number of families that have heard that girls are being sent out of the country. We knew this could never be kept secret long, but the dam has broken the last few days and weeks. Farzana and the others are trying to dampen expectations but already there are more girls ready than you can accommodate.”

Azita suddenly blanched as she realized that many would yet be left behind. She could never do enough. “And you and your family? Are you not in danger? Should you not leave with us?”

Archie started to speak but was cut off by the door opening again. This time a host of people entered including Farzana, Sayed, Agnes, and Carolyn, along with many of the former female teachers in the girl’s school.

Farzana went directly to Deena and hugged her warmly. "At last," she said.

After more welcomes, Archie gathered all assembled around him. "It is time to make our last-minute preparations. The morning will come soon enough."

The next morning, three large helicopters hovered into sight. By this time, there was little effort to conceal the identity of passengers nor the purpose of these fights. The race against time had begun … could the final evacuations occur before the regime invaded the camp in force and shut them down. Much now rested with Aalem who continued to play the ambiguous role of Taliban loyalist and spy who had infiltrated the camp and befriended those in charge to report out on any wrongdoings and determine what might be done about them. He sent a continuous steam of communications that morning, most of it consisting of carefully constructed disinformation designed to delay any immediate actions in response to the uptick in suspicious activity, or so he kept telling Doctor Singletary and others in charge.

After the crafts had set down, supplies were unloaded, though only a portion were the usual items essential to meeting the medical and human needs of a growing refugee camp. The remainder were materials that might be useful for the emigres as they made their way out of the country via the several escape tactics. Archie looked at what was going on and then at Aalem who observed the activity as he talked on his phone. Had he been too trusting? Would the camp suddenly be raided now when they were so vulnerable. A small doubt gnawed at his insides though he kept such doubts to himself. In the end, he dismissed such doubts. He prided himself on reading people and this was a good man. Besides, what else could he do at this late time?

The so-called head office team made its way to the camp headquarters. They included Karen, Ali, Atle Bergstrom, Tomas Modise, Luke Geoghegan, and several former students and teachers from the Masoud Education Center. All of the latter had emigrated in the past, with most teaching or mentoring or hosting newer arrivals from the country. When asked, more had volunteered than could be accommodated. Archie's residence was too small to hold the growing number of conspirators. As more entered the building, they found themselves in a large room that had been a reception area. A large table had been placed in the middle with chairs distributed around the periphery.

Ali looked about the room upon entering. She stopped when she spotted Azita. Both women looked at one another uncertainly. A buzz of unconnected conversation surrounded the two as they stared at one another, each waiting for the other to make the first move. It was Azita who did. She solely walked across toward the woman who had wed her adoptive father. It was a tentative walk of only a dozen feet or so, but progress seemed glacial until they could touch one another. At that point, the younger woman gave forth what can only be considered a strangled cry before collapsing into Ali's arms. They hugged for several moments in silence.

"I have been a complete ass." Azita blurted out.

"I have not been much better."

"No, no," Azita insisted, "this has been all my fault. I'm a stubborn, selfish girl."

Deena, watching this interaction nearby, struggled to contain herself. *'You can say that again,'* she wanted to say to her sister. Instead, she merely joined in the hug. "Listen, we can assign blame later, that will be my job." Deena chuckled briefly at her small quip. "Now we have more important work which, if we fail in it or tarry too long, we might not have to worry about past sins. Our only concern will be with the afterlife, and certainly we will not end in the same place." Deena smiled once more. She thought her wit quite excellent in that moment.

"Of course," Ali said as she wiped a tear from her eye. "It is just so good to be together again, as a team. Whether or not you believe me, I have missed that."

"Oh, yes, I do. Yes, I do." Azita said with meaning, wiping her own eyes clear of tears.

"To work," Archie cried out in a large voice.

Karen seconded his call. "Yes, there is much to do. But first, before we discuss the plans for the girls, I need to bring up an issue that Chris pushed on me. Can the Center survive our obvious large-scale flight of evacuees? There can be no hiding this from the Taliban powers. How will they react? Most alarming to him is the fate of the foreign senior staff, Archie, Agnes, and their daughter and son-in-law, the other medical personnel from Australia. For safety sakes, Chris suggested that they all consider being evacuated as well."

Her comments were greeted by a long silence. Then Agnes spoke. "My family and I have discussed the dangers many times, as you can imagine. I can state affirmatively that Archie and I intend to stay. You know, when we came, it was supposed to be a temporary thing, something to do early in our golden years before retiring to endless evenings around the barbie with our mates as we watched the sun set over the ocean. Those few years stretched on and any desire for a traditional place in the sun faded. We grew to love the people and even the place, with all its warts and problems. It was more than that, though. I'm not even sure I can put it into words."

"Perhaps I can," her husband interjected. "I recall an old fable of a young Prince who went out among his people disguised as a poor wanderer. He would ask those he met on his way for help, anything they might spare. When he returned to his palace, he brought with him one family, a young man and his wife and children. The prince's father asked who they were and was told they were poor and simple workers, no more than peasants. '*Why bring them here.?*' His father asked.

The prince replied, '*Father, in my travels, I asked many for help when those petitioned knew not my identity. Most turned me away, some gave me a little, a handful were even generous. But only this one gave me everything … all that he had.*"

Archie stopped as if he presumed all knew the meaning of his story.

His daughter, Carolyn, picked up his thread. "Just to make sure that all understand, my father means that we were given much as doctors in a Western country … excellent compensation, status in the community, country club memberships and nice homes if we wanted them. Society gave us much. But here, the people we worked with give us much more … some give us everything. You would be amazed. I would treat a poor family with nothing, and they would offer me their last goat or sack of grain. They knew we didn't charge, and I used to refuse at first. At some point, I realized that hurt them more. So, I would take some nominal payment, for their sake. But many would have given me everything."

Her husband, Kenji, spoke. "Some time back, we had this discussion about leaving, playing it safe. Initially, I thought this not a bad thought. Let us leave and perhaps return when things were settled. And then I saw my in-laws flatly refuse. They argued they could not leave in the face of such need. They pleaded with their daughter to leave however. It was one of the only times I have seen cross words between my wife and her parents. In the end, there was little more to be said. The daughter is a reflection of her parents and I, in turn, love their daughter. We will all stay and work with the people until we no longer can … or are dead. It is that simple."

Karen started to speak, then stopped, then tried again. "I was going to argue with you but even I can recognize when I'm beaten."

Instead, Aalem moved toward the table. "If I may, let me share what I know. I am a stranger to some of you so you may doubt my counsel, but I assure you I speak with a true heart."

"I have put my life in this man's hands." Archie noted in affirmation.

"You are a good friend. What I am about too share is my best guess as to what will happen but there are no assurances. Believe me, the politics among the Taliban leadership constantly shifts. Behind the righteous ideology lies much conflict for power. Some great sins are committed in the name of Allah."

Ali looked at the man with a puzzled expression. "I must admit, you do not sound like … what I expected."

Aalem laughed. "I know what is in your heart. You expected an uneducated buffoon. Too many of my peers in the Taliban are, I fear, like that. However, I enjoyed a good education and was able to travel abroad in my younger days. To anticipate your next question. I am with the Taliban because I was blinded by the vision of bringing peace to my country. There were so many factions fighting for power, this group came along promising to end the constant warfare and to bring a sense of virtue back to the land. In truth, the warlords of that era were suppressed for the most part. That was good. But the search for virtue became extreme, an excuse for a new kind of terror. So-called belief can become a veil behind which the greatest atrocities are hatched. I hate to admit that my recent work with them has been largely opportunistic, a way to make life easier for myself. I am ashamed."

Karen looked upon the man with only semi-concealed doubt, but all she said was "thank you."

"No matter the reasons." Deena said. "It is good to have you with us now." Inside, she also harbored concerns that this man might be a spy, perhaps playing the educated Taliban defector out to trap them all before his colleagues swooped in to torture them all. *'What choice do we have, now.'* She said to herself while supressing these slowly fading suspicions.

Aalem nodded to her and continued. "I have been doing my best to cover for what has been going on here. But the truth is known, and I could see the end days were near. I have good contacts in Kabul. I fact, I have been asked many times to relocate and take a leadership position … as you can imagine they need more competent leaders, those with an education who can speak English. They need such to interact with foreign countries and organizations, roles like that. It might have been a way for me to leave the country, on official business, but I could not help them in such a fashion. So, I have avoided that fate, or is it an opportunity. You can only say no for so long."

"I can imagine," Karen interrupted.

"I mention that to say I know what is coming. Very soon, the real Taliban will surface. In the internal political battles, the moderates have prevailed so far, moderate by their standards that is. For example, there are still girls being educated, fewer for sure but it is still possible. There are still women in jobs, even government jobs where they are having trouble finding competent male replacements. By the end of the year, that will end. The moderates are on the defensive and will soon lose out. The zealots argue that the revolution is being betrayed ... you know how that goes. All revolutions go through a process where the true believers consume those that they deem impure. Compromise is betrayal, dissent is treason. I have been most interested in what is happening in America. The Republican Party in that country so reminds me of the Taliban. As they became more extreme over the years, I noticed the wise men in their media kept saying this will end their influence and that political party will self-destruct. That never happened. Their extremists became emboldened, to the point where they violently attacked the government without any real consequences for those pushing such an atrocity. This happened even in good times in that country. Bad times make the situation more volatile. As the problems in Afghanistan mount, the moderates are losing ground. They have argued that the regime needs to present a good face to the outside world to regain foreign aid. But that is not coming in the amounts needed, so the extremists have made many gains in recent weeks. They argue constantly that the revolution is being betrayed."

"What are you saying, for us I mean, for what we have been doing and for the Center?" Azita looked impassive but roiled inside.

"That I cannot say at the moment."

"And for the people of Afghanistan, for the women?" Ali asked.

"For the country, all female education will be prohibited by law. All women will be banned from employment and banished to their families. I would expect public whippings, arrests, hangings, and beheadings to increase. And no one will come to our aid. The outside world is too tired of this place and the people … the people" He paused. "Let me just say the Republican Party in America is as strong as ever it seems. The people cannot be counted on." Aalem wanted to temper his cynicism but did not.

"And here …" Azita prompted him to say more about the fate of the operations named after her parents.

"Yes," I digress. "I have worked hard to keep the local Taliban at bay and the far away zealots in the dark. They are consumed with other fights and there are many. Groups are trying to get those who worked with the Americans, but were trapped here after the takeover, out of the country. There are thousands upon thousands of such families. Finding those so-called traitors is a priority of the government, fortunately for you."

"Thank Allah," Ali said before smiling awkwardly.

Aalem smiled back at Ali. "In any case, this area has never been a Taliban stronghold. Scattered resistance to their takeover last year continued until recently. The Masoud family, Pamir and Madeena, are yet revered by the elders. In fact, I remember meeting you many years ago." He turned to Deena.

"Me? I don't remember."

"You were here for a ceremony at the school named after you. My daughter would attend that school." He paused. "Two of my granddaughters are among those hoping to be evacuated."

All of Deena's doubts evaporated but it was Ali who spoke. "They will fly out in one of the first helicopters, along with their mother and you."

"Thank you." He said and turned to Archie. "My good friend, I ask you one more time. Please consider leaving with the others. You and your family are loved in this area and that may save you, and the Center, which the authorities need. And while I have made you sound innocent and well-meaning to my colleagues, I cannot guarantee ..."

"That decision, my good friend, has been made." Archie said softly but firmly. "You put your faith in Allah. I put mine in the Christian God. But you and I know they are the same, do we not?"

"Yes, we do, that is a certainty. I had to ask; you understand." The two men approached one another and hugged.

"Before we go any further," Karen inserted to break up what she considered an awkward moment, "there is one other person who needs to be on the first helicopter out."

"Who? Ali asked.

"You …"

"No," Ali sputtered, "Why?"

Karen fixed her with the no-nonsense look she adopted when her mind was set. "I will tell you why. If I get you killed, I could not go back to England. Your dear husband, and my dear boss, would kill me dead, perhaps several times over."

"Nonsense …" Ali got no further.

"Nonsense, you say. Nonsense." Karen's nostrils flared as they did when she was vexed. "The last thing Chris said to me before we left was that I should keep you safe or stay here myself. The Taliban would be kinder to me than he would be. He was not smiling when he said those words. And that was after he tried to get me to convince you not to come since he knew he had absolutely zero chance of winning that argument himself. Why in god's name did he think I would be more successful? By the way, you were supposed to stay in Pakistan to organize things there. That also was hopeless. Don't forget, I was there when you backed up Mary Kelly's argument that we could not deny Azita and Deena this, that we had to support their dream."

"And the dream of all those girls out there." Ali swept her hand toward the door. "Well, I can see he would be crushed at losing his … children. But I'm just his substitute spouse."

"What?" Karen now was so vexed that spittle shot from her mouth. "Are you listening to yourself. He loves you. Got that. Wow, and you are supposed to be so smart … dumb shit!"

"He does love you … totally." Azita said softly. "Dear Ali, never doubt that. That bothered me for a long time. Perhaps I saw his love as finite and any that went to you was subtracted from me."

"Dear Azita, please …"

Azita cut off her words. "Let me get this out. I suppose my mixed-up feelings came from my love for Amar … my anger at losing her. But I now see that was silly. This is what she would have wanted, you and father together. I cannot believe I was so blind. No, so selfish. It appears that intellectual smarts can only take you so far. Get on that plane. I beg you. You can help us in Pakistan, getting things ready there. There is much to do on that end. You know that is true. Please, for me."

Ali looked torn, but only for a moment. "Okay, for you … and Deena."

Ali turned to leave but Azita stopped her. "And one more thing. Please take care of him, Chris I mean."

Ali looked at Azita and then Deena. "We will take care of him … the three of us."

"Thank you …" Azita seemed on the verge of tears but kept it together. "I didn't …" She stopped, not sure where she was going with her thought. After all, there was work to do.

"Alright," Archie said as a way of regaining control. "I believe we have some time to get this operation off the ground. Is that your opinion Aalem?"

"Yes, they are not quite ready to do anything major right now. However, when they see all the activity taking place over the next few days, they will be alerted. It may still take some time for them to act. The other thing we have going for us is that the approval of others up the hierarchy must be obtained for any major initiative. That will take a bit of time."

"Like the Nazis in World War II." Archie said.

"What?" His daughter Carolyn asked.

"Just an observation … that war was still a fresh event in my youth. I read all about it, most of us kids did or listened to our fathers. Anyway, during D-Day, the invasion of Europe, Hitler's generals were reluctant to wake up the Fuhrer as the Allies stormed the beaches. Hours were lost as the reserves waited for orders which came too late. Let us hope that is what happens here."

"Let us pray for incompetence, on the other side that is." Farzana spoke for the first time in a soft voice. Then she spoke up in a more commanding tone. "Here is the basic plan. We start with the youngest children …"

She and the others continued for some time.

CHAPTER 23

Hegira – Flight

"The only thing we need more than hope is action. Once we act, hope is everywhere."

Greta Thunberg

The next morning, Azita woke early, after only a few hours of fitful sleep. As she stirred, her sister spoke out of the semi-darkness. "You cannot sleep."

"Who can?"

Deena responded "I was only pretending here so that I would not disturb you. Come, I want to walk a bit before it gets light, and the others awake."

After throwing on some clothes, they emerged from the tent they were using. Without a word, they walked away from the main camp which was now bursting to the seams with anticipation and desperation. The two sisters implicitly knew their destination, it needed not be verbalized nor discussed. It was a bit of a walk but soon they were at the classrooms that had been developed some time ago by the Masoud sisters. It was in these simple buildings that a generation of girls had been first educated, where their worlds had been expanded and personal ambitions became possible.

The oldest building had been the place where Deena had launched her private dream of educating Muslim girls. It now looked forlorn in the morning, bereft of spirit other than the sense of purpose stolen by perverted obsessions. They entered, flashing their torches about the room. The detritus of their recent employment were about them. There were unused desks and dust-covered books cluttering several shelves. There was a blackboard with a lesson in numbers yet evident, and maps remained pinned to the walls. This was far from the high-tech school rooms that would have ben found in many Western schools yet still unimaginable leaps ahead of what girls would now get in this troubled land.

Fingering the growing layer of dust on a desk, Deena whispered. “This is so sad, dear sister.”

Azita reached out to grasp her sibling’s hand. “No, it is not. It is a Providential incentive.”

“A what, Zita? Do you mean a motivation from Allah?” Deena broke into a smile at her sister’s language.

“I suppose, though I am struck that I no longer use His name. I’ve come to employ a more abstract label for those things we cannot imagine and certainly not measure.” She paused. “Is it not a matter of curiosity how beliefs, even the most embedded and instinctive values can erode over time, and in ways about which we are unaware. Until this moment, I have not fully admitted that I do not believe.”

Deena looked at her siter sharply. “And how does this make you feel?”

"That is the most surprising thing of all … I feel so little. It is as if one's core values are chiselled away by so many small cuts until, one day, an entirely different sculpture of the soul has been erected. Then you finally gaze upon this new creation and wonder, when did this happen and what is this that has been put in its place."

Deena reflected on these words before responding. "Don't you see? What has been put in its place has not been altered, merely its foundation shifted. You yet have much faith."

"Deena, you have become quite the philosopher. But what do those words mean?"

"We were taught that good comes from Allah, or some God. Without a belief in some divine presence, we would be without a moral core, or so we were repeatedly told. But look about you, figuratively that is, not literally. Think about Chris and Kay and Karen and Carlotta and even Chris's good friend Joshua. None of them believe in a God, not in a personal God at least, one who pays attention to our petty problems. For example, Amar drew inspiration from Buddhist precepts but that rested on guiding principles, not some ordinary notion of the divine. Yet, they are amongst the most beautiful people we know, the most devout in a way, wedded to a vision of the good that even the most believing of people seldom find in their own hearts. Ali cannot be counted among the Islamic faithful but is a believer in humanity. Is that not true?"

Azita pondered for a moment before responding. "That is so true, so obvious. I am ashamed how I lost sight of that fact."

"None of us are spotless, dear Zita. Many a time I had evil thoughts about you, thinking you a total shit."

"Not evil thoughts, merely objective observation. I'm often a total shit," Azita chuckled. "But think about this. We have been through so much in pursuit of what we think is the good. We have been shot at, wounded, kidnapped, threatened so many times, and seen our dreams dashed repeatedly. I suspect, after all that, it would be hard to sustain a belief in a benevolent God … unless such a divinity were merely testing us."

"True enough, but what kind of God would create a preferred species among his billions of galaxies and trillions of stars just to put them through a series of endless tests. Wouldn't such an omniscient and omnipresent Being have better things to do? Really!"

Azita sighed. "In truth, I agree though I cannot recall the moment I began to stop believing. Whose death were we grieving or which disappointment were we sharing when our doubts overcame our faith. There were so many challenges we faced, and the process though which belief is eroded can be so glacial, like tectonic plates moving beneath us. But here is what I think, or at least read somewhere. The best among us become our best precisely when we no longer rely upon some vengeful, calculating Providential figure."

Deena groaned. "Talk about being an inscrutable philosopher."

"No, listen. Which is better … to do good because one fears retribution by an angry deity or to do good because you have struggled through things in your mind and soul to arrive at some decent moral compass. I go with the latter. As I think back, I doubt Mama and Papa had any conventional beliefs, though they let us come to our own conclusions about things. Yet, their goodness was beyond question. They were spiritual above all, the most blessed of any God's creatures, were there a God who created things that is."

"Whether or not there is a God, whether or not we could possibly fathom such a being if it exists, we have been blessed I think." Deena asserted.

Azita nodded, "No doubt, dear sister. Perhaps it is a genetic gift, or the role models offered to us by our parents, both biological and adopted, or merely the products of our minds ability to connect the dots in terms of some mystery to move the species forward. Reasons matter less than what we have inside. I am confident of that." She then impulsively hugged her sister.

"What was that for? You are getting foolishly sentimental, silly girl."

"And you are not." Azita said through her tears. "I'm just recalling the times we almost lost one another ... the time we hid in a cave to escape the Taliban after Mama and Papa were assassinated, that moment you were shot as we exited our father's family home, or the time I was marched off by young radical bent on revenge. I thought I would surely die on that day."

"And don't forget your beating at the hands of the morals police when you were a mere child." Deena smiled ruefully. "But we did not die, nor waiver. Either we are being spared by someone or something beyond our imagining or we are just damn lucky."

"I shall choose the hypothesis that we are spared to continue our work. That's my story and I'll stick with it. But all this does present one unfortunate reality … that we may not be reunited in some afterlife."

Deena lightly hit her sister on the arm. "Are you insane? You think it would be good to spend eternity with one another?'

"You are so right. What was I thinking? No sane Deity would put up with the two of us bickering for all eternity." Azita laughed out loud. "Come, we have much work to do."

That morning was a bustle of activity throughout the Center. The first of many trucks and busses arrived from Kabul and nearby cities. Supplies were being prepared for those about to journey to a new life. Importantly, the final selection of the girls to be included was being conducted along with the determination of to which exit approach each girl would be assigned. Since those going by bus or lorry might be required to hike overland on occasion, the older and more fit were assigned to that group. But all had to admit, this was a subjective exercise for the most part. All the planners knew that they were making hasty decisions, and regrets were certain to occur. The worst part of this morning's frantic activity involved coming to grips with the fact that not all girls could go or explaining to parents why they could not go with those children lucky to be included in the evacuation. Tears and arguments rang through the Center though not to the extent anticipated. There existed a sense of resignation among the Afghanis. Yet, with the last-minute intervention of the full London staff and available resources, more planes, helicopters, and ground vehicles had been marshalled into service. Far from all, but more girls would now make their escape or at least make the attempt. Alas, it was never enough.

Those orderly days in the beginning, when just a few families were involved, were gone. Now, many parents were hoping to get their daughters out, many based on economic necessity since it was becoming difficult for some families to feed them all. Others wanted their children to escape in anticipation of the harsh prospects facing their female offspring. Parents recalled their own childhoods and what they experienced under the first Taliban regime.

A steady stream of messages came from Carlota Ciganda who was stationed in Jamrud on the eastern side of Torkhum international checkpoint at the beginning of the Khyber Pass, the traditional route used for centuries by forces bent on conquering the empire of the Hind. This was the pass through which British forces had marched with great confidence in the late 1820's only to see a few survivors escape back through this route through the mountains several years later. It had always been a site of great hopes and smashed dreams. Carlota and a team from London had sent vehicles and resources through Jalalabad and on to the camp along with useful intelligence. Those driving the trucks recorded where checkpoints were located and how diligent the staff were at each. At the same time, Sayed had sent a couple of his friends toward Faizabad, where the Badakhshan University was located. They also checked out any impediments on that route, whether trucks and busses could make it there absent harassment. The plan was to land larger aircraft there under the guise of bringing more relief from friendly international organizations and to depart again with a human cargo. It was all being done in such a rush. Carlota desperately wished they had more time.

By late afternoon, the first helicopter flight out was being prepared to lift off. Younger girls, those who had shown the most promise in the classroom were led onto the craft after emotional partings from their families. Apprehension and hope mingled with the afternoon heat and dust. It was the flight that Ali along with Aalem and his family were to use to exit what was now considered the danger zone.

Ali lingered near the aircraft, talking with Deena and Azita. She clearly was reluctant to board. "What are you waiting for, get aboard." Deena said impatiently.

"I want the two of you to know I never really opposed your dream. I was on your side."

"I know," Deena replied.

"*WE* know," Azita emphasized. "I heard you supported us in the argument with Chris about him not holding us back from carrying out our mission. That will never be forgotten."

"No matter what my husband and your father might fear. I know you need to be here, there is so much to do."

"You are so right, Dear Ali, which is even more reason you should get on that freaking helicopter. You are keeping us from our real work."

"You mean babysitting me is not real work. I just don't want to leave you, not at this moment. Can you understand that?" Ali's words were more of a plea.

Azita let a glimmer of a smile cross her lips before becoming so very serious. "I keep thinking about that attack on my father's old clinic in Kabul where I, Deena and I that is, grew up. It was a place of such wonderful memories. Then, when we were there on a visit, a young fanatic planted a bomb. My husband was killed, Josh's wonderful sister, a gifted doctor, also perished. Amar was weakened and became susceptible to Covid later. We lost three dear souls, and it could easily have been more. We are taking a big risk here, who knows how this will turn out. If we have learned anything in our work, it is that life is so tenuous. A few minutes earlier, and that bomb might have killed many more of us. Remember this, not even that horrific memory will deter us. If we succumb to fear, we are lost, our vision is lost. And yet, let us be sensible, we cannot risk all of us or … who will be left to take up our cause?"

"I know, but …" Ali started but was not permitted to finish.

"No buts," Azita virtually shouted. "Think about your husband. He is losing his best friend, probably as we speak. You should go to him. Don't even stop in Pakistan. Go back and comfort him. He lives by his quick wit, but we all know that is a mere shield, his Irish protection against all the hurt inside. What if he also lost us, and you, were you to foolishly stay here. Now, go to him. I beg you. Go!"

Ali looked at Azita carefully. "We have known one another for many years. Sometimes I think of you as younger sister. And yet, we really do not know one another, do we?"

Azita whispered, "I think not, but we can … when we all get back. We can. I promise."

At that, Deena intervened impatiently. "This is touching Hallmark moment indeed. But now get on the damn plane. I would hate for it to run out of fuel and crash somewhere in the mountains, just because we were blabbing away here."

With that, Ali got on the aircraft as Deena and Azita went off to other duties. Still the craft did not move. Aalem exited the craft.

"What is the matter," asked Archie who was helping supervising the comings and goings alongside Karen.

"Nothing," Aalem said. "I told my wife that I would be along on a later flight, that I still had work to do here."

"Additional work?" Karen was suspicious.

"Look about you, all this activity. Yes, there has been a sharp increase in traffic recently with more relief aid coming in and flights returning. But my Taliban friends, if that is what I might call them, have seen nothing on this scale before. They are sure to be suspicious. If I were to suddenly disappear now … you can imagine what they might think and do."

"I appreciate that, but …"

Aalem cut him off. "No arguments my friend. I will see this through, give protection and sow doubts among the true believers for as long as I can. I have many friends around here, men who fought the Russians in the old days and now are elders in positions of authority. We have a bond from those days when we put our lives on the line for one another. They still look up to me. I can help here in many ways, but I must be present to do so. You would be surprised at how many supporters you have in these mountains, surprised indeed. And perhaps we can find time for one more game of chess."

Archie realized what this decision might mean. He accepted more fully that this man was a true friend. Aalem might well be forfeiting his life for people he hardly knew. In the moment, that choice intrigued the elderly doctor. What prompts a man to make such sacrifices? What had prompted him to stay when safety and comfort were so easily obtained.

Archie flashed back to discussions he had with his father about World War II when the previous generation fought against the Japanese in the Pacific. Like many vets, his dad seldom talked about his experiences, but he did get him talking once, after so many beers one night under a canvas of Australian stars when the rest of the world and its cares seemed far, far away.

> *"Dad, do you still think about the war?"*
>
> *"All the time, son. There is nothing so bestial as war. There is no glory, none at all."*
>
> *"But you fought, in the Philippines as I recall," Archie had pushed.*
>
> *"And elsewhere, in too many places to even think about. Way too many."*
>
> *"Dad, I know you don't like to talk about it, and I understand that. Well, not really but I will try to honor that. Just one question, though, if I may."*
>
> *"I will give you one." His father grunted reluctantly.*
>
> *"Why?"*
>
> *"Why?" His father repeated as if not understanding the question.*
>
> *"Perhaps my question is 'how.' How did you get the courage to keep doing it even after you knew the horror of it all?"*
>
> *His father looked at him for a long time. "For the man next to you, even if you did not know his name. You did it because he depended on you, and you depended on him. Simple as that, and just as complex as that."*

Archie snapped to the present and gave a signal. The helicopter, with its horizontal blades rotating slowly suddenly roared as those same blades came too life. The machine rose into the sky, heading off toward the mountains to the east. The doctor then put a hand on Aalem's shoulder. "Perhaps we best get back to my office. We have things to which we must attend and perhaps a pot of tea. That would be nice … a pot of tea."

Aalem smiled. "And when this is at an end, perhaps a game of chess."

The Masoud Center became a hive of activity. Team leaders had to be selected for each escape mode. Travel packs had to be filled. Final selection of each girl had to be determined, both how they would leave and even whether they could leave. Those decisions were left to Farzana with the assistance of her former teachers, but Deena and Azita participated in many cases. Most decisions had already been, being based on the girl's academic potential, her maturity, and her eagerness to go. In a few cases, boys were selected, those who had exceptional academic potential and who had sisters also identified as emigres with great potential. In a few cases, it was a package deal or nothing.

The difficulty came when the obvious candidates were exhausted. What to do with those who appeared to have promise, but that potential was yet untapped or revealed. Deena knew from her own experience that not everyone flowered early. She would have been left behind as a young teen girl, seeking to evade her studies as her sister Azita increasingly showed academic prowess. At one point they took a short break.

"Zita, would you have selected me when we were young? Would you have thought me gifted enough, academically speaking?"

"What kind of silly question is that?"

"Just humor me, what would you have decided?"

Azita looked at her sister and saw she was deadly serious. After pausing to consider, she responded carefully. "For many years, no ... I would not have selected you. But then, miraculously, you blossomed."

"Exactly!" Deena exclaimed. "Yet, here we are making decisions. Some are based on good information, but many are guesses on our part. I so worry that we are making the wrong ones. How do we know who has promise and who doesn't? We are not Gods."

Azita took her sibling by the shoulders. "I am going to give you the same lecture you have given me on occasion. We cannot save them all. No one, and I mean no one, is more devastated by that reality than I."

Deena looked away, sensing that she bordered on petulance as her younger sibling donned the mantle of common sense. "Of course you are right. It is just that some of these decisions ..." She trailed off, knowing that there were no answers to her doubts.

"Part of my personal experience is helping me here. There have been too many times, as a physician, when one must decide with partial information or options clouded with doubt. Transplant surgeons make them all the time. Which candidate will get the liver or heart, and which will not and subsequently pass away? For me, those moments have come during triage in some of the camps in which I've worked over the years when resources or time were at a premium. Should I focus on this patient who requires so much time and effort or on the several in less immediate danger but whose chances of survival are better. At first, I was paralyzed until indecision could no longer be permitted. In time, I just chose. Oh, there was a kind of calculation involved but let's face it, these usually were not quantitative decisions, not in any exact sense. They were choices of the gut, bringing to bear all kinds of peripheral considerations and factors that would make me squirm upon more sober reflection. The ultimate trick is not to look back and question yourself."

"Can you do that?" Deena was incredulous. "That does not seem like you."

"Hah," Azita emitted a strangled chortle, "we know one another too well. I can block things out to a point, mostly out of some kind of survival instinct." She paused to consider an intruding thought. "As we talk, I'm reminded of something."

"What?" Deena asked when her sister hesitated.

"Probably not important, but there is a big difference in rich and poor countries. In poor sites, you can tell the loved ones that you did your best even when you know you chose someone else to help over their loved one. They will thank you for what you did which is unbearable for you since there is a lie involved. But in wealthy medical facilities, the patient's loved ones tend to look upon you with suspicion since they are entitled. *'You did your best'* they sneer as they look at you in ways that I somehow failed them because of my gender or skin color. If we were making similar decisions among privileged girls, it would be easier. But knowing that these families will accept what we decide … I mean they may beg but they will accept. That breaks my heart even more. There is one thing though …" Azita paused again. "Sorry, perhaps I'm embarrassed by this but … in my heart I tell myself I'll be back. I must tell myself that."

"And to the girls and their families … the ones turned away." Deena asked.

"I only promise to do the best I can to return one day." Azita said before quickly adding, "and this is not a lie since that is what I intend."

Deena looked around her. "Yes, I also must assume that we will be back. Hope is the ultimate narcotic for those who believe … people like us." Then she looked back at her sister. "Now, back to work or we will get no dinner."

As each group was ready, they were loaded onto the appropriate vehicle. More than once, Karen marvelled at the number of trucks and busses that arrived. Some were sent by the Guptas from Kabul, others from Pakistan from Carlota who managed things there. Still other from Faizabad and other nearby cities. Vehicles even arrived from Tajikistan to the wonderment of the local staff. When full of passengers, some went west to Faizabad's airport where medium sized planes were waiting. Others went south and then east toward Jalalabad and the Khyber Pass. The remainder boarded helicopters, which periodically came and went.

After a couple of days of such intense activity, Aalem sought Archie out early in the morning. "I am shocked they have not come yet, the authorities I mean. We must get the final ones off. There is no more time. My pleas and arguments now are falling on deaf ears. Are you determined to stay, doctor?"

"Nothing has happened to change my mind." Archie said blandly. "But you must get on the final helicopter, with Karen Fisher. If I'm not mistaken all the rest of the London staff have left on various busses … to bribe officials or whatever it takes to get through. Sometimes, a foreign presence makes local officials think twice."

"And you, my friend? You should get on this aircraft."

Aalem smiled. "Did you really think I would leave? I am staying to do what I can to protect you and your family, to help keep your work going here. What will happen to all these people if you are not here? I don't want to contemplate such a future."

Archie looked at his new friend, knowing that argument would be futile. "Then, let us make sure that Azita and Deena are on the final busses. Then it will be quiet again. We can have tea and that game of chess."

Many hours later, the final two busses made their way out of the camp and toward the east. Archie, Agnes, Carolyn, and the others waived good by and said a silent prayer. The subsequent trip would be arduous … a trial with many delays, arguments with local officials who had become increasingly suspicious the further away from the Panjshir valley they were. This flow of vehicles had become highly suspicious though the locals were exposed to conflicting information. Some believed these transports had an official okay and others concluded the opposite. Indecision and doubt increased with each passing hour. Deena was seated at the front of one of the busses when she saw a jeep coming toward them. It swerved to cut off any further progress of the vehicle. Her heart sank and she considered telling the driver to push on. Then she recognized the man jumping out of the vehicle.

"Sayed," she said as she got off the bus. Immediately, she was aware that Azita had joined her after exiting from a second bus, the last bus in the caravan.

Sayed said breathlessly, "Farzana and her group are being held at the border. No one knows what to do but there is great suspicion now. The only thing keeping them from being arrested is that there are officials at the border from several countries arguing for their release. I am not sure that will work now but praying it will. Confusion has favored us so far but … better that you not arrive at this moment and complicate things. They will know this is a mass escape."

Deena thought for a moment. "Here is what we will do. Take our bribe money, we have some left. Use it for your bus. We are taking our girls through the mountains."

"You don't know the way." Sayed argued.

"We will manage. We are very resourceful."

"Aach, wait a minute." He took the money and ran back to the jeep, returning almost immediately as the vehicle took off toward the border at a high rate of speed.

"What are you doing?" Azita asked.

"I will lead you?"

"You know this area?" Deena asked sceptically.

"Not by experience. But I studied geography in school and have an excellent memory."

"You are a crazy man, but I see why Farzana loves you." Azita blushed at what she revealed. "If we get out of this, we will see that you get to finish your education so that, in the future, you won't act like such a damn fool."

Sayed laughed out loud. "Gather the girls. It is not a great distance, but we are losing light." Then he pointed and spoke. "This way."

For hours he led the band of girls through a winding, and rough patch of ground amidst the hills and mountains on either side. They stopped frequently to let the girls rest and to try and keep them calm. As night settled in, a full moon made it possible to continue.

"Should we stop for the night?" Deena asked at one point.

"No, there is enough light. I'd rather keep going." He then pulled her away from the group. "Have you been hearing sounds behind us?

"Yes," she replied, concern in her voice.

"I have as well. I am thinking that they are following us. We had to make quite a sight, heading off into the hills. Surely, we did not escape without notice."

"You are right, we best keep going." Azita added.

The girls remained quiet for the most part, but the younger ones became increasingly cranky as the night wore on and the route through the surrounding peaks seemed endless to their young eyes. Sayed would take out a compass from time to time, look at it and say with confidence to no one in particular, '*it won't be long now.*' Azita wanted to ask him how a compass would indicate distance from their goal, whatever that was, but decided that would serve no purpose. They had cast their lot with him and that was that. She only hoped that Farzana's faith in this man was not misplaced.

At one point they arrived at some abandoned buildings, their original purpose now lost. They huddled for rest there and ate some food, trying to keep the spirits of their young charges up. Some of the girls were complaining of tired feet and small bruises from falls. They were all assured that the end was near.

Sayed walked away from the camp and seemed to stare at nothing. On his return, he whispered to Deena and Azita, "I can still hear them. I think they are gaining on us but I'm having trouble determining from which direction the sounds are coming."

"You were never a boy scout, were you?" Deena tried to sound witty but failed.

"Let us go, quickly." Sayed said with confidence. "We will make it."

With much groaning and complaint, the girls were organized, and the trek continued. The route seemed less arduous now, the terrain less hilly. They made better time.

"What's that?" one of the girls said, pointing at the sky where some object circled in the dark, something impossible to identify.

"Just our luck it will be a flying saucer and we'll be abducted." Deena tried to joke.

"Let's keep moving, girls. Not far now." Azita said while berating herself for an obvious deceit. Inside, her heartbeat faster. She was sure she now could hear noises nearby. Could they be arrested now when they were so close to freedom. Perhaps if she had not discarded her faith in Allah so casually. Perhaps this was His retribution … to permit hope before snatching it all away.

Then a bright light shone on them from overhead, soon there was another to their right and up on a small hill. Azita heart stopped for a moment, or so it seemed to her. She was about to yell run, as if that would do any good when a familiar voice said. "There they are." The words were in English with a British accent.

Out of the dusky morning gloom appeared Carlota and Ali and Farzana with a few other staff she recognized, and some she didn't. Ali rushed to Azita and hugged her with gusto. Carlota did the same with Deena and Farzana found Sayed. Many tears were shed in the moment.

"Where did you come from? Where are we?" Azita asked.

Ali answered. "You are in Pakistan, but you are walking in the wrong direction, back toward Afghanistan."

"Hmm, I think I forgot some of my geography lessons." Sayed said sheepishly.

"When you didn't show at the border, we assumed you went on some cockamamie trek. But I cannot say it was a foolish move. We had one hell of a time getting the final bus through. A good thing that guy arrived with the bribe money when he did. He could bribe them discretely. The natives know how, while we might have raised too many questions.

Sayed spoke, still holding Farzana. "That was my best friend, we taught together until recently. And that light above us, some thought it was an alien aircraft. Not me, of course."

"Of course," Farzana smiled.

"A drone," Carlota said with a laugh. "We had several hunting for you."

Deena wiped a tear from her cheek. "We thought you were Taliban following us. It is so good to see all of you." Then she turned to Ali. "Wait, aren't you supposed to be back in England. Didn't we tell you that."

"And you thought I would listen, foolish girl. Seriously, I intended to get on the next plane, but I talked to Chris. You are right about Josh. He is failing now. Chris will need me, but he insisted I stay here until I knew you were safe. Believe me. He gave me no choice. He could not even think about me returning until he was certain all of you were out of harm's way. Now I will get on the next plane out." There were more hugs.

Safety was not the end of the journey, nor the goal. In some ways it was just the beginning. Azita and Deena were taken aback by the number of foreign officials that had gathered in Abbottabad, where the locus of operations for the so-called *'girls-flight' project* had been set up. Representatives from the U.S., England, Canada, Australia, India, Spain, Germany, and New Zealand were there. They were also surprized that this city was chosen as the site to reorganize and get the girls off on their next stage of their *hegira* to freedom. It is the home of the Pakistani equivalent of America's West Point or the Royal Military Academy at Sandhurst. It was also the place where Osama Bin Laden hid in his compound for several years before being tracked down by high tech surveillance.

It was obvious to the girls that some deal had been struck with the Pakistan Government. Chris and his family must have called in a lot of chits to make all this happen so quickly. Other things surprised the two. They were told that the Singletary family had become heroes in Australia and the Gupta's were being lionized in the Indian Press. The decision had been made that an operation of this size could never be kept secret so that they might as well go with full disclosure. The optics apparently confused the Taliban who wavered between a quick and ruthless response and a slow one that permitted the evacuation to succeed before clamping down. They arrived in force at the Masoud Center some two hours after the last bus had left.

Karen Fisher caught up with Deena and Azita. "Well, it looks like I live to see another day."

"I'm sorry, what?" Deena responded.

Karen laughed. "I was never worried about the Taliban. But if either or both of you had gotten yourself killed, Chris would have done me in with his bare hands. I'm heading back with Ali, much to do on that end as well."

As she whirled to leave, Azita called out. "Karen, thanks for everything. Really,"

"All in a day's work," she said dismissively.

"And one more thing." Deena added. "Tell Chris we love him."

"Yes, oh please do that." Azita added with a choking voice.

At this Karen stopped. "Oh, he knows. You two do give him so much heartburn, but he knows that. However, he did say something about replacing you two with a couple of pet dogs. In fact, he specifically mentioned rottweilers."

With that she laughed and was gone.

CHAPTER 24

Refractive Reflections

> *"A good novelist does not lead his characters, he follows them. A good novelist does not create events, he watches them happen, and writes down what he sees. A good novelist realizes he is a secretary, not God."*
>
> *Stephen king*

Kay made her way into the room where Chris, Connie, and Josh's closest friends continued their vigil. "They are out," she whispered to her brother as she settled in next to him.

"All of them are out of harm's way?"

"Karen, Ali, and Cate have flown back directly; all the rest are safe in Pakistan with a few in Tajikistan, dealing with the massive logistics involved."

"Everyone!" He repeated.

"Yes, everyone involved in the education programs that is, as well as all our staff people. The on-site senior medical staff have decided to stay. I went around and around with them about the dangers they face but … they are just so dedicated. They make me ashamed of myself."

Chris assumed his all too recognizable impish grin. "Oh Kay, we are all so ashamed of you."

"Bite me, asshole," Kay shot back with her own grin, then turned serious. "I just hope that they do not fall into a political vendetta. I've grown to love those people."

"I've already made contact with some of my political friends … you know, to use back channels to drop a hint in Kabul that any harm that comes to our service personnel would not be looked upon kindly by the outside world."

"Damn you," Kay tried to look serious. "Every time I conclude you are totally useless; you go and do something like this."

"So, Azita and Deena are fine." He pushed.

Kay put her hand on her brother's shoulder. "Yes, don't you think I would have told you if they were not. Don't you understand the word *'everyone?'*"

"Sorry, I just needed to hear the words again, make sure I heard them right … just so I can breathe again,"

Kay hugged her brother. "You really are a softy."

"Shhh, our secret."

"How is he doing?" She whispered to while nodding toward Josh whose eyes were closed.

"The dead man is doing just fine," Josh said loudly without opening his eyes. Kay jumped slightly at his words.

“Don’t be alarmed,” Mo Greenstein said. “That’s his version of Irish humor. He’s done that to me several times.”

Josh slowly opened his eyes. “Well, the whole lot of you are like a bunch of old hens waiting for the rooster to croak. I hope you realize that none of you are in my will.”

“How the hell would you know anything about roosters and hens,” Carla came back at him. “Have you ever even been on a farm?”

“I saw one in the movies once.” Josh opened his eyes fully and looked about the room. “So, all is well in Afghanistan. Wait, I put that wrong. The country is going to hell in a hand basket, but everyone we love is unharmed.”

Bob Wilson moved his chair closer to his friend. “That’s right, I even said a prayer for them. Hadn’t done that in a while.”

“And they still made it out okay… even after this reprobate’s prayers,” Josh chuckled at his own wit. “Remarkable.”

Bob smiled. “You are still a funny man. And just to piss you off, I’ve said a prayer or two for you, even if you are beyond reclamation.”

“Hah,” Josh laughed which segued into a brief expression of pain. “What a waste but I appreciate the effort.” He looked about. “Where is Cate?”

Kay responded. “I just spoke with her and Ali. They are just back from helping with the evacuation and will be here momentarily. They rushed back to …” Kay stumbled with how to complete her thought.

"Be here to see the rooster croak? That is good." With effort, Josh raised his hand as he saw Kay blush with embarrassment. "No need to apologise for saying what is true. But, to change the topic, listen to me, there is a lesson for us all in this situation."

"And that would be?" His wife Connie asked as everyone instinctively leaned toward the dying man, afraid to miss anything in these moments.

Josh looked about and smiled again. "The secret to getting people to listen to your drivel … just convince them that you are dying."

"You are such an exasperation." His wife said though her eyes were wet with tears.

"That I am, but back to my drivel. We tend to think of them, the Taliban I mean, as so different than us, mostly because they wear different clothes and call their God by a different name. But make no mistake. The extreme right in America, or Britain or in any country, is no different. They would impose autocratic rule, they would entomb women in horrific shackles as they take us back to a patriarchal society, and they would rationalize all manner of oppressions as reflecting the word of God. They would end democracy. Over two centuries of effort to build something based on the consent of the governed, imperfect as it has been, would be swept away in their zeal for unvarnished power. Look a Bolsonaro in Brazil, the so-called Tropical Trump. After losing his re-election bid, he is copying Donald's playbook … crying fraud and asking the military to intervene. Can attacks on government institutions be far behind. I swear that if the January 6 leaders remain unpunished … I mean, only the foot soldiers have faced consequences so far … a terrible legacy will remain. They will learn that you can commit treason without penalty. We will see what political scientists call *'authoritarian learning.'* The current Trumpian playbook will be refined and spread around the globe. That is my fear, as I reach the end, that my native country remains blind to the dangers. They cannot see what is right in front of them."

Chris tried to calm his friend. "Relax Josh, Trump is fading from view. His chosen candidates are struggling. Fewer people attend his rallies. By next year, he will be done … *finito*."

"I wish I could believe that. Never forget that Naziism was fading at the very moment Hitler was appointed Chancellor. They had done worse in the most recent election just before his appointment. The pundits of that era felt that he had peaked, that his movement would soon be history, as would he. Then Papen, a moderate right-winger, who wanted another shot as Chancellor … wait, I've told that story before."

"No matter," Chris said, "we love your old stories."

"Okay then, Papen convinced Hindenburg that Hitler was a clown that could easily be controlled, at least until the Weimar Republic could beat back the surge of the Socialists. And so they made a bargain with the devil. And never forget, others will be eager to take his place, evil has no end." At this he sunk into a coughing fit.

"Josh is damn smart for a Mick," Carla intoned, "… but perhaps we best avoid politics."

"Thank you, my dear, for the compliment. I know that praise is not your strong suit." Josh said regaining control of his body.

Carla grunted. "You're right, Connie, he is such an exasperation."

“That I am but that has always been part of my charm.” Josh managed.

“Charm?” Chris echoed. “Anyone notice his charm?”

“Forget it, my friend. You simply don’t have an authentic Celtic wit. Your problem was being born rich. You never had to fight for stuff and humor is born from struggle … we all know that.”

Peter spoke up with a voice that cracked with emotion. “I can say one thing for sure. You would never tackle me on a football field now.”

“Says the slowest freaking running back in Boston.” Josh smiled at some boyhood memory. “But listen, I want to make sure you understand something. I’ve gone as far as I can with my final work. Gretchen, Ashok, and Amandeep have been great assets, thanks Chris. And before I faded, I did some sit-down interviews with Ashley. Chris, look carefully at all this stuff we’ve done. I’m putting everything in your hands.”

“That’s at the top of my list. No question.”

“Just remember, keep your focus on the long term, the big picture. Everyone else will be working hard and spending tons of money on the immediate battles like who will win the next election or, if the Republicans win the House or Senate in the upcoming election, can they be prevented from scuttling a functioning government just to prove their point?”

“What point could that possibly be?” Kay asked.

Josh looked surprised at the question. “That government isn’t necessary, except for the military and prisons and various means of controlling ordinary people. They are so hungry for power and so driven to get at the *'woke'* liberals, nothing is off the table."

"Wait," Kat piped up, "you're suggesting that the Republicans might consciously throw the U.S. government into bankruptcy by defaulting on our debts. That would result in unimaginable suffering and global chaos. Even they are not that insane."

"Think carefully, my dear benefactor. They somehow would get people to believe it is the Dems fault. Anyway, we've been at the precipice before. We talked about those moments during the cold war when the actions of one man saved the world from nuclear holocaust … the Russian sub fleet commander during the Cuban missile crisis who refused to go along with two other officers to launch their nuclear warheads when they suspected war had broken out."

"I remember," Chris nodded as he spoke, "and the Russian general in the 1980s who looked at his computer screen that said dozens of missiles were headed to his mother country and decided that this could not be true because the Americans were not that stupid. So, he did not launch theirs. He guessed right. We were not that stupid … back then. But the far right has lost touch with reality. Their only allegiance is to the well-being of the very richest of the rich and perhaps their whacko base. After all, the rich will always do well no matter what is happening in the economy or society or the globe. They would use a general breakdown to grab all remaining power. Why do it gradually by spending so much money trying to buy elections when you can take everything during a cataclysmic breakdown. No, no … a government default and the ensuing chaos might well serve their designs perfectly."

"That's quite an apocalyptic vision," Peter Favulli said. "But who is the hero now to step up to the plate and save us from Armageddon.

"You guys, I suppose." Josh now spoke quietly,

"Then we are in deep shit." Chris smiled.

"Got that right." Josh smiled back. "You know, I'm not totally against fighting the immediate battles. They are important for sure when you are playing defense, which democracy is in the States for sure … playing out a kind of desperate end game. All I am saying is that the real contest is the battle of ideas and values. Take your resources and energies and keep going after the big themes … cooperation over selfishness, community over isolation, reason over fear, democracy over demagogues, science over superstition, and the list can go on. We know what constitutes the good society where all are included and have the opportunity to succeed. Somehow the right has convinced half of America that such a world is a bad thing. They have sold us on a zero-sum world where every individual is in a desperate struggle with everyone else, so you better be armed to the teeth. Who in their right mind wants such a world?"

"I cannot believe the vision of the right will prevail." Kay tried but without conviction.

"I hope you are right, my dear. I really do," His tone did not reflect his words. "But I am counting on you to carry on the fight. They are driven by hate of what they see as *'woke' Americans*, those evil monsters driven by things like compassion, community, and civility." He seemed to lose his focus for a moment. "I've laid out all I can in my manuscript. Talk to Gretchen and the others."

"We will" Chris said. "And I promise, we will carry on."

Josh took a breath, so deep it startled those around him. Then he spoke again. "Funny, you get to this stage, and it is hard not to reflect. You know, things like what would I have done differently? How did I screw up? Well, there's not enough time to cover all my sins, but a couple stand out."

"No need to confess to us." Bob tried.

Josh chuckled. "Less a confession than an accounting. Wouldn't I be shocked if I woke up in front of St. Peter and had to account for my life? Holy shit."

"Hah, we'd all be screwed." Bob added.

"Not you guys," Josh looked at his old college revolutionary compatriots, "not one of you. You will be the first through the gates."

"Only if you put in a good word for us." Mo managed to say.

Josh continued. "I wish, though, that I had made amends with my father, Big Jim. I failed him. We argued so, and then I left. Before I could summon the guts to see him again, he was gone. I did make amends to my sister Rachel but only because she took the initiative. She literally had to bully me into a relationship again after so many years. And you guys," Josh weakly gestured toward his old college friends, "why did you track me down after four decades. I was such a coward, running away for so long. That … that causes me so much pain. And Connie, I knew I loved you long before admitting it. What form of cowardice is that? The worst, most unforgivable kind I think."

Connie moved to his side and stroked his hair. "Oh, dear man. We found one another, that is all that counts. Please don't beat yourself up."

"She's right," Peter interjected, "that's our job, and we enjoy it so." They all laughed at a line each had used for so long and so often. In the moment, it was more a way of releasing tension than expressing humor, but such a release was essential.

"No Peter, that is my job, and I would not give it up for the world." The voice came from the back of the room. Unseen, Cate, Ali, Karen, and Usha Nayer had made their way to the back of the crowd. Now people moved so that Cate could be get next to her uncle as Ali found a place next to her husband, taking his hand as she did. Cate leaned over and kissed Josh on the forehead but found herself unable to speak further.

"Thank you for being here, my dear. You so remind me of my sister."

"Mother was a saint." Cate managed to say.

Connie spoke up. "Yes, she was. In truth, I had given up thinking you were potential husband material until I met your sister and your niece." She nodded toward Cate. "After all, I had talked to Usha, and she told me what a pain in the ass you were to live with."

"An absolute pain. I was amazed you took him on." Usha Nayer added.

Josh focused on the woman who he had married for a while to keep her lesbian lifestyle a secret from her conservative family. "Usha, where have you been?"

"With Ali and Cate helping in Pakistan, but we all rushed back when we heard …"

Connie rushed her words as she saw Usha falter. "Yes, after meeting Cate and your sister, I realized there was hope for the Connelly clan and went in for the kill."

"We are so glad you did." Cate found her voice. "He was so pathetic until you rescued him from himself. Did he ever give you his lecture on male-female relations? Oh my God. When we all were in Vancouver for his retirement, he went on about this nonsense during a road trip up to Whistler."

"We can skip that, my dear, but I am so glad you're here. And Meena?"

"I'm sorry uncle, I insisted she stay and help in Pakistan. They need everyone. Did I err?"

"No, no," he hastened to add. "I'm being too selfish as it is. I am so glad she is in your life, part of your life."

"So am I" Cate managed to say but nothing more.

"Look how I've ruined the day for all of you. But I'm well practiced at it, ruining things. I gave all my friends here," again he motioned to his college crowd, "so much grief, and my father, my poor father." Now his eyes moistened. "All he wanted was a son to play football at Notre Dame. And I could have made that happen but walked away after I crippled that boy during a game. I said that was the reason but … I'm not sure it was. I think … I think I was afraid of failing him. I've often wondered if that's why I really quit. Perhaps I just took the easy way out by making it look like a principled stand. Does that make sense?"

"Listen," Mo said, "I thought I was carrying on my family tradition by becoming a college revolutionary, my grandfather and uncle were Bolsheviks. But they never ended up in jail, or at least they never admitted to it. Hell, I thought I was the one to screw things up big time."

"And me," Bob said enthusiastically, "I was supposed to become a Catholic Bishop at the least, probably a Cardinal with the red robes and all, if not the Pope. I was such a good young boy. Then I met you clowns and wound up in jail. I think my parents told everyone I had died." But he laughed as he said this.

Carla joined in. "I wanted to be a Rabbi, but my folks resisted that. They wanted me to marry a doctor and be a good Jewish mother. What were they thinking? I was an idealist, not a domestic goddess, but they couldn't see that. There were many, how shall I put it, *'discussions'* around the dinner table in my home. Then, my older brother went on to study fine arts. He was supposed to be a doctor. This was not turning out well for them. Good thing my younger sibling, by almost a decade, made plenty of money in Silicon Valley. I was saved within the family by his success, and really by him after getting out of prison. He financed our book shop."

"Boo, hoo," Peter chimed in. "No one has a story more tragic than mine. Do you know how a first-born Italian son is treated? I will tell you … like a freaking Prince. And I was an athlete to boot, and never got arrested."

"Bullshit," Josh said with a chuckle as his eyes brightened for a moment.

"What?" Peter looked offended. "I never got arrested, rather an accomplishment in my neighborhood."

"Not that, you idiot, the thing about being an athlete." Josh said firmly. "My sister could have knocked you on your ass."

"Okay, I've put on a few pounds since my playing days but …"

Josh chortled, then coughed. "A few, a few? You would need a crane to lift you on to a freaking scale."

Peter tried again. "Getting back to my main point, I was pampered and spoiled at home, treated as the prince of the family. You now, as it should be. Then, I made an unforgivable sin."

"You got involved with a bunch of radicals?" Kay asked.

"Hell no, I got out in time. No, my sin was becoming best friends with a Mick. My family was appalled, shocked, outraged."

Josh was enjoying himself. It was like old times. "Yeah, yeah, I became your friend because no one else would. I took pity on you. You think it was easy for me to hang out with some Mafia wanna-be thug from the North End?" Josh looked about. "In case anyone missed it, that's where the Italians hung out."

"This clown didn't even know what a cannoli was. Can you believe that?" Peter looked aghast.

"Peter," Carla interjected, "what if you had brought home a nice Jewish girl?"

Peter looked thoughtful. "Hmmm, good question. My folks thought of Jewish people as being smart and ambitious, that was good. So, if I brought home a good Jewish girl, that might have been okay, especially if she treated me like the prince I was.

On the other hand, if I had brought you home ..." He ducked as something whizzed by his ear.

As the group laughed, Chris leaned over to Ali and whispered in her ear, "*this is precisely why I wanted them all here. They've had these kinds of exchanges for weeks now.*" She kissed her husband on the cheek.

"You know, here's the thing that has always amazed me." Josh looked as if he was struggling with his thoughts. "Ever since we reconnected at my retirement event at UBC."

"University of British Columbia," Chris said to Ali who had looked confused.

"Right, ever since then, I have reflected on one thing. Why is it that our connection has been so strong, so ... what is the word ... intense?"

"I can't speak for the rest of you," Bob Wilson said with a straight face, "but I am doing good works by being friends with you losers so, you know, I'll have a better shot at heaven."

Josh rolled his eyes. "Nice try, asshole. Think about it. We were quite different in so many ways."

"True," Carla said. "Still, we had two things going for us. We believed in something, a purpose greater than ourselves. And we were young, not jaded by life or the accumulation of mundane experiences. You cannot replace those early connections I think, nor those first experiences which can seem so unique."

Josh seemed to drift off for several moments as if capturing lost memories, then he responded. "It matters not whether our purpose was correct or not, whether we were a success or failed, or even how we turned out according to the ordinary metrics of achievement. I feel we succeeded. I so feel that now, in this place, with all of you. We experienced something few do in their ordinary lives."

At that Cate let out a strangled cry. Josh turned to her. "And you, my dear. I've been asked many times whether I regretted not having children. My answer was always no, I never had a doubt about that. And there is a good reason for that."

"What's that unc." Cate managed.

"Obvious isn't it. I've known the best child possible. I could never possibly match her with one of my own." With that, Cate burst into tears. "Damn, I always make the girls cry."

"Thank you, uncle, for everything."

Josh looked away from his niece, afraid of his own emotions, and toward his new friend. "And you, Chris, you are the exception, you and yours I should say."

"Exception? I don't understand."

"Well, I met you later in life but that same bond was evident from the start. Like minds, like visions, and all that. A mystery I suppose. But it was there, nonetheless. If I were to have had a son, you would have been it."

"And for sure, if I had my choice of a father, I would have selected you, hands down."

"Of course you would, you could hardly do better. And besides, your real dad didn't set a high bar. In fact, the bar he set remained below ground," Josh said with his sly smile. "Now, I need my rest. So, I'll kick you out for a while, except for Connie. The rest of us can pick up with the insults later ... when we meet again."

Several in the group mumbled *'so long'* and *'see you later'* or some similar sentiment as they headed out of the room.

"Wait, one last thought." Josh's voice seemed weaker, more forced. "Remember Golding's classic, *The Lord of the Flies?*"

"Of course." Chris said as others nodded affirmatively.

"It changed our notion of children and society back in the 1950s. It drummed into people that man was essentially evil if left to their own devices. It was a triumph of the Hobbesian view of society over Rousseau's view ... we are basically evil and need social control to keep us from doing bad stuff as opposed to being basically good with the evils of society doing us in." He stopped to control unseen pain.

"A classic for sure." Carla filled in the temporary silence.

"But Golding was wrong, his was just a made-up story of kids lost on an island. In real life, six students from a Catholic School in the South Pacific had a similar challenge. They survived for 15 months on an uninhabited Island named Atta until they were discovered by accident and rescued. In real life, these kids remained civil to one another and cooperated with one another to survive against all odds. They were basically good and created a kind of working government. It was in the 1960s this happened. Remember that. It was the theory that, in our hearts, we are instinctively good that prevailed, not that we are evil."

"I will." Mo said, suddenly wishing desperately to be back in college with his old friend.

"We were the good ones ..." Josh said softly "Back in college, we were the good ones. That is my one certainty in life though I missed it at the time."

Peter let out a sound that resembled a strangled sob. "You guys were the good ones. I have no doubt about that. I wish I had stayed with you."

Josh forced himself to speak again, this time more loudly. "Some of you will recall the old aphorism, the one where the ancient wise man tells the young student that each of us has two wolves within our souls. One wolf is vicious, rapacious, selfish, and evil while the other is benevolent, kind, big hearted, and loving. These two are in continuous battle for dominance ... a struggle that takes place within each of us. '*Which one of them wins?*' the young boy asks, most curious as to the lesson being shared." Josh paused as if it were too difficult for him to continue. '*Which one wins ...*' he tried again.

Chris looked upon his dear friend and said quietly. "The wolf that wins is the one that you feed."

"Yes," Josh's eyes brightened for a moment. "Never forget that we are what we nurture. Now, I really need to rest for a bit."

The group slowly and reluctantly murmured last thoughts and left the room. For some reason, they were reluctant to disperse.

As Mo reached the exit, he turned. "Josh, I wish we had those long-ago years back, we would have done things differently."

Josh lifted his head slightly. "No we wouldn't; No way in hell."

They mingled and shared thoughts of the old days for some time when Connie emerged from Josh's room. Her face was ashen.

All looked at her, taken by her aspect. "He has passed." She said softly. "I think he knew when he sent us away. I think he wanted to do that alone, not to burden anyone … especially you people, his friends. He wanted to spare you." Then she sat and put her face in her hands until Usha picked her up and enveloped her in her arms. The two women who had shared Josh's life in an intimate fashion wept as they embraced one another.

Later, that evening, there was a gathering in a private room at the Hairy Hare. Mo, Carla, Bob, Peter, Cate, Usha, and Connie were there, along with Chris. These were the people that Connie had contacted when she realized her husband was dying. These were the people she knew Josh would want to spend his final days with. She often wondered whom she would choose when her time came. No easy list of candidates came to mind. Perhaps she had no comparable experience in her life where deep devotions were forged. Perhaps she could borrow her husband's fast friends.

She started the discussion once they were all seated. "Chris, we wanted to thank you, for bringing us over. I've felt guilty about relying on your generosity for so long. I wish you would let us pay …"

She got no further. "Another word about money and you will suffer a fate worse than death. You will not be permitted to leave the Hairy Hare and will remain here subsisting on their food and drink for the remainder of your miserable lives."

"That settles it, I'm good on the money thing." Peter said emphatically. "I thought your wife and sister would join us."

"They are back at work, there is so much to do with all these Afghan girls, mind-numbing arrangements to be made."

"Cate and I will re-join them soon. It is an all hands-on-deck moment." Usha observed.

"I am coming to an invaluable epiphany during all this."

"What's that?"

"I'm superfluous."

Carla mused. "I wish Karen was here, Chris. She would say that you have always been superfluous. I love that woman … she is such a firecracker."

"The two of you could be sisters." Mo observed.

Chris was tempted to retell the vignette about the interview in which he spontaneously decided to hire her despite a lack of qualifications but realized they all knew that story … he had told it so often. Instead, he said, "the only thing I was needed for during all this was to make some political calls. Now, that was critical but that was it. Then it was … get out of our way, old man. I'm becoming … useless."

Connie smiled, "I think that is a wonderful insight for all with delusional pretences to self-importance. I noticed the same thing toward the end of my research career. The younger, hungrier scholars were doing the heavy lifting. It is always good to realize when you have become obsolete."

Chris looked closely at Josh's widow. "How are you doing?"

Connie sighed. "I had a long time to prepare. My closest colleague back at the university, her husband had early Alzheimer's. She called it the *long good-by.* It went on for some seven years I think as his brain slipped away from him. When I consoled her when he finally passed, she told me it wasn't like that. By then, she had already lost him … he had left her much earlier. Josh was different of course. He was still sharp at the end. But I could see him struggling. He was ready. It was time. He really wanted to go; we must believe that. I do."

Carla took a deep breath. "I wonder if I will be ready when the time comes."

Mo snorted. "You won't even know it's coming. So no, you won't be ready. One night, when you are keeping me up with your snoring, I'll smother you with a pillow."

"I'm not the one who snores." Carla reacted before realizing she had fallen for his trap. "Asshole!"

Bob spoke in a serious voice. "There is one thing that has always bothered me … about Josh."

"What?" Peter asked.

Bob continued in a reflective voice. "He never could kick the guilt in his life … his father, his Irish tribe, and us. Even you, Connie. I know it is a Catholic, and maybe Jewish, thing but he had a bad case of it. He came to me, thinking I had some spiritual insight or silver bullet. I didn't, of course. I wish I had."

"And there was this girl in college … Eleni. When he ran off to Canada, he not only left us but her as well." Carla looked at Connie suddenly, wondering if she was treading on dangerous ground.

"Carla, I'm good about Eleni. I've known about her from the beginning. She was like his relationship with you guys, early and special and intense. I accepted that long ago, at least after I realized he did love me. I just wish I had enjoyed such an early connection with someone. but such was not to be. When young, I married sensibly and almost died of boredom. And if I ever find out that Josh, in fact, never loved me, I will track him down in the afterlife and break his kneecaps. And that would be for starters."

"Ah, the afterlife." Bob mused. "I can never figure out what I believe or, more accurately, what I want to believe. Face it, my friends, would you prefer a void, no consciousness, or some other state of being that lasts for eternity."

"Wouldn't that depend on the nature of the existence in which you are stuck." Mo mused.

"Good point," Peter chimed in. "Really, what about those poor souls who believe that they will be with their loved ones for all eternity. Come on, have people thought that through? Hell, we might be talking about the same family members they barely managed to get through the last Thanksgiving dinner with."

"Absolutely," Mo nodded in agreement.

"You mean like being stuck with your wife." Carla added, looking at her husband.

Mo started to respond and caught himself. "Er, a blessed eternity for sure."

"Nice save, asshole," Carla smiled.

Chris came to his rescue. "Or think about Azita and Deena. They have been driven by a singular passion, or maybe a related set of passions. Their lives have become dedicated to freeing Muslim females from the worst form of patriarchy, giving young girls hope. Think about it, they've given up so much for this dream, lives of comfort and conventional success. So many times, they have risked death, came close to it, for what … an impossible dream."

"Any more impossible than yours, or ours, when we were younger." Peter added.

"What if," Chris went on, "there are these infinite number of universes that string theorists argue exist. Is it possible we jump from one reality to another at our passing? If so, perhaps we jump into a parallel universe where our fundamental aspirations are realized."

"Right there, that's why I dumped you," Usha said with a chuckle.

"What do you mean?"

"Chris, your thinking has always been so flawed. If that were true, what would explain the millions born as untouchables in India? Surely, that was not their aspiration in a previous life."

Connie joined in, "Good point, and who would be born again as a Trump supporter in America … a hellish outcome by any standards."

"No," Chris said slowly as he thought of a response. "If beings were jumping across universes, we could hardly surmise what situation they existed in before."

"But," Bob persisted, "to make the next life worthwhile, would we not have to be aware of where we were, what we had experienced before? The satisfaction comes in the comparison, no?"

Chris thought for a moment. "You got me. We have no freaking idea. But that is the one thing that makes me look forward to the end, perhaps finding out something about life's greatest mystery. That possibility motivated Josh. I recall him musing during one of our recent talks that, *'wouldn't it be great to know that answer?'*"

Bob sighed. That reminds me of one of my favorite poems. I spent my time in the monastery reading and becoming literate. This one I memorized, titled *Fear*, spoke to me.

It is said that before entering the sea

A river trembles with fear.

She looks back at the path she has travelled,

From the peaks of the mountains,

The long winding road crossing forests and villages.

And in front of her,

She sees an ocean so vast,

That to enter

There seems nothing more than to disappear forever.

But there is no other way.

The river cannot go back.

Nobody can go back.

To go back is impossible in existence.

The river needs to take the risk

Of entering the ocean

Because only then will fear disappear,

Because that's where the river will know

It's not about disappearing into the ocean,

But of becoming the ocean.

Carla adopted a faraway look. "Gibran. I recognized it … loved him back in college."

"The poet hit on something for sure." Mo said in a quiet voice. "You cannot go back. All adventure is before us. Nothing we did before matters. Only what we do next counts. I've watched Azita and Deena closely. Their vision never flags no matter the setbacks. Neither should we, no matter how things turned out in our early years. We fought for the things in which we believed. Those things have not changed."

"No," Chris said, "they haven't. Fighting for a better world never grows out of date."

Peter grunted. "Remember when people believed in mediums and their ability to communicate with loved ones on the other side."

"Sure," Mo responded, "the guy who created Sherlock Holmes, Sir Arthur Conan Doyle, was a huge believer in that nonsense."

"Nonsense for sure," Peter mused, "but I wish we could. I would love to have one more conversation with that Mick son-of-a-bitch."

Connie saw the mood declining into sentimentality and decided to shift gears. "Enough on things we cannot alter. Here is my question. What are we going to do next?"

"Wow, I hadn't thought about that," Mo said thoughtfully. "Probably whatever my wife tells me I'll be doing."

"You two will be married forever," Connie laughed. "But seriously, what's next?"

They all looked at one another, waiting for someone else to venture a thought. It was Carla who spoke first. "I have been thinking on this, even before Josh left us. Earlier, I had been thinking that Mo and I could buy a place in Tuscany, or maybe on the Costa del Sol, or in a seaside villa in Portugal or perhaps Costa Rica. I'm sure my rich younger brother would kick in some more to make his older sister happy, and to get rid of her at long last. Wouldn't it be nice to spend the final years in peace and sunshine?"

"Really?" Mo stammered. "Hmmm."

Carla continued. "Hah, don't panic ... though I did think about that, sort of. Then Josh's final words caught me. Why did he end with that parable? He knew he was about to pass when he did, so why that? I'm convinced it was his last message to us, and very intentional. So, what was it all about?"

Peter snickered. "Anyone know a good medium to get us in touch with the departed. I'd love to ask him now."

"Perhaps his way of telling us where our personal salvation lies?" Mo asked.

"Precisely," Bob enthused. "We have to read his manuscript, and talk to the students who helped him, but I believe it is all about his vision of *'feeding the better wolf within our soul,'* not as individuals but as a societal collective."

"I see," Mo joined in. "He always talked about this dark cloud, the Irish pessimism, which had dogged him through life. But I think, toward the end, that sense of cynicism was being pushed aside. Perhaps it was being closer to the work that Azita, Deena, and Ali have been doing, watching their unending faith and optimism in the face of insurmountable obstacles and continuing setbacks. Their example finally washed out his own despair. At long last, he kicked that dark cloud that always haunted him."

"Yes," Carla enthused, "he left a blueprint in his final work and wants us to pick it up and run with it. Is that what I'm hearing people saying?"

"Usha looked at the others. "You mean we would not scatter now that he has passed. We would remain together, stay together, and devote our remaining time to his vision."

"Yes," Carla said emphatically. "We would take on the challenge of altering the default position of American politics, of politics in the Western world. That's what he asked us to do."

"Why not?" Connie added. "He kept going back to this theme of appealing to the better angels of people, of going after the fundamental premises that govern our beliefs and behaviors. You know, focusing on collaboration as opposed to competition, community over individualism, opportunity over inequality. He talked to me a lot about such things in his final weeks."

"With me as well." Cate said at least. "I think … I think he was not willing to ask outright. He didn't want to push us but hoped we would come to this ourselves. He wanted us to be the river in that poem, to keep moving ahead. Yes, that's it. He wants us all to find our sea and become part of it. Well, I'm in. Of course, that's easy for me to say since I've pretty much chucked my career with the Foreign Service."

"Me too, if my wife doesn't kill me." Peter added. "I probably was going to stay to provide security consultation to the Crawford empire in any case."

Carla looked at Chris, "and by the way, most of us have pensions or savings so we don't need to be taken care of. Is that clear."

Chris looked quickly at Bob, whom he knew did not have his own resources. "Let's not talk about that now. I'll shake whatever we need from my sister Kat's tight fists. I mean, after what we just spent on this wild-eyed scheme to evacuate half the female students from Afghanistan, this is nothing. And get this, Karen tells me that Ali, Deena, and Azita are talking about going into Iran where women also are rising in protest. You guys will be pocket change though I'll likely be selling my blood to afford food at the Hairy Hare."

"To remaining together," Carla raised her glass as did the others.

"And to Chris finding a better place to eat." Usha added as everyone cheered.

Cate spoke up. "The last time I chatted with my uncle, in private at least, he told me that the best and worst time of his life was when he was with you guys in college, she nodded toward his old friends. He said he never felt more alive than he was during those days. I asked him why. He said it took him a long time to recapture such a sense of purpose … doing good for the world, as he saw that good."

"And the worst part?" Carla prodded.

"Oh, I thought that obvious. When he left it all behind, including the people he loved so much. It took him his whole life to forgive himself for that."

"Yes, he shared all that with me as well." Chris observed. "You guys being here with him at the end. That helped him find peace at last. He knew you had forgiven him."

"But he was happy in these last days, at peace like I've never seen him before." Cate added in a soft voice.

"I noticed that as well," Chris murmured.

"Yes," Cate beamed, "he kicked that guilt of his and, just as important, found his purpose again, even if others would carry it on … his best friends."

"That makes sense," Chris picked up the thread of thought. "He told me a day or so ago that America, and others, were like an addicted person seeking the bottom. The country had spiralled down a path of hate and vitriol, where the old conservative values had been replaced by simple and unreasoning hate for those who cared for the world. But like all addicts and drunks, the bottom would come. I mean, really, you can only indulge in know-nothingism, rampant mendacity, horrific authoritarianism, extreme division, and the euphoria of an anticipated Armageddon or Rapture for so long before the hate wears you out. Waiting for the rapture where your enemies dissolve in blood and gore can exhaust and frustrate you beyond measure."

"And then?" Carla asked.

Connie now spoke. "You seek the other side, the better angels within us that he was sure were there. Mr. Dark Cloud understood this clearly at last, that we had these better angels. When I realized that, I knew he was ready to go. I'm convinced of this. He knew we would not let him down."

Chris sighed. "At moments like this, when there is a large loss or, conversely, a large joy, I get reflective."

"We all do," Mo added.

"But these are different, they are *refractive reflections.*" Chris said with meaning.

"What?" Connie asked.

"Well, refractive reflections are special." Chris continued. "They are our most profound thoughts and emotions. What makes them different is that they are filtered through someone special to us, like light through a prism. What comes out the other end is refined, pure, differentiated, and unique. Josh has been our prism. Well, that is how I see it. That's my story and I'm going to stick with it."

"To my uncle's dream of a better world." Cate affirmed.

"And my husband's vision of the good in all of us." Connie echoed.

Peter stood. "To my good friend from my youth who taught me that there were decent Micks in the world. Not many, I suppose, but I did know one."

"And to the best Mensch I've ever known." Mo declared as he raised himself of his chair.

"To Jeremiah Joshua Connelly," Chris raised his glass as all stood up.

Every glass was raised. Tears flowed. No one bothered to wipe them away.

EPILOGUE

"Extremists have shown what frightens them most: a girl with a book."

Malala Yousafzai

There were many emotional reunions at Abbottabad and nearby sites in western Pakistan. Former teachers and students and program staff from Afghanistan hugged each other and cried as they realized they were safe, that their friends were also safe, and that a new life awaited. They could hardly imagine such a new world but looked toward the future with anticipation and more than a bit of apprehension. Carlota and Karen, with the help of key staff such as Atle and Tomas took charge of the logistical demands that would occupy them all for several weeks. When Cate and Usha returned, they pitched in, especially talking through the emotional issues many of these girls faced. In most ways, this was a high for all the staff, a dramatic break from the routine that governed their professional lives. These periodic high points afforded them drama, apprehension, emotional release and, most of all, a sense of accomplishment.

Azita and Deena found Farzana and several of the other former female teachers. They all took a few moments to think about what they had just experienced and perhaps consider what might lie ahead. They relived those moments when they were stopped and harassed by ominous and well-armed men, about frightening delays on airport runways, about all the bribes and other subterfuges employed to keep going when danger lurked. The most rewarding vignettes, however, involved the kindness of people, average people, who seemed to sense the purpose of these desperate *hegiras* and wished the migrants well. Some gave the girls food and drink. That might have merely been Afghani hospitality. Or, it might have been that some of those witnessing these flights wished that they also were going.

The conversation eventually touched upon what they had accomplished. '*We will be famous all over the world, like Malala,*' one of the teachers exclaimed.

"We won't but Deena Masoud likely will, even more famous than she now is." An anonymous voice proclaimed.

"No!" Deena said sharply. "There will be no publicity. The people in England insist upon this. I insist upon this. Eventually word may get out but not from us. Better not to embarrass the new regime, who may take it out on the families back in the villages or the staff who remain at the service centers. We will keep this as quiet as we can. Understood!"

"Listen to my sister," Azita added. "This is but a tiny victory, so much remains to be done. It is like the raindrops that form a rivulet that no one sees, which then joins others to become a brook and, with time, a river that cannot be stopped. But that beginning rivulet, if noticed, easily can be diverted and become useless. Do you understand?"

There was a general affirmation.

After more sharing of emotions and laughter and some tears, Azita made her way to a quiet spot to compose a message.

Dear Chris … As you undoubtedly know by now, we are all out now and safe, as safe as anyone can be in this uncertain world. I know I have been such a disappointment to you as of late, sullen and uncommunicative and acting like a colossal ass. I am so sorry. Being here and experiencing the hopes and fears of these girls has reminded me in a powerful way just how fortunate I have been and what you and Amar and Ali, yes Ali, have given me. I have made amends with your wife, and likely owe her so much more in that regard. She will not recognize me upon my return. ☺

On the journey to the border, when I was not panicked about our imminent fate, I thought hard on my recent behavior. I don't have a complete understanding but here is the best I can do. I have seen so much suffering and death in my life, more than anyone should. I started treating the ill and damaged when I was still a child, which continued on a grander scale as a physician where I labored in some very difficult sites in the middle east and elsewhere, including the more challenged parts of London. You would think that would have given me some sort of protection, a kind of emotional immunity.

Apparently, it didn't. The personal losses kept mounting, with my parents, my brother, my first fiancé and then my husband, and all the people I had grown close to through you, Rachel and Ricky and Jules and the list goes on. I guess the proverbial straw was Amar. She was like losing Madeena, my mother, all over again. At first, I coped but the effort to accept it proved enormous and perhaps too much. Then, when it looked as if you had moved on with Ali so easily, my composure broke. It should not have I suppose but it did. I am somewhat ashamed of my humanness, my mortality. I suppose, from time to time, you must let the pain out. You cannot put up a brave face forever.

I have one thing to ask of you. Don't go and put yourself in harm's way. I know you keep asking me not to do that, and I keep doing it anyways, so I'm well aware that this sounds utterly hypocritical. Well, it is. However, you must realize that you are the embodiment of my papa … Pamir. Even now, I still think of him as papa, so wise and kind and such an inspiration to me, as our mother was to Deena. To be honest, you are not so wise and kind, but you come very close. (I so hope you smile at that.) If I lose you, I'm not sure what I would do, though I'm sure following you into hell where we all know you are headed, likely will be involved. ☺

Seriously, Chris, you have meant so much to me, from the first day when you arrived in the camp to fire Amar and wound up marrying her and taking my sister and I back with you. That act burned a place in my soul, a good kind of fire. It turned my life around, gave me opportunities I never imagined, and a sense of hope that seemed beyond my grasp. That is why I do these crazy things, defy you and take such risks. I simply want to give other girls a similar chance.

One more piece of honesty. I wish I could say with confidence that I would be a good girl from here on in, no more foolishness. But I cannot since I know that would be a lie. Now there is so much unrest in Iran, women of all ages are rising up and speaking out against the misogyny rampant in many parts of the Islamic. And we know it is not just there. In America, the Republicans are taking pages from the Taliban and striking out against females in that land. We can never rest. The forces that would take us back keep rising up again and again.

But that does not matter. Each of us does what we can, for as long as we can. You surely could have had an easy life, one in which you were not always worrying about an unruly daughter who would not listen. I do regret I have brought you so much pain. But, at the end of the day, I doubt either of us would have it any other way.

Know this, dear father,

I love you so …

Zita

Some time later, in Oxford England, Chris read the email. He printed out a copy and left it for Ali to read. Then he locked himself in his office and shed several tears in private.

In the weeks that followed Josh's death, several seminal events occurred. The American midterm elections occurred. Despite many prognostications of a *'red wave,'* the Democrats held the Senate while the Republicans barely took over the House, an outcome that shocked the pundits who predicted something of a landslide in that chamber. Most of the candidates championed by Donald Trump were defeated, as were many of those who still denied the legitimacy of the 2020 Presidential election. Once again, the punditry was in full voice, arguing that Trumpism was in retreat and that American Democracy had held firm against a mildly serious challenge.

Chris and the team that organized themselves around Josh's vision, including Gretchen, Ashok, and his sister, began to organize a new campaign. One unexpected addition to the team was Ashley Boyd, Chris's former student, who drafted some other colleagues from the media world. They knew how to present a good story and had many contacts in that arena. As the team effort expanded, the campaign evolved in its unique direction. Moving forward, it was less oriented toward immediate political battles and more toward the fundamental assumptions and premises that underly the choices and values that inform individual choice. It was Josh's vision.

Chris did his usual thing of reaching out to his network of friends and associates in the media, the philanthropic world, and academia for partners and additional talent and support. Kat tapped her contacts in the business world for additional resources. Like many contemporary initiatives to shape opinion, it was marketed carefully to niche audiences. Some parts of the message were designed to embolden and encourage those already a part of the *'woke'* flock. Other parts were designed to reach those who were not but might be reachable, like those in rural parts of swing states in America and Britain. As Josh had pointed out, most large issues in recent years were decided by a thin portion of the population. By 2024, the campaign was taking off.

There would be one additional loss in that year, occurring just as the Spring season was awakening. Mary Kelly's vigor suddenly declined. Despite her advanced age, this inevitability took her children by surprise. She had always been spry though life except during the period when she hid her grief in alcohol. That was some time ago. She became younger and livelier after she stopped drinking, but age eventually caught up to her as it does for all. One day, she called her surviving offspring around her.

The Crawford children would speak of these moments often in the future:

> *'I was hoping my Azita and Deena might join me today.' She protested.*
>
> *Chris responded, 'I'm sorry mother, but this has come on quite suddenly and they are off in Iran, continuing their educational work with women. They will see you when they return.'*
>
> *'I fear not, I shall be gone very soon.'*
>
> *Kay spoke, 'You will be with us for a long while, I'm still a good doctor.'*
>
> *'Yes, you are, my dear, a very good doctor and I am so proud of you. But there comes a time when nothing can alter destiny. Besides, I am ready.' Mary raised her hand up when her she saw further*

protests coming. 'No need for that, one knows. Christopher, you let them go this time I hope, no effort to lock them in their rooms.'

Her son smiled, 'No mother, I learned my lesson. As you told me, one must let the bird fly from the nest, no matter what it cost. To clip their wings kills the ones you love in another way. Besides, who listens to me? Surely not any of the women in my life.'

'You should be proud of them. I am not proud of my first reaction when I heard that you were taking them as daughters so many years ago, but that was a short- lived reaction. One day, they will make you proud, perhaps a Nobel Peace Prize…" Mary coughed at the effort to speak.

"Just relax mother." Chris said softly.

Mary went on, "Now son, if you want the women in your life to listen to you, perhaps you could try making some sense occasionally.'

At this, Chris's two siblings guffawed. 'Isn't that the truth.' Kat said.

'Now, now, girls … be good to your brother.' Mary managed through more labored breaths.

"I will," Kat responded.

"So will I," Kay managed.

"Thank you, girls. I have had many wonderful things happen in my life and, as you well know, one horrific tragedy, the one I ended myself but way too late. But you three, each one of you, has brought me such great joy. Given your father, my one great mistake, I thank God every day that none of you turned out like him. You have been such pure pleasure for me. You made this life of mine worthwhile…'

Mary then closed her eyes as her children moved closer, concerned. After Kay felt for a pulse, she noted that their mother was yet alive, but noted to her siblings that the end might be very near. Her three children stayed by her bed until her stay on this earth ended an hour later. Each of them mentioned something they wished they had said before she passed, then comforted themselves with the notion that perhaps she could still hear what was in their hearts even though each was a non-believer in any traditional notion of an afterlife.

"She still believed," Kat murmured almost to herself.

"In us?' Kay asked, not sure what her sister meant.

"No, in God." Kat responded

"That has always been a comfort to her." Chris said distractedly.

"She is probably the better for it, better off than we cynics I mean." Kay suggested.

"Realists you mean." Chris tried.

"Yes, realists." Kay sighed. "You know, I remember something Chris said to me a long time ago ..."

"Wait, you listened to me?"

"Yes, my dear brother, to my everlasting regret and embarrassment." Kay smiled broadly. "You pontificated something like the following. *'In the first century in Israel, Christianity was a community of believers; then Christianity moved to Greece and became a philosophy; then to Rome where it evolved into an institution; and on to Europe where it emerged as an encompassing culture; and finally to American where it became big business.'*

"Oh sure, I think I was in high school when I came upon that."

"Had to be," Kay said sadly, "I stopped listening to you after that. Yet, who is to say that mother, clinging to what we see as primitive beliefs, was not the happier."

"Or the only one of us getting things right." Kat said quietly.

Later, Ali, Cate and Cate's partner Meena met at the Hairy Hare joining the three siblings. No one kidded Chris for bringing them there. After talking about their latest loss for a while, Chris raised his glass. "I think I am finally learning a lesson."

"About time," Kay responded immediately.

"Hah," Chris smiled, "I knew you wouldn't keep your promise to mother, you know ... to be nice to me." He smiled even more broadly for a second. "But the lesson is this. Longevity in life matters little. If you can look back and say, '*I did my best,*' you will be at peace, and all will be good."

All those assembled agreed.

Over the weeks and months that followed the great *Hegira,* the girls who had escaped were evaluated, prepped, and sent on to suitable sites across Europe, India, Australia, and North America. Naturally, word of this remarkable feat spread, some articles appeared, but it never made it to the front page of the media. They had sexier stories to cover. Yet, the world quietly noticed. The Masoud name, along with that of Professor Shaheed Al-Hussein gained notoriety and respect.

More importantly, there were few repercussions in Afghanistan. The regime chose to ignore '*the great escape,*' rather than suffer any international embarrassment by exhibiting how incompetent they were. Everyone complied with this conspiracy of silence as best they could. At the Masoud Center, Aalem continued playing chess with Archie when he was not helping run operations. The Taliban threatened all the staff for a while, making much noise about their displeasure but seemed satisfied with imposing a few new rules on the Center. Shockingly, they never came for Aalem, who continued to play chess with Archie. It was as if the great *hegira* never happened. However, Aalem's prediction that the regime would harden, especially toward women, did occur on a larger scale throughout the country. There was much lamentation across the land.

In Oxford, Sayed Aktar and Farzana Balkhi married in a mosque with Esrin looking on happily. Both parents would continue their educations, but everyone who knew the family recognized that Esrin was a future intellectual star. The girl was quick, inquisitive, and filled with boundless energy. Deena and Azita took her under their wing though argued more than once about who was the girl's role model.

"Esrin takes after me." Deena would say.

"Don't be silly," Azita would respond, "she looks to me for guidance."

Ali heard this oft repeated spat between the two siblings one day. "Listen to the two of you. She takes after her dad or, more likely, is being inspired by Maddie. Anyway, does it really matter. The truth is, she might well be better than both of you. No, all three of us." Then with a smile, she added. "Think on it. Esrin and Maddie are our legacy, just like so many of the others. Just be proud, that is all."

"For once, Ali may just be correct." Azita laughed lightly.

"Of course I am," Ali smiled. "While I'll grant that Maddie takes after you, isn't it obvious that Esrin takes after me."

The three women laughed generously before returning to their life's work.

> *"Some things you must always be unable to bear. Some things you must never stop refusing to bear. Injustice and outrage and dishonor and shame. No matter how young you are or how old you have got. Not for kudos and not for cash; your picture in the paper nor money in the bank either. Just refuse to bear them."*
>
> *William Faulkner*

THE PLAYERS

<u>Connelly Clan</u> [Related to or associated with Joshua Connelly]

*Jeremiah Joshua (Josh) Connelly … Professor at
UBC who fled America during the 1960s.*

Corinthea (Connie) Chen … Josh's wife and chemistry professor at UBC.

Erika ………………………. Connie's daughter by a first marriage.

*Rachel Connelly [deceased] … Josh's sister, a physician,
who reunited with Josh after 4 decades.*

*Usha Nayer … Lawyer, close friend of Josh
who became Rachel's partner in life.*

*Catherine (Cate) Connelly … Rachel's daughter, had
worked for State Department in Jordon.*

Meena Muhaisin … Rachel's partner, they met in Jordon.

*Peter Favulli … early friend of Josh, had a career
in FBI, wounded protecting Jules.*

*Morris (Mo) Greenstein … early friend of
Josh during their anti-war period.*

*Carla (Shapiro) Greenstein … another friend
from college days, now married to Mo.*

Bob Wilson … a third friend of Josh's from college, recently left a monastery.

<u>Masoud Clan</u> [Related to or associated with Azita and Deena Masoud]

Pamir Masoud [deceased] … the patriarch of the Masoud clan, doctor and humanitarian.

Madeena Masoud [deceased] … wife of Pamir, university teacher before the Taliban took over.

Majeed Masoud [Eldest brother-deceased] … died fighting the Taliban and for the northern alliance.

Azita Masoud … physician whi idolized her father, Pamir.

Ahmad Zubair [deceased] … husband of Azita, died in bombing intended for his wife.

Deena Masoud … Sister of Azita, educator, devoted to her mother's work.

Madeena Amar Zubair [Maddie] … the daughter of Azita and Ahmad, born after Azita almost killed.

Ben Kaplan [deceased]… early boyfriend of Azita who committed suicide.

<u>Crawford Clan</u> [related to or associated with Chris Connelly]

Charles Crawford Sr. [deceased] … Patriarch of the Crawford clan and right-wing zealot.

Prof. Shahed (Ali) Al-Hussein … Colleague of Chris's at Oxford, his current spouse.

Mary (Kelly) Crawford … estranged wife of Charles senior, wealthy in her own right.

Charles (Chuck) Crawford Jr. [deceased] … first born and presumed heir to the dynasty.

Christopher (Chris) Crawford … the surviving son and creator of the ISO.

Kristen (Kay) Crawford … Chris's twin sister and medical doctor.

Katerina (Kat) Crawford … The youngest of the Crawford children and head of the family business.

Richard (Ricky) Jackson [deceased] … Chris's best friend through his life.

Juliana (Jules) Jackson [deceased] … Ricky's sister, former lover to Chris, TV personality.

Amar Gupta [deceased] … Chris's first wife, they met in Afghanistan.

Ajinder (Aji) Singh … Amar's brother, Astrophysicist visiting at Cambridge.

Jamie Whitehead … Husband of Kay, they met in Afghanistan.

Emeritus Don Sir Charles Howard … Supporter of Chris's projects at Oxford.

Emma (Em) and Elizabeth (Liz) Crawford … children of Chris and Amar.

Ashley Boyd … former student of Chris, now a British TV personality.

Gretchen Willingham; Ashok Kaur; Amandeep Kaur (sister).

ISO Staff [People who work for ISO or with Kay Crawford]

London staff:

Karen Fisher … now CEO of Chris's international organization (ISO).

Carlotta Ciganda … long time staff member originally from Spain.

Patrick Collins … From Northern Island, linguist, govt. relations.

Luke Geoghegan … Headed Toynbee Hall in London, in charge of ISO services.

Tomas Modise … African born (Botswana) staff member.

Atle Bergstrom … Handles ISO finances, was in Chicago, originally from Norway.

Afghan Staff: Masoud Center and Kabul.

Dr. Archie Singletary … From Australia, now working in the Panjshir Valley.

Agnes Singletary … Archie's wife, a nurse.

Dr. Carolyn Watanabe … Archie's daughter, working with her father now.

" Kenji (Ken) Watanabe … Carolyn's husband, Japanese and Philippino descent.

" Bahiri Gupta … Working in Kabul, originally from India.

" Ferhana Gupta … Bahiri's spouse, an Afghan who met Bahiri in medical school.

Farzana Balkhi …. Education advocate at the Masoud Center.

Amooz Aktar … elder of an Afghan village.

Sayed Aktar … his grandson.

Chicago staff:

Josef Spiglanin … day to day manager, originally from Poland.

April Song … Data analyst, originally from Korea.

Pamela Stuart … poor rural southern youth who made it to Harvard, authors reports

ABOUT THE AUTHOR

THOMAS J. CORBETT is emeritus senior scientist and had been a long-time affiliate of the Institute for Research on Poverty at the University of Wisconsin–Madison, where he served as associate and acting director for a decade before his retirement. He received a doctorate in social welfare from the University of Wisconsin and taught various social policy courses there for many years in the School of Social Work. During his long academic and policy career, he worked with governments at all levels including a stint in Washington, DC, where he helped develop President Clinton's welfare reform legislation. He has written scores of articles and reports on poverty, social policy, and human services issues and given hundreds of talks across the nation on these topics. In addition, Dr. Corbett has consulted with numerous local, state, and federal officials on various poverty, welfare, and human services issues both in the United States and Canada. Among many other things, he has testified before Congress, worked with the Wisconsin and other state legislatures on important social issues, and served on an expert panel for the National Academy of Sciences. His most recent fictional works include ***Oblique Journeys*** along with the first three volumes of a trilogy: ***Palpable Passions, Ordinary Obsessions and Felicitous Fates.*** His other sole-authored works include several non-fiction books: ***A Clueless Rebel, A Wayward Academic: Reflections from the policy trenches***, and ***Our Grand Adventure,*** and ***Confessions of an Accidental Scholar***. He has also co-authored several works and written too many book chapters to mention. His latest academic work, the 2nd edition of ***Evidence Based Policymaking*** was coauthored with Karen Bogenschneider was released by Routledge Press. Now long retired, the author resides in Madison, Wisconsin. You can find more information at www.booksbytomcorbett.com

www.ingramcontent.com/pod-product-compliance
Lightning Source LLC
Chambersburg PA
CBHW020616310726
48979CB00008B/1504/J